DARK VICTORY
STELLA BLED BOOK FOUR

A.W. HARTOIN

Dark Victory

Stella Bled Book Four

Copyright © A.W. Hartoin, 2021

Edited by Dj Hendrickson

Cover by:Karri Klawiter

This book is a work of fiction. Names, characters, places and incidents either are products of the author's imagination or are used fictitiously. Any resemblance to actual events or locales or persons, living or dead, is entirely coincidental.

All rights reserved. Except as permitted under the U.S. Copyright Act of 1976, no part of this publication may be reproduced, distributed or transmitted in any form or by any means, or stored in a database or retrieval system, without the prior written permission of the publisher.

❦ Created with Vellum

ALSO BY A.W. HARTOIN

Historical Thriller
The Paris Package (Stella Bled Book One)
Strangers in Venice (Stella Bled Book Two)
One Child in Berlin (Stella Bled Book Three)
Dark Victory (Stella Bled Book Four)

Young Adult fantasy
Flare-up (Away From Whipplethorn Short)
A Fairy's Guide To Disaster (Away From Whipplethorn Book One)
Fierce Creatures (Away From Whipplethorn Book Two)
A Monster's Paradise (Away From Whipplethorn Book Three)
A Wicked Chill (Away From Whipplethorn Book Four)
To the Eternal (Away From Whipplethorn Book Five)

Mercy Watts Mysteries
<u>Novels</u>
A Good Man Gone (Mercy Watts Mysteries Book One)
Diver Down (A Mercy Watts Mystery Book Two)
Double Black Diamond (Mercy Watts Mysteries BookThree)
Drop Dead Red (Mercy Watts Mysteries Book Four)
In the Worst Way (Mercy Watts Mysteries Book Five)
The Wife of Riley (Mercy Watts Mysteries Book Six)
My Bad Grandad (Mercy Watts Mysteries Book Seven)
Brain Trust (Mercy Watts Mysteries Book Eight)
Down and Dirty (Mercy Watts Mysteries Book Nine)
Small Time Crime (Mercy Watts Mysteries Book Ten)

Bottle Blonde (Mercy Watts Mysteries Book Eleven)

Short stories

Coke with a Twist

Touch and Go

Nowhere Fast

Dry Spell

A Sin and a Shame

Paranormal

It Started with a Whisper

For those who sacrificed so that we might be saved.

PROLOGUE

There wasn't a thought in his head, not a single one. Abel Herschmann walked across roll call square with his previously active mind curiously quiet. He saw the new prisoners entering Dachau in his peripheral vision but didn't bother to give them a good look. He hadn't any curiosity left.

Several dozen men sat with their bony bottoms on the gravel, hammering nails into boards and then pulling them out again. Abel threaded his way between them, not meeting their eyes or hearing the weeping. Some guard had come up with the idea, genius in its insidious evil, as a punishment. At first, Abel had thought this simple hammering was benign and it was, compared to having your hands bound behind you and being hung by them from a pole. But the senseless activities were a special kind of torment that affected the mind terribly and Abel had seen more than one man come apart at the seams after spending a few thirteen-hour days hammering or digging a hole only to fill it back in.

Jakob had told him hopelessness was the enemy and that's where those punishments excelled. The old man was the wisest person Abel had ever met as well as the bravest. He kept his wits about him, despite illness and injury, to give Abel a name to help him survive in Dachau.

"Adam," whispered a man as he passed.

Abel gave the slightest of nods to acknowledge the voice of a bookkeeper from the Jewish barracks, but he didn't hesitate or answer. The guards were watching and it would do neither of them any favors. He'd learned a lot in his eighteen-month internment, but the most important was not to think. It was a rare time when Jakob had been wrong. His sweet and naturally hopeful nature leaned toward happy distracting thoughts. He'd advised dwelling on pleasant memories of childhood or friends or holidays, but those thoughts only tormented Abel. They were so far away that he was no longer quite sure they had happened. He'd discovered during a particularly long punishment of moving sand from one pile to the next and back again that not thinking was the key.

So a man given to thinking in vivid imagery and full complex sentences in multiple languages learned to turn it off and found the specter of insanity that had been barking at his door disappeared entirely. Now the guards ignored him and it was considerably easier to pretend to be a communist bricklayer named Adam Stolowicki when he didn't think about Oxford, his beloved books, his friends, or, most importantly, Stella. That beautiful young woman had to go, pushed into a corner of his mind, where her smile and charming naïveté didn't twist his soul with longing. That was the kind of thing that showed on a man's face and made him a target. Abel was blank and obedient. He'd become a master bricklayer and memorized a mountain of useless facts on communism, making him both convincing and useful.

Abel would do what he had to for survival's sake. It was only a matter of time. He'd given his name, his real name, to Michael Haas a second before his friend's release and Michael would save him. It would happen. He was so sure he'd even stopped thinking about that. Wondering if today was the day was pointless and inefficient. Let the others waste their time. He'd told them his secret to survival and counseled them on their pain as Jakob had done for him, but some couldn't or wouldn't follow his advice and there was nothing he could do about that. Some would whisper and plead as the bookkeeper was just then. They could not be led away from it. Abel heard a boot connect with flesh and a howl burst out in protest, bringing more guards and more pain. Some survived with hope like Jakob and Michael, a path much harder in Abel's opinion. The guards didn't like hope. Blank was better.

In silence with his quiet empty mind, Abel Herschmann approached the guard standing next to the Jourhaus door. He'd eyed Abel critically, looking for something to target or suspect.

Finding nothing, he asked in a guttural kind of German accent most often spoken in factories or fields, "What do you want?"

"I was ordered to come to the Jourhaus," said Abel without any interest at all.

"What for?"

"I was not informed of the reason."

"Do you deserve a reason?" asked the guard slyly.

There was a time when Abel's heartrate would've skyrocketed. He'd have flushed and broken out in a sweat, but now he merely stared straight ahead and said, "I follow orders. I do not question them."

Mollified, the guard stepped aside. "Weiß is waiting for you in his office. Don't make him wait." He said it like Abel had some kind of control over his situation and might just decide that angering the assistant to the camp commandant was a swell idea. Both notions were ludicrous, but neither one made the slightest impression on Abel.

"Yes," he said. "May I open the door?"

The guard shoved his shoulder. "Unless you want to walk through it."

"I will open the door."

"Do that."

A nearby prisoner sweeping the gravel tensed up and backed away. Abel saw the move. Once he would've been dismayed, but, for him, this wasn't a tense exchange. He had no interest in the outcome because he couldn't do anything about it.

"Do I have permission?" Abel asked simply.

The guard was puzzled but said, "You do."

Abel opened the door and walked inside the Jourhaus, feeling the warmth of a heated building for the first time since the time he was there with Michael. Jakob had somehow arranged to have their designation changed from Jews to communists and it had been a terrifying experience. There was no terror now. He explained himself three more times before standing at Weiß's door and giving it a single knock.

"Come," barked the SS officer and Abel walked into an office with a large window overlooking the men hammering and the beating that was still taking place. The SS Weiß sat behind a cherrywood desk that was at least a hundred years old. Its neoclassical elegance was completely out of place in the white-walled office replete with metal filing cabinets and photos of Der Führer, the high command, and Nuremberg rallies covering the walls.

Weiß sat on a rolling office chair and signed a series of papers, stacking them in a basket next to a bronze-colored SS desk eagle. It looked like an oversized paperweight and if Abel had been thinking he'd have wondered what on Earth it was for and why anybody would put such a hideous symbol on such a beautiful desk, but he wasn't thinking and he merely stood waiting in silence.

The SS signed three more papers, tossed them in the basket, and finally looked up saying, "Who is she?"

Abel's blank mind had nothing. He hadn't seen a woman for five months, not since Michael stumbled into the arms of one just outside the gate and he didn't know who she was.

"Sir?"

"There's a woman here asking for you," said Weiß as he leaned back in his chair and steepled his fingers.

"I don't know who that is," he said with complete honesty. He thought he felt a flicker of interest inside himself, but it was quickly gone.

"You don't?"

"No."

"She knows who you are." The SS shuffled around the desk and found a folder. "Adam Stolowicki."

Abel remained silent. There was no right answer.

"You don't know any women?"

The answer to that would seem obvious. Of course, he did. All men knew women at least in some capacity, but in Dachau the simplest answers could be death. Three months ago, a new arrival had been asked during a work detail what color the sky was. The prisoner had said without hesitation that the sky was blue. The guard had beaten him into unconsciousness because the sky was currently grey as it was an overcast morning. The man was lying and he died for it. Abel had been working near him and he'd seen it coming. They all had. That guard roused them that morning and they knew him well enough to know he was spoiling for a fight, but they hadn't said anything to the new prisoners. Abel bitterly regretted it, but in the end, it made his silence more profound.

"Not since I've been here."

Weiß watched him with dark eyes. He was a brutal man, but not the kind that beat men to death over the color of the sky. He would, however, have no difficulty sending Abel to the medical block for what would be called treatment.

"I guess not," the SS said finally. "This would be a member of your family?"

"I have no family, except an aunt in Prague." He left out Adam's sister Helena in Vienna, a risk he took without thought. Adam had died for a moment of decency on that hellish night in Vienna when they'd been arrested. Abel would not repay the man by turning the SS's eyes on his sister.

"This aunt has money?"

"No."

"You're sure?"

"Yes."

"So, who is this woman who has come here for you?" the SS asked.

"I don't know."

He flipped through the file. "I remember you. Michael Haas was your friend."

"Yes."

"Have you heard from him?"

"No."

Prisoners were allowed mail intermittently and Abel had received a letter from Adam Stolowicki's aunt, a caustic woman who said she was glad that his parents weren't alive to see him in jail. Jail, as if Adam had been picked up for purse snatching or something equally minor. Dachau was hardly jail. Jail would be a holiday. He hadn't answered her, since he wasn't her nephew and because her last line was quite pointed. "Serves you right."

"Have you heard from anyone?"

"My aunt," said Abel.

"What did she say?"

"That I was a *Dummkopf* and also ugly."

The SS's mouth twitched. "Maybe she changed her mind about you."

"I doubt it. She also said she was ashamed of me."

He drummed his fingers on the desk. "Is she small? Tiny?"

Abel was able to accurately describe Adam's aunt since Jakob had seen her, a large woman with a beaky nose and bad teeth.

"That's not her. What is your organization?"

"The Communist party of Poland."

The SS frowned. "A dirty, conniving Pole."

Abel was originally categorized correctly as a Jew when he arrived since it was assumed that everyone on the train was. It turned out Adam Stolowicki wasn't Jewish. Usually, once a person was labeled, they were stuck, but Jakob had managed to take Jew off Adam's list of so-called crimes. Unfortunately, the stain of what remained was still enough to hold him. Being a Polish communist was the reason Abel hadn't been released when many of the others arrested on the Kristallnacht were. Michael had, fortunately, been turned into an

Austrian communist and had, according to the Nazis, good Aryan blood.

"Why do we keep you?" muttered Weiß.

Abel knew he wasn't referring to release. The SS was asking why he was still alive. Many of the Poles were beaten or starved to death. But they were not silent, their minds filled with justifiable rage that they couldn't contain.

While Weiß pondered Adam's continued breathing, a gunshot went off in the square. Neither man reacted. It wasn't unusual. But then another fired and another and another. Weiß looked up, his dark brows knitted. "What is it?"

Abel looked out the window and saw several guards firing into the air and cheering. "A celebration."

The frown grew deeper. Celebrations weren't common unless it was about a prisoner's death and even that was usually met with indifference.

"What about?"

"I can't tell," said Abel.

More gunshots went off and Weiß jolted to his feet. "Stay here." He marched out, leaving Abel to stare out the window at dozens of congregating guards. Curiosity didn't come. He simply watched the joy of his tormentors and waited until the SS came back to decide his fate.

After fifteen long minutes, Weiß came back wreathed in smiles with a beer in hand and a touch of foam on his upper lip. "You are curious about the commotion?"

Abel wasn't, but he said yes.

"A great day for the Fatherland. All these months of quiet restraint are over." He took a big gulp of beer and raised the mug to the men in the square who raised theirs to him.

Abel wouldn't have described the Nazis as restrained, but it pleased them to think they were. They often bragged about not killing a prisoner as if it were some kind of virtue.

"You are not asking questions?" the SS asked, still smiling.

"Did a country surrender to the Fatherland?"

Weiß pointed at him. "Good guess, but no, not yet. We have attacked and overwhelmed Norway and Denmark."

"In one day?"

"Today. This morning. What do you think of that?"

Abel had to answer and he did so honestly. "I'm not surprised."

"No?" asked Weiß.

"I heard what happened to Poland," Abel said.

The SS nodded and drained his beer. "This is your lucky day." He pounded his knuckles on the desk.

Abel very much doubted his idea of luck was the same as Weiß, but he nodded.

"It's not much, but I will accept it. My wife still longs for a boat." He pulled out a sheaf of forms, signed several, and then stamped them. "Get your things from the barracks and report to the intake area for your papers."

Abel stood in front of the desk, his blank mind frozen and unable to comprehend what was happening.

"You're straining my good will, Stolowicki."

"I…"

"You are released to that woman whoever she is. You should thank the Führer that today is a day of triumph."

Abel nodded, took the papers and walked woodenly out of the door as Weiß yelled for another beer. The square was awash in guards, celebrating both Germany's triumph, which they took for granted, and the possibility that they would be heading for the front. He walked through the men and passed unmolested, which was a first. Other prisoners who hadn't learned that curiosity killed the cat were coming to see what was going on. Abel was the only one going in the other direction and he found his barrack empty, except for the two men who had died the night before and hadn't yet been removed.

Abel looked down at his belongings. There was nothing he wanted, but to leave without his tin cup, bowl, and spoon would be seen as odd. He tied them in a bundle and looked at the man on the bunk next to his. Abel hadn't known him well, a frail newspaperman from Nuremberg accused of making anti-Hitler pamphlets. He claimed he was innocent and Abel had no doubt about that. He hardly looked like the type to stand up to Hitler and he'd only lasted three days, dying in a fit of wheezing in the frigid April air. Another death amid so many others, but Abel wouldn't forget. Like Michael, he wouldn't forget or forgive.

He walked out and made a beeline for the intake area as ordered. There were yells and screams as men were forced back to work. The celebration had been short-lived. To Abel's surprise, there wasn't a guard on the door of the intake area and he walked straight in without being challenged. He managed to find an SS Unterscharführer in an office who wasn't drinking or particularly cheerful. Abel had reported to him before when he needed bricks. It was a lengthy conversation about why he needed brick to build a wall that he was ordered to build. Haverbeck was the kind of guard who didn't think he was a guard because he kept inventories and ordered supplies instead of holding a rifle and kicking prisoners, but it was no different and Abel would remember him as well.

"Yes?" Haverbeck asked in what could be considered a friendly voice if the person speaking didn't have lightning bolts on their collar.

"I've been released." Abel handed over the papers and Haverbeck, surprised, examined them.

"But you're a Pole," he said.

"Yes."

"And Weiß agreed to release you?"

"Yes."

Haverbeck leaned back and smiled. "How'd you get so lucky?"

Abel said nothing. He had no idea.

"Well, this isn't my department. Find a clerk."

"I would, but they're all gone," he said.

"Gone?"

"Everyone is in the square."

"Who's intaking new prisoners?"

Abel shrugged and Haverbeck got wearily to his feet. "You'd think they've already surrendered, but they haven't, you know."

"I know," said Abel.

Haverbeck gave him a sharp look. "They will."

"I know."

Satisfied, Haverbeck went into the hall and Abel followed, not knowing what else to do. The SS yelled at a clerk drunkenly weaving down the hall and told him to get Abel's papers before rushing off to where the new prisoners would be categorized and disinfected.

The clerk stumbled around until he found Adam Stolowicki's papers right where they ought to be filed under S. The camp was nothing if not organized. He shoved the papers into Abel's hands and gave him some civilian clothes, demanding that he give back his uniform. Abel stripped, carefully keeping his privates out of sight in case the clerk had noticed his designation as a communist not a Jew, and quickly put on the clothes that were both dirty and way too small.

"Get out before I change my mind," said the clerk. He said it like there was a chance that Abel might object and beg to stay in prison. Before the clerk could get any ideas—it was evident from his eyes that he was starting to—Abel hustled out a side door and headed toward the Jourhaus again. He found himself unsteady as his mind so quiet for so long, awakened. The clerk had not stopped him. No one had stopped him. Everything seemed fuzzy around the edges. He passed the line of men coming into the camp for the first time. Their frightened faces, he could see them, and he could not stop his mind from wondering who they were or if they would survive. They shook and he shook. Abel felt he was in their line, not walking in the opposite direction with release papers in hand. It was all a dream; a fantasy he'd had so many times early on that he finally thought it was real.

Abel passed some guards and cringed for the first time in months, but they took no notice. It felt wrong and even more unreal and empty. He expected to leave. He believed that Michael would save him, but that moment wasn't full of elation, only confusion. Abel was Adam, a Polish communist that the SS thought they ought to have killed. There should be protests at his leaving alive and unmaimed or at least anger and ridicule. Those were served daily, but there was nothing. They didn't care. The guards didn't care and Abel's mind, fully awake and thinking, knew that he was nothing and no one in that place and to those men. The prisoners he was passing, shivering from the cold and fear, were nothing, too. He grieved for them.

The gate was open and he squeezed through under the mocking "Arbeit macht Frei" and stepped out past the walls of Dachau, smelling the fresh air and trying not to weep. He stumbled past several guards who ignored him and heard a new prisoner hiss, "How did you get out?"

"I don't know," he said and continued past the men to a road he could only vaguely remember and that's when he saw her. He might not have noticed such a tiny little woman dressed in drab old-fashioned clothes in any other circumstance, but in a world where there were only men, she couldn't have stood out more if she were dressed in scarlet satin and dancing a jig. It didn't hurt that she had her eyes pinned on him with such intensity that Abel felt it in his chest and he was a little bit frightened of this stranger who had saved him, despite her grey hair, wrinkles, and being the size of a prepubescent boy.

He walked over slowly and when he loomed over her, she looked up and said, "Come on. I haven't got all the day to waste on you."

Abel looked around. The SS had said a woman, but somewhere inside of him, he still expected Michael. His friend never said anything about this tiny stern woman and Michael knew how to talk. He told Abel everything about his life and no one matched this woman who was staring up at him with irritation and just a touch of disgust. He took a step back.

Her face softened and she took his arm, speaking softly in Austrian-accented German, "Don't be a fool. Chances like this don't come easy or cheap."

He hesitated. He couldn't think what to do. Where were they going? What would happen?

A guard called out. "You there! Get in line!"

She squeezed his arm. "You must come now."

There was crunching on the gravel, high black boots. He knew the sound well and it never brought anything good. He started walking with her, slowly, dragging his feet and feeling all the fear he'd pushed

A.W. HARTOIN

away for months. He was breathing hard like he'd been running and sweat ran down his face. Where was Michael? Jakob?

"Hurry, you fool," she hissed.

"I don't know you."

The tiny woman yanked him down to her level and she whispered in his ear, "Stella wants you to get away."

Her name. *The* name.

His mind cleared. Stella. The one he was living for. He could remember her and he could feel and think and hope. He picked up speed and they cleared the crush of new prisoners.

"Hey! You! Let me see your papers!"

Abel started to look back. He had papers, but she jerked him forward. "No. Forward. Only forward."

"Who are you?"

"Hildegard." She seemed to think he understood who she was and he went along and soon the guard lost interest. There were plenty of prisoners to occupy him. They walked on into the town. It could've been a long time or short. Abel wasn't sure, but Hildegard said, "Very good. We will make the train."

She led him to the Bahnhof and she bought two tickets to Munich. Abel wanted to say he didn't want to go to Munich, but he had no idea where he did want to go or how to get there. It didn't matter though. Hildegard wasn't interested in his opinion anyway. That much was clear. It was also clear that people were noticing him and taking a wide berth. He knew he looked odd with his small clothes and maybe he smelled. He probably did smell. Embarrassment washed over him and surprise after that. He didn't think embarrassment was something he could still feel.

Hildegard guided him to an empty section of the platform, giving the other passengers dirty looks and muttering insults under her breath. Then they stood there and he had a chance to look at his savior. Her iron grey hair was pulled back in a tight bun under a flat unfashionable hat and her clothes while clean and well-kept were far from new. How had she bribed Weiß to get him out? His mind jolted from thought to thought. It had grown undisciplined from disuse, but it kept coming back to the same thought.

"Hildegard?"

"Yes?"

"Is she safe?"

The tiny woman gave him what he suspected was a rare smile and pulled a bit of newsprint from her pocket. He took it with dirty, shaking hands and looked down at a photo and article dated January 1, 1940. There she was. Stella, smiling at some swanky dinner party in London. Safe. Whole. Well. His hands shook harder and Hildegard took the paper from him and tucked it away. He began to cry silently and people began to look and comment. He didn't care. She was safe. He didn't get her killed. He gave her the book and she survived.

"Thank God."

"Yes," said Hildegard. "I do. Many times a day."

The train came into the station drowning out the other passengers' interest. Hildegard gave the porter their tickets and helped him climb the stairs. He almost couldn't do it. His knees knocked and he shook with the effort, but she got him on and into a compartment, pulling closed the curtain that served as a door firmly behind them. She sat down on the seat opposite, her little feet nowhere near the floor and swinging like a child's. "Can you eat?"

The train pulled out of the station and away from Dachau. He looked out the window in a daze. He would've pinched himself, but he hadn't the strength.

Hildegard put a sandwich wrapped in well-used wax paper in his hands and he stared down at it, wondering if it was really there.

"Stella didn't risk everything to have you starve with food in front of you," she said. "Eat."

He took a bite. It was an excellent sandwich made of *Fleishkäse* and a fresh *Brotchen*. But it was hard to chew. He hadn't had anything truly solid for so long it felt large and unwieldy in his mouth. Hildegard dug around in a little rucksack on her hip and produced a flask. "Take a sip, but not too much."

He sipped and then sighed. Apfelwein. Heat flooded his body with just a sip and he relaxed back against the cushions to eat his sandwich. Hildegard kept a sharp eye on him as she pulled out a set of knitting needles and began work on a hairy green scarf. He had so many questions bouncing around in his head, but Hildegard didn't look like she had the patience to answer more than a few or even one.

"Did Stella send you?" he asked when the Apfelwein had made him substantially braver.

She started to answer, but the curtain yanked open with a jolt and a well-dressed man slipped inside the compartment. "No, I did."

Abel stared up at the man whose full rosy cheeks stretched into a warm smile. So familiar but also not.

He sat down, still smiling. "It's me, Abel. It's Michael."

Abel dropped the sandwich and grasped his friend's hands, unable to contain his tears. "It's over. It's really over."

"No, my friend," said Michael. "We've only just begun to fight."

CHAPTER 1

The hammering echoed through the warehouse, joining the cacophony of activity and grating on Stella Bled Lawrence's frayed nerves. The workman placed each of her carefully wrapped parcels into a nest of straw and then looked at her for approval, which she gave without hesitation.

Outside, men shouted orders and complaints. Bells clanged and so many ships were blasting their horns, Stella had no idea how anyone knew who was warning of what or why. She'd thought, at one point, that she would start to understand the significance, but the last three months had taught her that no one expected a woman to understand the intricacies of ships and shipping and men grew annoyed at her questions, so she stopped asking them. Standing out was not her mission and a curious woman asking questions on the Rotterdam docks definitely stood out and for more reasons than one.

"Micheline?" one of the workmen asked as he lit a thick brown cigarette and smiled.

"Yes, *Pieter*?" She emphasized his name because it amused him and was rewarded with laughter as she walked over to check the inventory. Dutch informality was something to get used to even though her handler Park-Welles had warned her. She'd made mistakes in the beginning, but instead of correcting them, Stella decided to go with it. She was Micheline Dubois from the more formal Belgium and she tended toward last names and honorifics. Park-Welles would not be pleased. It was a good thing he didn't know the half of what she was up to and there was no reason he should. She'd accomplished everything he required and what he didn't know wouldn't hurt him.

"Is everything correct?" Pieter asked.

Stella flipped the page and scanned each line for issues. There wouldn't be a problem. The Dutch didn't make mistakes as far as she could tell. Business was like a religion and they took it very seriously.

"Perfect as expected," she said. "Are you ready for the next crate?"

He nodded and two of the men put the lid on her first crate and began hammering it closed with ferocious blows that made Stella's chest tighten, but she didn't show it. She showed only the appropriate weariness for a woman who'd been working and traveling for months. That was easy. She was tired. More tired than she thought a person could be and remain awake.

Pieter waved her over to the next crate and began pitchforking hay inside. "How delicate?"

Stella wrinkled her nose. "Medium. No glassware or porcelain in this one."

She and Pieter moved to a packing table and picked up some of her purchases. Stella chose a cuckoo clock of amazingly intricate design from the Black Forest of Germany and Pieter picked a watercolor by Ernst Huber in a simple but well-made frame. He glanced at the clock that was almost garish with its carved leaves, birds, and bucolic woodland scene complete with a young boy, cows, and a Saint Bernard.

"Your American has interesting tastes," he said.

Stella smiled. By interesting, Pieter meant bad. He wasn't fond of the heavy German and Austrian antiques she'd brought to the warehouse for him to pack. "He doesn't have to have good taste," she said. "He's rich."

"What will he do with it all?" He wrapped the painting in brown paper and then gauze before placing it in its own box.

She shrugged. "He's getting married and wants a European-style house to surprise his bride."

"So, you'll buy anything?"

"Not anything. I buy what I think might interest him."

"What if he doesn't like it?" Pieter asked.

"He'll sell it and tell me to buy more."

He placed the painting in the shipping crate and covered it with hay. "It's a good time to buy with all the refugees."

"That was the thought," said Stella, getting a twinge as she looked at the workman's face. He'd asked questions before, but there was something different about the way he was asking now, tentative with a touch of hope.

The two other men came over and asked for a break, which Pieter eagerly agreed to. Stella's twinge got worse.

He waited until the men had left and then asked, "Do you pay good money?"

"I pay what's fair," she said, placing the clock in a box and sealing it.

"Even to the Jews?"

She picked up a small, battered cardboard box secured with a string. "My employer is a fair man and has plenty to spend."

"On all sorts of things." He picked up the inventory list and looked at her expectantly.

Stella pulled the string and took out a collection of small silver spoons, the kind a tourist might buy. Pieter raised an eyebrow and she said, "They are solid silver and since they won't be taking their honeymoon in Europe, I thought these might be fun."

"How many?"

"Twenty-eight."

"All individually tagged?"

"As you see."

"Bertha Auerbacher?"

"Mr. Rutherford likes to know the provenance of each piece," said Stella. "I don't think you need to note each individual spoon, just call it a collection."

Pieter looked at the spoons and said softly, "She must've hated to let them go."

"They usually do." She wrapped the spoons in gauze and put them back in their box. Bertha Auerbacher had hated to let them go. It wasn't an exaggeration to say they were her prize possessions. The old lady had worked for a German family in Frankfurt for forty-five years, working her way through various jobs from scullery maid to housekeeper. She traveled with the family and collected the spoons on her travels. They were the only things she had that were worth anything and she gave them to Stella.

The trust people placed in her, a woman they didn't know, was at times overwhelming and frequently humbling. Bertha had been fired and thrown out of the family home six months ago, but lucky for her, she knew one of the families on Stella's mother's list and she managed to escape Germany to The Netherlands with them. Francesqua's list of friends and acquaintances for Stella to help during her work for the British Secret Intelligence Service had grown since December even as Stella checked people off. Her mother and Florence, her Uncle Nicolai's young wife, had been busy, constantly writing letters and sending telegrams to whoever they thought might help the people on the list. The soft-spoken ladies weren't above haranguing friends and members of Congress about visas and money for the destitute fleeing Hitler.

As a result, Stella was well-funded and Bertha had enough money to survive. The old lady had held her hands and repeated the names she needed to retrieve her spoons. The Earl of Bickford of Bickford House in Derbyshire, England and B.L. Imports of New York, New York. Once she had the addresses down pat, Stella left and moved on to the next person on her mother's list.

She tucked the little box in next to the painting and swallowed the sadness that threatened to overwhelm her. She had the worst feeling that sweet old lady would never come for her spoons and when Stella got that feeling, it was hard to shake.

"Are you all right?" Pieter asked.

"Just tired. I've never traveled so much in such a short period of time."

He efficiently wrapped up a pair of silver candlesticks and said quietly, "If you don't buy now, you may not have another opportunity."

"That's why I've been working so hard."

"And now you're done?"

Stella heaved a sigh. "I think so. Finally, I can go home and put my feet up."

"I thought you had a few more weeks," Pieter said with an odd note in his voice.

"I was going to go back to Denmark, but that's not possible now," she said.

"The invasion changed many things."

"For me, it's good news."

"You are happy to be done."

"Yes, of course." She smiled and said it offhandedly, but she was more than happy. Three months was a long time to keep a cover, especially since she was constantly moving and meeting new people. Her side mission of the list put her in jeopardy if anyone noticed and she knew she was beginning to make mistakes. Little things like dropping her very specialized native French speaker accent that was trying to use non-fluent Dutch. She would speak Dutch too well as she was fluent or the French accent on the Dutch would drop. Park-Welles had warned of exhaustion and slipping. His advice was to get out as soon as possible if it began to happen and it was well past time. The Nazis' invasion of Norway and Denmark wouldn't be the last and she wanted out before the situation got worse. The Phony War wouldn't be phony for much longer and she needed to see Nicky. It'd been so long that she couldn't remember his scent or the way his arms felt around her. He'd be flying missions to protect Britain and anything could happen.

"These two are the last?" Pieter placed two parcels on the table.

"That's it." Stella wrapped up a small portrait by Renoir that her father would be thrilled to see again. It belonged to his friends, the Bachners. Stella was surprised when she met them in Brussels that they didn't recognize her. She imagined her father, despite his stern demeanor, had shown them pictures of her, but the couple and their children readily accepted that she was Micheline Dubois, a Belgian businesswoman who specialized in art and antiques. She gave them a reference letter written by her father recommending that they trust Micheline and send their art to America through her. They were happy to do it. Stella always expected a barrage of questions and doubts, but they never came. The people on the list were desperate and it made them trusting. She paid them a good amount and handed over several letters written by someone Francesqua finagled into giving recommendation letters and financial guarantees for their visas. Everyone got letters and that was the thing that worried her the most. If anyone took notice of the number of letters coming out of America, they could trace them back to a woman who only turned up in business in February. Another thing that Park-Welles could not know and he would send her back to continue both missions, none the wiser.

"Micheline?" Pieter asked so quietly it was almost a whisper.

She looked up from the inventory. "Yes?"

"I think I have a lead for you, if you don't leave too soon."

"A lead?"

"Objects to buy," he said and his face flushed. "They're not furniture or large. I could pack them for you and you could post them to the American."

His eagerness took her aback. Pieter was never eager. Calm, patient, organized would be how she'd describe him.

"Where are they?"

"Amsterdam."

More sadness settled on her, adding to Bertha's that was still pressing down.

"I don't intend to go back to Amsterdam," said Stella with a businesslike attitude that didn't betray how she felt. "Would it be worth it?"

Pieter choose his words carefully. "It depends on how you think of worth."

The other men came around a stack of metal containers, holding sheets of newspaper with piles of pickled herring littered with chopped onions. One handed a paper to Pieter and said, "We would've gotten you one, Micheline, but you don't like onions."

This set off a round of good-natured chuckles. Stella's dislike of the cold herring that the men ate was well known. She'd tried it and, in her opinion, onions didn't improve the situation. When she suggested a roll, they teased her the next three times she returned to ship her purchases until she bought them a barrel of the slimy stuff and suggested they bob for them like apples.

"Only joking," he said, handing her a roll. "Here you go."

She narrowed her eyes at him and took the perfectly innocent roll. "What are you up to?"

The smell gave it away. Full of onions.

"Wilhelm!" She launched the roll at his head. The lanky workman caught it neatly but was rewarded with a shower of onions. Laughter burst out of the men and others came to have a look. Pieter explained that Belgian ladies couldn't eat herring and proceeded to hold a herring over his head. He tore off chunks and gobbled them down like a seal.

Stella put her nose in the air. "I'll be back when you're done with my crates."

"Don't be mad, Micheline," pleaded Wilhelm.

She winked at him and said, "I'm not mad, but I'm not eating herring either." She picked her handbag up and walked with exaggerated dignity out of the area. Behind her, a man said, "Quite an interesting lady."

"A little on the old side for me," said Wilhelm.

"As if she'd have you," said Pieter. "You're a skinny bastard."

"How old do you think?"

"Hard to say these days."

"The hair is unfortunate."

"But she has a mind for business."

Stella left them discussing her qualities with a smile on her face. Too old and unfortunate hair. She'd never gotten a better review.

Stella walked out of the warehouse making her way through the narrow roads and paths clogged with trucks, workmen, and the occasional suit. She was the only woman, certainly the only businesswoman that came into the working section of the Rotterdam docks not far from the cargo ship that would take her crates to New York and safety.

In the distance at the end of the canal, she could see the luxury liners and felt a pang. Some would be headed for the States, New York or New Orleans. Part of her wanted to step on one and leave Europe's troubles behind. Knowing what was going to happen and being unable to warn anyone about it was one burden Park-Welles hadn't warned her about. The Earl of Bickford had. He knew more than a little about clandestine warfare and his advice was typically more practical than Park-Welles' who hadn't ever been in the field.

She walked toward an area close to the hotels where she could get something other than herring. Leaving the working section, the people changed more to tradesman, clerks, and potential passengers. Market stands popped up and she got a whiff of spices and fresh flowers. It was tulip season and the madness was on. Sellers were everywhere and shipping had gone into high gear. Even with a war on, it seemed people still wanted flowers. It didn't hurt that The Netherlands was neutral and thought they would remain that way. Part of Stella's job was to find out what the people thought of the war and of the Nazis. Would they fight when it came to it or capitulate? What would they do after their country fell? Would they work with the British to fight covertly or meekly follow orders?

As she moved from country to country meeting contacts for the SIS and buying antiques, she asked questions, but mostly she listened in bars and restaurants. The contacts were forceful, sure of the impending fall of whatever country she was in, but the ordinary people, bakers, teachers, maids, they didn't think it would happen to them. Nobody thought the Nazis would invade and take over with ruthless efficiency like they had in Poland. This was The Netherlands or Belgium or whatever, they would say. Totally different. Not a target. The awakening would be rude, and the changes in attitude slow. Belief would take a long time. The Poles were still struggling.

In every country, Stella wrote her reports, detailing current attitudes and local sentiments on future resistance. For The Netherlands, she wished she could say for certain whether or not Pieter and his fellows would fight. They had a strong national sense and a pride that shouldn't be underestimated, but the Dutch were pragmatic, always weighing the pros and cons of any situation. If they resisted the Nazis, organized and thoughtful, they'd be good at it. The Belgians would fight, underground, if necessary. So would the French, but it wouldn't be fast. Factions there were quite diverse and immediate cooperation unlikely. The British couldn't count on a local groundswell when the Nazis made their move. It'd be a slow pooling of pushing back that would grow and nobody had time for that. Stella had spent countless hours listening to officials and military and she didn't think any of the governments could withstand a full onslaught. They simply weren't prepared, so if the French fell, the Brits would be going it alone for a good long time. She put all of that in her last report that went out through the American embassy in Amsterdam by diplomatic pouch. At least that's what she thought happened. Her contact was a high-class prostitute who had a connection. Stella didn't really know her, but she was very reliable and had a British mother.

It was a grim outlook and she didn't think it would do any good, but she'd done what they asked and now she could leave. The smell of fresh croquettes led her to a stand with a husband and wife frying little Bitterballen. She bought a cone of beef and chicken Bitterballen topped with a healthy dollop of mustard. Wandering away, she stood against the railing overlooking the canal, watching the seagulls and dreaming of Nicky. She'd finish her paperwork, sign the necessary documents, and get on a train. First to Belgium then on to Calais where she'd become Charlotte Sedgewick, a British nanny returning home on a ferry to Dover. She might stay a couple of weeks or a month, depending on what they decided to do with her. The SIS wasn't thrilled with using a woman, but they couldn't deny her success. The Churchills liked her, especially now that the earl's son Albert worked as a private secretary to Clementine Churchill, a more important position than one would think. She knew everything that Winston knew and now so did Albert.

Stella smiled. She would get to see Albert, a cheering thought. He'd come out of his funk of unhappiness and found a way to serve his country during the crisis and he didn't need to be whole to do it. He was on her side and he made sure the Churchills stayed there.

Three Bitterballen left. As she nibbled at a chicken one, a man came to the railing near her, but she wasn't worried. Her new identity kept most men away. It turned out her face was easily made older with thick eyebrows, under-eye bags, and a crown of frizzy auburn hair. The most she got was pity for her ringless state and that was fine by her.

She kept nibbling and thinking, slowly becoming aware that the man was inching closer as he ate his disgusting herring the Dutch way and drank a beer from a tall chipped mug. The closer he got, the more her heart sank. It was too well done to be an accident and no man in his right mind would make a pass at Micheline Dubois at eleven in the morning. So she waited for him to speak and she was on her last Bitterballen when he finally did.

"Fancy meeting you here."

She glanced over and he lowered his collar helpfully, although she didn't need it to identify Oliver Fip, the very first spy she'd ever encountered. He was not one of her contacts and there wasn't a single reason for him to connect with her a day before she left. Except, of course, for the bad one.

I won't be leaving.

CHAPTER 2

*O*liver sipped his beer, his face turned slightly away from her, but she could hear him plainly. She'd been given a new assignment and it came from the top as he put it.

"This wasn't my idea, you understand," he said.

"I didn't say anything."

He nodded. "I can tell you aren't happy."

"What's the assignment?" She didn't want to discuss happy. Happy had nothing to do with war.

"It's fairly simple."

"I doubt that or you wouldn't be here right now."

She looked over at Oliver and found him essentially the same as when they met, hidden behind a bookcase in Hans Gruber's library. He was still thin, blond with angular features, but now he carried scars that resembled pockmarks up his neck and the side of his face. He'd taken no trouble to cover up these things and was dressed as a rough working man in thick overalls and heavy boots.

"You are to return to Amsterdam and make contact with two men and evaluate them."

"For what?" Stella asked.

"One is a suspected Nazi spy and the other may be willing to work for us," said Oliver into his beer.

"Sounds like a job for someone who isn't me."

"I agree."

"Then why am I doing it?" she asked. "I've been here for months. I'm done."

"You've a friend who campaigned for the assignment."

"What friend?"

"Someone in the Admiralty."

Albert. That sweet man.

"Hopefully, you can use your established connections and make short work of it," he said.

"How long do I have?"

"They asked for two weeks, but I've told them a month."

A month!

"If I stay that long, I might not get back," said Stella, her mind on Nicky.

A smile touched the corner of Oliver's mouth. "Then you'll have to make short work of it. Don't worry. I'll be watching."

"Watching me? Why?"

"You're slipping and I'll be there to make sure you don't fall." Oliver hung another herring over his mouth and smacked his lips after biting off a chunk.

Stella gripped the railing. The desire to flee, to not take the assignment was almost too much. "If you don't think I'm up to it, then you do it, and I'll return to the nest."

He grimaced and then admitted, "There have been several attempts, but they've gotten nowhere."

"So, I'm not the first choice."

"No."

"Second?"

"No."

"Great. I'm the last resort before the invasion or should I say *invasions*," Stella said with venom.

"I'm glad we understand each other," he said softly.

"You don't look happy about it."

Oliver pondered a tugboat chugging by and spewing black smoke into the blue sky. "It's past time for you to go. You've made considerable connections."

"That was my job."

"Not among the Jews."

She took a breath and licked a bit of mustard off her thumb. "How long have you been watching me?"

"Long enough to know that someone will notice your…sympathies."

"I've purchased items for my client."

He nodded. "A genius cover. I will give you that."

It was a great cover and it pleased her to have it acknowledged. She and the earl had come up with it. The buyer shopping for foreign clients was easy enough. The particular client they picked was the genius part. Dilbert Rutherford III. He was a real person and if someone cared to inquire about her client they would find him just as fabulously rich as advertised. That wasn't the best part. Stella knew Dilly Rutherford personally and while sweet and well-mannered, Dilly was considered far and wide to be the dumbest man ever to draw breath. The Rutherfords and the Bleds knew each other well and Stella had been friends with Dilly since she was five, but every time he met her it was the first time. He had no idea who she was. Stella had once watched him mount his horse backward and ride around for ten minutes utterly confused as to why he couldn't see where he was going. If anyone asked Dilly if he'd hired a woman in Belgium to buy antiques, he wouldn't have any idea if he did and no one would expect him to. He was always coming up with harebrained schemes and hiring people to do ridiculous things like build the world's largest slingshot on his roof. That was a narrow miss. He was going to slingshot *himself* until his mother got wind of the plan and dismantled it, saving her dimwitted son's life.

"Thank you," said Stella. "I'm rather proud of that one."

"People have made inquiries about Dilbert."

"Have they?" She yawned.

"Not a single blip of a problem, but you've got to change your ways," he said.

"I'm doing the job the import company hired me to do," she said.

"At market value or above."

She wrinkled her nose. She'd hoped he wasn't aware of that.

"I don't know what you're talking about."

"You pay too much. There will be questions. The word is out among the Jews that you will pay fairly," said Oliver with feeling.

"I'm trying to help them survive," said Stella.

"And that is the issue. You shouldn't. Desperate people sell prize possessions for pence, but you're paying pounds."

"I can't rob them."

"Everyone is robbing them," he said. "You can't be any different."

She looked away and folded up her paper cone. "Whatever you say."

"Listen to me. This private mission is putting you at risk."

"I have no private mission."

"You do and we are willing to overlook your interests but intervening in the Visa process can't happen again."

"I don't know what you're talking about," she said.

"Yes, you do. It was noticed and noted by more than one person," said Oliver. "You can't force things. You can't interfere."

Stella shrugged. She did what was right. No regrets.

"What you're doing," he said, "it can't go too far."

Stella's voice went up. "Nothing is too far."

"It is if we lose you."

"You sound like you care."

Oliver went quiet and then said, "I'd be dead if it weren't for you. Don't think I've forgotten it."

Stella had wondered if he'd mention their connection or if he even remembered how she'd helped treat him after the attack on Hans' brewery, stolen Peiper's plane, and flown him out to a safe house, leaving Nicky and Hans behind.

"How are you?" she asked quietly.

"Well enough to serve my country."

"No one questions your injuries?"

He chomped on another herring and then said, "It's actually helped. I survived a boiler explosion, you see. I'm lucky to have use of my arm and I work hard. I don't complain."

She looked at his left hand lying limply on the railing. "What about the hip?"

He shrugged. "I limp or not, depending on my effort."

"But the arm…"

"Doctors call it nerve damage, but I have good use of it, considering." To illustrate, he used his left hand to raise the mug to his lips. He did it, but Stella could tell it took effort to force the fingers to close and hang on. "I'm grateful for my life."

"So, you're going to hang around watching me like a creepy old man?"

"You'll never know I'm there," he said.

Stella leaned over the railing to look at some seagulls perched on a pylon and snapping at each other. "I knew you were in The Hague two weeks ago having a coffee at Grote Markt Square. Eating an appelflap, too, as I recall."

Oliver exhaled sharply. "Very good."

"Thank you."

"Nevertheless…"

"Have you been told to watch me? Are those your orders?" Stella was losing patience. She'd proven herself time and time again. First in Germany and then Poland and Czechoslovakia and they were still sending men to dog her steps and using her as a last resort. She followed orders. Mostly. She definitely got results. What more did they want?

"Not officially," said Oliver.

"Then you should officially go away."

"And risk you? No."

"I don't want a watcher. It will cause problems. Someone might spot you. What's *that* going to do to the mission?"

"No one will," he said. "I guarantee it."

"I spotted you," she said.

"You are a professional."

That silenced Stella for a moment. No one in the SIS used the word professional in regard to her, except Cyril Welk and he was unreliable to say the least. She usually got baby spy or Mata Hari, which was bad on so many levels. Either she was a child and incompetent or a harlot that could only get the goods by sleeping around.

"That's nice to hear," she said finally.

"What?" he asked, genuinely puzzled.

"That I'm a professional."

"You couldn't be anything else and survive in this game."

"Still, you should attend to your own mission," said Stella.

"You are now my mission." He slid his paper with one remaining herring toward her. "I'll be in touch."

She gripped the railing and turned to protest, "That's not—"

Oliver was gone, just that quick, melting into a crowd of passengers lugging suitcases and fat baskets of supplies for their journey.

Turning back to the water, she moved in front of Oliver's herring, feeling under the newspaper and finding a slim packet. She tossed the herring to the seagulls, folded the paper up, and tucked the packet into her jacket before turning around to walk swiftly back to the warehouse.

The area was surprisingly quiet. The hammering was done. The crates securely closed. Most of the men had gone off to lunch or were loading the multitude of crates onto the trucks waiting outside to haul them to the ships. Wilhelm waved to her from the back of a green truck and she hurried over to give him his customary tip and then the other workman, Andreus, popped out from behind another truck to get his.

"Is Pieter still here?" she asked.

The men made long faces.

"Paperwork," said Andreus.

She thanked them and hurried inside to find Pieter bent over the table checking off items on a list with his herring still on its paper next to him.

"What was the name of that family in Amsterdam?" Stella asked.

CHAPTER 3

The train pulled into Amsterdam Central Station, all grinding gears and creaking metal. Stella sat packed into a compartment with two men and an exhausted mother of four. It wasn't a long trip, but the children had managed to whine, cry, beg, and wet their pants in maddening succession. It was miserable and smelly, but she was lucky to get a ticket at all. Tuesdays were always busy and with the twin invasions of Norway and Denmark, everyone was on the move and there was an undercurrent of nervous tension that Stella hadn't felt before.

"I wish you good luck, my friend," said one of the men, a Dutchman with a gruff manner but extraordinary patience for the children.

His friend, a Dane who could barely stay still for five seconds straight said, "I wish I knew what was happening."

"They won't bomb Copenhagen. They need the port to take Norway."

The Dane shook his head. "I wish you to be right, but to get control, they will. My mother is ill. We cannot move her and her flat is near the palace. They will bomb it first and so many will—"

"Shush," hissed the mother. "Have you no decency? There are children present."

"I'm thinking about my children," said the Dane. "You should think about yours. They are coming."

The mother clutched her baby to her chest and her oldest, a five-year-old girl with a runny nose and enormous blue eyes said, "Who's coming, Mama?"

Mama glared at the Dane. "No one is coming. We are neutral."

"So were Norway and Denmark," said the Dutchman with a sigh.

"We are different," she said stubbornly, but Stella could see the fear in her eyes.

"What is neutral, Mama?" the little girl asked.

"It means we are a place of business and we don't take sides. It would be unreasonable to damage a profitable relationship and replace it with nothing but strife and difficulty." She looked at Stella. "Is that not right?"

Stella had been silent for the entire trip. The sadness had gotten worse as the train barreled on in the opposite direction from where she wanted to go, but there wasn't a way to avoid a direct question. "It depends on the goal."

The men looked at each other grimly. The goal. The Nazis certainly weren't interested in peace and profitability.

"What's a goal, Mama?"

The mother grimaced, none too happy with Stella's answer, but she didn't argue with it. "Shush now. We've arrived. Papa will be on the platform."

The train halted with a jolt and the men stood up, grabbing their valises and helping the mother with her large suitcases.

"Ma'am?" the Dutchman asked. "Are these your cases?"

"Yes. Thank you," said Stella with a small jolt. She still hadn't quite gotten used to being called ma'am. Ma'am was for her mother. Even in disguise, she still didn't think she was in ma'am territory yet.

"Can I bring them down for you?"

"Yes, please."

He got her cases. The Dane, despite his anxiety, offered to carry the mother's suitcases and she went first into the packed corridor. Stella glanced out the window at another train where people were shoving their way on before passengers could disembark. Not exactly a panic, but not normal either.

The Dutchman helped her into the corridor and forcibly pushed their way through as new passengers got on and tried to get by. He cursed under his breath and said, "As if this will change anything."

They finally got onto the platform and Stella thanked him, breathlessly. He tipped his hat and then turned to embrace the Dane. The men said nothing as they parted, but an understanding passed between them. Stella had seen that kind of look between Nicky and Abel on the way to Vienna. At the time, she hadn't known what it meant. Now she did and it worried her greatly. There were times when she missed her naiveté. She missed not knowing that trouble was coming and that there was no stopping it.

But that Stella was gone for good. The new Stella, some would say the improved Stella, walked past the mother tearfully hugging her husband and entered the terminal with a cool detachment that she'd learned from her husband.

She'd gotten to know Amsterdam's Central Station and wasted no time walking through. The highly decorative arches with stone and brick were no longer something of note but routine, although it was one of the prettier stations she'd traveled through. That thought almost made her stop in her tracks. She could see it, the hideous things to come. Swastikas hanging from those arches and the SS marching through in their stiff, haughty way. She could hardly bear it. Another city desecrated with their ugly symbols. And it would happen. She had no doubts about that.

A boy ran in through the tall doors and waved a newspaper. "Denmark surrenders! King Christian capitulates to save his people!"

Gasps rose up all through the station and Stella rushed out, pushing out the big doors to run into the square. The briny sea air was a relief after the compartment and crowded station, but the sadness was so heavy, almost like a solid structure in her chest. There would be boxcars. There would be Abels dead in them. She couldn't think. Where was she going? Why did she have to be there?

"Ma'am?" asked a kind older gentleman. "May I help you?"

"Oh, I forgot which…" Her Dutch was perfect. She automatically mimicked his voice, a habit she was struggling to break. "I forgot which way to the trams."

The man pointed out the direction. "It will be all right. We are safe."

She nodded and rushed off, trying to calm her mind and breathing. The city was always a hub of trade, but it was busier and everyone was buzzing about Denmark's surrender. That helped. Those voices of worry and fear brought her back to the job and this, in many ways, was new information. The platform next to the tram tracks was crowded and opinions on the Danish king's decision flowed freely. The crowd had great sympathy for the king and his desire to save the population while at the same time criticizing surrendering with barely a fight.

"They're under the boot now," said a man.

"Norway has vowed to fight," said another.

"The British will save them."

"With Hitler sitting a ferry ride away? Hopeless," said a woman.

"We're next."

"The queen will negotiate."

"The prime minister certainly will. There must be a way."

"They tried negotiation in Munich."

"Look where that got the Czechs."

The tram rattled up and Stella pushed her way on with her bags. It was a mistake. She should've taken a cab, but she hadn't been thinking. Park-Welles would be happy, at least. The public sentiment had changed in the space of a day and she was there to observe it.

As the tram made its way down Damrak, Stella realized she had no plan. She'd automatically headed towards Dam Square and the Hotel Krasnapolsky. It was a bit of an indulgence and one that Park-Welles had not approved of. The officious bureaucrat had told her to stay in some hovel in an unfashionable part of the city, but Stella hadn't been about to do that. While Micheline wasn't a smart, young thing she was in the employ of wealthy Americans. The clothes she wore were very nice if dull. Her watch wasn't a Cortébert, but it was Swiss and 18k gold. People noticed these things, even if Park-Welles didn't. When Micheline gave her hotel to people, they automatically took her seriously. She was successful but not too successful.

One of her contacts in Copenhagen had passed on the message from Park-Welles that she should not return to the Hotel Krasnapolsky or any hotel like it. It was an order she felt free to ignore. Her choices were working. She got appointments with the best art dealers and every merchant was happy to deliver to a good hotel. Imagine delivering a Pissarro to some rat trap in a bad neighborhood. She had bought one from a dealer in Bruges for her father. She tried to find out its provenance, but the dealer was cagey on the matter. He was very suspicious of her and started asking questions about her history that were a little too on the nose, but as soon as she said she was staying at the Hotel Dukes', he was happy to box it up and deliver it there. No more questions.

But arriving at Hotel Krasnapolsky in a tram with suitcases and a briefcase in tow, now that would cause comment. So, at the next stop, Stella got off, walked around the corner, and hailed a cab. The driver was confounded as to why she hired him to drive four blocks, but she said, "I didn't want to spend too much."

He nodded approval and away they went to Dam Square with its lovely shops and good restaurants. She would spend what she liked if she couldn't see Nicky.

"You heard about the Danes, ma'am?" the driver asked.

"Yes, such a shame. What do you think will happen?" Stella asked.

"What happens whenever those cabbage-eaters force their way in." He grimaced. "You're not Dutch. Belgian?"

"Yes, from Wallonia province."

"You won't be safe there either."

"The Nazis will invade Belgium?"

"And us. I wasn't sure before, but with the North taken, it's only a matter of time," he said. "I have family in Poland."

"The invasion was such a shock. Have they come through it all right?"

"No, ma'am, they haven't." He stopped at the front of the hotel and she paid him with a generous tip, placing her hand on his rough jacket.

"I'm so sorry," she said.

"They're the ones who will be sorry if they come here. I'll make sure of it."

"You won't be alone."

"No, I won't."

"Do you have a card, by chance?" she asked. "I might need another ride."

He shook his head, suddenly grim with thoughts of the future.

The hotel doorman opened her door and helped her out, his face lighting up. "You are back, Micheline," said Daan. "We thought you wouldn't return to our beautiful city."

"I wasn't going to, but there's been a change of plan."

"A lot of things have changed today."

"Yes, they have."

Daan got her bags out of the trunk and she watched the driver. The poor man lit a cigarette with shaking hands, but it wasn't grief. Stella knew grief. This was tightly controlled anger, the kind of anger they'd need in the coming months.

"Ready, ma'am?" the doorman asked.

Stella straightened her shoulders. "I am."

He led her into the hotel and another doorman opened the door for them. She walked into the lobby and smelled the smell of cleanliness and good linens and found herself smiling.

"You look quite pleased to be back," Daan said.

"I wasn't, but I am now," said Stella.

"Yes?"

"There are worse things than being in Amsterdam."

Stella stripped off her jacket and kicked off her shoes the moment the bellhop left. She was known as a good tipper and he was happy to see her, too. All the staff were. Micheline Dubois was no trouble at all. Being in and out for the last three months, she'd gotten to hear a few stories of less welcome guests. A few of them sounded a whole lot like her Uncle Josiah. The naked drunk trying to climb into a fountain in the center of a square especially. Stella was careful not to ask for any names, because it probably was Uncle Josiah and she'd rather not know. The Hotel Krasnapolsky was her parents' favorite hotel in The Netherlands and they'd been there often, which was another reason she picked it. Park-Welles would have a fit if he knew, but her reasons were sensible. No one would imagine that Stella Bled Lawrence would be a spy and stay at the hotel where her parents were well-known. It was ridiculous. Someone would recognize her. Someone would remember that face so like her mother's and talk.

But, of course, they hadn't and Stella had the advantage of knowing a lot about the staff, hotel, and area before she got there. Uncle Josiah talked about the different doors he'd used to get in in the middle of the night and told a hair-raising story about climbing up to a female guest's room on the third floor and getting in through the window. He used only his fingers and toes to do it. No ladder, like he was some kind of monkey or squirrel. But where there was a woman, Josiah Bled found a way. Francesqua had been horrified at the story. Because of the story itself—the lady was married—and the time he chose to tell it, during a Daughters of the American Revolution meeting that he'd wandered into. Josiah thought it was hilarious. He couldn't go in the normal way. People kept coming and going in the lobby and halls. He might be seen.

He was seen. By the police and arrested. The charges were dropped, thanks to the lady, but Francesqua was never allowed to host a meeting again. No loss in Stella's opinion, but her mother was upset and Uncle Josiah was banned for a month. Stella was grateful for those stories. Her uncle got what he wanted typically and he taught her a lot about perseverance. And perseverance was exactly what she needed to get a job done that she'd rather not do.

She sat down at the dressing table and plucked off her wig. Her own hair was matted and sweaty underneath and it was a relief to feel air on her scalp, not something she'd ever appreciated before. She gave her head a good scratch and then stripped. The hotel was lovely with plenty of hot water and soft towels. Two weeks. She could do two weeks. It wouldn't be so bad. She took a long bath and scrubbed off the lingering smell of grubby children and sweaty men.

Oliver's packet was hidden in her suitcase's secret compartment as yet unopened. She hadn't been anxious to see what was inside, a kind of stubborn rebellion, she supposed, but after she'd rinsed her hair and combed it, the curiosity came. Two men in Amsterdam. Two men that had been elusive. Male agents had their turn and now it was her job. She got out of the bath and wrapped herself in the plush robe the hotel left for her.

The packet looked like all the other packets, brown, simple, and sealed. It wasn't any fatter either. That meant they had little information for her and that wasn't a good sign. Stella used her nail file to slit open the packet and let the papers within slide onto the bed. The contents were simple. She was to get close to both men and provide an analysis of their loyalties and liabilities. Stella had been taught how to do that kind of thing, but it was a first for her. She'd done courier work, observation, and reporting. Who had a mistress? Who owed money? Who gambled? Those things were easy. She didn't have to speak to the target at all. Watch and learn. People thought they were so mysterious. She'd followed a Czech official, who'd quickly signed up with the Nazis, for exactly three hours before she found out he had a lover that happened to be a man. If he thought he could survive the war by being a stormtrooper, he was mistaken. The Nazis sent homosexuals to camps for no other reason than that and he wasn't exactly stealthy. SIS had filed that information away, thinking it might be useful. It was distasteful but necessary she was assured. Stella wasn't sure she bought that, but the man was arresting Jews as fast as he could, so she decided to think about it later.

"Who are we interested in," she said to herself and flipped to the next page. "Hm. Interesting."

Stella was to cozy up to a Dutch aristocrat, Baron Joost Van Heeckeren. The baron was wealthy and not political, but he employed Jews in his house and the family import export business. He didn't run the business and had a reputation as a playboy and partier, but he had extensive contacts in government and knew the royal family. He was fifty-seven and unmarried and had been heard saying that he wouldn't leave the country if Hitler came. The Führer could lick his boots. Stella assumed that was the reason for the interest and she could see it. An aristocrat willing to stay and who favored the Jews. The Baron Joost Van Heeckeren was a high priority.

Next was a less pleasant fellow, but there wasn't much information on him personally. Jan Bikker was thirty, married, and heir to the family hotel fortune. The Bikker family was secretive about politics and finances, not unusual for the Dutch, but he was married to Anna Hartman, daughter of Paul Hartman, described as a rabid fascist and a member of the NSB. None of that made him a spy for the Reich, but he was in and out of Germany with a frequency that got him flagged. Bikker and his wife were athletes and spent a lot of time in Bavaria, hunting, hiking, skiing, and the like.

Stella had spent enough time in Berlin to know that meant nothing, just like employing Jews meant nothing. Bikker was a former Olympic speed skater. Maybe he just liked the sport in Germany. Maybe his wife wasn't a fascist like her father. The baron might be the kind to hire Jews when it was convenient and would drop them when it wasn't. Poor Bertha thought her German employers cared for her. It broke Stella's heart to see the pain on the old lady's face when she spoke of being turned out. "I did nothing. Nothing. I was a good worker and I don't even go to synagogue. I don't understand. I did nothing wrong."

Stella took a breath and pressed that memory away with the others she couldn't bear. Sweet Hanni being dragged down the stairs in Berlin for owning a radio. Rosa dead on the train station floor in Venice. The Sorkines in the water. Too many memories. Pain for another time. She scanned the descriptions again and their slim details. It was enough to get her going but gave no clear path. Those men were very different and would require different approaches. As far as she could see, Micheline was suited to neither. She was a rather unattractive businesswoman and obviously an old maid. That was hardly going to draw a ladies' man in. She couldn't suddenly take up boozing and carousing the night away. And Bikker was no better. Getting into a party or bar was one thing, but how could she approach Bikker? Try to sell him antique skis?

There was no use torturing herself. Ideas would come. They always did, so she memorized the men's addresses and tore the papers into tiny pieces. Once they were flushed, she unpacked and ordered room service before laying out what she'd come to think of as her props. A framed family photo taken in Bruges. A French copy of *Gone with the Wind* and packet of letters in French from various family members and tied with a ribbon. Various city maps, a jewelry box for purchases, and her ledgers got stacked on her dressing table, noting the purchases that she made for Dilly and other clients in America. She had two sets of makeup. Micheline's makeup, which was scant as befitting a woman who no longer hoped to attract a man, and Stella's makeup with the specialized brushes, pencils, and shadows she used to become Micheline. Stella's makeup got hidden under the wardrobe and Micheline's sad collection sat in front of the mirror, just some powder, a pot of mascara that she never used, and nude lipstick in a shade that would make Joan Crawford's lips disappear.

She tended to her frizzy wig, combing and shaping it, not to make the hair look better but more to make it look like Micheline tried to make it nice. It wasn't, but she had to play the hand she was dealt.

Someone knocked on the door and called out, "Room service."

Stella rolled her own hair onto the top of her head and yanked the wig on. She pulled down strands in a curtain around her face since some of her makeup had come off in the bath and answered the door with a smile and a big yawn. The waiter was new to her and thrilled with the handsome tip. He'd remember her money, not so much her, just the way she intended.

She put the tray on the bed and took off the cloche to reveal a large plate of Stampot, her favorite Dutch dinner. It wasn't really just called

Stampot and the staff enjoyed correcting her on the matter. Her favorite was a combination of Hutspot, a mashed combination of potatoes, carrots, and onions, and two versions of Stampot, mashed potatoes combined with a mysterious green vegetable and the other one had apples and sauerkraut. All topped with a juicy sausage.

The smell rose up and wrapped her in a veil of steamy mouth-watering yumminess. So comforting, like Bubble and Squeak in England, although that was harder to get. She asked for it at the Savoy once and quickly learned that her favorite thing was for *those* people. If you were poor, you ate fried up leftovers in a mash. It certainly wasn't for ladies of quality, so Stella would go to the less swanky side of London to get the comfort she craved. She did not tell the staff at the Savoy that the elegant Lord and Lady Bickford introduced her to the stuff and had it often when there weren't any guests at Bickford House. That's when Stella knew she was family. She got the Bubble and Squeak, not poached salmon or anything with watercress.

She dug into mounds of mash and took out the one prop she had that wasn't a prop, not really. It was hers. Property of Stella Bled Lawrence, although there was nothing in it to indicate who she really was.

Der Totale Krieg, the book that she originally borrowed from Irma in Berlin in exchange for her German copy of *Gone with the Wind.* Stella opened it to the flyleaf and read the name, written in a neat hand at the top. Irma Koch. Stella still couldn't sort out her feelings on the girl. She'd shown kindness and consideration. She grieved for Hanni in prison, but she was also a Nazi to the bone and would've turned in Stella and her dear friend Maria in an instant, if she'd known who they were. People were confusing and nothing simple. She hadn't known that before Berlin.

Stella's finger traced down to the names she'd written under Irma. Just first names, so they couldn't be easily traced if the book were discovered by the wrong people. She just wanted a reminder, in ink, of why she was there. Abel topped the list and then Rosa and Karolina. Raymond Raoul and Suzanne, the Sorkines. Under them she'd added Hanni, Maria, and Ruth. Maria and Ruth were the same person, but to Stella, they were separate and she kept them that way on paper and in her mind. Maria, the girl who wanted to marry and was a good German Aryan and Ruth, the young Jewish girl of extraordinary courage.

She unscrewed her fountain pen and wrote a new name. Bertha. Stella simply couldn't leave the old lady who'd touched her heart off the list of those she cared for and would track down after the war.

There was one more name, one she was a little ashamed of writing. She tried hard not to write him down. It didn't do to dwell on that person, but he came back. He kept coming back and in the end, she wrote his name at the bottom of the flyleaf away from all the others, like he was contagious. Maybe he was. Maybe Ulrich von Drechsel had infected her in some strange way with his wounds and his strength. He'd loved her and she'd given him hope in the worse kind of betrayal. And there he was at the bottom of the page. Ulrich the unforgotten. He came to her mind almost as much as Abel. Neither man would leave her alone. One a friend. One an enemy. How odd the mind was. How odd the heart.

Stella turned to the bookmark near the back and began to read. If you've got an enemy, you must study him, the earl had told her, and study she did.

CHAPTER 4

Two weeks had gone by. An unbelievable amount of time and Stella cursed Oliver Fip for being right. It would take a month to get what she needed on the baron and the businessman and she'd be lucky if it only took that long. She'd wasted two days visiting her business contacts to see if anyone knew the baron or Bikker. One or two had met the men, but nobody ran in their elevated circles. An elderly watchmaker that Stella had purchased an antique clock from described Bikker as a cold fish when he'd come in to pick up a repaired wristwatch. That wasn't a good sign, but he did have several antique clocks that the watchmaker had serviced.

So, Stella went to Bikker's office and tried to make an appointment. She said she had some fabulous clocks he might be interested in and was summarily rebuffed. It was obvious that without someone Bikker knew introducing her, he wouldn't consider a meeting. She had to turn to observation and tracking. Both were wholly unsatisfying with such a dull man as Jan Bikker.

On the other hand, the baron was rumored to be friendly, if you were lucky enough to accidentally run into him, so Stella started hunting around Amsterdam for him in bars and restaurants, not daring to go directly to his house without an introduction or a legitimate reason. She knew enough about aristocrats to know not to just show up. The earl had taught her that.

Stella put miles on her shoes going from café to café, restaurant to restaurant, but the Dutch were nothing if not discreet. She couldn't find out what places he frequented or when he'd last been seen. She needed a way in, but the best she could do was to plant herself across the canal from the baron's elegant address to see if she could spot him. The house wasn't what Stella expected for a baron. Despite being three times the width of the average canal house, Baron Van Heeckeren's was rather dull with a flat roof, typically large plain windows, and a front door with a glass oval, simply etched.

She watched the Baron's front door for hours on day four. It never opened, not once in seven hours and Stella felt herself sinking down. The sadness returning. She wasn't getting anywhere and she had to. Men could fail and no one would mind. If she did, it was a black mark that she couldn't erase. It didn't help that the battle for Norway continued with the British engaging. Nicky could be there, even though the fight was so distant. There were aircraft carriers. He could be on one and she wouldn't even know.

Just when she was considering giving up, the servants' entrance opened. The double doors were directly under the formal entrance down a set of wide steps so that Stella could only see the top of the highly polished wood panels. People had gone in and out of those doors all day with small deliveries of the papers, milk, and other essentials, but this was the first time someone was coming out that wasn't a delivery person. She sat up straight and put some coins on the café table.

She was in luck. Three women came out and Stella recognized the sturdy practical coats and shoes. Maids. That front door still hadn't opened and maids didn't go out en masse when their employer was home, so Stella jumped up and hurried after the women, tracking them to a neighborhood bar. After slowly working her way into the women's group, two young girls and an older lady, by accident that, of course, wasn't an accident, they began to chat about the bar, the food, and the weather. Not the most exciting topics, but Stella could keep them going for as long as necessary until she could turn to something better. The young girls weren't cooperative since they were in pursuit of a barman who had no interest in them, leaving her with the tired older woman, a stocky redhead with white at the temples and plenty of smile lines.

Stella chatted up the maid only to find out that the baron was off in St. Moritz supposedly enjoying the last of the ski season. The maid confided that the baron really didn't ski. He was there to enjoy the spas and seduce a young woman lately married to a man older even than the baron and ugly as a walrus.

"Will he be successful?" Stella had asked, trying to get the measure of the baron.

The maid chuckled. "Maybe, if she's bored."

That told Stella a lot and the maid was helpful, if a bit expensive. It took a lot of Jenever to loosen her tongue. Cornelia did like her gin. Stella thought she might have a problem, but it was to Stella's advantage and she took it. They accidentally ran into each other twice more over the weeks and became friends, since they were about the same age, or so Cornelia thought. Stella was able to convince her that while she was a successful businesswoman, they were really two of a kind. Women who worked and had to get by on their wits instead of looks and connections.

Since Stella had assumed Micheline as a cover, she'd gained a new respect for women like her and Cornelia. Stella'd been blessed with connections, money, and a certain amount of looks. Micheline had none of those advantages and it was evident every time someone met her for the first time. She had to prove herself, make herself important and heard. It was tedious and exhausting.

As she watched Cornelia walk into the café two weeks after returning to Amsterdam, she knew it was the same for her, only she'd been fighting that fight for a lot longer than three months. The maid spoke to a waiter at the door who had his mouth turned down as he greeted her. Stella watched him question Cornelia the way he questioned her and Stella had the urge to walk over and give the pretentious little prig a good smack. Yes, he was young and handsome and

Cornelia was middle-aged and dumpy, but that gave him no right to act like she couldn't have a coffee and a pastry with a friend.

Stella was about to give in to the urge when Cornelia pointed her out and the little snot gave way reluctantly. Cornelia stomped over, yanked out a chair, and dropped down, making the chair creak.

"What a day I've had," she said.

Stella leaned forward and asked, "Was he giving you trouble?"

"Yes, of course. He knows I'm a maid and doesn't think I'm good enough to eat here."

"Ridiculous. If it makes you feel better, he wasn't happy about me either."

Cornelia lifted a woolly brow. "Really? You in your fancy coat and bag?"

"They're not that fancy," Stella whispered. "I got them from an estate sale for guilders."

"You *are* a smart one." She glanced at the door. "Look at that."

Two young women, dressed at much the same level as Cornelia, came in and went directly to a table. The snotty waiter didn't intervene, but he did rush to take their orders. Stella was still waiting. She was lucky to get a menu, which she shared with Cornelia.

"Oh, to be young and pretty," Stella said.

"And dimwitted. The tall one might be out of a job soon."

"Really?"

"She's been stealing from the corner shop, but he's on to her now."

"Who is she?" Stella asked.

"Marga Kübler and the other one is Ester Isaksohn. They work at your hotel. Haven't you seen them?"

Stella had, but the girls made no impression, certainly not as much as the waiter. She had to wave at him for a third time in an attempt to get some service. He looked annoyed but came over reluctantly after he brought coffees to Marga and Ester.

"Yes?" he asked with a sneer.

Stella ordered the most expensive coffee and pastry and offered the same to Cornelia who agreed offhandedly like she ordered the best daily. He raised his pomaded brows and pursed his lips.

"Problem?" Stella asked.

"You'll be paying for this?"

"Who else?"

He spun around and went back to Marga and Ester. Soon the three of them were sharing a laugh presumably at the older ladies' expense. The manager came out and spoke sharply to the waiter and he rushed back into the kitchen.

"Finally," said Stella. "What an obnoxious trio."

"They wouldn't be a trio if they knew anything about each other," said Cornelia.

"Do tell. I've had a terrible day trying to drum up business and getting nowhere at all."

"Well, those two *flapdrols* are Jews and Siert, he's the last person they would want to know."

The manager came over with a tray and served their coffee and pastries with an apology and an excuse.

"Yes, he is young," agreed Stella.

"Not that young." Cornelia was a good deal feistier than she looked.

The manager's cheeks colored and he apologized again before dashing off to wipe down the bar.

"As if Siert is some sweet young man right off the farm," said Cornelia.

Stella sipped her coffee and kept an eye on the window. She'd picked that café because it was near Jan Bikker's home and she'd been trying to pin down his movements. "Definitely not sweet. Does he not like Jews?"

Cornelia laughed. "He's in the NSB. You know about the NSB?"

"Certainly, but I don't know any National Socialists, not here anyway," said Stella, perking up. This could be useful.

"You don't know that you know any, but you do. They're everywhere. They have seats in the senate now."

"What would he do if he knew about the girls?"

Cornelia grimaced. "I don't like to think. They're silly and Marga's a thief, but I wouldn't want them to get hurt."

I wonder if they'd say the same about us.

Stella caught the girls giving them superior looks, quite full of themselves. How could they be so unaware? Young and pretty meant nothing to the Nazis. For a second, Stella could hear Hanni's pleas, her sobs, and she was a German, an Aryan.

Cornelia touched her hand. "Micheline? What is it?"

She was slipping. Feeling. She had to pull herself together. "Oh, just tired."

"Of the world, like me?"

"Yes, but I think they're coming." Stella lowered her voice. "The Nazis."

"I think so, too. Why would they not? We're right here and our military is nothing to theirs."

She gestured to the girls. "Don't they know?"

"You'd think so. Marga came from Germany with her family years ago. They didn't leave because it was good. And…"

Stella leaned in. "Yes?"

"They were fired from Bikker's. That's why they work at Kras."

Cornelia knew all the details, the way maids who've worked in the same neighborhood for twenty years do. Marga and Ester had worked in the Bikker Grand Hotel on the Herengracht. The fashionable and expensive canal was the place to work and the girls had been lucky to get their jobs. Cornelia wasn't sure how they did it. The Bikkers did not like Jews as a general rule, but somehow the girls managed to work for them for two years without a problem. But they were silly and bragged at a bar about having jobs when the refugees were flooding in. They got there first. Someone overheard, realized they were Jews, and told the hotel. This was just after the Polish invasion and anti-Jewish sentiment was running high with so many refugees flooding into the city.

"Stupid girls," said Stella.

"That's not the half of it," said Cornelia with a grimace.

"What else could happen? This isn't Germany."

"But the Bikkers are like Nazis. They keep it quiet, but we know."

Stella ate her pastry, her eyes alit with casual interest. "What did they do to the girls then?"

"I heard the son, the heir to the whole company, came and told the girls they could keep their jobs if they told them the truth," said Cornelia.

"About what?"

"If there were any other Jews working there."

"Oh, no. They didn't," Stella gasped.

"They did. Two cooks and a doorman. My friend Yannj was one of the cooks," she said. "They were all fired. All, even the girls. Stupid fools. Yannj had to leave. She didn't want to, but she couldn't find work."

"Where did she go?"

"America. She's in a place called Ohio," said Cornelia. "She writes."

"How did she do it?" asked Stella. "I buy from the Jews. They say they can't get visas to America."

It turned out Yannj was lucky and prepared. She and her husband had gathered all the necessary documents. It was a laundry list, including a sponsor to guarantee them financially and security documents to say they weren't a threat to the States. The luck came in that Yannj had gotten to know a certain American diplomat who stayed at the hotel. He worked at the American consulate in Rotterdam and got Yannj through the endless queue quickly.

Stella held her breath. Help at the consulate. She could use that. The prostitute was useless in anything other than communications. She wasn't going to give up her connection in the embassy. He was probably a client. "Who is this American? He sounds kind."

"Oh, I don't remember. He had a funny name. You know Americans," said Cornelia.

"Yannj didn't mention who helped them?"

She frowned slightly. "You're very interested."

"People fascinate me, like those two girls over there. They don't think at all. The American must have broken some rules to get the visa for your friend. He's interesting, too, in a different way."

"He is now that I think about it," said Cornelia. "And he probably has money. That's what you're thinking, isn't it? Tell the truth."

It wasn't. Money was the last thing on Stella's mind. Visas. If she could find that American, she could find a way to get him to give Bertha a visa and the others, too. The States weren't filling their quota. There was space. They were just making it so damn hard to jump all the hurdles. Even Francesqua's influence wasn't as good as someone on the ground right where she needed them.

Stella smiled. "You know me too well. He might like antiques. Everyone has family. Maybe they'd like a souvenir of his time here. I've bought things and I have to sell them. If he has a wife, even better."

"A wife that likes antiques."

"A wife that likes jewelry. I've bought so much I don't know what I'm going to do with it and buyers here are getting more scarce."

"What about your American?" she asked.

"He wants art and things to decorate his house. Can't get enough of it, but jewelry doesn't interest him."

Cornelia ate her pastry and pondered a man with a bride that didn't want jewelry. She did not approve of Dilly Rutherford III, the big cheapo. "Why did you buy it then?"

"Well, I had to, didn't I? It was such a deal. Too good to pass up and our other American clients might like it."

Her friend stiffened slightly. If Stella hadn't been paying close attention to her cues, she wouldn't have noticed. "The Jews are selling. Yannj had to sell everything she owned to pay for their tickets."

Be careful.

"Yes, I know. It's a buyer's market, but I'm fair. You can ask anyone."

"But you're a businesswoman." Cornelia wasn't satisfied and Stella had to thread the needle carefully. Oliver was right about her generosity getting out.

"I'm no Bikker," she said.

"Thank heaven for that." Cornelia laughed. "They're coldhearted bastards."

As if on cue, a coldhearted bastard walked by. Jan Bikker in an overcoat and hat walked across the street and out of view. Stella had followed him and studied him for days, looking for a way in, but there didn't seem to be one. The man was discreet to say the least. He wasn't social or at least hadn't been in the last three weeks. He biked. He worked. He didn't go out to restaurants or bars. Stella had yet to locate someone who called him a friend or even someone who knew a friend of Jan Bikker.

"Do you know them?" Stella asked.

Cornelia scoffed. "Nobody *knows* them."

"Oh, I thought that you worked at the hotel or something."

"I've always worked for the baron and his father before him. Good men. Kind. Generous."

"I didn't know that," said Stella.

Cornelia gripped her cup. "What have you heard?"

"Nothing really. The baron doesn't collect anything, so he's no help to me." She smiled and sighed.

The maid relaxed. "Oh, yes. The baron doesn't care for art or antiques. You won't sell to him, but…"

Stella smiled. "You have an idea?"

"Buy my coffee?"

"I would've anyway."

"The baron likes parties. He loves a good time."

"How in the world would that sell a diamond necklace? I've got three."

"He knows people, all the best people and some of the worst."

"Like the Bikkers?"

"Yes, that's how I'm acquainted with them or her anyway. She comes to the house."

"Who does?" Stella asked with feigned confusion. "Jan Bikker?"

"No, not him. He's no fun at all. The wife."

Stella made a face. "You don't mean that the baron and Jan Bikker's wife are…"

Cornelia smacked her arm. "You are as silly as those stupid girls over there. He's old enough to be her father."

"That doesn't matter to some, like that woman in St. Moritz."

"It would matter to Anna Bikker. She has ambitions and that's why she comes."

"I don't understand," said Stella.

Cornelia wiped her mouth and said, "You pay and we'll take a walk."

Stella shrugged and said, "All right, but I don't know what you're getting at." She really didn't, but the wife was a way in. She hadn't thought of that. She'd been concentrating on Jan and had barely seen the wife. They didn't do anything together.

"You'll see," said Cornelia. "Hurry up or you'll have to buy me another pastry."

Stella would've bought her dinner, a turkey, a ham, five pies, or whatever she wanted. Cornelia was worth it.

Cornelia stepped off the tram onto the wide and very busy Westermarkt. The street was double wide and packed with shoppers and people hurrying home after a long day. The smell of fresh waffles and Bitterballen filled the air along with flowers and a hint of exhaust. It smelled like car exhaust to Stella, but there weren't any cars that she could see. Men bicycled by with large carts attached between their handlebars and front wheel. Handcarts were everywhere and hauling everything from firewood to children.

The women dashed between one barrage of bicycles and the next to make it to the Prinsengracht, a wide canal clogged with barges and boats. They crossed and walked down the avenue on the side, dodging a horse and wagon hauling bulging sacks. Stella had never seen horses hauling anything until she got to Europe and now the sight was so common, she hardly noticed it or the occasional pile left on the cobblestones.

"Have you been here before?" Cornelia asked.

"A few times," Stella said.

"When you're buying, not selling."

She nodded. No one was buying in that area of the Jordaan. It was working class, not a bad neighborhood but not one where antiques and diamonds were seen either.

"This way." Cornelia turned onto a narrow side street with weeds growing between the tall, skinny houses and the sidewalk. Rough wooden stairs led up to the plain first floor doors in this area and there were no servants' stairs underneath, but there were quite a few bicycle carts. They passed one with a pair of chubby babies sitting inside sucking their thumbs. Stella couldn't imagine leaving her babies sitting alone outside, but it wasn't uncommon and the babies didn't seem to mind.

"Here we are." Cornelia pointed at an extremely narrow house, four stories tall with the usual hook on the pediment to haul up heavy loads to the higher floors and a set of stairs that sagged to the point of splintering. The whole structure leaned over the street like it was bowing to its inevitable disintegration and Stella wondered how it continued to stand.

"Why are we here?" Stella asked.

"You told me that it's best if you know a lot about your buyers so that you might give them exactly what they want."

"There's a buyer here?"

Cornelia bumped her shoulder. "There was. This is Anna Bikker's family home. She grew up here and her parents shared this house with two other families until she married Jan Bikker."

"Where are they now?" Stella asked.

"Out in the country where no one need meet them."

She's ashamed. Shame is useful.

"So, this is a secret."

Cornelia yawned and buttoned her coat's top button against the early evening chill. "People know. We just pretend not to know."

"I have an uncle that people pretend about," said Stella, surprising herself and immediately regretting the admission.

"A bad uncle?" Cornelia asked with a smile. "We all have them."

"A drunken one. He does things like wandering into other people's houses and sleeping in their beds. Everyone knows, but they don't say anything."

"Nice neighbors."

"Tolerant anyway," said Stella. "So, if this is sort of a secret, how do you know?"

Cornelia took her arm and they walked down another block to a charming little house, painted blue with a bell-shaped gable. "This is where Yannj lived. She knew the family. Her landlord knew the mother, I think. My point is Anna Bikker is *this* place not that house on Keizersgracht, but she is doing everything she can to act like she's not. She comes to see the baron to meet his friends, eat his food, and see how the house is run. He knows everyone and everyone knows him. Anna Bikker wants to be like that, but it takes more than study to attain it."

"He's a charming man then."

"The most charming. He was born that way and has so much energy for life and fun. Anna Bikker isn't like that at all."

"What is she like?" Stella asked.

"She wanted Marga and Ester arrested. Yannj, too, as if the hotel had been harmed in some way. They were all good workers, except Marga."

"She might've stolen from them."

"If she had, I doubt she'd live to tell the tale," said Cornelia.

"Sounds like some Germans I know."

The maid nodded grimly. "Very like the Germans, the Nazis anyway."

"But Anna likes jewelry and fine things?"

"She does and she has no taste at all."

"How did she happen to marry a Bikker? It seems an unlikely match."

Cornelia screwed up her mouth and frowned. "I don't know, but we can find out, if it will help."

It's time.

"You are certainly earning your finder's fee," said Stella, beaming.

"Finder's fee? I was just trying to help your business."

Stella took her arm and squeezed. "And you are. Very much. I often pay a finder's fee to those who help me with lucrative sales. It's good business to help people who help you."

Cornelia beamed back at her. "You are almost Dutch in your thinking."

"Thank you. That is quite a compliment," said Stella. "Now what was the mother's name?"

"I don't remember, but Flore will know." Cornelia marched up the stairs of the blue house and pounded on the black wooden door.

Stella chased her and asked, "What are we doing?"

"Asking Flore, Yannj's landlord."

"Right now." Stella feigned surprise, despite her heart leaping with joy. Information was good. The thin edge of the wedge.

Cornelia bumped her with her hip. "I have to earn my fee, don't I?"

"You are and then some."

The door opened a crack and a little old lady with white hair and a lace collar peeked out, squinting behind tiny wire-rimmed glasses. "Yes?"

"Flore, it's me, Cornelia, Yannj's friend. I thought I'd come for a visit," said Cornelia in a charming social way that made Stella wonder if she learned it from her boss. It wasn't Cornelia's natural way.

"Oh, my dear. Of course," said Flore. "Come in. Come in."

The little old lady opened the door to reveal a narrow hall with rag rugs and smelling of floor wax. Cornelia introduced Stella as her dear friend and she was greeted as such.

"I was just going to have my evening tea. Come and join me," said Flore and she led them into a tidy little sitting room with lace doilies on the furniture and old-fashioned oil lamps on the side tables.

They sat down and Flore hurried off to the kitchen, but then poked her head back in. "Perhaps coffee for you, Cornelia?" Flore asked with a wink.

"Lovely, my favorite."

The ladies shared a laugh that Stella didn't understand, but she was in on the joke a short ten minutes later. Flore offered both coffee and tea along with little sandwiches. Cornelia had coffee that Flore poured a generous amount of Jenever in.

"My favorite," said Cornelia.

Flore gave her a wicked smile. "I know. Yannj's too. She misses it."

"Have you heard from her lately?"

"I had a letter last week. She's got a new job and is making more money. It's at something called a department store."

Cornelia turned to Stella and asked, "What is that?"

"Oh, it's a store with lots of different sections like one for hats and shoes and another for men's coats."

"All in one place?" Flore asked. "The store must be very large."

"They are," said Stella. "In New York, they are enormous."

"New York? Are you American? You sound Belgian."

Stella congratulated herself. It never got old. She loved her accents being recognized. "I am, but I work for Americans much of the time."

"Do you?" Flore leaned in and Stella told the old lady about her business and she was properly impressed with all the travel and interesting people.

"That's why we're here," said Cornelia.

"Really? I can't buy two-hundred-year-old clocks or fancy necklaces."

Stella smiled. "Actually, I was hoping that you could tell me about Anna Bikker. Cornelia thinks she might be a good buyer for me."

The old lady's face, so sweet and pleasant, balled up and her lower lip poked out. "That girl? She's no good. No good at all. She was a Hartman, a good family. They lived right down the street. You couldn't say a bad word about them, but the daughter…no. She married that Jan Bikker. Do you know that he never came to see them here? Never. Not once. They were allowed to go to the wedding, but then he shipped them off up north."

Not a bad word about a rabid fascist father?

"What's she like?" Stella asked. "The daughter?"

"Terrible. Always looking for a way up. No loyalty to her family or her neighborhood. What was the next thing, the better thing. That was Anna Hartman."

"How in the world did she meet Jan Bikker?" Cornelia asked.

"Well, it wasn't an accident. I can tell you that."

Stella and Cornelia glanced at each other puzzled, but they didn't have to ask for the story. Flore couldn't wait to tell it. Anna's mother, Isa, had told her the whole tale, embarrassed and bewildered by her daughter's ambition. Anna had spotted Jan Bikker in the newspaper during the run up to the 1932 Winter Olympics. There were profiles of local athletes and Jan was a speed skater. Anna was working as a secretary at a tea importer. It was a good job, but it wasn't enough. She was never going to be rich and she told her mother she wasn't meeting the right kind of men. By right, she meant wealthy.

Stella had to give it to Anna Hartman Bikker. She knew what she wanted and she wasn't afraid to give it all she had. The girl studied Jan Bikker. She followed him around town to find out where he liked to go, where he bought his suits and hats. Then she followed his dates, finding out what he preferred. She even befriended a few of them to get the skinny on how he behaved, his likes and dislikes. Then Anna Hartman transformed herself into what Jan Bikker wanted. She learned to hunt and ski. She dyed her hair blond and lost weight. She spent every dime on the right clothes and changed her accent to match his and when the moment was right, Anna Hartman began going to his skating club. From there, it was easy, Jan Bikker found her, a tall blonde who liked everything he liked, who ate the same foods, had a passion for sports, and Germany. He proposed before he had any idea who she really was or where she came from, exactly the way she planned.

"And he just married her?" Stella asked. "Without knowing her family?"

"Yes, he did," said Flore. "Well...I heard he had them investigated first."

Cornelia frowned. "For what?"

Flore grimaced. "What do you think? To make sure they weren't Jewish. That's what her mother told me. She was so upset."

"Because it was insulting?" Stella asked, guessing an NSB family wouldn't like the inference.

"Because it wasn't love, it was a transaction. If Anna had been the smallest part a Jew, there would be no marriage. That's what I remember the most."

"What's that?" Cornelia asked.

"Isa calling it a transaction. She said Jan Bikker had no moral center. It was all transaction."

"Everything was about looks then. He didn't fall for a person at all."

"That's right, but Anna didn't care. She gave the right impression. She said the right things and she got what she wanted." Flore snorted. "Well, she hasn't really, has she?"

"Why not?" Stella asked. "She's rich."

Flore offered her the sandwiches and Stella took a triangle of gouda and egg salad. "Because Anna Bikker is Anna Hartman and everyone knows it. She hasn't got the taste and style that fancy people do. She can only imitate it and no one mistakes her for an aristocrat or a lady. I saw her just the other day in the Vondelpark. She was complaining about no one respecting her here. She likes it better in Germany. They have respect, she said." Flore looked like she might spit on the floor she was so disgusted.

"She may get her wish with the way it's looking," said Cornelia. "I heard that the government is negotiating with the Nazis."

Stella looked up. "Negotiating what?"

"Whether they will attack us or not."

"I hadn't heard that."

Flore sat frozen in her little armchair, seeming older than ever. "You don't really think they'd attack. They consider us Aryans, don't they?"

Cornelia patted her hand and then poured her some more tea. "Yes, they do. Don't worry. The queen will think of something."

"Where did you hear that?" Stella asked. "About the negotiating. I didn't see it in the paper."

"I know a maid at the palace." Then her friend frowned. "Does it matter so much to you? You're not Dutch."

"Belgium can't be far behind if they're coming here. Many of the French think they will attack them to get to Britain and there we are right in between."

"I hadn't thought of that."

"We're all in this together," said Stella, making her hand shake slightly and Cornelia gave her back a rub, comforting them both at the same time.

"You're right we are." Then to change the subject she said, "Flore, can you think of anything that would help Micheline to sell to Anna?"

Flore poured Cornelia another jot of Jenever and nodded, "Tell her you have rich people's things. She'll like that."

"They're all rich people's things. Who else would have diamonds?"

"I mean, tell her they belonged to someone special." She put her cup down in the saucer with a clunk and gave them a grin. "I know, tell her the jewelry was stolen from German dukes or princesses. She'll love that."

Stella sat back and pursed her lips. "That would make them stolen goods. I could be arrested and they're not stolen."

"Who did you buy them from?" Flore asked. "That has to be a story."

She hesitated, but Cornelia didn't. "She bought them from the Jews, but she's not cheating them."

"I hope not. Some of those merchants wouldn't give Yannj half of what her mother's rings were worth. Poor thing." Flore looked down into her cup and for a second Stella thought she'd changed her mind about Micheline, but then she looked up and said, "You know, Yannj's mother was quite well to do."

"I don't think so," Cornelia said.

"Yes, she was. Her grandfather owned several banks and they had summer houses and even boats."

Cornelia drank her Jenever coffee and pondered that information. "Are you sure? She never told me so."

"Well, she was a maid, just like you and she didn't want to seem like she was anything else."

"She didn't want me to feel bad?"

"Or think she was too stupid to save the family fortune or something like that. Of course, she couldn't. It was nothing to do with Yannj."

A.W. HARTOIN

"Did she mind being a maid?" Stella asked, thinking about growing up the way she had and ending up a maid. What would she think or do? She really couldn't say, but she knew she could survive like Yannj. She'd proven that time and again.

"No, I don't think so," said Flore. "She was never bitter. She did mention that horrible Anna trying to get her arrested. Can you imagine? They knew each other, lived right here on the same street and there's Anna Hartman screeching about how Yannj should be arrested for nothing. She didn't wrong her in any way. Micheline?"

"Yes?" asked Stella.

"You should tell her they're diamonds and sell her paste. She's too stupid to know the difference."

"I like the idea, but my merchandise is the real thing. I can overcharge though."

Flore clapped her hands in delight. "Do that. Yes, do. Tell her you bought them from Jews who…who…foreclosed on some German aristocrats. She'll love that."

They all laughed and Stella thought about it. She could do that. Anna Bikker sounded like the type who would enjoy a story of wicked Jews falling on hard times, but she'd have to play the part. That was no problem, but Cornelia, so well-informed, would find out.

"But I'd have to really do it," said Stella dabbing at the corner of her eyes, careful not to smudge her faux crow's feet.

Cornelia wiped her eyes aggressively with a big cotton handkerchief and then blew her nose lustily. "Do what?"

Stella wrinkled her nose. "You know, pretend to be like her. I told you I'm no Bikker, but she'll like the story better if she thinks I am."

Flore laughed. "Yes, yes. Be one of those NSB people. Say you love Germany and the Führer."

"That might be too far," said Cornelia. "Anna's not crazy."

We'll see about that.

"I'll play it by ear," said Stella before turning on Micheline's brand of charm and asking Flore about her life. She wasn't disappointed. There were interesting people to be found in every country. Flore and her husband were retired bakers, but he'd died ten years ago. That was when she started taking in boarders for cash and company.

"I haven't got anyone just now," she said. "My last got married and dear Yannj has moved to America. It's so nice to have you here. I do get lonely in this big house."

The old lady was very chatty and they stayed long into the evening talking of everything from cheese to Italy. Flore and Cornelia had always wanted to go, giving Stella a chance to tell a multitude of stories. She gave them experiences she had before it happened in Vienna, before she lost Abel and became a different Stella, so different that it seemed like she was truly talking about someone else entirely. Stella managed to work in asking about Yannj's American diplomat in Rotterdam, but Flore couldn't remember the name either. She did promise to look through her letters to see if Yannj wrote about him and Stella went into a funny story about a misdirected letter that Florence had told her about.

The ladies enjoyed the stories and she enjoyed telling them about eating spaghetti for the first time and seeing the Trevi Fountain, even though it made her miss Nicky so much it hurt. He was part of her story, but more and more he seemed relegated to the past.

When Flore began nodding off, Cornelia and Stella stood up, thanking her profusely for letting them barge in and drink all her Jenever and coffee. Flore was delighted and asked them to come back soon. They said they would and stepped outside into the dark, chilly night, linking arms.

"Do you have enough information to sell to that dreadful Anna?" Cornelia asked as they walked back to the tram.

"I do," said Stella. "All except one thing."

"What else could you possibly need?"

"An introduction."

Cornelia laughed. "Oh, that."

"Yes, that. I tried to make an appointment at Jan Bikker's office, but he wouldn't see me. His wife doesn't even have an office and from what you and Flore say she'll turn her nose up at me straight away."

"The baron is coming home on Friday."

Stella's stomach tightened, but she said with a yawn, "How is that helpful I'd like to know."

"He'll have a party, a welcome home. He always does and we've already started the ordering for it."

"I'm sure Anna Bikker will love it if she manages an invitation," said Stella.

Cornelia nudged her, smiling, and asked, "How much is my finder's fee?"

"Fifteen percent of my profit on whatever pieces I sell to Anna."

"She'll be invited. I'll see to that."

"Nice for her, but what about me?"

A bicyclist came careening out of the dark and they jumped out of the way in the nick of time. Stella still couldn't get used to so many bicycles. They were absolutely everywhere.

"You should come, too."

"Me? At a baron's party? You can see me, right?"

"I can and you are very respectable."

"Cornelia, you're very kind, but I'm not an aristocrat. I can't pretend that I am any more than Anna Bikker can."

"You don't have to. The baron enjoys all sorts of company and you're an interesting woman."

"Am I?"

"Of course, you are. A woman working alone without any man at all and you know wealthy Americans. You've been to New York."

"It's not as exotic as you make it sound," said Stella, feeling that it was probably quite exotic to most people and she'd always taken it for granted. Shame on her.

"I'll tell him I met you at a gallery and he should send an invitation to your hotel," said Cornelia. "He's always after intriguing conversation and you never know who you'll meet."

"As easy as that?"

"Certainly. We're talking about Baron Joost Van Heeckeren. He's not like anyone else."

"What should I expect?" Stella asked.

"Anything. Absolutely anything."

CHAPTER 5

Anna Bikker did not disappoint. Stella had a picture in her mind of the sort of woman she was looking for as she walked past the Bikkers' front door for the fifth time the next morning. It was getting harder and harder to look casual and her feet were starting to ache. So far, she'd bought flowers and walked past. Gone to a café, had coffee and then walked past. Purchased meat at a butcher and walked past. She didn't know what to do with that. Then she bought some rolls and walked past. She bought a handy carrying basket for her purchases and walked past, each time changing her look slightly. Hat. No hat. Coat. No coat. Scarf. No scarf.

Stella was beginning to think Anna Hartman Bikker was a figment of Amsterdam's imagination. Where was this woman? Jan Bikker had left promptly at eight and headed in the direction of the Bikker Grand Hotel. He returned at noon, stayed an hour, and went back in the same direction. Deliveries came. Trash went out. Servants bustled around in full view behind the large windows, dusting and then dusting again. Apparently, there was a frightful amount of dust in the Bikker house. It was useful to be able to see inside and Stella appreciated the Dutch dislike of curtains. Anyone could see into the main rooms and she was that anyone. Park-Welles had said it was something to do with Calvinism, but the concierge at her hotel had told her it was honesty. The Dutch don't draw curtains on their main rooms because an honest man has nothing to hide. Interesting concept, but in Stella's experience everyone had something to hide. She knew because she was so terribly good at finding it, but that wasn't proving to be true with Anna Bikker.

Walking across the canal, Stella looked in at different rooms, trying to spot the elusive lady of the house but never did. Just maids dusting, arranging, and dusting again. She didn't have a view into what might be an owner's bedroom and Anna could be holed up there, but it was three o'clock in the afternoon. Was she ill or out of town? Stella was about to give up when the front door of the tasteful house opened and a woman of about twenty-five came out. Anna Bikker. It had to be. She was tall as the Dutch almost always were. At least five or six inches taller than Stella. She was very thin with blonde hair that was obviously not natural, not with those brows.

Anna Bikker put her nose in the air and walked down the stairs to the street in a way that was overly careful as if she thought someone was watching. Someone was, but not who she imagined. Stella knew women with that air. They thought they were the center of everyone's attention and it made them stilted and, frankly, odd. Those were wealthy American girls, usually in love with Nicky, and stunned that Stella had captured his heart without spending hours with a book on her head, learning to play the harp, or having elocution lessons. Watching Anna walk down the street, Stella began to notice more and more how much Jan Bikker's wife stood out and not in a good way. It took a minute and then she got it. Anna Bikker did not look Dutch. Cornelia said she'd know her when she saw her because you couldn't not see her. It wasn't a compliment although her friend insisted that Anna was attractive.

Stella kept her distance and wondered where on Earth they were going. Unlike the rest of Amsterdam, Anna didn't get on a bicycle. She didn't take a cab or drive and they kept walking and walking, but Anna was not dressed for a trek. Stella didn't know what she was dressed for; if her outfit hadn't been so expensive, she'd have thought something akin to prostitution. Anna stopped to speak to a woman appropriately dressed in conservative day clothes and Stella stopped ten feet away at a vegetable stand, close enough to hear the ladies chatting about a party. The appropriate woman wanted to speak about a function on Sunday, something to do with orphans, but Anna kept bringing up a party she'd been invited to that the other woman clearly had not. Stella had no affection for either woman, but the conversation still made her cringe.

"It will be quite an event," said Anna.

"I'm sure it will," said the woman, "but on Sunday we must see if—"

"All the best people will be there."

"As you said. Now Fenna Janson says that if we can each bring two guests to hear the speakers, the fundraising will be very much improved."

Anna tossed her hair and held out her hand that had three bejeweled rings on it. "I suppose I could talk to someone about it at the party. There will be so many people there."

The grocer approached Stella and, not having any other alternative, she bought potatoes, one beet, and asparagus. More food she had no use for. While the man wrapped up her vegetables, she caught him glancing at Anna with disgust. That had to be unusual. She was obviously wealthy and right at the edge of his stand. Normally, the man would've approached her to ask if there was anything he could get her, but he didn't. He stood back with a sour milk look on his face and then turned to Stella with a polite smile, but he kept glancing at Anna, his face changing on a dime, and Stella could see why. The more she looked at the woman, the more she understood what Flore was talking about. The average person walking by, rich or poor, young or old, was dressed a certain way. They were understated to a one. That's not to say without style for they certainly had that, but it wasn't overdone. Quality over quantity was what came to Stella's mind.

Anna Bikker didn't appear to have the Dutch mindset when it came to dress. She wore a mink coat, the only one Stella had seen that spring day and it was a Wednesday afternoon, for heaven's sake. But that wasn't enough for Anna. She had a red hat plastered with feathers of three different varieties, a jeweled pin on the right side and a hatpin with a heavy pearl and diamond cluster at the end. A woman could have one of those things, but certainly not all of them and not at three o'clock in the afternoon. To make it worse, Anna's stiletto heels matched her hat with multiple bows and large buckles.

Stella found herself wondering who in the world designed them and the answer came just as the man tucked her asparagus in her basket.

"Your shoes are very distinctive, Anna," said the appropriate woman. "Wherever did you get them?"

Anna apparently didn't have an ear for tone because she stuck out a shapely leg and said, "Madam Milla, but they were so plain. She hasn't picked up on the latest styles out of Paris yet. I had the bows added. Can you imagine these shoes without bows, just buckles? They'd be nothing at all. Anyone could wear them."

"Anyone would, I'm sure," the woman said dripping with sarcasm that Anna was oblivious to. "Madam Milla is quite a talent."

"I couldn't even wear them to coffee much less an event like the party on Friday. I told you about the party, didn't I?"

Friday. The baron's big do. Thank you, Cornelia.

Stella paid the man and they shared sly smiles at Anna's expense before Stella walked away past the ladies.

"Yes, you did," said the appropriate woman.

"Did I tell you that I got a special invitation just this morning?"

"You did. I really have to go. My…daughter is waiting."

"Oh, well, if you…"

Stella lost the conversation at ten feet but then stopped to adjust her own very plain brass shoe buckle. Happily, Anna swished by in a cloud of perfume that might very well have been more than one brand. Stella stood up, adjusted her basket, and then strolled after her, hoping she wouldn't have to buy anything else. The basket was getting heavy.

Two turns later, she got a good idea of where Anna was headed. Dam Square where Stella's hotel was. Convenient, if a bit of a walk. There were tons of cafés on the square and restaurants, too, but Anna sashayed straight across to the Hotel Krasnapolsky, ignored the doorman who tried to help her, and a second doorman had to run to open the door for her because she certainly wasn't going to open it herself.

Stella followed her slowly. Anna didn't seem to be the sharpest tool in the shed, but she had managed to snooker Jan Bikker into marrying her, so anything was possible. Stella didn't want her to notice a drab, frizzy-haired woman always on her tail, but she needn't have worried. By the time she was inside, Anna was already going through the doors to the hotel's famed winter garden without a glance back.

"May I help you, ma'am?" an unfamiliar desk clerk asked.

"Yes, please. I'm so ridiculous. I went out walking and I found myself looking at meat and produce."

"We have very good shopping here."

"You do and I bought quite a bit. Could you please take my basket and put it in your icebox? I have a person in mind to give it to, but I have to have a coffee first."

The clerk took the basket and said, "Yes, ma'am. Would you like to go to our café for coffee? Or I could send it to your room."

Stella tapped her lips like she had to give the choices some thought. "How about the winter garden. It's lovely in there and so airy."

"I'm sorry. We are setting up for an event. There will be a wedding on Friday and we are having the pleasure of hosting the reception. Our café is open or the restaurant, if you prefer."

"Oh, I thought I saw a woman go in the winter garden just now."

"That was...that lady must be going to another section of the hotel."

Ah...I see.

"Then I would love some coffee in the café," said Stella.

The clerk took her into the café and she managed to get her favorite table. It came with a view of the lobby and the square. Then the clerk hurried off with her basket and Stella pulled out a handy little book and pencil that she pretended to write facts and figures for her business in until a young lady arrived at her table.

"Good afternoon, ma'am."

Stella looked and there was Marga, the thief and betrayer of Yannj. She covered the internal jolt and said, "A café creme and apple pie."

"Would you like whipped cream?" Marga asked.

Stella waited a split second to see if there was a glimmer of recognition, but Marga's eyes were vacant and disinterested. "Yes, please."

Marga nodded and ambled off. Several other patrons tried to get her attention, but the girl was in her own world, a very good thing for Stella and a little curious. Marga had focused quite a bit of energy making fun of Stella and Cornelia twenty-four hours prior. Stella was wearing the exact same brown suit and shoes. Her hair was still frizzy and auburn and her face lined and tired, but Marga showed no sign that she remembered her. That made her either stupid or incredibly self-absorbed. Marga clearly wasn't discreet, but she had managed to keep a job at Bikkers for a while and get another after being fired. Stella decided to bet on the latter and if she played it right, it could be useful.

An unacceptable amount of time later, Marga ambled back into the café, carrying a tray with a coffee but not pie. Another patron demanded her attention by literally getting up and blocking her path. That was the only way he could pay his check and Stella didn't see a bright future at the Hotel Krasnapolsky for Marga Kübler.

Marga allowed people to pay their checks with a few sighs and one eye roll before coming to Stella and plucking down her coffee and dish of rum baba with half-melted vanilla ice cream. That wasn't anywhere close to the apple pie she'd ordered, but it wouldn't do to mention it.

"Hard day?" Stella asked as she picked up the lukewarm cup.

"They all are." She wasn't looking at Stella but staring at a wall.

"Can I ask you something?"

"Did I get it wrong?" Marga squinted at the rum baba and it looked like there was a hint of a thought that it wasn't what Stella ordered.

"It looks delicious. I wanted to ask you something else, but you may not think it appropriate."

That got the girl's attention. Inappropriate was her wheelhouse. "Yes."

"Right before I came into the hotel, there was the most extraordinary woman in front of me."

Marga perked up. "A film star? We get film stars sometimes." She named a few people Stella had never heard of, but she was very impressed.

"She might be a film star. She was very fancy and when I asked about her," Stella lowered her voice even though no one else was left in the café, "no one would say who she was."

"Really? What did she look like?" Marga pulled out a chair and sat down.

It took Stella two seconds to recover, but then she said, "She was very tall and blonde."

"That's half the city." Marga touched the long dark hair that lay in lovely waves down nearly to her waist. She really was very pretty with clear porcelain skin and enormous dark eyes. It was a shame that those eyes held no hint of intelligence.

"I know, but she was wearing a mink coat. Today. In the afternoon."

Frown lines formed between Marga's eyes and Stella continued. "She had the fanciest shoes I've ever seen, bows and buckles. Her hat was amazing and her jewelry. So many rings. She must be American, right?"

Marga rolled her eyes at Stella's ignorance and then glanced at the door to the kitchen. "She's Dutch. Her name is Anna Bikker and she's an awful, nasty *kutwijf*."

That wasn't a word you heard in polite company, but Marga showed no sign of knowing that.

"Is she a guest?" Stella asked with rapt attention.

Marga laughed much the way she had at them yesterday. "She's not a guest, but she does like to *visit*."

"Oh, I bet I know what that means."

"Yes, and she acts like she is above everyone. We know who she is. Mink coats don't change it."

"Change what? Who is she?" Stella asked.

Marga told her a surprisingly accurate account of Anna Hartman Bikker's rise from working class to wealthy. Flore was right. Everyone did know.

"You'd think she wouldn't want to jeopardize all that work," said Stella.

"What work? She doesn't know work. Do you know that she had me fired and it wasn't even fair."

"Fired from where?"

"Some horrible woman came to the hotel—"

"This hotel?"

"No, no. I worked at the Bikker Grand then," said Marga impatiently. "She came and said I didn't do good work. But I did and my friend, too."

"But she fired you anyway?"

"She wanted us arrested. We told them who wasn't doing good work, but she wanted us arrested anyway."

It was almost too much, but Stella managed to keep a straight face. "For not working well? I don't understand."

"I know, right? I told them what they wanted, but we were still fired."

"But not arrested?"

Marga's version of the story included a visit from the *politie* at her family's home. She was questioned, accused of lying, and possibly stealing because why would you lie if you didn't intend to steal. In the end, after a good deal of crying, and her father's pleas, the *politie* let her and her friend off with a warning. The young woman didn't show any fear. She was outraged, but it was hard to tell about what. She never said what she was lying about. She was bright enough to do that, but she had no regrets about telling the Bikkers what they wanted to know. There was betrayal, but it was all against her. Stella doubted she'd given a single thought to Yannj and the others since it happened.

"Now this horrid Bikker woman comes here," said Stella.

"Yes, she does and I think about telling all the time, but I would probably get fired again for…something."

"I wonder if she knows how lucky she is."

"Anna Hartman thinks she's special, not lucky."

"It doesn't take a special woman to do what she's doing," said Stella.

Give me a name. Give me a name.

"And if you know, everyone else must, too."

Marga smiled. "They pretend they don't. It's the Dutch way. You're not Dutch?"

"Belgian. I have noticed that they ignore the obvious sometimes."

"Yes, they do. Lotte even has to leave the office, if you can believe that."

A man appeared at Stella's table and said sharply, "Marga, what are you doing?"

She jumped up, blushing. "Oh, I…"

"It's my fault," said Stella quickly. "I was lonely sitting here and she was keeping me company since there are no other guests. Please don't punish her for kindness."

The last bit might have gone too far. Marga probably wasn't known for kindness, but the café manager bought it anyway. "If you insist, Micheline."

"Thank you, Dirk. She…" Stella looked at Marga questioningly but only got a blank look in return.

"Marga," said Dirk in exasperation. "Her name is Marga." He shooed her away and then asked Stella, "Are you sure she wasn't bothering you?"

"Not at all. The girl is silly but entertaining in her way."

"I'm glad you're entertained by her. I assure you we are not. Can I get you anything else?"

"No, I'm fine. Thank you."

He went into the kitchen and Stella heard a few sharp words drifting out of the backroom as she sipped her ice-cold coffee, allowing herself the smallest of smiles.

Anna Bikker emerged from the depths of the hotel an hour and a half later. She blew through the lobby and was out walking before Stella could toss some coins on the table.

"Madam Dubois," Dirk came over in a rush as she snatched her coat off its hanger, "what is the matter?"

"I've lost track of time. I'm going to be late for my appointment." She slammed her hat on her head and he helped her on with her coat.

"What time is your appointment?"

"1700. It was so hard to get. I must not be late." She grabbed her handbag and dashed for the door.

"Let Sim call a cab for you or Albrecht."

"No, no. It will be fine." Stella hurried through the door, taking a split second to thank the doorman before going across the square and checking her watch. Luckily, Anna's mink and red hat were like a beacon. She could see that getup for a mile and it was a good thing. Anna was in a huge hurry and practically running through the streets with the mink flapping in the breeze. Stella's legs couldn't hope to catch up and she did lose sight of Anna several times, but since she had an idea of where she was going, it wasn't hard to guess her path.

And Stella was right. Anna Bikker was in a huge rush to get home and she made it just in time. Stella watched her dash up the stairs and through the big open windows she could be easily seen throwing her coat at one maid and her hat at another before disappearing into the depths of the house. Stella passed the house, crossed the canal, and walked back up on the other side. She shuffled through her handbag and came up with an Amsterdam map. Pretending to look for her location, she didn't have long to wait.

Jan Bikker came striding down the street with his long legs at exactly 1715. He went in, spoke to the maids, who nodded emphatically and took his hat and coat. Jan went to a room that looked like a library and sat down. At least, Stella assumed he sat. He disappeared from view. She waited for another five minutes to see if Anna would appear to greet her husband, but she didn't show, and Stella retraced her steps back to her hotel.

"Madam Dubois," said Sim at the desk. "Did you miss your appointment?"

"Please call me Micheline."

The clerk blushed with pleasure. The hotel staff took longer than Pieter and the workmen to use her given name. They liked to be invited and she was working her way through the ranks as a regular guest.

"Micheline," he said. "Were you late?"

"I was three minutes late, but he forgot completely, so I've rescheduled with no problem."

"That's very good."

"It is and a relief. I do have a business to run," she said. "I'll be back down in a minute. Can you get my basket for me? I need to deliver it."

Sim said he would and Stella went upstairs to her room and allowed herself to flop down on the bed for a moment. She could've gone straight to sleep, but she'd made a promise and now was the perfect time to keep it.

Her makeup needed a touch up, but her tiredness helped the situation. Stella didn't remember ever having purple smudges under her eyes before coming to Europe. She wondered if she did but just didn't notice them. With a little shadow she made them even worse and was pretty sure she added another five years.

She combed her wig, pinned it more firmly to her sweaty head, and put on a fresh coat of nude lipstick before frowning at herself in the mirror. "Micheline, you need serious help."

Since there was no help to be had, she got out *Der Totale Krieg* and found a letter tucked way in the back. The sadness threatened to return, but Stella Bled Lawrence reminded herself of how much she'd found out in the last two days and rushed off to do her duty.

CHAPTER 6

Stella had been to the *Jodenbuurt* before but not often. The friends and acquaintances on Francesqua's list typically had some money and were spread out across the city and the Jewish quarter was fairly crowded. She'd heard it called a ghetto in a very nasty way, but it was just a neighborhood, not unlike Flore's. It wasn't Westerbork and the people she'd talked to were very happy to have come legally and not to be interned in the refugee camp. Only two families on the list had been stuck in the camp and that was more than enough. The camp had challenges of its own.

By the time Stella stepped out of the Hotel Krasnapolsky, the square had cleared out. Daan wanted to call her a cab, but she decided to walk since it wouldn't take long and it felt good with the canals all sparkly and quiet after the evening rush. There were more people out in the *Jodenbuurt* and Stella fit right in with her basket and clothes not made for garnering attention. She asked at a market for Eiger Menswear and was directed down a few side streets where she found the shop starting to close. It was a typically narrow building with the shop on the first floor and flats above. The shop had large windows with etched glass giving the year of establishment 1912 and the offerings, men's ready to wear and expert tailoring for all sizes and styles.

The shop was neat and prosperous with nothing to show it was Jewish, and with a sigh, Stella thought how the Nazis would make short work of that.

"Excuse me," she asked the older man as he pulled a rack of ready-made men's shirts inside.

"Yes?" he asked.

"I'm looking for the Dereczynski family. I was given this address for them."

The man hesitated and looked her over, not exactly suspicious but a little reluctant. Stella would've been suspicious. She suspected everyone now and it wasn't a trait that she was proud of.

"I know the family," he said without giving anything else away.

"A man in Rotterdam gave me their information. He thought they have some items I might be interested in buying."

The man scoffed. "Them? No. They have nothing. Refugees from Poland. They left with their lives. Nothing more." He pulled the rack inside and started to close the door, but she persisted. A promise was a promise.

Stella put her hand on the doorjamb so he would have to slam it on her fingers or relent. As expected, he relented but not without irritation.

"Who are you?" he demanded.

She gave him her card. People of all persuasions loved a card. Anyone could have absolutely anything printed up for a price, but people seemed to think they were official.

"Licensed buyer for B.L. Imports of New York, New York," he read slowly.

Using *licensed* had been Stella's idea. It sounded terribly important and government sanctioned, but Park-Welles objected. There was no such thing as licensing buyers for importers, but she talked until he got tired of her talking and she got her *Licensed buyer*. Stella was right. People were impressed and it got her toe in the door more than once. New York, New York didn't hurt either. Besides, nobody knew what went on in America. For all they knew dogs got licensed to pee on trees.

"What do you buy?" he asked, bringing the card within an inch of his face.

"All sorts of things that might interest my clients. Antiques, jewelry, books, small pieces of furniture. Americans like to have a bit of the old world in their new houses."

He gave her back the card. "You won't find anything like that here. Don't you know where you are?"

"I do," she said primly.

"You don't or you wouldn't be asking for antiques. We have what we need, nothing more." He tried to close the door and to his dismay, she stuck her hand in again.

"Do you know where I can find the Dereczynski family or not?" she asked.

"They have nothing or they would've sold it to me."

I'm sure you'd pay a good price, too.

"Sir, I have a job. I intend to do it, so I can go home," said Stella.

He was a big man and he leaned over her smallness to say in a gruff voice. "They are Jews."

"Yes, I know."

"You think Polish Jews have antiques for you?" He was starting to sound as if she was stupid and it was wearing.

"I was sent here to find out. I don't *think* anything."

He grumbled something offensive about Polish Jews and opened the door for her. "They are in the attic with the mice. Don't hit your head."

Thanking him burned, but she did it as diffidently as possible. She was a disinterested party after all, but she was starting to question Pieter sending her here. He'd been evasive about who they were. Friends of his father's cousin or something equally unlikely, but she'd agreed to come and he'd been almost tearfully grateful. She didn't know what to make of it.

She also didn't know what to make of a family of four living in an attic four stories up a staircase so narrow her elbows touched the walls. Pieter assured her they would have something for her to buy, but the shopkeeper had a point. Surely, they would have sold it to get out of that attic.

At the top of the stairs was a low door, not five feet high and without a proper doorknob. There was just a hole and she could hear children's voices and smell dinner. Something with cabbage.

She knocked and a chorus of excited young voices urged the father to answer the door. They had a visitor. It was obviously a first. The door opened and a tall man with a mop of dark curly hair stooped under a low ceiling peered down at her in surprise.

"Can I help you?" he asked in Polish once he'd recovered.

Stella's Polish wasn't as good as her Dutch, but she answered readily and his shock grew.

"Who sent you?" he asked, nervously.

"May I come in?" Stella asked.

He waved her in, but she could tell it was out of politeness and he was deeply afraid. She couldn't blame him. She'd seen Warsaw. You'd have to be a fool not to be wrapped in a blanket of anxiety after what happened to the Jews there and was probably still happening for those not as lucky as the Dereczynskis.

Stella walked past a wall with a row of coats on metal hooks into what passed as a living room. She didn't have to duck or crouch. There were advantages to being small.

In the corner of the room, an extremely thin woman with long blonde hair in a single braid was bent over a pot on a hotplate. It was the only source of heat in the chilly flat and a stack of dishes sat next to the hotplate, all chipped and mismatched. She turned around and exclaimed in Polish with an upper-class accent that her husband shared but wasn't quite the same.

"Hello. Forgive me. I was expecting our landlord. He comes early for the rent," the wife said.

Her husband made a faint grumbling noise, but quickly said, "We are lucky that he would take us. He is very generous."

The wife smoothed her apron to hide her expression which contradicted her husband in every way. "Yes, yes, of course. May we help you?"

A.W. HARTOIN

"My name is Micheline Dubois and Pieter Visser sent me."

Both husband's and wife's mouths dropped open and before they could close them, a little girl about six with her mother's dark blond hair came out from the back lugging a three-year-old. He was a big boy and she could hardly carry him. "He won't stay in the bed, Mama," she said, her brown eyes on Stella, alert with interest.

The boy wriggled out of his sister's arms and landed with a thump on the floor and a wail erupted from him. Like with Stella's little cousins, Myrtle and Millicent, a lot of noise came out of such a small creature and she resisted the instinct to cover her ears.

His sister didn't. She made a face and said, "Quiet, Ezra. It's your own fault."

"He's ill, Leonarda. Have some sympathy."

Leonarda's face grew furious and she looked at Stella. "My name is Lonia."

Her mother plucked Ezra off the floor and gave him a taste of dinner, but he wasn't thrilled with whatever she was cooking and wailed all the more. Downstairs, someone yelled and hit the ceiling with something.

"You must quiet him," said the husband. "They're getting less tolerant every day."

The wife looked around frantic and Stella spoke up. "Perhaps I can help." She dug under the cloth she had over the basket and came up with a roll. The boy lunged toward it, but the mother said, "We couldn't possibly take your food."

"You could and you'd be helping me," Stella said.

They looked doubtful, but another pounding from their neighbor convinced them. The boy tore into the roll like he hadn't eaten in days and Stella feared that might not be far from the truth. It wasn't a large pot on the hotplate.

"May I have a roll, please?" asked Lonia.

With parental permission, Stella gave the girl one and watched her take a delicate bite and then smile up at her with angelic appreciation.

I will help them. No matter what.

"As I said," Stella began, "Pieter Visser sent me. Do you have time to talk business?"

The wife poured a kind of cabbage and potato soup into two bowls and took the children into a back room. Lonia wasn't happy to leave, but she obeyed with regret.

The husband introduced himself as Józef and when his wife returned, he introduced her as Weronika.

"I don't understand," said Weronika after offering Stella a chair. "You know Pieter Visser?"

Stella gave them her card and watched as they examined it in confusion and not a little wariness.

"Pieter works for the export company I use in Rotterdam and we've gotten to know each other."

"And he sent you here?" Józef asked. "Why?"

She indicated the card. "I'm a buyer, primarily for Americans. He thought you might have something to sell."

They weren't convinced and she got out the letter. "He wrote this to explain. I hope it will help you to trust me."

Józef took the envelope and broke the seal. Weronika sat down beside him and they read it together. Weronika wiped a tear away and clutched her husband's leg. The couple was as Pieter described them, elegant, well-spoken, and a bit delicate. She was a Polish aristocrat from the Umiastowski family and he was from the Jewish Dereczynski family, upper class but not nobility.

"I apologize for doubting you," said Weronika. "We don't get many visitors. We are strangers here."

"I understand completely," said Stella. "May I ask what Pieter said?"

"You don't know?"

"I didn't ask."

Józef was still looking down at the letter and didn't answer. Stella suspected he was having a hard time getting ahold of himself. She didn't blame him. It'd been a long, hard fall from where he'd been.

"Pieter said you are good and honorable. He says," she glanced at the doorway to the back, "that he would trust you with his children."

"High praise. I'm honored by his faith," said Stella. "Can I ask you something?"

Józef looked up and said, "I would deny you nothing."

She had to swallow hard before continuing. The pain on his face. She'd seen it so many times before, but it was always like the first time. "How do you know Pieter? He didn't say and Rotterdam is a long way from Poland."

Weronika smiled, transforming her pinched features into true beauty, and Stella couldn't help but think that this face, this elegant composure that spoke of good breeding and education was what Anna Bikker was trying to fake. But there was no faking that and piling on pricy furs didn't make a bit of difference. Weronika wore a shapeless cotton dress and a woolly sweater that wasn't originally her own and she was more classy than Anna covered in her guilders.

"I can see why you would be curious and it is funny how these connections happen," said Weronika. "I've known Pieter most of my life. His father was a master woodworker and my father hired him and three other men to build a staircase in our new house when I was five."

"He brought Pieter with him to Poland?"

"Pieter's mother had died and there was no other family to leave him with, so my father gave him permission to bring his son. It was unusual, but Johannes was extremely skilled and an important part of the team. They stayed for ten years on the estate and I grew up with Pieter. My father was a generous man and Pieter was intelligent and hardworking. He didn't have his father's talent, but he was educated on the estate and made himself useful."

"Ten years to build a staircase," said Stella. "How big was it?"

"Huge. Our house, you understand, it was a palace," Weronika was slightly embarrassed at the admission and glanced around at their place with its cobbled together furniture and frayed fabrics, "but it only took two years. The staircase was a masterpiece and my father hired the team to make all sorts of other pieces, mantles and cornices in our other houses."

"Your father can't help you?" Stella asked without thinking and it was mistake. She knew the minute it slipped out.

"He died five years ago," said Weronika.

"I'm sorry to hear that," said Stella.

Weronika looked down at her red, cracked hands and the silence grew between the three of them. Stella struggled to think of something appropriate to say but came up empty. It was all so horrible. It had to be or they wouldn't be in that attic.

"As Pieter said, I'm looking to buy—"

"My father's gone, too," said Józef, coming alive and flushing.

Weronika's head jerked up in surprise. "Oh, my dear, you don't have to—"

"He…died unexpectedly." The words burst out of Józef like an old abscess finally lanced.

Stella knew what *unexpectedly* meant. Suicide. Terrified people took the only avenue of escape open to them. It happened in Vienna and Prague, everywhere the Nazis took over. It would happen in Amsterdam.

"I'm so sorry," she said.

"He did it during the siege of Warsaw." Józef deflated and put his head down.

"Who did what?" Lonia peeked out from behind a ragged curtain that separated the living room from the bedroom.

Józef gave her a stern look and his child withdrew with wide eyes. Stern wasn't an everyday occurrence in their home.

"It was not uncommon during the invasion," said Weronika. "We all lost someone in one way or another."

Józef touched her hand lightly. "Weronika's mother and brothers died in the bombing. Three of my cousins as well."

"I'm sorry I made you think of it," said Stella and she meant it. She had to be more careful. Weariness was no excuse.

"No," said Weronika. "It is a good question. We've lost everything as most of our countrymen have. Józef's publishing company is gone. His remaining family scattered to the winds. We have no one." She said it with resignation but also pride. She might be delicate, but Stella thought if given half a chance she would survive.

"You have Pieter," said Stella and a glow emanated from Weronika, but Józef slumped down. Depending on a woodworker's son couldn't be easy.

"We do. Pieter is a godsend," said Weronika. "As you are."

Stella caught a glimpse of Lonia peeking out again and she winked at her. Lonia gave her a shy smile and a little wave. A sweet child. A child in danger.

"Was Pieter right?" Stella asked. "Do you have something to sell?"

"Yes, I—" Weronika said, but her husband grabbed her arm.

"No," said Józef. "We aren't that desperate."

His wife took his hand off her arm and said simply, "We are." Then she went to a corner of the room and dug into a pile of books. She came back to the chairs with a shiny wooden box inlaid with ivory, mother of pearl, and gold filigree. She put the box into Stella's hands. "This is what I saved. We sold everything else to get here."

"Weronika." Józef put his head in his hands.

"Pieter is giving us this chance. We can't waste it. Who else would buy from us at a decent price?"

He didn't answer and Stella opened the box. Her breath caught in her throat. Weronika really was a woman from a palace. It was quite a collection. The main pieces were a Victorian set, a necklace with a pendant of sapphires, pearls, and diamonds, matching earrings, and a delicate tiara. She also had a multi-strand pearl collar with a diamond clasp, three rings with high quality stones, rubies, emeralds, and more diamonds, and Stella's instant favorite, a brooch with two enameled peacocks, diamonds, and a large opal in their beaks.

"These are incredible," Stella said. "I never expected so much or such quality."

"They are family pieces," said Weronika.

"Are you sure you want to let them go…for the time being?" Stella asked and Józef's head jerked up. "What do you mean?"

"I mean that things can be sold and then given back."

The pair stared at Stella and then looked back at Pieter's letter.

"He says you will give us a name and we must remember it," said Weronika. "What does that mean?"

Stella was shocked at the depth of Pieter's knowledge, but she simply said, "It means exactly that. I will buy your pieces and tell you where they are going, so you can get them back later if you so choose."

They just looked at her.

"My clients are people of sympathy and considerable means," said Stella. "They are not without palaces of their own. Profit is not their first consideration, shall we say."

"We will never be able to buy them back," said Józef bitterly.

"Never is long time."

"It is forever."

Stella responded by getting out her notebook, examining the pieces and totaling up her offer. She held out the page to them. "It is your choice, of course."

Weronika gasped. "Not really. Surely you won't pay that much."

"I'm fair and so are my clients," said Stella, very businesslike.

"I don't know what to say." Józef was shaken by the sum which was probably close to retail value. It was over what she normally paid, but the Dereczynskis were worse off than every other person on Francesqua's list. Oliver would be furious if he knew, but Stella didn't regret it. Someday the Nazis would get the boot out of Poland and they would get their palaces back. These were the kind of people who would see it as a duty to pay her back in full. Even if they couldn't, the pieces would be returned, and it was money well spent.

"Do we have a deal?" Stella asked.

"We don't want charity."

"It's not charity. It's business," said Stella, even though it was, but they didn't need to know that. Józef was shattered enough as it was.

The couple took each other's hands and Weronika said, "Yes. It's a deal. Thank you."

Lonia came out from behind the curtain. "No, Mama. You said those were to be mine when I am big. Don't sell them. I can get a job. Bram down the street is a sweeper. I could be a sweeper, too."

Tears rolled down Weronika's cheeks and Józef's head went back into his hands. But this wasn't the first time a child had objected to their future possessions being sold to Stella. She sat up straight and ignored her aching heart. "So, you are the heir to these beautiful pieces."

Lonia nodded. "I want to have my birthright. You can't have them."

"You're right. I can't. I'm not a birthright kind of person."

"What do you mean?"

"I don't wear this kind of jewelry and I never will. I'm a connecting person. I connect people with people who can give help when needed."

"Like Tante Truus?" Lonia asked.

Stella feigned ignorance although she knew Tante Truus personally. "Geertruida?"

Weronika swallowed hard and said, "Geertruida Wijsmuller-Meijer. She put Ezra and Lonia on the list for transport to England, but we were too late for the official transports. We're hoping there may be another way."

"They're not going," said Józef. "I will not send my children to strangers."

"They must go."

"I will not allow it."

The parents faced off and Lonia put her fingers in her mouth to suck. Six wasn't very big at all.

"Lonia," said Stella, "you're right. I am like Geertruida in my own way. I'm helping your parents and these precious things are going to England, like you, to stay safe during the war."

The little girl's eyes brightened. "My parents can have me back. Can we have them back?"

"You can."

"Can I have them if I'm in England?" Lonia asked.

"I don't see why not."

"She's not going—"

Weronika's hand went out like a snake and grabbed Józef's arm. He jerked away shocked at his frail-looking wife's determined face.

"Mama?" Lonia asked. "What was that?"

"A bug," said Stella quickly. "Your mama makes decisions quickly and correctly."

"You don't know," said Józef.

Stella met his eyes and said quietly, "I've spent considerable time in Germany and I assure you that I do."

He looked back at Pieter's letter, his eyes going over the words again and again. "All right."

"I'm going to England?" Lonia asked.

"If it can be arranged, yes."

"And Ezra?"

"Yes."

Lonia ran in the back and could be heard telling Erza about the great adventure they would have in England to get Mama's jewelry.

Back to business, Stella got out her pocketbook. "I have a little over one third with me. Would you accept a check for the rest?"

"Certainly," said Weronika.

Stella handed over the cash and wrote the check. "I do have something to ask of you and it's very important."

"Name it."

"I need you to destroy Pieter's letter and promise me that you will lie when you tell people about our transaction."

"Lie? Why?" asked Józef.

"Because I should pay you a quarter of what I have or even less. That is not something my clients and I would like people to find out."

"By people you mean…"

"Yes. They are coming, quicker than you think. In fact, they are already here. My safety depends on you. This is my business, but they might not like it."

Józef and Weronika swore on their children's lives to give a small sum, a sum that would be taking terrible advantage of them. Stella hoped they would keep their word. Unlike the others on Francesqua's list, she didn't have friendship to bind them and even that hadn't worked.

"One last thing," said Stella, pulling her basket in front of her. "You may think I'm silly, but I have a hard time saying no."

"That does not surprise me," said Józef with his first hint of humor.

"When I talk to the market sellers, they're so lovely and eager. They have businesses, too, that they must keep going in these difficult times."

"Yes?"

"Well, I want a pear and I end up with…" She whipped back the cloth and they leaned forward, "all this. I'm staying in a hotel with no cooking facilities and I don't want it to go to waste."

"But it's so dear," said Weronika. "We can't take your food."

"I said you'd be helping me and you would. I won't feel so weak if you take it. The beef did look very good and I thought of my mother's Carbonnade Flamande. The next thing I knew he was wrapping it up." Stella held out the packet of beef.

Weronika's hand shook when she took it and she whispered, "Thank you."

The rest of the basket was emptied quickly and Stella cursed herself for not bringing food to everyone on Francesqua's list. It was such an obvious thing to do.

"You must keep the pear, at least." The look on Józef's face said he knew the food had nothing to do with her wanting a pear or her mother's stew, but he said nothing. Stella couldn't decide if he was happy or ashamed, maybe a bit of both. She was just glad he accepted. The food really did have to go to someone.

"Miss?" Lonia stood in the doorway, holding back the curtain with one hand and a large stuffed bear in the other.

"Yes?"

"Are you going to send the box to England right away?"

"I plan to. Why do you ask?"

Lonia came into the room as if someone was behind her holding her back with all their might, but she kept coming with her stockinged feet dragging on the rough floorboards.

"No, Lonia," said her father. "Go back to bed."

The little girl glanced her father's way, but she was as determined as her mother and kept on coming until she stood at Stella's knees. "Will you take him with you?"

"Don't be silly, Lonia," said Weronika. "She's a businesswoman. She has to make a living. She can't buy your bear."

Lonia looked her straight in the eyes and Stella looked straight back. Her training was good or she might've cracked with the well of feeling rising in her chest. "Let me see. Who have you got there?"

She took the bear, a good one as it turned out. A Steif and an early, too. Stella had her own Steif, a cuddly cinnamon colored one named Muffin. Lonia's bear was older and blonde with the button in the ear and the all-important white tag.

"Was he your mama's first?" Stella asked. "Maybe your grandmother's?"

"How did you know?" Lonia asked.

"I can tell. It's my job to know."

Tears pricked at the edges of the little girl's eyes. "You don't want him because he's old."

"On the contrary, I want him more because he's old. He's worth more."

"You can't be serious," said Józef.

"I'm entirely serious."

"It's too much."

Stella looked at him. "It's never enough. Once again, I speak from experience."

"They have to get on that transport," he said.

"I would put my children, if I had any, on without a second thought."

Lonia poked Stella's knee. "What about Masło?

She laughed. "You named your bear Butter?"

"My mother did," said Weronika. "She always loved good butter."

"Don't we all." Stella made Lonia an offer and the child considered carefully before making a counteroffer. "Twenty guilders."

"Lonia!"

"Sold," said Stella, "but I take him now and no complaining."

Lonia stood straight. "I won't complain. I want Masło to be safe like me."

"All right then. Are you good at remembering?"

"Very good. Very very good."

Stella cocked her head to the side and asked, "What about your parents?"

Lonia wrinkled her nose. "They forget to punish Ezra when he's bad."

"He's practically a baby. That's usual for parents. They do like those little ones."

Her nose wrinkle grew bigger. "Yes, they do."

"But Ezra can't remember things, can he?" she asked.

"Not at all. He's useless."

"Lonia," said Weronika. "He's little."

"Still useless."

"But you're useful and you can remember, like your parents," said Stella. "I need you to remember how to get your things later after the war and when you're in England."

Lonia became very serious and Ezra's uselessness was quite forgotten. "I'll remember. I want Masło back and Mama's jewels."

"You can't write it down. You just have to remember with your brain."

They all three nodded.

"The Earl of Bickford of Bickford House in Derbyshire, England. He's buying your bear and the jewelry."

They all three repeated the words in a singsong rhythm to help them remember.

"Good and if the earl isn't available or there is some sort of problem, B.L. Imports of New York, New York. That's the company I work for. You can call an operator or find us in the telephone directory. A secretary will assist you."

"They'll know who we are?" Józef asked.

"I include an inventory with all my purchases and I will label every piece you sell me. They'll know."

"Even Masło?"

"Even Masło," said Stella. "Give him a kiss and we'll tuck him in my basket."

Lonia gave her bear a kiss and a cuddle, reassuring him that he'd be fine in England and it wouldn't be so very wet. Then she said goodbye and held out her hand. Stella paid her and put the jewelry box under Masło. Then she stood up and said, "Thank you for seeing me. It was a pleasure doing business with you."

They shook hands and Józef held the money and check to his chest. "Thank you, Madam Dubois. We owe you a great debt."

"Come and get your items. Then we will be even."

He just looked at her, unable to say more.

"Will you be seeing Pieter again?"

"I think so. My business won't take too much longer I hope."

Weronika took her hand. "Tell him thank you for us. We appreciate everything he's done to help. He's the reason we got in. He wrote letters and we didn't have to go to Westerbork." Her voice broke.

"I'll tell him." Stella nodded to each of them. "Goodbye and please do put the children on a transport as soon as Tante Truus can arrange it."

The parents nodded and Stella went out the little door onto the rickety staircase, descending into the darkness.

"I told you they didn't have anything." The shop owner wasn't exactly nasty, but there was a bit of enjoyment in his face.

"It was a disappointment, but that's business for you. Sometimes you get a great deal. Sometimes a waste of time," said Stella. "Do you have a telephone?"

He grimaced. "Yes but calls cost."

"I'll pay. I'd like a cab back to my hotel. Nothing's worse than walking after a fruitless journey."

He made her hand over a coin before he called and charged double what it really cost, but Stella didn't care. The sadness was pressing down again and she could feel that family up there. She could see them in that hovel, trying so hard to keep going.

The shopkeeper walked her to the front and unlocked the door. "I bet you won't keep trying to buy here," he said knowingly.

"I will. For a little while anyway. There's some stained glass in a shop I'd like to see, but I might go up to Groningen instead."

"What for?"

"A cabinetmaker died and I heard he had a collection of pocket watches that his son wants to sell."

"And that's how you make a living?" He shook his head in disbelief.

"People have things they don't want and Americans like things from the old world. It gives them history. They won't come for themselves to shop so I do it for them. The arrangement suits us all."

"What's your company?"

"Fugazi Incorporated."

"Fu…what?"

A black Renault cab rolled up and the driver peered out at them with a sneer. The look was so familiar and unpleasant, Stella wished she'd just walked. The nasty comments and queries wouldn't be worth it.

"Thank you, sir," she said to the shopkeeper. He started to ask her something, but she dashed out to the cab. The driver had gotten out but hadn't opened the door for her. Stella almost shouted at the man's insolent face staring at her over the roof. What did it matter if she was a Jew or not, if she had money? Why did he care? Why did they all care? Months in training and on the ground had never answered that question to her satisfaction and the driver looked like a dull clod, so she doubted he had any reasonable clues about his hate.

"Well?" she said.

"I don't drive Jews."

"I'm surprised you came into the *Jodenbuurt* then."

He pointed at the shopkeeper and said, "He said you weren't a Jew."

"There you go then."

"You look like a Jew."

"What does a Jew look like?"

That befuddled him and he stuttered some nonsense about hooked noses and greedy hands.

Stella sighed and gave him a level stare. The man didn't know what to do as men of his ilk never did when confronted.

"She's Belgian," said the shopkeeper.

"Shut up, Jew whore!" The driver looked at Stella and asked, "Are you Belgian?"

"I am."

He gave the shopkeeper a rude and wholly unnecessary gesture and got in. She followed suit and nearly pointed out that there were Jewish Belgians as well as French and Americans and Canadians as well, but there wasn't much of a point and so exhausting. The driver slammed his hands on the steering wheel and shouted blasphemies at the shopkeeper through the closed window, which got him shouts in return. So much anger and for what? Stella couldn't imagine the point of any of it and to her dismay, the driver wasn't done. He kept yelling as he attempted to start the car. For a second, Stella thought all the angst would be for naught. The cab's engine sounded like someone was shaking a bag of hammers, but the thing rumbled to life under protest and they sped down the street at a disappointing ten miles an hour. Next time, she would walk. Or buy a bike or a mule. A mule would be better than the driver, who continued to mutter and actually spit on the seat beside him.

"Where are you going?" he asked as they took a corner at five miles an hour and got a chorus of impatient honks for their trouble.

"The Bikker Grand," she said to test his reaction.

Stella would have to walk a ways back to the Hotel Krasnapolsky, but it was worth it. The driver smiled grimly and nodded. "That is a good one."

"It is very nice," she said.

"And now I know."

"Know what, may I ask?"

"Why you were there at the Jew shop?"

She gave him a sly smile she knew he would like and flirted. "But I haven't told you anything."

He set his shoulders and assumed a superior tone. "You are staying at a *good hotel,* so you are *working* the Jews."

Good hotel had never had such ominous connotations. She'd remember his inflection and use the phrase to her advantage.

"That's one way to put it," she said.

"Wringing them dry, are you?"

"If it wasn't me, it would be someone else."

"You won't hear any complaints from me."

Stella sniffed and said, "Good. I've had enough complaints for one evening."

He laughed and shared a few choice stories of his own, not realizing how petty and cowardly he sounded. The man was fifty if he was a day and he was bragging about tossing a brick through a shop window at two in the morning like a petulant child.

They rolled up to the front of the Bikker Grand and she got out after giving him a generous tip. You never knew when an ugly bigot would come in handy and it garnered her a gap-toothed grin and some kind of hand sign she wasn't familiar with. She smiled and went for the doorman, who was looking exceedingly doubtful at her basket and lack of luggage. So she came close and widened her pale blue eyes at him before speaking in a heavier Belgian accent so there could be no doubts what side she would be on.

"Excuse me," she said. "I'm staying at the Park Canal and I don't think it's to my liking. Do you have any vacancies?"

He picked right up on her bread crumb. The Park Canal was butted up against the Jodenbuurt. "Yes, ma'am. We have a few rooms available and as you see we're far away."

She tightened her mouth and narrowed her eyes. "And you're very careful about your guests. Do you screen? I do not want to be... surprised again."

"The Bikker Grand has the highest standards."

"I heard it's owned by a very *good* family."

"The very best."

She nodded and looked up at the fine façade. "I'm glad to hear it as I will be staying for some time. I wouldn't want any concerns over the coming weeks."

The doorman leaned forward ever so slightly. "Have no fear. We will fare very well."

"Excellent. Some of the hotels I enquired at didn't seem quite sure. I think I will be back. Thank you for your insights."

"My pleasure," he said smugly. "Can I call you a cab?"

"No, thank you. That last one." She gave a little shake of her head. "I wouldn't want to deal with that again."

"Oh, I see." The doorman frowned in the direction the cab had disappeared in, doubtlessly wishing he'd taken note of the cab's number. "I can make a request for a *good* driver."

"No need. A little exercise is called for. *We* must be strong."

"*We* will be."

Stella said goodbye and walked away humming the famous melody from *Rienzi*. She thought she caught him joining her in a few notes as she turned the corner. Of course, he did. What was it with Wagner anyway? She much preferred *Carmen*, but she supposed an opera about a gypsy wasn't ever going to fit the fascist ideology.

When she was well-enough away, Stella switched to the Toreador song and found herself skipping along the canal to her hotel. Bullfights and pretty girls that would definitely do. The Bikker hotel was filled with Jew-hating Hitler-welcoming scum and she was that much closer to getting the measure of Jan Bikker. He would collaborate with the Nazis when they came. That was a cinch. But was he a spy already working on the inside to hurt his country's chances? That would take some more digging, but not that night.

The Hotel Krasnapolsky was lit up across the square and since she was getting looks that suggested she might be mad, Stella stopped being happy and became quiet and dignified as befitted Micheline Dubois. She couldn't wait to be Stella Bled Lawrence again, even if it was for a short time. She wanted to be Nicky's wife, Albert's friend, but most of all, herself. Herself was getting harder to remember.

"Micheline," said Daan. "You've been working late."

"Hello, my friend," she replied with a little sigh. "I have to now while I still have the chance."

"You shouldn't worry so much. We are going to stay neutral like the last time. War is not good for business."

She nodded. "You're right, of course, but I only hope the Reich agrees."

"They will see sense. The Germans cannot fight everyone." He opened the door for her and she thanked him before heading into the lobby. She would've gone directly to the elevator, but Ludwik waved her down. The portly Polish concierge was flushed with excitement and held out a large envelope like it might go up in flames any second.

"Madam Dubois. Micheline." He stopped in front of her panting. "I...this came for you two hours ago. I've been waiting for you to come back. I would've messengered it to you had I known where you were, but I didn't so I couldn't. Two hours is a very long time and I am very sorry for the delay."

"What in the world is it, Ludwik?" she asked. "Breathe. It can't be that bad."

"It's not bad at all." He held out the thick buff envelope with her name and hotel written in beautiful calligraphy on the front.

She took it and felt the weight of the good vellum. "Interesting. Looks like a wedding invitation, but I don't know anyone getting married."

Impatiently, Ludwik turned the envelope over in her hand to show the return address. "It is from the Baron Joost Van Heeckeren. I didn't know you knew the baron. He throws the most spectacular parties," he lowered his voice, "but perhaps not the most appropriate."

"Well, I don't know him, but I did meet an associate of his. She mentioned a party on Friday."

"That could be it."

Stella fixed a look of confusion on her face. "I didn't think I would be the baron's sort of person."

"Everyone is the baron's sort of person if you are interesting."

Does that include Nazis?

"But am I interesting?" she asked. "Why would he invite me?"

Ludwik was about to jump out of his skin, so she decided to put the poor man out of his misery and open the envelope then and there.

"Look here, Ludwik." She held out the embossed invitation to the concierge, "it is for the party on Friday. A *soirée intime* this time."

"The baron does not have small parties. It is quite an opportunity for you."

She sighed. "I don't know. I'm not an aristocrat as you well know."

"You are a businesswoman, Micheline. You will make such connections."

"I could use a few new buyers. My contract with the Americans won't last forever." She squared her shoulders. "I will have to have a new dress."

Ludwik was very careful with his reply and she appreciated it. "A new dress would be appropriate." He didn't say that she was dull and sturdy, which she certainly was.

"And perhaps I can order the hairdresser for you. This is a special occasion."

Oh, no!

"That's not necessary. I have my combs and tonic."

Ludwik covered his dismay and said, "Yes, of course. Would you like some dinner?"

Stella ordered her favorite Stampot again, comfort was in order, and then she went into the elevator with her prized envelope.

Thank you, Cornelia.

Her dinner arrived quickly and came with congratulations on her invitation. She didn't know if that was a good thing or a bad thing. She definitely didn't expect being invited to a party to get so much notice, but there was nothing to be done about it now.

She listened at the door for a moment before turning the key in the lock and taking off her wig. Ludwik was right. It needed serious help. She'd have to give herself a party hairstyle with what amounted to a giant reddish ball of lint. She had considered having a second wig at the start of the mission in case she needed something fancy, but the idea was discussed and discarded. That was extra space in the secret compartment of her luggage and wigs were fat.

She pulled the suitcase out from under the bed and plopped it next to the basket. Feeling along the seam in the leather exterior, she found the right part and used her nails to open a gap and pull out a slim sheaf of papers. Her mother's list. Stella added the Dereczynski family with each member's name and approximate age. She marked them as Polish refugees and gave the address of the shop. Then she opened Weronika's jewelry box and made an inventory of every single item, ending with Masło the bear.

Settling back on a pile of pillows, she tried not to think of that small family in the chilly attic while she ate her huge dinner and wrote out each individual tag and attached them to the pieces. She got out her little sewing kit and stitched a paper tag to Masło's original Steiff tag, naming Leonarda (Lonia) Dereczynski as his owner. The name was so long it barely fit and she couldn't get Lonia's face out of her mind. She wasn't anything like Anna Wildholtz from Berlin and yet she was. Both were vulnerable for reasons they couldn't control. Being only half Jewish hadn't protected Anna and she doubted it would protect Lonia or Ezra either.

She finished her dinner and her work, packed the jewelry and the list away, and then laid back in her comfortable bed with her warm blankets and decided what to do next. She held Masło to her chest and breathed in the scent of a little girl who had such faith in her and knew she wasn't done with the Dereczynski family quite yet.

CHAPTER 7

The rain came down in bone-chilling sheets and attacked Stella's window with gusto. If this was what they meant about April showers bringing May flowers, it wasn't worth it. She stood at the window, holding a coffee cup and cursing the fact there wasn't a big enough umbrella in the world to protect her from that mess. She only had two pairs of shoes and one pair of boots, and they would be waterlogged. It took forever for anything to dry out in The Netherlands or Europe in general, if she was being honest, and now she had a laundry list of things to do with getting a new dress on top of it.

Once upon a time, she'd loved rain and snow especially. Those were the best days with her mother. Francesqua would come into her room and announce in a dramatic way that wasn't typical of her at all that it was raining or snowing or hailing or sleeting and they couldn't possibly be expected to do anything at all. Then Stella and her brothers would run down the hall to her parents' room because their father would be long gone. Nothing kept Aleksej Bled from the brewery. Without his presence, they'd jump on the big bed and wrestle until the housekeeper brought them breakfast in bed. They'd eat together with Francesqua and then she'd bring out the games. They'd play The Landlord's Game, Reversi, and Stella's favorite The Wonderful Game of Oz. When they tired of those, they'd get the cards and play Whist and Hearts. They'd stay in bed all day, listening to the storm rage, warm and safe until Father came home. Fifteen minutes before his usual time, they'd pack everything up, run to get dressed and rush to various spots around the house to act like they'd been doing something constructive. Aleksej wasn't fooled, but he pretended he was and Stella never knew how much her father knew about those wonderful days. Maybe Francesqua told him what they did or maybe seeing Stella with her French workbook was enough to give it away. She wished she'd thought to ask her mother about it, but she was only just now remembering all the wonderful things about Francesqua Bled. She'd been so busy being thwarted and stubborn she'd forgotten who her mother was.

Weronika seemed like that kind of mother. Stella could imagine her playing games with the children on whatever kind of cobbled together bed they had and telling them stories about how happy they'd be in England. It was a good day for it. Stella watched a man run across the square with a golfing umbrella, but he needn't have bothered. He was soaked to the thighs and just as he passed her window, he slipped in a puddle and fell in spectacular style. His umbrella broke and his briefcase skittered across the cobbles to land in a bigger puddle.

"This is going to be miserable," she said and went to pack up her basket. The cloth over Masło and the jewelry box wasn't enough. She tucked a towel over the Dereczynski's family treasures and put on her coat before setting her breakfast tray outside the door.

She double checked to make sure nothing important had been left out and then locked her door, pocketing the large brass key. The elevator operator was waiting and greeted her familiarly as most of the staff did. They talked of her invitation. There was no one that didn't know about it apparently.

"I hear you will have a new dress for the occasion," he said.

And no detail had been left out of the tale.

"I think I will."

The elevator stopped with a jolt and he opened the door. "Do you have to go out right now? It's a terrible morning for shopping."

She patted her basket. "I made some purchases for my clients in America. I have to ship them immediately."

"Surely there is no rush." His face went all somber and she hated to ruin his mood.

"Maybe not, but my clients are not patient people."

He rolled his eyes and shrugged. "Americans."

She laughed and went off past a couple coming for the elevator. Instead of going straight into the lobby and out the front door, Stella went toward the winter garden like Anna Bikker had, past the café with Marga strolling around giving guests their morning coffee and papers under the watchful eye of a stern-faced Dirk. Stella had been hoping to ask her a question or two about Lotte and why she avoided her office, but with Marga's boss there, she couldn't.

Gritting her teeth, she walked on, following what she thought was Anna's path into the guts of the hotel. She took two turns and found a row of offices down a dimly lit hall. A young man with a harassed expression came hurrying toward her with a stack of folders. He saw her and stopped short. She couldn't tell if it was because she looked like a guest or because perhaps she didn't. The worst thing was, he'd slow her down.

"Can I help you, ma'am?" he asked.

"I do hope so," said Stella laying on her accent a bit thick. "I'm looking for where Lotte works."

"Are you a guest?"

"Yes. I'm Micheline Dubois. I only wanted to ask her something."

The young man beamed at her as different as different could be. "Congratulations on your invitation. I hope you'll tell us all about it. The baron's parties are legendary in Amsterdam."

Maybe this wasn't such a waste of time.

"Would you please tell me why? Everyone says they are exciting parties, but no one says what they are like."

"We can't say because we don't know. I don't know anyone who's been to one and his staff is very discreet."

That was true. Even Cornelia was quiet on the details even after a good deal of Jenever.

"Someone must know something," said Stella. "I'm getting quite nervous about it."

"Well, people are seen going in and there are often costumes. Very elaborate. Once, I heard, the baron hired acrobats and flame throwers."

"That's extravagant. How do you know?"

"They set the house on fire and it was all over the papers. It took months to repair and then he threw another party and had the flame throwers on the roof instead. All the best people are invited." The young man practically glowed. "And now you're one of the best people and a guest of ours."

Stella was very sure she'd never brought so much joy to anyone without even trying. It was a little overwhelming to realize the invitation was a social coup and a triumph that the hotel shared by association. She couldn't be quiet little unknown Micheline anymore and that wasn't good for the mission or her.

"I'm told I must be interesting to get an invitation, but I don't think I'm very interesting," she said.

"Well, you've got one, so you must be," he said. "Please excuse me. The chef is waiting."

"Wait. Lotte's office?"

"Oh, yes. I'm sorry. Down the hall on the right. Mr. De Jong's office."

He hurried off and Stella went for the office, trying to formulate an excuse for going in. She didn't know who Mr. De Jong was or what he did for the hotel. Unfortunately, the names on the door didn't clear up the question. Mr. Luuk De Jong and Mr. Willem Elek. That's all it said and she couldn't claim a billing problem or give a compliment on bedding or service.

She took a breath and knocked gently.

No answer, so she opened the door to find a little room with a desk and typewriter. On either side of the room were two doors. One for Mr. De Jong and one for Mr. Elek. Still no clue what they did for the hotel.

"Hello?" she called out since neither door seemed the better option.

To her surprise, both doors opened immediately and she knew exactly why Anna was coming there.

"May I help you?" both men said at the same time and then laughed. Mr. De Jong wouldn't be the office Anna Bikker was interested in. He was about sixty with a pot belly and a beard that resembled steel wool. On the other hand, Mr. Elek was tall with a chiseled jawline and dark hair that went back from his face in glossy waves.

"I don't know which way to turn," said Stella.

The men chuckled again and the older one said, "I'm Mr. De Jong, the hotel manager, and this is Mr. Elek, the assistant manager."

"It's a pleasure to meet you," said Stella. "Did you used to have a girl here?"

"Oh, yes. Lotte," said Mr. De Jong. "She's gone and broken a tooth, poor girl. She'll be back tomorrow."

"That explains it." It wouldn't pay to be too pointed in her knowledge of the unknown Lotte. "She helped me with directions once and I thought I'd come back and say hello before I went out for the day."

"Sorry to disappoint you," said Mr. Elek. He had a musical voice, a touch foreign. Hungarian. That was it.

"It's fine. Sorry to bother you." Stella quickly stepped out in case they, too, knew about the invitation. Anna knew Mr. Elek very well unless she missed her guess and she didn't want him telling her anything about Micheline Dubois. That would not help her cause at all.

"That's all?" asked Jelle. The workman hefted a hammer and looked at her expectantly.

Stella held up her palms. "I haven't been as successful as I hoped."

"It's no trouble," said the manager, Jacobus.

He looked worried, but then again, Jacobus always looked that way. Stella wondered what his expression would be when the Nazis rolled in. His forehead simply couldn't crumple any more than it already was.

"You've always been so helpful," she said. "I'm going to look at some stained glass, but I'd like this group out immediately. Do you have any crates going to England that it can go in?"

Jacobus's head jerked up. "England, not New York?"

"My American clients don't care for jewelry, but vintage pieces are still popular in London. I think I have a buyer. Why?"

"No reason. It's just rare for you to send things to England instead of New York."

"That's true, but I must fill each client's list." She smiled and asked, "Will it go out soon?"

"Immediately. We have crates of bulbs and it can go with them." Jacobus did manage to frown more deeply. Stella thought for a second that the skin of his forehead would fold over his eyes. "You are concerned your purchases won't get out?"

She straightened her shoulders and became more businesslike. "Frankly, I am. I heard a day or two ago that your government is negotiating with the Reich. Who knows how that will go."

Jacobus gripped his clipboard tighter. "I had heard that myself."

"Isn't that good?" Jelle asked. "They must be discussing our neutral status and making arrangements for goods and services."

"Many countries have negotiated with the Reich," said Jacobus. "It only gets them invaded."

"We will not be invaded. We're neutral."

"They invaded Norway and Denmark. Norway will fall anytime now."

The little group went quiet and then Jacobus said, "I will make sure your purchases are on the next ship out." Then he handed her the inventory. She checked it and signed. The Dutchman quietly left, deep in thought and she suspected in need of a dram of the Scotch he kept in his desk drawer.

"So, I'm closing it then?" Jelle asked.

"You are. Thank you."

He looked down at Masło's woolly face and said without looking back at Stella, "You bought a Jewish child's bear."

The shipping company knew who Micheline Dubois was and where she was getting a lot of her purchases, but Jelle was the first to comment on the fact.

To soothe him, she said, "I bought a woman's bear. She had a greater need for money than a stuffed toy. I was fair. I always am."

Jelle was mollified and placed the wooden lid over Masło's face and positioned a nail. "I thought you would be." He hammered in the nails one by one and then asked, "Why aren't you gone? I thought your buying was done."

She sighed heavily and said, "I thought so, too, but things change. My company asked for more and I had a lead, so here I am."

"You're tired. You should go home."

"I will as soon as I can." Stella tipped him and then headed back out into the rain that had not relented one bit. She was soaked to the knees, but there was a cab driving by the warehouse and stopped with a jolt when she waved. She just jumped in and shook her umbrella before folding it at her feet. There was a time when she wouldn't dream of doing such a thing, but she could barely remember it.

"Where are you going, ma'am?" the driver asked.

Stella pondered the question and searched for the right answer. Close was as safe as she dared to be. She named a café safely outside the Jodenbuurt but walking distance to her destination. Sometimes close was too close.

"Yes, ma'am. Terrible weather we're having. You ought to be at home," he said with fatherly concern and she wondered if he'd be so kind if she gave him her real destination. People surprised her, but not nearly enough.

"I wish I was, but business takes precedence."

"You are in business?" he asked with surprise that wasn't insulting and Stella took comfort in that at least. She explained her business and the wealthy Americans taste for all things European. He nodded with interest and drove her to a small house on a backstreet so narrow that they had to wait their turn before driving down it.

The driver peered up through the rain-spattered windshield. "You're buying here?"

"One can hope," she said.

He stopped and she gave him a perfectly appropriate tip so that he would have no additional reason to remember her and hurried away to the café while trying to listen through the pounding rain on her umbrella to see if the cab left. He did without hesitation and she dashed down the street until she almost entered the Jodenbuurt and knocked on the plain but well-made door.

After a few minutes, a maid answered. She threw up her hands and said in her strong Greek accent, "Micheline, what are you doing out today?" Rena pulled Stella inside and relieved her of her umbrella, coat, and hat.

"You have come for more information? You are still buying? I thought you would leave."

"I had a new request and I thought Mrs. Keesing—"

"Elizabeth. It is the Dutch way. You are friends. You must be familiar," insisted Rena. She'd come to The Netherlands shortly before the Nazis moved on Czechoslovakia, knowing she'd lose her job. Rena could've returned to Greece, but she'd taken to the Dutch people with a vengeance, just the way she did everything. Full commitment. That was Rena.

"Elizabeth. You are right. I should forget my formality."

Rena nodded primly. "Good. While you are here, you must be Dutch."

Stella couldn't help but think Rena would make a fine agent. She was fearless if nothing else. Stella had once seen her smack a young NSB member right across the mouth for being nasty to a Jewish bookseller and Stella feared for her safety once the Nazis invaded. That kind of thing had to put the Greek maid on some kind of list.

"I will do better," said Stella. "Is Elizabeth here?"

"Where else would she be in this weather?" Rena led Stella through the narrow house to a toasty sitting room where Elizabeth Keesing sat on a lounge covered in blankets and reading a Dutch edition of *The Little Mermaid*.

"Elizabeth, look who is here, Micheline," said Rena in an odd tone she often took with her mistress.

"Rena, do not speak to me like I'm a child," said Elizabeth. "I'm ill, not an idiot."

"Children are not idiots." Rena crossed her arms. She was mother to six, all bright bulbs and seriously troublesome because of it.

"Some are. Have you met the butcher's new boy, Johann?" Elizabeth looked at Stella. "I was able to go out to the shop last week and that boy believed that a chicken thigh was veal. I couldn't persuade him otherwise."

"The boy is ignorant," said Rena. "It is not the same thing."

"Johann is both," said Elizabeth and Rena's lower lip poked out slightly.

"I will get you tea." The maid turned around, stomped out, and practically slammed the door behind her.

Stella took off her wet shoes and put them next to the blue tiled stove in the corner of the room. "That's going to be trouble."

"Rena is always in a fit about something," said Elizabeth. "There's no avoiding it."

"Are you bothering her on purpose?"

Elizabeth smiled, transforming her face briefly from pale and strained to mischievous. "Maybe a little."

"How are you feeling?" Stella asked.

"The same." That was Elizabeth's standard answer and Stella had learned not to press in the three months they'd known each other. Rena had whispered once that it was her kidneys but hadn't gone farther than that. Even the earl didn't know and he'd been friends with Elizabeth for years after serving in the Great War with Elizabeth's husband. The earl was there when the young man died and he'd kept in touch with his friend's widow. Elizabeth's dislike for the Germans who killed her husband was well-known. What wasn't well-known was her love of children, particularly Jewish children. The Reich declared the Jews to be their enemy, so they were automatically

Elizabeth's friends. She'd never remarried and had no children of her own. She'd been helping Jewish orphans and refugees with her money and considerable gift of persuasion since 1933. Elizabeth Keesing was Stella's main contact in The Netherlands and the only one who knew her connection to the earl.

"Glad to hear it, although your choice in literature had me thinking otherwise," said Stella as she sat down in a plush upholstered armchair and put her wet feet up on the footstool close to the hot stove.

Elizabeth looked down at the book. "Oh, this. I've been thinking about the Danes."

"And you wanted to be more depressed?"

She tossed the book on a side table. "You're right. Enough of dying for love." Then her eyes, so tired and worn, fixed on Stella with a sharp intelligence that most would miss due to the pallor of her skin. "You didn't leave on schedule. I can't say I'm pleased."

"I'm not either, but here we are."

"You were directed to make contact again?" Elizabeth was doubtful. She'd connected Stella with all her friends that could be reliably trusted to fight the Nazis once they took over and all of them had been evaluated. Stella had met with some and put others on a list of possibilities, depending on what she observed. "I haven't met anyone new for you to contact or...has something happened? The rumors are flying. Rena keeps me well-informed."

"Nothing's happened. I do have some questions for you," said Stella.

Rena knocked on the door and brought in a tea tray. She served and then ordered Stella not to tire Elizabeth out before leaving. Stella wondered if she'd made a mistake. She'd noticed Elizabeth's hands were thinner. The veins and bones stood out in stark relief under bone-white skin.

"Don't worry about tiring me out," said Elizabeth. "I started out tired. You won't make any difference. Ask your questions. You know I'll do anything to help."

"Is Truus here in Amsterdam?" Stella asked.

"No. I'm afraid she is traveling. She may be in Paris, but she mentioned Greece, too. I'm not sure where she is at the moment. Have you come across more children to help?" Elizabeth sat up straighter and her hands grabbed at the blankets.

"I have. Will she be going into Switzerland again?"

"I couldn't say. How desperate is the situation?"

"Well, they're all desperate, aren't they?"

"They are, of course. Orphans?"

"No. Two children. Polish. In the *Jodenbuurt*. Six and three."

"Are their parents healthy and able to care for them?" Elizabeth, always practical, asked.

"Yes, but you know what's coming," said Stella.

The two women looked at each other for a moment. Neither one wanted to say it out loud and Stella had told Elizabeth her instincts on what would happen to Jewish children. She'd managed to get rid of Oscar von Drechsel, but she wasn't fool enough to think the Obersturmbannführer was the only Nazi to come up with a systematic plan to eradicate the Jews. She had only hoped to delay it and she had for the time being.

"When Truus comes back, I'll see what I can do," said Elizabeth finally.

"I'll pay for the transport."

"Will you?"

"I will."

"Micheline, you can't be connected. Your work is vital."

"I've done this before," said Stella.

Elizabeth pursed her lips. That wasn't strictly true. She'd never paid. She'd merely told the families on Francesqua's list who might be able to get their children out. Elizabeth thought she only came across them during the course of her regular work and it wasn't a topic that came up often. Only twice, in fact. Most of the people on the list were aiming to get everyone out together and with the money and letters Stella provided, they were able to. Two families were still waiting in the enormous queue and they decided to get their children out alone. Stella didn't know how it was accomplished, but five children were smuggled into England outside of any Kindertransport list. If it could happen for them, it could happen for Lonia and Ezra.

"This is a great risk for Truus, you know," said Elizabeth.

"I know. I would do it myself if I could, but I'm otherwise occupied."

"With the reason you came back?"

"Do you happen to know Baron Joost Van Heeckeren?"

Elizabeth frowned deeply. "You're not getting involved with him."

"I'm not getting involved with anyone," said Stella. "Do you know him?"

"I know of him and I recommend that you avoid the man."

"Why? He's thought to be sympathetic."

"Yes, but to what?"

"Why haven't you mentioned him before?"

Elizabeth stiffened. "Why haven't I mentioned a ridiculous fop who seduces married women and consorts with Nazis and gangsters? Why, you ask? Because he's the sort of person a young woman should avoid at all costs."

Stella smiled. "I'm not a young woman. I hardly think I'd be enticing to a member of the nobility."

"Nobility," she spat. "Would a true member of the nobility have dinner with Dries Riphagen?"

Stella had no idea who Dries Riphagen was, but he didn't sound like a good contact for her. "I've heard only good things about the baron before this."

She rolled her eyes. "Because he's wealthy and throws outlandish parties, I imagine. He invites Nazis to those parties. Germans are invited."

"Interesting."

"It's not interesting. He will collude with them against his own people."

It was interesting. The reason Elizabeth hated the baron was the exact reason he might be useful. He knew Nazis. They liked him. Everybody but Elizabeth seemed to. If you wanted to find out what your enemy was up to, you had to get close. The baron was close.

"You don't know that," said Stella. "Perhaps he's cultivating friendships for a good reason."

"What good reason? To get special treatment when it happens, that's why. Go home, Micheline. You've done your work. Go home."

Stella hated to ask for fear of upsetting Elizabeth further, but she had no choice. "I heard something about a Jan Bikker. Do you know who—"

"You cannot be serious. Jan Bikker is practically a German. I wouldn't be surprised if he's working for them."

Stella sat silently and just looked at Elizabeth, who'd managed to bring a tinge of pink to her cheeks as she ranted about his trips to Bavaria. "We all know that he loves Germany. He probably lost at the Olympics to give them a better chance." She paused to take a breath and then saw Stella looking at her calmly. "Oh."

"Yes."

"You think he might be a…"

"I don't think anything yet. When you say *we*, who do you mean?"

Elizabeth relaxed back into her lounge and took a deep breath. "Us. Our people. The anti-Nazis of my acquaintance."

"Is it well-known outside that group?"

"Oh, I don't know. Probably not. He's not in any organizations that I know of."

"Well, he's not sympathetic to the Jews. I heard he fired some girls for being Jewish."

"I hadn't heard that, but I'm not surprised," said Elizabeth. "It's not unusual though."

"He moves in elevated circles?"

"I don't know what you mean by elevated, but the Bikkers are an old family. They know people in the government and the nobility, not to mention business."

"Has he ever done anything that would be considered anti-Dutch?"

Elizabeth wrinkled her nose. "No, but that doesn't mean he hasn't."

"It means there's no reason for people to think he'd be working for the Reich in a quiet capacity."

"I wouldn't trust him as far as I could throw him."

"But would other people, not of your ilk, trust him?" Stella asked.

She sighed and the pink was completely gone. If anything, Elizabeth was paler than before and distressingly grey. "I suppose they would. He's rich and well-known because of the hotels. You know how silly people are about money."

Stella did, much better than Elizabeth could ever imagine. It gave people a predetermined opinion without having ever met you, good or bad. How many times had she said Bled only to see judgement cross someone's face? Elizabeth was no different. She judged the baron and Bikker on their money and what they chose to do with it. Skiing in Germany and knowing gangsters didn't mean those men would betray their country. It meant only that they had opportunities others didn't have.

"I should go," Stella said. "You're exhausted."

Elizabeth closed her eyes. "How long will you stay?"

"Not long I hope."

"Micheline?"

"Yes."

"They're not stupid."

"Who?"

"Those two men. We talk a lot, the people of my ilk as you put it, and nobody thinks they're stupid. They could sniff you out. You are getting to be known. I was relieved when I thought you were gone."

"I'll be careful," Stella said as she tugged on her still-damp shoes. "Try not to worry."

"About the children…" Elizabeth trailed off.

"I'll give the information to Rena."

"She still doesn't know about you."

"Good."

"But she's not stupid either."

Stella stood up and then took Elizabeth's icy hand. "I'm counting on it."

CHAPTER 8

The door closed behind Stella and she grabbed the handrail to make her way down the waterlogged steps to the flooded street. If anything, the rain was worse and gusting down the street in waves that turned Stella's umbrella inside out and nearly took her wig off. She clamped her hand on top of her head, shoved her umbrella back the other way, getting it flipped back into position, and ran down the street toward the nearest tram. She should've let Rena call a cab, but she didn't want too many people seeing her come in and out of that house. Elizabeth might be an invalid, but she knew who the Nazi sympathizers were and they knew about her, too.

Besides, the tram wasn't far. Stella had been through far worse. If she could get through flooded Venice on wrecked feet, rainy Amsterdam on good feet was miserable but easily done. She turned the corner and saw the stop ahead. Usually, it was full, but the rain had kept people away. Stella was the only one at the stop when the tram rolled up, clanging its bell and half full of bedraggled passengers who rushed off, muttering curses about the weather and splashing Stella as they stomped away.

Stella got on and found an empty row. To her dismay, a man got on right after and he came to sit behind her, smelling of musky cologne and sweat.

"Is this necessary?" she said down into her handbag.

"Yes," said Oliver and he continued to breathe down her neck, when he wasn't coughing or sneezing, for the next six stops until she got off at the Spiegelkwartier, home to all the best antique shops and art galleries. Every shop had something interesting that her father or uncles might like to have and she'd spent a good deal of time there shopping for her client. Dilly Rutherford curiously having much the same taste.

But she didn't go toward the shops where everyone knew her. Smelly Oliver fixed that. Instead, she turned the other way toward the Rijksmuseum. It would've been another favorite place if it hadn't been emptied of its treasures at the start of the war. Once upon a time, the museum had been high on her list, but Stella never had a chance to see it. Abel was planning to bring them after they'd had their fill of Italy and Greece, but Vienna changed all that. Now Frans Hals *The Merry Drinker* (Uncle Josiah's favorite) was hidden away in the countryside thanks to a farsighted minister who didn't like the sound of Neville Chamberlain's so-called "peace for our time" and canceled the sandbags and steel shutters, choosing to hide the art instead. Stella could kiss him. What a wise man.

So the museum wasn't open, but Stella rushed through the streets with Oliver somewhere behind. She wished she could lose him, but that wasn't possible. His legs were longer and he was totally impervious to weather. The one glimpse she'd gotten made her question his sense. Oliver was soaked with no umbrella, a runny nose, and bluish lips. And he wasn't dressed in his usual working man attire, overalls and a rough coat either. Oliver wore a heavy black raincoat, a good canvas fedora, and shined shoes. She'd never seen him dressed well and couldn't imagine what he was up to.

The bridge over the Singelgracht was filled with slow-moving cars but empty of bicycles for the most part. A few determined bikers pedaled past in rain slickers with their teeth bared in furious concentration. Up ahead, the Rijksmuseum stood in its gothic glory.

There was mist around the towers and the windows were dark, making the famously welcoming museum seem as ominous as the country's situation surely was. When Park-Welles had briefed Stella on the Amsterdam situation, he became almost poetic. "Dark museums show how much they know," he said. Her handler didn't mean the Dutch people, but the government, the ministers, they knew.

She turned right and hustled down a couple short blocks to a small café. It'd been recommended by another contact in The Hague. The coffee was good and all sorts of people knew it. Mr. Pontier or so he called himself said she could hear things there, if she cared to listen. She did care and she did listen. She'd learned a lot for her reports. The café was loud and a mixed bag. Everyone from Jews to Dutch nobility went there and did they like to talk. Stella couldn't help but think that Dutch openness would do some people in, but for her purposes it was grand.

A man carrying a battered umbrella let Stella in the café's rickety door and then rushed out into the rain with a grimace. She walked in and found the place about three-fourths full as usual with smoking men and women of every class, but it sounded like it had twice as many people in it, they were so boisterous. It was lunchtime and they were all reading newspapers and loudly discussing the situation whether it was the weather or the Germans, it was all loud.

Stella hung her soaked coat and broken umbrella on a peg and then squeezed into her favorite spot next to the green-tiled stove. The café might not have been her best idea. The entire place smelled like wet wool and feet. Sausage and coffee were in the mix, too, but those lovely scents just made the other ones worse, not better.

A harried waitress came over and asked if she wanted the special. Stella didn't bother to ask what it was. It didn't matter. If she could eat turnip water masquerading as soup, she could eat anything. "Yes and a coffee, too."

"Can I sit here?" Oliver asked, indicating the chair next to her. "I'm frozen and I need the heat." He blew his nose on a handkerchief for effect.

The waitress grimaced at his red nose and eyes. She looked at Stella, who said, "Certainly."

Oliver plopped into the seat and blew his nose again.

"Do you want the special?" the waitress asked.

"If it's hot, I want it."

"It's Hachee."

"I'll take it and a coffee with milk," said Oliver, using a French accent that wasn't the greatest in Stella's opinion.

The waitress hurried off and Oliver blew his nose a third time. Stella tried not to lean away from him in disgust, but she couldn't help it. He was very juicy.

"I'm not feeling very well. I apologize," he said, holding out a hand. "Sebastian Martin."

She reluctantly shook his hand and said, "Micheline Dubois."

Oliver switched to French. "Belgian. Very nice to share a table with you."

"You're welcome," Stella replied also in French.

Nobody was paying them any mind and the closest table was filled with workers who were smoking, drinking and laughing all at the same time. They couldn't care less about a couple of French-speaking foreigners. The smoke from their table created a noxious cloud that was nearly intolerable, but it did obscure them in a blue haze. It was hard to make out the features of the people sitting across the room and that was a good thing even though Stella's eyes were burning.

Oliver leaned over to her and asked, "What do you think you're doing?"

"Waiting for Hachee, I guess."

"You know what I mean."

"I don't," she said. "Blow your nose. You're about to drip."

He blew his nose and then to her dismay, he lit a cigarette. Just what the place needed, more smoke. He took a drag that got cut off by coughing, not that it stopped him from trying again.

The waitress brought their coffees and Stella stole his little pitcher of warm milk for herself.

"Hey," he protested.

"Live with it. This stuff looks like tar."

"You brought us here."

"It's usually good, but that waitress is new. She must've made the coffee."

He stole his pitcher back and poured the milk in his tar dramatically. "I'm waiting for your explanation."

"For what?"

"Why you were there?"

"Where?"

"The invalid's house."

"Oh, that."

"Yes, that."

They drank their coffee for a few minutes while listening to the workmen rage about a pay cut. Oliver blew his nose and made a terrible grumbling sound in his chest when he tried to clear his throat.

"You really are sick," she said.

"You thought this might be a cover?"

"Why not? Who'd want to get near you? I know I don't."

He growled at her and then went into a fit of coughing. "This is thanks to you."

"I don't see how."

"You could've been out of here, but you're up to something that has nothing to do with the mission and I've caught this cold waiting around."

"I'll have you know I asked her pertinent questions about the two you're after."

"Oh, really?"

"Yes, she's lived here all her life. She knows people."

"So well that you waited three weeks to ask her?"

He had her there, but she persisted. "I didn't think of it before."

"No more children. No more art. Do your job."

"I am."

"It's taking too long."

She sneered down into her cup. "If it was easy, someone else would already have done it. Isn't that what you said?"

"Not exactly."

"Close enough."

"I want you out."

"That makes two of us," Stella said and smiled up at the waitress. She brought two bowls of thick stew and baskets of bread.

Oliver blew his nose and grabbed a bowl. "Have you gotten anywhere at all?"

"Yes."

"Well?"

"Eat your soup."

They ate for a few minutes and Stella gradually got warm enough to start caring about Oliver's chest.

"Have you been to the doctor?"

"What do you think?"

"I think you should go to the doctor."

"I saw you go into the Jodenbuurt. Why were you there?"

"I'm a buyer. I was buying."

"No more of that," he hissed over his spoon.

"It's my job. Do you want people to think I don't have a job?"

"Do your job at the shops where you won't cause talk."

Stella took a large bite of soup. Beef and onion, such a hearty, comforting combination. It made her think of the beef she'd given Weronika. "No. I'll do what I see fit."

"*They* will cut you loose, if you don't comply."

"No, *they* won't. I'll deliver."

He glanced over, his red eyes sharp with interest. "You *have* gotten something."

"I have."

"Tell me."

"An invitation to a party."

Oliver clenched his teeth. "A party? Don't you understand? We don't have time for that. They are coming."

Stella blew on a steaming spoonful. "So many *theys*."

"The invasion is probably two weeks away or less."

"A party is a way in. I'm getting in."

"Slowly," he said.

"Whatever it takes."

He looked at her sharply. "You mean that?"

"Of course. What about you? Whatever it takes?"

"To stop them, yes, everything." His eyes were bright. It could've been fever or fanaticism. Hard to say. "All will be given."

She thought of Nicky with longing tightening her chest. "Or taken."

"Do I hear regrets?"

"Yes. Only a fool feels no regret, but I'm not going to feel any more than I absolutely have to."

"Do not contact the invalid again. We won't be using her anymore. Her interest in the children is getting too well known."

"I don't take orders from you," said Stella.

"Or anyone, it seems."

"I do, but I choose what's best."

Oliver ate his stew with a flush creeping up his neck. It made the scars darken and stand out even more, reminding Stella of what they'd been through together.

"You have to go to a doctor," she said.

"I will, if you promise to hurry it up," he said.

Stella didn't answer. Instead, she mopped up the dregs of her stew with the bread and checked her watch. When she moved to stand, he grabbed her thigh to make her stay seated, so she took a last, horrid sip of the coffee. "What?"

"You have to hurry. We're running out of time. They won't make a stand," he said into his handkerchief before blowing his nose so hard people actually turned to look.

"The Dutch?" she asked with a look of disgust on her face, getting her expressions of sympathy throughout the smokey room before everyone returned to their discussions and cigarettes.

"They're negotiating for continued neutrality," said Oliver. "They will fail."

"I know."

"How do you know?"

"People talk. You think there aren't maids in the palace and government offices?"

Oliver tried to speak but ended up trying to clear his throat. It sounded like he was shaking a box of rocks. Stella waved at the waitress and edged away from Oliver in the politest way possible, both as an act of theatre (they were strangers, after all) and as self-preservation.

He spat into his foul handkerchief and asked, "Do they say that the government and the palace are preparing to evacuate?"

A chill went through Stella. It was inconceivable. They would run for it and leave their people to be occupied by the most repressive government on Earth. "Without a fight?"

"They're hopelessly outmatched in training, weaponry, tanks, you name it, they don't have it."

"I think they'll try," she said. "The mood is shifting the closer it comes."

"Perhaps, but not for long," he said. "I'm telling you party or no party we want you out as soon as possible."

"Why? I went in and out of Poland and Czechoslovakia with no issues. They're occupied."

"You are needed elsewhere. It seems there are shoes only you can fill."

"Why didn't you say that in the first place?"

Oliver blew his nose again and said, "I wanted to see where you were at."

He sounded odd and it wasn't just the cold.

"With the mission?" It seemed an obvious question, but his tone made it otherwise.

"Where your head's at."

"And?"

"It's with the Jews. This obsession of yours is a topic of conversation and it's doing you no good. Don't go there anymore. I'm begging you."

She glanced over and saw the sincerity in his eyes, his fears for her, but only her. How she envied Oliver and his sort. For them it was about winning the war and only winning the war. Humanity didn't come into it. Oliver didn't see the people. Sometimes all she could see was them and the winning so distant. And what was winning if you lost everything that mattered?

"I'll do my best," she said.

"Like your country, I suppose," Oliver said bitterly.

"We will come in. We have to."

"With what? Rusty wrecks and mild condemnations?"

"Roosevelt is doing what he can," said Stella, feeling shame at her country's reluctance to stand up for their allies.

"In other words, nothing. Winnie is begging, but they won't budge. You know that."

"When Churchill is prime minister he will be able to do more to persuade Roosevelt," she said.

"Will he?" Oliver asked.

"Yes."

"Your people don't have a horse in the race. They won't do anything until they do."

"You're wrong."

A muscle in his jaw twitched but Oliver didn't comment. There was nothing left to say on the topic. The waitress came over and he insisted on paying for Stella's lunch in a way that was both sleazy and pathetic as if he were trying to seduce her with beef stew. The waitress clearly thought he was pathetic, not to mention gross. She, too, encouraged him to get to a doctor, mostly to get him out of her café. He agreed and helped Stella to her feet, insisting on walking her out into the deluge. Her broken umbrella was no match for the storm and Oliver took her by the arm, practically dragging her to a shop where he bought them both good umbrellas and tossed hers away.

"I'll want to hear about the party."

She nodded.

"There must be results or you're out, if I have to drag you away."

"Give it a try. I dare you."

Oliver looked out at the flooded street teeming with cars, bicycles and carts, his icy blue eyes filled with irritation and exhaustion. Both were expressions Stella was very familiar with. Her mother sported one or the other nearly all her life, but it never stopped her or Uncle Josiah.

"If you weren't so valuable to the war effort…"

"You'd push me into traffic?" she asked with a small smile.

"Something like that," he said. "Results this weekend."

"You're giving me no time."

He shrugged. "If your party is the in you think it is, that should be enough to form a final opinion."

"Fine, but remember things change."

"Not this time."

Stella rolled her eyes and then dashed across the road narrowly avoiding getting hit by two bicycles and a truck. When she glanced back, Oliver was bent over and hacking into his handkerchief. He might not be alive at the weekend.

She turned back and hurried across the canal, looking for a last time at the Rijksmuseum. If Hitler took it into his head that the Dutch weren't Aryan after all, he might bomb them into oblivion in a week or two. He had that option and who would stop him? If Oliver was right, no one. Absolutely no one.

CHAPTER 9

Four hours later, Stella walked into the Hotel Krasnapolsky cold, wet, and thoroughly exhausted. She'd done her job and it had nothing to do with the list. She'd bought multiple panels of stained glass, four paintings, two tea sets, an incredible French sewing box in tortoiseshell and mother-of-pearl that supposedly belonged to the fabulous Thérésa Cabarrús. It was the right age, Napoleonic, but Stella seriously doubted the woman famous for her beauty, lovers, and salon spent much time sewing.

"Micheline, my goodness, you are damp." Ludwik rushed up and the concierge took the basket out of her grateful hands. "Daan! Daan! Come get this coat!"

The doorman ran over and took off Stella's coat. He reached for her hat that had once had a stiff brim but was now flopping in her face, but she took it off herself and handed it over. "Can you have them cleaned? There's mud and who knows what."

Ludwik agreed that everything must be cleaned and sent Daan off to the laundry with her things. He looked her over and then at the basket. "You've had a busy day."

"Shopping. Shopping. Shopping."

"For your clients?" He held up the heavy basket.

"Take a peek. I couldn't resist bringing it back with me instead of having it sent to the shipper. It's so lovely."

Ludwik looked under the oilcloth covering the basket and made an appreciative noise. "A beautiful box. What is it for?"

"Sewing."

His kind face crinkled up in doubt. "Sewing?"

She explained the box, but he had to see the tools inside to believe anyone would make such a beautiful box for such a mundane activity. It wasn't the Dutch way at all; despite being Polish in origin, Ludwik was very Dutch.

"Remarkable," he said with disapproval.

"I know. I know, but my client will like it."

"What will he do with it?"

"He'll put it on a sideboard and tell everyone it belonged to a famous French revolutionary who nearly died in the Terror."

"This is a good thing?"

"It's a conversation piece."

"Americans need these things?"

She leaned forward. "Yes."

He grinned, but then said, "I see you have not done the shopping you should have."

Stella drew a blank and the concierge sighed. "Your dress. The party is tomorrow and you have no dress."

"Oh, that," she said. "I'll just wear something I have."

He drew back in horror. "To the baron's party? You cannot."

Stella couldn't help but tease him a little. "It'll be fine. No one will even notice what I wear."

"The baron will notice and you will not be asked back. He is a man of taste and refinement."

And appetites.

"Well, all right, Ludwik," she said with an exaggerated sigh. "Tell me you have a plan because all I have is a sewing box."

The concierge smoothed back his thin, oiled hair and steepled his fingers. "I have a surprise for you."

"I thought you might." Stella smiled.

The Kras had excellent service and if they could anticipate Uncle Josiah's needs and keep him out of jail, Ludwik could handle clothes.

"I put in a call to Madam Milla," he said in triumph.

"And she is?"

"A personal designer to the baron. She has done costumes for him and designed the sets."

Sets?

"Ludwik, I know you're trying to help, but there's no way I can afford that kind of designer. I need something less silk and more cotton."

He waved that away. "It is done and she is coming."

"How much money do you think I have? My company only pays for my room and meals."

"There's another surprise."

Please, no.

"Don't say jewelry," said Stella.

"See you do know something about a society party."

I do and I should've known better.

"I can't possibly—"

Ludwik leaned over and said, "I have arranged for you to borrow the items. Milla will bring a selection and she will choose all. You don't need to worry."

"Am I borrowing the clothes, too?"

He turned her toward the elevator and handed her over to the operator, who maneuvered her into the tiny space. "Not to worry."

"I am worried," she said. "This could cost me a month's pay."

Ludwik winked at the operator and said, "Milla's cousin's nephew is married to my niece. So she will take good care of you. It is a challenge. She loves a challenge. Up you go. I will call and she will come. One hour. Be ready."

With that, the door was closed and Stella couldn't think what to do. This Milla couldn't get too close. Her face was Micheline. Her body wasn't.

"Don't worry. Madam Milla will take good care of you," said the operator.

"So I hear."

They stopped on her floor and he let her off saying, "I will have the kitchen bring up your favorite dinner?"

"Yes, thank you. Wish me luck."

"You don't need luck. As Ludwik said, she loves a challenge."

"Am I supposed to take that as a compliment?"

He said yes, but his eyes said no. In a way, it was a compliment. The whole hotel thought she was hopeless, just like she was supposed to be, but still it kind of stung.

Shaking off the remnants of her old vanity, Stella went in her room, took a quick bath, and redressed in a pair of loose and concealing pajamas. Her wig was worse for wear, but she had no time to fix it before her dinner arrived and shortly after Madam Milla. None of her training had prepared her for that.

Madam Milla strode into Stella's room looking like she stepped right off of *Vogue* magazine, but in a way *Vogue* could never have imagined. Milla was nearly seven feet tall in her six-inch heels, thin as a beanpole, wearing makeup Max Factor would've envied and a black and white suit with both checks and stripes. Her hat, fire engine red to match her heels, was as large as a dinner platter and just as flat. Madam Milla was also a man.

How Stella knew was hard to say. How did she know when Uncle Josiah was drunk ten feet away from the back? How did Florence know that Millicent would start wailing two minutes before she did? "Here it comes," Florence would say while looking at her perfectly pleasant child and then the eruption would happen, never failing to shock Stella with the accuracy.

Instinct. It had to be, because the illusion was truly remarkable and Stella stood back as Madam Milla swished her hips around the room, examining the clothes in her wardrobe and her scant makeup on the dressing table. She was not impressed.

"It is very good that you call for me," she said, holding out a long black cigarette holder with an unlit cigarette fixed to the end.

Greek? Hungarian? French?

"Ludwik said you would find me a challenge," said Stella.

Milla's dark brown eyes went up and down her body with an expression of extreme disappointment, like a mother with a dumpy daughter, which Stella supposed she sort of was. "Yes, but we will have no trouble with you. Paola!"

An older woman about sixty-five hustled in, wreathed in smiles. She was the absolute opposite of her boss, five feet tall and nearly as wide with grey curly hair tucked halfway under a beret. "I'm here. Shall I bring the rack?"

"Please do," said Madam Milla as she began to circle Stella like some kind of high fashion jackal.

Paola wheeled in a rack of fabulous clothing and to Stella's surprise it wasn't only dresses. There were coats and suits, too. This was going to be a challenge. She was Micheline Dubois. Dumpy and plain was her calling card.

"Ludwik was correct with your measurements," she said. "He has a good eye."

"What would you like first?" Paola asked in a strong Hungarian accent and Stella wasn't sure who she was talking to. She was the customer, but it didn't really feel that way.

"The café down by the lobby is open, yes?" Madam Milla asked.

Startled, Paola looked at Stella.

"I think so," said Stella.

Madam Milla jutted out a bony hip and said, "You've had a long day, Paola, in all this rain. Go down and have a nice dinner."

"Oh, no. I'm fine."

"You're tired and cold. Have a rest." She was kind but firm and Paola relented. She left and closed the door quietly behind her. Madam Milla went to the door, leaned back on it and struck a pose. Very Vogue.

"You are not ugly."

"Um…thank you."

"And you are not a woman of—" she waved the cigarette up and down Stella's form "—thirty-five or forty years as Ludwik said."

The hair on Stella's arms stood up under the level gaze of Madam Milla's inscrutable eyes.

"I have my mother's skin," she said.

"The wig is a disaster. Throw it out. Burn it."

Stella couldn't speak. Madam Milla knew. Instantly, just the way Stella knew about her.

Taking a breath, she gathered her wits and thought of escape routes. "I'm sorry you don't like my hair. Perhaps this isn't a good idea. I'm not really your sort of client."

"You'd be surprised." Madam Milla's voice was husky but not particularly low. Uncle Josiah would've called it a whiskey voice and Madam Milla was undeniably sexy. It was the strangest thing to look at her and call her a her, when every instinct said she wasn't a woman. But she was, too. Very confusing.

"I don't need a dress. I'm fine," said Stella.

Madam Milla tilted her head to the side and narrowed her large eyes. "You are going to the baron's party, are you not?"

Not now.

"Maybe." Stella tried to stop herself from searching for stubble on Madam Milla's chin, but she couldn't help herself. Her eyes couldn't stop looking, even though there wasn't any. How did she do that? Nicky couldn't go three hours without a touch of stubble.

"Maybe? An invitation to the baron's is a triumph." Her eyes were searching, too. They roamed over Stella's hairline, her eyes, neck, and hands. She was seeing Stella, really seeing her, and Stella fought to control her breath.

"I know."

"It no longer has meaning to you?"

Careful.

"Certainly, it does, but maybe such events are not my place."

"And you will not go?"

Stella went over to her wardrobe and all her practice of inhabiting Micheline fell away. She was shaky, her voice tremulous. Park-Welles had taught her what to do. In fact, she'd been retrained after being tracked by Ruth in Berlin. The sweet young Jewish girl hadn't known Stella was a spy, only that she was escaping Germany. That turn of events had turned out in Stella's favor, but this was wholly different. She was to get out immediately if this happened. If she had to kill Madam Milla to do it, that was acceptable, at least to the SIS it was.

She found a dinner dress in violet silk and held it up. "I'll wear this. It's fine and it fits. You can leave and join Paola for dinner. I'm sure she'd enjoy that."

"I'm sure she would," said Madam Milla, "but I cannot leave."

"Of course, you can." Stella hung up the dress and went for her handbag. "I'll pay you for your time."

"My time isn't the problem."

Stella continued to get out her pocketbook and tried to calculate what it would take to get Madam Milla and her clothes out of the room. She'd give her anything, everything to just get out. "How much?"

"He is expecting you," she said.

"Who?"

"The baron."

"He doesn't know me. We've never met. I doubt he'll notice what I wear or whether I'm there or not." Her voice had grown tight and odd, but the accent hadn't slipped so that was something.

"The baron knows who you are and is looking forward to meeting you," she said.

Oh.

"That's right. You know him, don't you?"

"I do and, more importantly, he knows I'm dressing you for the evening," she said.

Stella took a breath and gathered her wits. It wasn't easy. Madam Milla was so unexpected and frankly, unnerving the way she stood there calmly watching Stella struggle. "That's no problem. I changed my mind. Clients do, don't they?"

"Not my clients. Getting an appointment with me is harder than getting," she pointed at Stella's invitation on the dressing table, "that."

"Oh, well, I don't mean to insult you," said Stella. "We're just not a good fit."

She waited, but Madam Milla didn't move. She was thinking. That much was clear, but what did such a person think of? Where did she come from? Stella had spent plenty of time in Amsterdam and she'd never seen anyone like her. The boys at Valkyrie in Berlin were the closest, she supposed. They loved their costumes and would often dress in the girls' costumes for a laugh. Stella's favorite, Rolf, had once put on a dirndl and done a dead-on impression of Stella, bringing the room to hysterics.

Looking at Madam Milla, Stella saw that she was a performer, but why put on that performance? What would be the point?

"We are at what is called an impasse, I think," Madam Milla said after a moment.

"No. This is simple. I pay you for your time and you take your beautiful clothes away for someone else," said Stella.

"I could do that, but then what would happen?"

I get out of Amsterdam as fast as I possibly can and try to explain this disaster to my superiors without sounding like a crazy person.

"Nothing."

"That has not been my experience," said Madam Milla.

"Experience with what? Customers?" Stella asked, her heart pounding.

"People. I'm adept at the reading of people. I have to be."

Don't panic. It's fine.

"A useful skill, I'm sure."

"And one we share," said Madam Milla. "You know. I know. We, the both of us, know."

"I don't know anything, except that I'm tired and I'd like you to go."

"You knew the moment you saw me." Her voice grew a tad deeper. "A survival skill, yes? Another thing we share."

"I'm just a buyer for wealthy Americans."

"What are your intentions?"

"I intend to go to bed," said Stella. "Please go."

Madam Milla got a little tortoiseshell lighter out of her tiny handbag and lit her cigarette. "Usually I'm in the cage alone and trying to find a way to escape. But we are in this cage together. A new and uncomfortable experience for me. You are the same. I can tell this."

"I don't know what you're talking about. There's no cage. I'm fine. You're fine. Everybody's fine."

"I can't let you go and not only for myself. I am a patriot. And you are not Micheline Dubois. Are you even Belgian? Or is that fake as well?"

"Nothing's fake and I am Micheline Dubois. Ludwik told you who I am," said Stella.

She laughed. It was not feminine but also not male either. "Ludwik. Dear Ludwik. He doesn't know. He has an eye for figures, but not an eye for the truth. He does not know about me and we have known each other for years. He could know you for years and never see the makeup around your eyes or the wig that has just a little too much hair for a normal person or that your hands are much too young for a woman of middle years."

That's when Stella started thinking about her weapons. Park-Welles, given her needs in Berlin, had seen fit to issue her a decorative pen that, with a press of a button, shot out a razor-sharp icepick, lock picks, an explosive device in a pack of cigarettes, and double her normal cache of pills, ill, kill, and energy. None were handy and even if they were killing Madam Milla in her hotel room was hardly an ideal solution.

"I'm a normal person," she said with more conviction. "I just want you to go. That's all I want."

"This is what I want as well," Madam Milla said. "But I cannot risk myself or my country."

Is it possible? Could she be...like me?

"You're not risking anything. I don't know anything."

Madam Milla reached up and plucked her amazing hat off her head, taking the glossy dark hair with it. "Do you still deny?"

Stella stared. Madam Milla wasn't any less feminine without her hair. But she became unsettling. Yes, that was the best word. Her real

A.W. HARTOIN

hair was the same glossy dark color but chopped short like a man's, but otherwise every feature was female.

"See. You were not surprised," she said. "Who sent you and why are you in Amsterdam?"

"How do you do that?" Stella asked, not bothering to conceal her amazement. "It's absolutely brilliant."

"Oh." For the first time, Madam Milla's cool composure cracked and a flicker of pride or perhaps it was vanity crossed her face.

Not a spy.

Stella made a decision. Oliver would be furious, but it didn't matter since she would have to leave immediately, job undone, anyway. She may as well find out what she could. If she was anything like the boys in Berlin, Madam Milla was sweet and unlikely to expose her. The last thing she would want was exposure.

"Ludwik really doesn't know?" she asked.

"No, he doesn't." Without her hat, Madam Milla became shy and a bit fearful. The exposure wasn't planned and now that it was done, she reminded Stella of a dog that had been kicked more often than not.

"And you really are…" Stella asked.

"I am," said Madam Milla. "I take it you've never seen anyone like me before."

"Has anyone?"

She smiled and showed small very white teeth, too small for a man of her size. Stella suspected they'd been filed down to make them less prominent. A genius idea really. Madam Milla thought of everything, like Stella's unaged hands. Now that it'd been pointed out, it was painfully obvious.

"Of course," she said. "I'm not so unusual in my world."

Stella crossed her arms and gave her a sideways glance. "I think you're very unusual. Which world doesn't matter. Does Paola know?"

"She's my mother," said Madam Milla.

"Really? She's so…short."

She looked at the cigarette that she had yet to take a puff of, walked over to Stella's side table, and snubbed it out on the ashtray the maid had left there. "You aren't going to tell about me."

It was a statement, not a question, but Stella asked anyway, "Why would I?"

"People do." She put her hat and wig back, growing instantly more self-assured the moment her head was covered. "They like to. They enjoy it."

"I wouldn't," Stella said truthfully.

"You wouldn't want to be exposed either."

Stella sat down in the armchair next to her bed and put her feet up. "We haven't agreed that I have anything to expose."

"This is true, but I think now that you wouldn't do this to me anyway," said Madam Milla. "You're not…mean."

"And you would know?"

"I would. I have to."

It was a sad thing to admit, but Madam Milla did it without sentiment or sorrow. It was a fact of her life and an unescapable one. She reminded Stella of Maria telling her that she was really Ruth, a Jew living in the world of Nazis. Maybe it was the same in a strange way.

"You're right, of course," said Stella. "Now what about you?"

"You think I might be mean?" she asked striking another pose.

"I doubt it, but I haven't got much experience."

Madam Milla watched her for a moment and then asked, "Why are you in Amsterdam?"

"I'm not going to answer that."

"You're not going to tell me that you buy from the Jews and pay much too much."

For crying out loud.

"I don't know that I do," said Stella.

"I do. Ludwik does." Madam Milla went to the dressing table and sat down. "Why do you think I'm here? Because some dumpy woman of a certain age needs a—"

"I'm not that old!"

She laughed again. This time it was looser and full of genuine mirth as she examined her perfection in the mirror. "You might as well be with that wig."

"This could be my real hair."

"It could, but it is not. The brows are well done. This is what saves you." She got out a tube of lipstick in a gold case and applied it with a deft hand. "You know that you must tell me who you are."

"Or what? You'll expose me? I don't think so."

Madam Milla pursed her lips and then said, "Why do you want to go to the baron's party?"

"Who says I do?"

"Cornelia."

The air went out of her lungs in a silent whoosh.

"She's very fond of you," said Madam Milla, turning to look at Stella and propping her elbow up on the dressing table. The picture of elegance. "I thought it was a fast friendship, but now I see you and it's not a mystery."

"I like Cornelia very much."

"She believes you to be a kindred spirit of a certain age and I ask myself why would this girl do this thing to Cornelia? Could it be that she is like the man in the canal?"

"Canal?"

"A tailor from Delft with an interest in his neighbors. He asked questions. Very many questions."

"About?" Stella asked.

"The government. The Jews. The NSB," she said. "You are interested in the Jews."

"I buy from them. That's true."

"You are kind," said Madam Milla.

"I'm fair," said Stella.

"Few are fair these days. They take advantage."

Stella stayed silent. That she was so well-known and understood wasn't good. How far had this information gone? Who else knew?

Madam Milla turned back to the mirror and turned her face from side to side, evaluating her perfection with a critical eye. "But you don't ask about the government or the NSB."

"What did the tailor want to know?" Stella asked.

She smoothed a brow with the tip of a finger painted scarlet. "Who was friendly to the Germans? Who would flee if they came? Where would the government go if they fled? How would they get there? Very many questions."

"Yes," said Stella. Too many. "Sounds like he was for Germany coming."

"This is why he took a swim."

"They killed him?"

Madam Milla turned and crossed her shapely long legs. "He had an accident."

"Accidents happen when you want your country to be overrun."

"Yes, and now you see how we are caged together."

"Are you threatening to throw me in a canal?" Stella asked.

"Not me. Never me," she said. "But were it to be known that you are not who you say you are and are friendly to the Jews. There are some that would put these pieces together and…"

"And it's the same for you? A dip in the canal, if the wrong people knew."

She nodded. "We are in this bad place together."

"I'm not a tailor," said Stella.

"You don't care about the government?"

"Not my concern."

"What is your concern?" Madam Milla asked. Her face was impassive but her eyes intense.

"Does Cornelia know about the Jews and my…generosity?"

"Yes."

"Does the baron know?"

"If Cornelia knows…"

Stella took a breath. This was a horse of a different color and could be useful.

"And I'm still invited," Stella said.

Madam Milla nodded.

"I've heard that the baron has many friends in many quarters."

"He does," she said. "You find those friends interesting?"

"I do, but not as interesting as where his loyalties lie," said Stella.

Madam Milla stood up, a languid movement, and went to her clothes rack to sift through the dresses. "They lie with us."

"Us?"

"His country. The Dutch. You and I."

"I'm not Dutch," said Stella.

"Aren't you?"

"No."

Madam Milla took a gorgeous forest green dress with accordion pleats down the bodice to an embroidered belt in black off the rack. She held it up and gestured to herself. "Like me, I think you are close enough."

"You trust that I won't tell?"

"I do."

"May I ask why? You don't know me and as you pointed out, neither does Cornelia," said Stella.

"You weren't repulsed by me. Even after you thought about it, you weren't."

"Um…no." The thought had not occurred to Stella. Many things did repulse her. Nazis in general. Oscar von Drechsel specifically. Hate. Stupidity. Turnip soup. The list was long, but a man dressing as a woman was not on it. She found that she couldn't care less, especially since it was looking less likely that Madam Milla was going to betray her.

"You were thinking it over," said Madam Milla with a touch of amusement.

Honesty was working so Stella decided to stick with it. "I was and I can't think of a reason to care about what you do. You're not hurting anyone."

"And you've really never known anyone who wasn't…quite the same before?"

Stella thought about Uncle Josiah, the boys in Berlin, Ruth, Mavis at home in St. Louis and she laughed. "I've known a lot of people who aren't quite the same, but you are unique."

"Unique is what I have always wanted."

"You've achieved it and then some."

She held out the dress. "This will cover you, but it will seem like it's not."

Stella stood up and took the dress. The silk was so fine it felt like running water under her fingers. "So we have an agreement?"

"Tell me your name."

Stella set her shoulders. "Micheline Dubois."

"You're real name."

"Micheline Dubois."

"I will tell you mine," said Madam Milla.

This surprised Stella immensely and spoke of a need Madam Milla's visage didn't convey. It saddened Stella. Madam Milla knew she was a spy of some sort, by definition she wasn't a person to be trusted, but the need to be known was stronger than logic.

"I'd be honored to know it, but it wouldn't be safe for you."

She pulled back. "Safe? But you will not tell. You promised."

Stella didn't promise, but there was that pesky need again. "Some people get thrown in canals. Others have different more painful fates."

"I don't…"

"A person never knows how they will react until they face it."

"What?"

"Pain."

"Oh. You think you might get…"

"The less people know the safer we are," said Stella.

Madam Milla handed her the dress. "This is the story of my life."

"And mine."

She looked away, blinking rapidly. "Try it on. I can make alterations if they are needed."

Stella decided the trust was worth expanding on and unbuttoned her pajama top. She slipped it off and her bottoms, too.

"You are not shy in front of me." Madam Milla stepped back in surprise. "I thought you would go in the bathroom."

"Remember when I said I know others who weren't quite the same?"

"Yes."

"Well, let me tell you about Berlin."

Madam Milla lit up while she helped Stella dress. Stella told her about an unnamed club she worked in in Berlin and the boys she met there. She got Madam Milla laughing, belly laughing. She'd probably revealed too much, but it was worth it. That laugh hadn't been so well used in a long while and besides she was supposed to make contacts and connections. So Madam Milla wasn't what Park-Welles had in mind. She wasn't a clerk in Bikker's hotel or a valet in the royal house. So what? She was Dutch and she was on their side.

While chatting, they decided on a dress, the green one. Stella was deeply in love with the style and the concealed pockets. Every dress should have pockets in her opinion. Then they moved on to shoes, a coat, hat, and stockings for the baron's party. Madam Milla told Stella what she knew about the baron, but it wasn't a lot. There was a secrecy there and Madam Milla knew it, too, but she couldn't say what it was about. She didn't think it had anything to do with a leaning toward the Nazi regime, but she admitted that she could be wrong.

"I think Cornelia would know," said Madam Milla.

"You never asked?"

She shrugged. "I don't like to pry, but she would not tell me if I did anyway. She and the others are very protective of the baron. They love him."

"How protective?" Stella asked.

"They are Dutch first." Madam Milla was strong on that and Stella didn't doubt her, but it was worrying. Where there was something to hide, there was something to exploit. The Nazis were all about exploiting.

Madam Milla stepped back from the finished product and had Stella twirl. "Very good, but I must insist you give me that wig."

Stella fluttered a hand over her heart. "My hair? I can't take off my hair."

She rolled her eyes and held out her hand. "It is a mess and ugly."

"That is the point."

"Give it to me. I will make it better."

Stella gave her the side eye. "Maybe, if you tell me about someone."

"And who is that?"

"Jan Bikker and his wife."

She drew back. "Why would you be interested in them?"

"*We* should all be interested in them," said Stella.

"I see what you mean. They are not kind to the Jews. Cornelia said that she told you that."

"Not unusual though, is it?"

"No, but they do care for Germany."

"The Dutch have close ties with Germany. The Nazis think of you as Aryan."

"Not me," she said. "I am also Hungarian, remember?"

"Right," said Stella. "I forgot. Do you dress Anna Bikker?"

"I have."

A mysterious answer that brought a smile to Stella's face. "Do tell."

Madam Milla didn't know Anna Bikker well, but the woman was as Stella observed, tacky and over the top. She would not listen, had no taste whatsoever, and worst of all, she had altered a Madam Milla dress after it was delivered.

Stella grimaced, thinking of the shoes with the bows and buckles. "Did she add sequins?"

"Yes."

"More than sequins?"

"Yes."

Anna Bikker had taken a velvet evening gown with impeccable lines and an understated elegance and added sequins, gold braid, and crystal droplets.

"She looked like a cheap chandelier," said Madam Milla.

"No one would think *that* was your work," said Stella.

"I lost customers. This is a business of taste and I did not look well with that dress." She held out her hand expectantly.

Stella hesitated. The wig, no matter how awful, had become a part of her persona. She was oddly attached.

"How would your American clients say it? A deal is a deal."

"They do say that, but they aren't so good at living their words."

A.W. HARTOIN

Stella reached up and whipped the wig off her head, striking a pose in an imitation of Madam Milla. "Happy?"

Madam Milla took the wig and tossed it on the bed with disdain. "Awful thing. It should die. Now let me see who you are." She moved in close and cupped Stella's cheekbones. Her hands were so large they wrapped around her head so that her fingers touched in the back. She moved Stella's face left and right and then shook out her light brown hair.

"I remove my previous comment," said Madam Milla, stepping back and jutting out a hip.

"What comment?"

"That you haven't done a good job."

"You didn't say that."

"I was thinking it."

"Well, thanks for the retraction," said Stella. "What did I do right?"

"The hair."

"Really?"

"It is so bad, frizzy and—" she waved her hands around in disgust "—it conceals you very well. You are quite pretty." She started rearranging Stella's hair in sweaty waves over her shoulder and wiping off the makeup. "Yes, yes. I could do so much with you. So very much. The figure it is sadly short but well-proportioned. Very good."

"Thanks. Help me off with this dress."

Madam Milla helped Stella out of the clothes and she put on her big pajamas again while the designer worked on her wig.

"Don't make it too much better," said Stella.

"It is impossible to make it *too* much better. We will settle for not hideous."

She combed out the wig's frizzy locks and worked them into what might pass for curls if you didn't think curls should be smooth and shiny. Then she picked out a jeweled comb and strategically placed it behind the right ear.

"Not good at all." Madam Milla looked Stella over as she sat on the bed legs crossed and feeling more like herself than she had in months. "You must go like this?"

"Like Micheline? Yes."

"Why?"

"I am Micheline."

"The baron likes pretty young girls and you have the charm. That would be better."

"It's too late now," said Stella. "Besides, what would Jan Bikker like?"

She made a face that barely changed the smooth lines of her face. "He would like nothing. You could not seduce him even as you are now."

Stella was a bit hurt. She knew she wasn't a femme fatale, but it would be nice to think she had some seductive skills. "Why not? Anna did."

"Yes, and he is thought to be a fool," said Madam Milla.

"Does he know that?"

She laughed. "No. He sees nothing but himself."

"Maybe that's why all Anna's flash got her noticed. He can't see the subtle only the spotlight."

"Don't take him for stupid. He is not."

"I won't underestimate him," said Stella. "Can you tell me anything else?"

She shrugged. "I don't know him well. He never comes to the baron's parties and I saw him at the Bikker house, but he would not speak to me."

"Why not? His wife hired you. Didn't he like the dress?"

"He didn't like her hiring me," she said.

"Why not?"

"I told you I'm Dutch *and* Hungarian. I brought Paola with me and he knew right away. He didn't want us in his house."

"But you didn't tell them she was your mother," said Stella.

"No. Only the people who *know* know, but he looked at me closely. At first I thought he might guess, but what he guessed was that I was Hungarian, too."

"He guessed you were a Hungarian, but not that you're a…"

"No. People believe what you tell them." She smiled. "You are a rare exception."

"Hungarian," said Stella. "You're Hungarian."

She frowned. "Yes, I am."

"This might sound farfetched, but do you know other Hungarians?"

"Of course, I do. We are a small community."

"Do you know Mr. Elek that works in this hotel?"

Madam Milla smiled. "Of course. You have an attraction?"

"Not at all," said Stella. "What do you know about him?"

She ignored the question and went over to Stella's dressing table and looked at the makeup. "Where's the rest?"

"What?"

"The makeup you use to disguise your face," said Madam Milla.

"Why?"

"I will show you how to do the hands and neck."

Stella had the designer turn her back and then got out the makeup that was concealed under the wardrobe. "Here it is."

Madam Milla looked it over and Stella had the distinct feeling she was looking for clues as to its origin. She waited patiently. There was nothing to find. Generic makeup. It could be Dutch or French or Russian.

"This is very plain and simple," she said, looking dissatisfied.

"That's best. Why make it complicated?"

Madam Milla gestured to her own face. "I like complicated."

"You're a professional."

"As are you." She sat Stella on the bed and showed her how to shadow her hands to make the bones slightly more prominent and then adding the smallest amount of blue tint to the veins, making them seem bulbous and protruding.

"There," she said. "You like this?"

Stella held up her hands. "It's subtle, but it does make it better, a lot better actually. How about the neck?"

Madam Milla worked on her neck at the dressing table so she

could see how to shade the barely perceptible lines and age her dewy fresh neck a good fifteen years.

"Tell me about Elek," said Stella as another line was added.

"I don't know him well, but as you said, he is Hungarian and extremely handsome." There was a warmth to her voice that got Stella's attention.

"He is pretty stunning, but what else?"

"Just that he works here at the hotel as you know. I think his family has been here a long time," she said evasively.

"Elek knows Anna Bikker, right?"

Madam Milla jerked up from where she was working on a line on Stella's décolletage and said, "How did you know that?"

Stella told her about following Anna Bikker and how she disappeared into the back of the hotel. Madam Milla was doubtful until Stella told her about Marga in the café and her inference about Elek.

"You think they're having an affair?" asked Madam Milla.

"I'd put money on it."

"That is…unexpected." The warmth was gone.

"Why? People have affairs. She's attractive if classless."

"I thought he had more taste." She shook her head. "I don't think so. No."

"Do you know him well enough to say that?" Stella asked.

Madam Milla and her mother celebrated the holidays with other Hungarians. They'd had Christmas dinner together in December. It didn't happen every year. Sometimes it was Easter or New Year's. They were casual acquaintances, but Elek had brought young women to the parties more than once. His choices were quiet, demure girls with traditional values.

"Beauty isn't a factor?" Stella asked.

"They were pretty girls, but not remarkable. Elek was the prettier of the pairs and very well spoken. The girls hardly spoke at all. I've heard him discuss literature and music. He likes the theater and dance. I think he may paint watercolors, but I am not sure." The warmth was back.

"Nothing like Anna Bikker then."

She scoffed. "Anna is smart enough to ensnare her husband and no smarter. I doubt she has read a book in years. I have seen her at the theater, but she does not pay attention to the stage. She is there to be seen herself."

"How do you know that she knows Elek?" Stella asked.

"Because when I was at the house, Jan Bikker noted that we were Hungarian and not fully Dutch. I asked if he knew any other Hungarians and he said he didn't, but that Anna did. Then she made a big fuss how she doesn't know Elek anymore. He was not her sort of person at all."

"How did she act?"

Madam Milla closed Stella's makeup containers and thought about it for a moment. "Embarrassed, I think."

"To have known Elek?"

"Yes and that her husband threw it in her face."

"I wonder how they know each other," Stella mused.

"Attractive people have a way of finding each other, don't you think?" Madam Milla said.

That was true, but they were having an affair. It seemed out of character for Anna Bikker, a woman who'd gone to such trouble to marry well to jeopardize that with a tryst. And Elek worked at a rival hotel to boot and was nowhere near Bikker's social status. Anna gilded the lily on every occasion, but not with her lover. Very odd and it said something about her. It said something about Bikker, too. Stella just didn't know what.

"She's not as attractive as he is," said Stella.

"And he is a bookkeeper. Why would Anna make love to a bookkeeper? It does not make sense to take that risk."

"He's the assistant manager, but I don't think that's much better."

"He was a bookkeeper at Christmas," said Madam Milla thoughtfully.

"When was your appointment with Anna?" Stella asked.

"Over a year ago. Why?"

Stella picked up her pocketbook and sat down on the bed.

"They've known each other for a long time then, so the affair has been going on for a long time."

"Maybe. Does it matter?"

"It means Jan Bikker either isn't very observant or he doesn't care."

She nodded. "Most men would care and he isn't thought to be stupid." She hesitated. "This is important for us?"

Stella smiled. "We need to know what kind of man he is if we are to understand what he'll do. He won't be at the party though."

She shook her head. "No. He's not social. He only works."

"That's what I thought."

"This makes him hard to know?"

"It does."

Madam Milla gathered up her things, sewing kit and measuring tape, and put them in a basket on the bottom of the rack. "Anna is social."

"Yes. That is what I'm hoping."

"You need her to know Bikker?"

"It's all I've got."

"And you will come to the party?"

It might be a mistake, but one had to take risks and follow instincts. The job couldn't be done without those elements. Otherwise, you were just a tourist taking notes.

"I will."

"Then I will make sure that the baron likes you," said Madam Milla.

"Is that essential for knowing Anna Bikker?" Stella asked.

"She doesn't come for the food. She comes for the connections and if he likes you, she will whether she does or not."

"Anna Bikker sounds about as deep as a puddle."

Madam Milla smiled and then the amusement drained off her face. "She is, but I fear her husband is much deeper."

"That's what we have to find out."

She came over and sat on the edge of the bed, taking Stella's small hands in her long elegant ones. "My cage is a gilded one. I am glad to share it with you."

"I've never been fond of cages, gilded or otherwise," said Stella.

"But it's where we must stay for safety's sake," said Madam Milla.

"My cage has an exit. Does yours?"

"I don't know."

Stella thought for a second and then said, "I don't think I know either."

CHAPTER 10

Stella walked into the Hotel Krasnapolsky laden with packages and gratefully handed them over to the concierge on duty, Johannes, not Ludwik, before going to the café under the guise of having lunch. She was terribly hungry after hours of following the exceedingly dull Jan Bikker and his ridiculous wife, but she had another purpose as well.

The day started out dull and it stayed that way. Bikker left his house bang on time and went to his hotel where he stayed for thirty minutes. Then he went to an accounting firm, two separate importers, a doctor, and a flower shop, where, oddly, he bought no flowers. All the names were typically Dutch, but Stella took note of every single one. All morning he went in with nothing and came out with nothing. None of the visits took very long, thirty minutes at most, and it seemed to Stella that these were the kind of errands that could be accomplished with a phone call or, at least, a flunky could've gone.

To Stella's relief, he then went back to the hotel, where he stayed put and Stella got to have a cup of coffee and rest her feet. It was a lot of walking and she didn't appreciate it.

When Bikker didn't reappear after an hour, Stella decided to return to his house and see if she could get something going there. On the walk, she worked up a reason to knock on the door. Going to the baron's party. Need help. So well-known in Amsterdam. Blah. Blah. Blah. Stella seriously doubted Anna would be the least bit interested in mentoring her, but it was a way in. If she was going to have definitive answers for Oliver by the end of the weekend, she had to use whatever she had. At the very least she could get in the door and take a look around. She didn't expect to see Nazi paraphernalia on the walls, but you never know.

It seemed like a good idea, but it never got off the ground. Just as Stella was heading up to the house, Anna emerged, looking just as garish as before, if not more so. She wore an ankle-length red fox fur coat, even though it was fairly warm out, and topped that off with a gold lame turban. The turban had a ton of peacock feathers sprouting out of the front. Peacock feathers. Stella didn't consider herself to be a fashion genius, like Madam Milla, but that hat was painful to behold. It did, however, make it easy to follow Anna and it was fun to watch other people's reaction to her getup. She walked along the canal like she owned everything she saw, oblivious to the looks of consternation or outright laughter.

Stella expected her to go back to the Hotel Krasnapolsky to see Elek. That seemed like the kind of thing Anna would wear to meet her lover, but she went instead to a salon for hair styling. There were no windows and Stella couldn't see in, but her curiosity at what in the world Anna Bikker would do to her hair almost got her to stay for the duration, but exhaustion won out and she went back to the hotel to get on with her other focus for the day. Marga Kübler and the girl did not disappoint. Well, she didn't disappoint Stella. Her employers were, no doubt, a different story.

Stella sat down at her favorite table where she had a good view and watched Marga drag her feet around the café, occasionally rolling her eyes and sighing. Dirk came out from the back to prod her into action, but the effect was short lived. There weren't many customers, but Marga was so slow to wait on anyone. So slow that Dirk sent another waitress out from the back. It was Ester, the other girl that had sold out Cornelia's friend Yannj at the Bikker hotel.

Dirk pointed out Stella waiting at her table and Ester walked over, faster than her friend, but her feet weren't on fire. "What will you have?" she asked.

"A menu," said Stella, wondering if the girl would recognize her from the café with Cornelia, but she wasn't really looking.

"Don't you have a menu?"

"I wouldn't ask for one if I did."

Ester looked down with surprise. "Oh, I'm sorry. I'll get one."

The girl hoofed it into the back and returned within three minutes. Stella had settled in to wait for at least fifteen, but there she was and with a smile, too.

"Here you are. I apologize for the wait. Can I get you a coffee?"

"Yes, please."

Ester hurried off and Stella watched Marga amble around giving people the napkins she forgot and dropping silverware. If she hadn't talked to her before, she'd have thought she was dimwitted, but she was more lazy than stupid. Mostly, Marga Kübler didn't care. Stella couldn't help but wonder what would happen to her. She'd had little experience with the working class before Vienna, counting Mavis as her only friend in that category, but in Berlin she'd gotten a good taste of the working life. The girls at Valkyrie worked incredibly hard. Stella was tired at that very moment, but she reminded herself that it was nothing like working all night at a club.

Marga didn't seem to have any of the work ethic that the Berlin girls and Mavis displayed. Ester was better and not a thief as far as Stella knew, but neither girl would've lasted at Valkyrie, despite their pretty faces. There had to be a way to get what Stella needed out of them. She'd used money in several instances in the recent past, but those girls couldn't be trusted to keep their mouths shut for more than five minutes.

Friendly sympathy. It's worked before.

Ester brought her coffee, putting the cup down roughly so that it spilled.

"Do you know what you want?" she asked.

Stella ordered a *boterham* with ham and cheese.

"That's all?"

"For now," said Stella. "You must be so tired. On your feet all day?"

"Yes. I get so tired." Ester glanced over her shoulder. "He won't let us sit down at all."

"That's very mean. Girls get tired, just like men."

Ester's face became superior and she tossed back her light brown curls. "We work harder than him and he sits all the time."

"I heard that from Marga," said Stella conspiratorially.

"You know Marga?"

"She's served me before. I like her and I told him so."

"Did you really?" Ester asked. "That's nice."

"She was about to get in trouble, but I couldn't let that happen. She was cheering me up with some stories and I like to help where I can."

Ester came in closer. "Stories."

"Oh, you know. Just a little fun gossip. You should ask her."

She grinned. "I will. Be back in a moment."

Stella's *boterham* arrived in record time with Ester and Marga, looking very curious.

"I do remember you," said Marga.

Stella wasn't entirely sure that was true, but she went with it. "I hope Dirk didn't give you any more trouble after I talked to him."

Marga giggled and Ester joined in. "He didn't, but he wanted to know how I amused you."

Stella smiled and whispered, "What did you tell him?"

The girl hadn't a clue and she shrugged. "Just jokes, I guess."

"I saw him," said Stella, lowering her voice. "I see what you mean about him."

The girls were blank.

"Mr. Elek. I met him. Oh la la."

The girls giggled again and elbowed each other. Behind them, Dirk was hovering but unwilling to interrupt a conversation that a long-time guest was enjoying.

"He's very nice, too," said Marga. "I thought he might like me."

"He does," said Ester.

"Or you."

"Maybe."

Stella sipped her coffee as the girls went back and forth about who might've attracted the attention of the handsome Mr. Elek. From Madam Milla's description, Stella would've said neither featherbrain stood a chance, but he was sleeping with Anna Bikker, so one never knew.

"I thought you said Mr. Elek *knew* Anna Bikker," said Stella when there was a break in the chatter.

Both girls sneered in unison and Marga launched into her tale of woe again, but Stella hadn't the patience for it. "What an awful woman and so tacky. I saw her wearing a gold lame turban today. It was the most hideous thing I've ever seen. What does he see in her? Both of you are much prettier and younger, too."

Marga pulled out a chair and sat down. It was almost too much for Dirk. The man was wringing his hands in indecision. She'd better hurry it up.

"Well, I shouldn't really say, but—"

Ester pinched her shoulder with a look of panic on her face. Not so dimwitted as her friend. "Marga, don't."

"It's okay. Who would she tell?" Marga asked with a kind of condescending authority that made Stella clench a fist in her lap. As if being middle-aged and unattractive took away every power a woman might have including speech. How did Cornelia put up with it without smacking people on a daily basis?

"I've no one to tell and I'll be leaving town soon anyway," Stella confirmed although it pained her immensely.

"See," said Marga. "I told you."

Ester tried to intervene again, two bright spots of pink on her cheeks making her even prettier. "No, we could get in trouble and I need this—"

"I heard that they grew up together and that's why he likes her," said Marga. "They were sweethearts until she married that nasty bastard Bikker for the money."

"Where did you hear that?" Ester asked breathlessly, her fear forgotten.

"You know."

"No, I don't."

Marga widened her eyes at her friend and Ester got it. "Oh, right."

"Who told you?" Stella asked.

"Nobody."

"It must be somebody very interesting."

Ester shook her head. "No, no. Just somebody. Nobody really."

"Is this a good story, too?" Stella asked.

"Well," said Marga.

Ester pinched her hard on the shoulder and Marga yelped in protest. This was finally too much for Dirk. He rushed over and said, "Girls, don't be bothering the customers with your chatter."

The girls looked at her expectantly and Stella had to hide her frustration. "Oh, they're not bothering me. They're sweet and amusing."

Dirk frowned in disbelief, but he let the girls off without a reprimand. "Micheline, they can't be amusing to you. You're a woman of business and they're…"

"Young and silly?" Stella suggested.

He sighed. "I hope that's all they are. I wouldn't trust them, if I were you. I was told to hire them because of their pretty faces. The management thought it would bring customers in."

"It hasn't."

"Oh, no, it does, but they can't be made to work. I don't understand it. I've heard some…not very good things about them from colleagues at other hotels. They should be grateful for their jobs."

"They're young," said Stella.

"I hope they didn't trouble you with too much nonsense."

Not enough nonsense unfortunately.

"Not at all," she said. "Let me tell you a little secret."

Dirk leaned over and it was a fair way to go, being fully Dutch and over six feet tall. "Yes?"

"I'm thinking of writing a book and I need characters."

"Those two for characters?" he asked.

"One must have some humor and they inspire humor," said Stella.

He chuckled. "They inspire irritation for me."

"But you're trying to manage a café and I'm trying to find a plot."

"You have the better bargain."

"With those two, yes," said Stella, "absolutely."

He left her to eat and finish her coffee. She tried a couple more times to entice Ester into giving up who told her about Elek and Anna, but the girl was definitely the smarter of the duo and wouldn't go near it.

With regret, Stella finished and instead of doing what she wanted, going up for a nap before the party, she did what she had to, find the information the hard way or at least the long way.

Flore answered the door after the fifth knock and Stella feared that she'd forced the old lady up out of a deep sleep.

"Oh, no," Stella exclaimed. "I've woken you."

Flore threw up her hands. "Micheline! No, no. I was just closing my eyes for a minute or two. Please come in."

"I wouldn't want to bother you."

"I love visitors. You know that." Flore opened the door wide and ushered Stella into the small sitting room where there was a little fire in the grate and a cold cup of tea on the footstool. Flore hurried to take the cup away and said, "Would you like some nice hot tea? It's getting chilly out there."

"Speaking of tea." Stella got packets of butter, tea, and a very nice ham out of her basket. "I didn't want to come empty-handed like last time."

Flore flushed with pleasure. "You didn't need to, but it's very nice that you did." She went to the kitchen to put the kettle on and Stella took off her coat. She sat by the fire and listened to Flore whistling a little tune she didn't recognize. Happiness pervaded the little house and Stella didn't get to experience that much anymore. Most houses were frightened and for good reason. Flore's was a break from all that and it reminded Stella of her grandmother's house Prie Dieu, not that they were alike on the surface at all, but Flore did remind her of her imperious grandmother. She wasn't severely fashionable like Evangeline Bled or as tough, but there was the same generosity, good intentions, and warmth in both women and their homes. Evangeline hid her kinder qualities so that some couldn't see them at all, but Stella knew the truth and always found a comforting hot chocolate at Prie Dieu when her mother's criticism had been too much to cope with. Grandmother understood. She'd raised Uncle Josiah and lived to tell the tale. A daughter more interested in brewing beer than coming out parties met with her approval. Uncle Josiah had been very interested in coming out parties and he ruined quite a few of them.

"Here we go." Flore came in with a pot of tea and a selection of cookies. "You look like you could use a treat."

Stella couldn't speak for a moment.

"Micheline? Did I say something wrong?"

She shook her head. "No. It's just that my grandmother used to say that to me when I turned up at her house out of the blue."

"You miss her," said Flore.

"I do. Sometimes I forget that, but I do."

Flore poured the tea and asked, "So what have you been up to?"

"Well," said Stella with a smile, "I have news on my quest to sell to Anna Bikker."

"Tell me you got paste diamonds to sell her," said Flore with a wicked glint in her eye.

"Sorry no, but I do have an invitation to Baron Joost Van Heeckeren's party tonight and she'll be there."

Flore clasped her hands together and exclaimed, "Wonderful. Cornelia did that, didn't she?"

"She did. She is a miracle worker," said Stella.

"I hope you have some very gaudy things to sell to that horrid Anna. She's so stupid the more horrid the better."

Stella grimaced. "I have seen her a couple of times. Her clothes and hats…"

"I know. She never did have any taste at all. Just because something has a shine doesn't mean it's a jewel."

"Jan Bikker certainly didn't know that."

Flore laughed out loud. "Serves him right."

Stella sipped her tea and leaned forward, "I did happen upon a little information that might serve him right, too."

"I do love a good gossip. What has that Anna done?"

"Well, I was in the café at my hotel and a girl there told me that Anna's having an affair with someone there."

Flore drew back. "No. Surely not. If Bikker found out, he would… well he'd divorce her, that's what, and she'd have nothing."

"I think it's true. I saw her there and she stayed for a long time. Why else does a woman who owns a hotel go to another hotel?"

The old lady ate a delicate little butter cookie and thought it over. "I can't think of a reason, but who would have her. Most men aren't as easily fooled as Jan Bikker. Who has she entrapped this time?"

"A man called Mr. Elek." Stella watched as Flore's face lit up with recognition and then consternation. "What?"

"Oh, I…who is this Elek?"

"An assistant manager at the hotel. Do you know him?"

"I knew a family called Elek, but they've moved away," said Flore.

"All of them?"

The old lady didn't answer, but asked, "What was the man's first name?"

"Willem, I believe," said Stella.

She relaxed back in her chair and sighed. "Well, it's not him then."

"Who did you think it was?"

"Oh, no one. It's not him."

Stella poured Flore some more tea and gave her an innocent expression as she asked, "How do you know it's not for sure?"

"The man I'm thinking of is called Béla Elek, not Willem."

"Well, I saw Willem Elek and was he handsome. I can see why Anna Bikker would like him," said Stella.

"Handsome you say?"

"Very and tall with this dark wavy hair. He could be a film star."

Flore's forehead puckered. "You think Anna Bikker went to see him at your hotel?"

"I know she did and apparently it happens a lot. The other man in the office leaves when she comes or so the girl told me, but it's probably not the Elek you're thinking of. I couldn't see why such a handsome intelligent man would be interested in a married woman, especially Anna Bikker. The girl told me they grew up together. She didn't tell me where, but oh…that would mean here on your street."

Flore had grown quite pale and Stella started to regret asking her, but it was just an affair. As bad as those could turn out, why would Flore be so concerned?

"Are you all right?" Stella asked. "Do you need to lie down?"

"Tell me what he looks like again," she said.

Stella described Willem Elek in much more detail and then Flore asked her to get an album on the bookshelf. Stella pried it off a shelf stuffed full of books and brought over the fat album with its well-thumbed pages and put it on Flore's lap.

"What are you looking for?" Stella asked as the old lady bent over to go through the pages.

"I think I have a photo from when they were children. We had a street fair and I organized a treasure hunt."

"A picture of Anna and Béla Elek?"

"Here it is."

Stella knelt beside Flore's armchair and looked at the black and white photo. A group of children were gathered in the middle of the street wearing broad grins and gesturing to a boy, about fourteen, at the center. He held a tin cup trophy aloft with a huge smile of triumph on his face. It was Willem Elek.

"Is…that him?" Flore asked, pointing at the boy.

"Yes, absolutely, but his name is Willem now."

"I thought he left with his family."

"Where did they go?"

"England," said Flore. "His father lost his job and had a hard time getting another one. The girls got harassed on the street and they became afraid when the Nazis took Austria and then Poland, so they left."

"Are you saying that the Eleks are Jews?" Stella asked.

"Yes, they were. They are. That's why they left. Béla was going, too. I'm sure he was," she said.

"They got visas for the whole family? I thought that was hard to do," said Stella.

"It wasn't so hard for England, because they have quite a bit of family there. Béla's uncle is a physician in London and several aunts live in Hastings."

They looked down at the photo and Stella searched for Anna.

"There she is," said Flore without being asked to point her out.

Unlike Willem Elek, Anna was pretty hard to recognize. She had dark hair and was plump with knobby knees and a genuine smile on her face. Nothing like the Anna Stella had been watching. She was pretty in a clean, fresh way and had her head tilted toward Willem slightly as she stood next to him with both her hands fastened on his arm, sharing the win.

"She looks so different," said Stella.

"Yes, this was before she started doing little jobs so she could buy what she thought were fancy clothes, but she was always putting on airs and saying things, even then."

"Saying what?"

"Oh, she'd tell people that she had rich relatives in Paris. Once she told a neighbor who told her to pick up her trash that she didn't have to do such things because she had royal blood."

Stella wrinkled her nose. "Really?"

"Yes, it embarrassed her parents. Her mother would tell everyone that she just had a good imagination." Flore slammed the book shut and slapped her hands down on the cover. "This is her doing. It has to be."

"Béla staying?"

"Yes. I never imagined…it was a childhood fancy and now you say they are having an affair?"

"It looks that way. They were an item back then?"

Béla and Anna had known each other since they were small and were always in a big group of kids that ran together. About the time of Flore's photo, it changed and they became something more, but Anna's father had joined the NSB and the Eleks, while not particularly religious, were Jewish and weren't keen to change that.

"So, the parents broke them up?" Stella asked.

"I thought so. Neither family was happy about it and then I stopped seeing them together. They'd turn their faces away from each other in the street."

"If her father was in the NSB, he must've been very adamant."

Flore shook her head. "He was, but it's not what you think. Paul Hartman was a nice man, but he was a metalworker and had arthritis. He needed to move out of that work. He joined the NSB so he could get an office job."

"Did he?"

"Yes and he moved up fast." She paused and thought about it. "Maybe that's where Anna gets it. Paul always knew just what to say to get what he needed. He told a neighbor that the NSB was easy if you give them what they want."

Interesting twist.

"So, he wasn't really a fascist?"

"He was, but it was more a matter of convenience. If the communists had offered more to Paul, he'd have been a communist."

In a way, that seemed worse to Stella than being a true believer. Fascist for money or was it really that straightforward?

"He didn't want his daughter with a Jew," said Stella. "What would he have done, if she didn't give him up."

"Paul was never one to spare the rod," said Flore with a deep frown. "I can't believe Anna did this. Her father got worse about the Jews as he went up the ladder. It helped his career."

"Well, she married Bikker. How did the Hartmans like that?"

"Paul was quite pleased. He told everyone how he would be moving up and maybe working at the hotel in a suit and tie."

Stella put the album back on the shelf and warmed up Flore's tea. "That didn't work out for him."

"Not a bit and off they went. No big job. No advancement," said Flore. "I just can't believe Anna and Béla would have an affair. It's so dangerous for the both of them."

"Maybe they thought no one would find out," said Stella.

"You did and you weren't even trying."

Well...

"I am interested in selling to Anna, so I had a vested interest in what she was up to."

Flore scowled. "Up to. Right. This was her doing."

"Béla not going to England? How could she do that?"

"She got him a job at the Bikker hotel after she got married, but they don't hire Jews. She had money. She must've gotten the false papers and made him change his name."

Stella didn't point out that Béla Elek was a grown man who was intelligent and capable. Anna Bikker didn't make him do anything. He wanted to. He must love her. Why else would anyone go against their family in the way he had? And Anna was going against her family too and risking the marriage she'd worked for as well. Love? It must be. Stella fell in love with Nicky instantly and without reservation and he with her. What would they have done if their families had forbidden it? Give each other up? Fat chance.

"She's more complicated than I thought," Stella mused almost to herself.

"This is a problem for you?" Flore asked.

"I had planned to do as you said and tell her that I got the jewels from Jews that *took* them from good Germans, but now, I don't know."

"The affair doesn't make a difference."

"Doesn't it?"

"I think Anna is like Paul, an opportunist. She will want what you have if you sell it right," said Flore.

"But what is right? She loves a Jew," said Stella, feeling more sure of that by the moment. "Can she love a Jew and hate Jews at the same time?"

Flore made a face. "Love. What does she know about anything but her own wants? If she loved him, she'd want him far away from here, safe with his family. Not where the Nazis could come any minute."

An unexpected blossom of sympathy bloomed in Stella's chest. Love wasn't so easy or clear cut. Love burst through barriers. Love thought it could change what was unchangeable. Love was, in many ways, just hope by another name.

"She tried to conceal him by making him Willem," said Stella.

It was Flore's turn to warm Stella's tea. "I suppose that's something. What is it about her that the boy I knew would become someone else to be with her?"

"I couldn't say, but maybe tonight I will find out."

"Who cares?" Flore waved that thought away. "Just sell her the most gaudy things you have and go home. Profit. Worry about that."

There are all kinds of profit.

"I am, believe me," said Stella. "I wonder if you found the name of the American diplomat that helped Yannj get her visa through so quickly."

Flore's eyes widened. "Oh, my goodness. I completely forgot about that."

"Profit made me think of it."

"Profit?"

She smiled at the old lady. "I sell to Americans. He might be in the market for a few nice pieces that I happen to have on hand."

"Yes, of course. This is good business. You know someone who knows someone. I understand."

"So did you find it?" Stella asked.

Flore sighed and said apologetically, "No, I'm sorry. Dear Yannj didn't write about him, but I did write her and ask."

Stella wanted to howl in frustration. A letter to the States and back? That would take forever and a day.

"Thank you and don't worry. There are more Americans where he came from. Now I just have to figure out what Anna wants most."

"Oh," said Flore. "That's easy."

"Is it? When I came here, I thought she was one thing and now she's another."

"Little Anna Hartman always wanted to be better than everyone else."

"I should offer to make her better?" Stella asked with a smile. "I can do that."

Flore winked at her. "I know you can."

CHAPTER 11

Stella Bled Lawrence had seen some parties in her life. All sorts of parties from her mother's staid tea parties where everyone ate delicate little sandwiches and spoke only of appropriate things to Uncle Josiah's raucous celebrations of anything from the Kentucky Derby winner that he had inevitably lost money on to the launch of a new brew. The police would come with batons at the ready to beat back the drunks and if there wasn't at least one naked person staggering down the avenue, Uncle Josiah considered the evening an abject failure. Stella remembered with a little horror that the first naked man she ever saw wasn't her husband. It was Uncle Josiah's morbidly obese friend, Herbert, who'd snorted something out of a fish tank, painted himself red with tomato ketchup, and led the cops on a merry chase. Her mother had cried for three days when she realized it.

And Bled parties weren't the only parties. Nicky's mother threw plenty of soirées, too. They were in Newport where the wealthiest Americans discussed money, drank buckets of champagne, and had elaborate scavenger hunts where they would find clues like llamas or potted eucalyptus trees imported from California. There were plenty of drunks, but they rarely got naked according to Nicky. He had, as a child, caught people in a compromising position in the butler's pantry. He wouldn't tell her who it was, only that senators shouldn't act that way.

With all Stella's party experience, she'd never seen anything like the Baron Joost Van Heeckeren's party. Apparently, nobody else had either because she had to worm her way through a crowd a block away just trying to get there. The canal was completely blocked with onlookers and the authorities were trying in vain to get boats and people moving.

"I hope this is worth it," she said to herself as she squeezed between a couple of butchers still in bloody aprons and had someone try to relieve her of her handbag.

A perimeter had been set up and Stella ended up pressed against wooden fencing, unable to see a way in other than launching herself over the pointy pickets. They were up to her armpits, so that wasn't happening and she had to admit that staying outside had its charms. The baron's large house had been transformed, no longer the boring building with regular unremarkable features. The house was covered in red satiny fabric, suspended from the cornice. Loops and twists in the fabric revealed some windows and concealed others. In each visible window was a performer. Some were singing an aria. Others were dressed in Arabian costumes and doing magic tricks or having monkeys climbing all over them in a kind of swarm. One window had marionettes and another had a woman who was getting less dressed by the moment.

Stella started smelling smoke and she couldn't imagine what would happen next when the crowd gasped in unison. She looked up to see a woman emerge from a tiny little window at the top of the house. The house's hook for moving things in and out of the upper floors was above her and she looped a rope over it. A long red ribbon rippled down from the hook and the woman wrapped herself in it before launching herself out. People screamed and panicked, but the ribbon caught her and she began to do a kind of suspended ballet as an orchestra played in the background.

"He's in a good mood," said a man next to Stella.

"This is the best one yet," said another.

"I liked the circus one the best," said a woman.

"But the elephants!" exclaimed a man. "What a mess!"

"The camels weren't too good either."

"I loved the clowns."

"Remember the Venice theme?"

"I liked the Roman one better," said a man.

"You liked the half-naked girls," said a woman and that brought up a chorus of laughter.

Stella went up on her tiptoes and tried to find a gate, but no one was going in. What was she supposed to do? The invitation gave no instructions. She was to arrive at ten and present herself at the door. It was a bit early and she checked her watch. Two minutes till. Was she expected to be late? Was that a Dutch thing she hadn't heard of before?

Another gasp exploded from the crowd and she looked up. The woman was snaking her way down the ribbon in no apparent danger, but the crowd wasn't looking at her anymore. Stella had to shift and turn to look back to the left. At the house next door, a window had opened and a man dressed like *Arabian Nights* came out and hooked a rope over the hook above his window. Then Stella watched in amazement as he constructed a platform using the hook and planks. Another man at the baron's did the same thing at his window. The woman on the ribbon reached the bottom, but instead of letting go, she began to run back and forth, building up speed until she was swinging back and forth, getting surprisingly high off the ground. Then the man at the neighbor's house brought out a hook on a rope and threw it at the ribbon. He missed on the first try but got it on the second. The crowd cheered as he and another man hauled the woman up on her ribbon to their platform. She did a bow and a pirouette before disappearing inside. The men secured the ribbon to their hook and a barrage of fireworks went off from behind the crowd. Everyone turned to watch the incredible display and when they turned back to the house, a man came out onto the platform, threw a strap over the ribbon and launched himself off the platform. Stella screamed along with everyone else as he zipped along the ribbon and magically ended up on the other platform.

"He can't just have them come in the front door," said a man behind Stella.

"He'd never do anything so mundane for the first party of the season," said a woman.

"It's not as good as the balloons."

"Says who?"

"Me. They were beautiful and this is so dangerous."

Then a woman came out onto the platform, looking abjectly terrified, but she got across without falling and then a man and so on. Stella watched, increasingly amazed that people of all ages and sizes were willing to do that and then it dawned on her that she had to do it, too. Her chest got tight as she looked at that thin ribbon and pictured it fraying.

"Oh, no," she whispered.

A man put a hand on her shoulder. "Are you all right?"

"I'm…I'm…"

"What is it?"

"I'm invited," she managed to mutter.

"To the party?" he asked in wonder.

Stella nodded and was pummeled with questions. Who was she? How did she manage such an opportunity? She could honestly reply that she had no idea. She couldn't remember why she was going or why she would ever want to do that. The crowd moved her away from the fence and she found herself at the door to the next house where there was a pair of men behind another fence, also dressed as characters from *Arabian Nights*.

"She's got an invitation," yelled a man.

Several people were being let in through a narrow gate and Stella noted that none of them looked particularly thrilled at what was coming. One of the men came and looked her over, clearly noting the quality of her Madam Milla clothes. "Good evening. Do you have your invitation?"

Stella produced the envelope and he quickly read her name. "Ah, yes. Your first time to enjoy an evening with the baron?"

"It is." Her stomach was in knots and her voice came out squeaky and not at all self-assured.

He smiled with sympathy. "You will be fine. What kind of a party would it be if the guests died?"

"That's not as comforting as you think," she said, and he laughed as he opened the gate to usher her to the door of the house. "Is this house the baron's, too?"

"No, he's just borrowed a part of it for the festivities." He opened the door and Stella was in. The residence was a typical Amsterdam house albeit an expensive one. The art was good, she noted, and the carpets the best quality, but she didn't have much time to look around before being herded to the stairs.

I can do it. It won't be that bad.

A woman at the foot of the stairs took her coat, hat and handbag to be put in the cloak room. "You won't need them where you're going."

Stella very nearly threw up, but she went up a couple of stairs dragging her feet. Since when was she afraid of heights? She flew planes, for crying out loud. The answer was simple. She was afraid the moment she saw that woman on the ribbon. It was uncontrollable. She couldn't think her way out of it. She'd have to zip over on that ribbon. Either it would work out or it wouldn't. Stella didn't like the odds.

"There you are," said a woman behind her and Stella looked down to see Cornelia inexplicably dressed in Victorian costume. "I was worried that you wouldn't read the fine print."

"Fine print?"

Cornelia had her come back down the stairs and led her deeper into the house. "It gives this address instead of the baron's as the place of the party."

"Oh, right." Stella gulped.

"Are you all right?"

"I…uh…"

"Is it the ribbon?" she asked.

Stella nodded, unable to speak and she hated herself for it.

"You don't have to do it."

Thank you.

She sagged against a wall. "What a relief."

"I didn't know you were afraid of heights."

"Neither did I," said Stella. "Why aren't you in Arabian costume?"

Cornelia laughed and patted her hair that had been done up in a sort of giant puffed up bun. "The baron says the Victorians were obsessed with *Arabian Nights*."

"Were they?"

"I don't know, but I'm wearing a corset. It's the worst thing to happen to me since mumps."

Stella poked her side and it was like poking the wall. "Unbelievable."

"I take it you didn't see how they got the cable set up."

"Cable?"

"The baron spent months on this party." She stepped back. "And look at you. Madam Milla does good work."

"She's incredible."

"I was glad Ludwik called her," said Cornelia. "I couldn't have gotten you in. Come this way."

She led Stella through the back of the house into a courtyard that was on fire. She shrank back. "What in the world?"

"This is the other way in," said Cornelia.

"Through fire?"

"It's not so bad." She explained the loops and hoops of flames. Stella simply had to walk through a maze to get to the party. She made it sound simple even as a woman ran by with her dress on fire, being chased by a man with a bucket. "She'll be all right." The woman was doused. "See."

"Cornelia. This is insane. Who would come up with this?"

"The baron." For the first time, Cornelia looked testy and Stella could not say something like that again, although she wondered why. It was obviously crazy. Even crazier, people were doing it. Running into the fire, screaming, cursing and, occasionally, crying.

"I can't believe it," said Stella, since she couldn't think of anything more reasonable to say.

"You have to see this to believe it." She took Stella's arm companionably. "And it's worth it once you get to the other side."

Stella stood there frozen. She couldn't run into fire. She absolutely couldn't. It was impossible. If Gabriele Griese came back to life and held a pistol to her head, she could not run into that fire. "I can't."

"There she is," said Cornelia.

"Huh?"

Cornelia pointed and Stella saw Anna Bikker emerge from the house in a dress of white velvet with a train and pink satin flowers that looked rather like nipples from a distance, and something long and fuzzy hanging off the drapey, cape-like back of her dress. The whole thing was so tight she could barely walk and her hair was enormous. She had two big rolls on either side of her face and then a spray of ringlets in the back with jeweled combs and several flowers.

"Wow," said Stella.

"You should've seen her last time."

"It couldn't be worse than that," said Stella.

"Never underestimate Anna Bikker and oh, I can't believe it," said Cornelia. "Look."

A man came out of the house as Anna posed and waited to be admired. Jan Bikker walked in with a bad smell kind of a look on his face. When he realized people were looking he quickly turned it to a faint, unconvincing smile. He and Anna discussed the fire hoops and maze.

"Surely she's not going in there," said Stella.

"Are you kidding? Of course, she is. All the best people are on the other side."

As if on cue, Anna pulled up her skirt as much as she could and hobbled into the maze. Jan dashed past her, disappearing into the glow. Quite a guy.

"You should go now." Cornelia nudged her. "That couple there looks like they'll panic. You want to get through before them."

DARK VICTORY

"I'll do the ribbon." Stella said it without thinking. It just popped out.

"You're sure?"

Stella pushed down the panic and reminded herself she'd jumped out of trains with the SS hot on her trail. She could ride a ribbon fifteen feet.

"Yes."

Cornelia took her back in the house and up the narrow stairs to the third story. She waited in line with Cornelia who told her that she'd done it and it wasn't so hard. You just couldn't let go. There was no chance whatsoever that Stella would let go. She was more worried about going hysterical on the platform.

"Are you coming in, too?" she asked the maid as a man held out his hand to help her onto the platform.

"As soon as all the guests are in," said Cornelia. "That's when the fun starts."

"I certainly hope so. This hasn't been any fun so far."

"You old fuddy-duddy. Live a little."

Or die. Either way.

Stella took a breath and stepped up on the platform. The man put a kind of cable in her hands. It had wooden handles on either side for her to hold and seemed sturdy enough.

"Look here," he said when she wouldn't look up.

"I'm looking."

"You are not."

"Just tell me what to do," she said.

He laughed. "You will be fine. Put the cable over the cable and we will push you off. It takes five seconds and you are over."

Cable?

She looked up and there was a cable, a real steel cable hidden cleverly behind the ribbon so that it looked like one was riding the ribbon, but it was really a cable. "How did they get this cable over without us seeing it?"

"Tricks and sleight of hand. The baron's specialty. Ready?"

She wasn't remotely ready, but she nodded and he was right. Five seconds and over. She was on the other platform being cheered by dozens of people on the ground watching. Her legs were wobbly and she felt worse than she had after jumping off trains or nearly getting killed by Peiper's boy in Venice. Like the very blood in her veins had gotten molten and fried her brain. Uncle Josiah had described a feeling like that after he'd nearly gotten executed during the Great War and he likened it to sticking a fork in a socket. He would know. He'd done it enough.

"Come this way," said a maid in Victorian costume and Stella stumbled into another world. *Arabian Nights* came alive at the whim of a Dutch aristocrat. The house was tented on the inside. Every wall covered with silk. There were snake charmers, acrobats, and baby camels. For a second, Stella thought they were stuffed, but no, they were alive. Each room had a slightly different theme from genies to Aladdin to the Forty Thieves. One room was all sea monsters and Stella assumed that had to do with Sinbad, but there wasn't any reference point. She wandered around, completely overwhelmed by the belly dancers and sword swallowers, so much so that she'd almost forgotten why she was there when she heard a man say, "I heard she was a Jew."

Stella stopped to watch a snake charmer dancing with an enormous snake around her arms and neck, carefully edging closer to the conversation of three men wearing prim and proper black suits with their heads together as they drank goblets of champagne.

"I think she is. How else could she be so exotic?" said one with a bald head and large belly.

"She's Hungarian. That's exotic," said another.

"I'd like to see how exotic she is," said a third, who kept glancing around to see if anyone was listening. Stella kept her eyes enthralled with the charmer but her ears on them.

"A Jew? No. Disgusting."

"Bikker hired her to dress his wife. She can't be a Jew."

"He married the wife," said the bald one. "I wouldn't listen to him."

The men laughed and began discussing Anna and it was not flattering. Stella felt a twinge of pity. She was trying so hard to be admired, but she was really digging a hole.

"He could divorce her."

"She suits him. She'll do whatever he wants."

"She better."

"I don't know about that," said the suspicious one. "I heard she was a friend to the Jews."

"That was years ago."

"Bikker would know. He had her looked into."

"He's thorough. No worries there."

"He could try a little harder with the rest."

The men murmured agreement that Jan Bikker wasn't trying very hard with the government. He had influence but wasn't using it. He hadn't joined the NSB or even attended a meeting. This information wasn't in Stella's brief. Paul Hartman was in the NSB and Oliver deemed that to be a factor in Jan Bikker's loyalties, but not joining himself was a bigger issue in Stella's mind. Bikker was obviously anti-Semitic and made no bones about it. If he didn't go all in with the local fascists that meant something.

"He's going to do better," said the bald man.

The suspicious one snorted. "He'll wait to see which way the wind blows."

"Didn't you see him? He's here."

"You must be joking," said the third man.

"Not at all. He came in with that wife of his."

The men discussed what this meant but really had no clue. They backed up Stella's information that Bikker wasn't social, he didn't work a room, or care for much other than business. They were befuddled by the change and came to no conclusion other than the wife had somehow persuaded him although they didn't credit Anna with either brains or talent.

A belly dancer slithered in and gyrated around the men totally distracting them from anything but lust and Stella moved away to search for Bikker. She had to see him in action. She knew why he was there, even if the men didn't. Leopards changed their spots but only for a good reason.

She wandered into a large dining room where enormous skewers of meat roasted in front of a pair of fireplaces at either end. Cooks shaved off slices of sizzling meat and tucked them in round, fluffy bread loaves to the delight of the guests. They ate what they were calling peasant food and moaned at its deliciousness. In the corner, a woman was using what looked like a duck press to make juice out of exotic fruits like pineapple and guava. Stella took a glass but declined the shot of rum that was supposed to go in it. She had to keep her wits about her, but it was difficult not to indulge in the champagne that every other servant was offering. She missed champagne and it was pink, too. Her favorite. If she hadn't eaten before she came, she would've been distracted by the food. The air was thick with the smell of spices she couldn't name and roasting meat that could've been lamb or beef or who knows what.

Stella wove in and out of conversations, greeting people warmly as if they were acquainted and people responded in kind. The champagne was flowing and no one but Stella was being restrained. She heard their joy and fears. Some of the guests believed that their country would avoid the fate of Poland and Denmark. It simply wouldn't happen. Other groups were sure it would and were talking of escape. There were murmurs about how they would be treated and plenty of fear on that score. Some thought the Germans were a business opportunity. None of it changed what Stella had previously reported to London and she became frustrated.

After an hour of wandering around, she still hadn't found Jan Bikker or his wife. Presumably the baron was there somewhere, but she hadn't found him either. She had discovered that Cornelia and Madam Milla were right about the baron. He didn't appear to take any sides. From her eavesdropping, she'd found Jews and Gentiles, NSB members and people who hated them, harebrained socialites and university professors. Stella had to admit they were all interesting in their own ways with different experiences and opinions. No one was particularly shy or secretive. That would change soon enough. A couple of government officials spoke of German troops moving into position. They calculated the invasion to be less than a week away, at the most two. Instead of panicking, they'd decided to enjoy life while they could in a fatalistic take on their future. England would get no help from them.

Stella went down the stairs in hopes of finding her way out into the courtyard to look for Cornelia, but then someone tapped her on the head when she stepped on the stairs. There was Madam Milla standing in a doorway, looking like she ought to be in a movie about a temptress involved with espionage. Very Mata Hari and it made Stella smile. She would never be cast in such a role.

"You find me amusing?" Madam Milla asked.

"I find you stunning," Stella came over and lowered her voice, "and brave."

"Brave?"

Stella glanced meaningfully at her décolletage. Madam Milla's dress had a plunging neckline and a bare mid-riff. It was beaded and embroidered, but somehow looked right and appropriate for the setting at least. This was what Anna Bikker wanted to achieve but would never manage.

Madam Milla bent over to whisper in her ear. "I must stay in sight. What is hidden is intriguing."

"Or suspicious."

She nodded. "Have you met our host yet?"

"I was just looking for him."

Madam Milla led Stella through a series of rooms to a library with walls completely covered in books. There were even free-standing shelves sitting next to comfy armchairs and a large desk that instead of having a blotter and ledgers, had trays of little cakes that looked like Aladdin's lamp and another woman pressing juices. In the center of the room was a small table surrounded by men sitting in folding chairs. They were smoking from a weird brass contraption on the table with individual stems snaking out of it. Stella couldn't imagine what it was, but the room smelled like her Uncle Nicolai's smoking room after a bad day.

"Baron," called out Madam Milla.

A man popped out of his seat like he was sitting on a spring. "Milla, my love. How are you?" He put his stem on a hook on the side of the brass contraption amid protests that he ought not leave. He soothed them by ordering another round of champagne and squeezed out of the group.

During her time in England, Stella had gotten to know a few aristocrats beyond the earl and his family. She'd have to say Winston Churchill was the most unusual. During a weekend at the Churchill home, Stella had seen him go into a meeting with the military wearing a dressing gown. He dictated in his bathtub and he was forever taking a bath. But her favorite oddity was the outfit he called a romper, a kind of onesie that he had in a variety of colors, including pale green and pink. But Winston Churchill had nothing on the baron.

The man working his way across the room was thin to the point of being gaunt and he didn't trouble to hide it. He wore an outfit like the performers were wearing, a kind of sleeveless vest, no shirt, pants like balloons, and no shoes. On his thin blond hair, he wore a tiny fez identical to the ones the monkeys were wearing and he had on more jewelry than Anna Bikker and that was saying something.

The baron got to them, bowed, and did a spin. "What do you think? Cornelia says that I have gone too far. But what is a party if you don't go too far?"

I've found the Dutch Uncle Josiah.

"I think you are vulgar, inappropriate, and possibly indecent," said Madam Milla.

He threw up his hands. "Success."

They exchanged cheek kisses.

"And you," he said, "are beautiful, exotic, and stubborn."

"Stubborn?"

The baron looked at Stella and winked. "She still won't go to bed with me."

"Well, you are vulgar, inappropriate, and possibly indecent," said Stella with a smile so wide it hurt her mouth.

"So many compliments whatever shall I do?" He grinned back at her and asked, "And you are?"

"This is Micheline Dubois, Cornelia's friend."

"I invited you?"

"You did," said Stella.

"Well done me." He took her arm. "You must be interesting. Cornelia knows what I like. Let me introduce you to the world."

"The whole world?"

"The whole world of Amsterdam. Everyone that matters is here and you must meet them."

He led her away from Madam Milla who was accosted by a drunk who insisted on lighting her lit cigarette. She gave Stella a little finger wave and blew out a perfect smoke ring.

"This is Julius," the baron said. "He's a terrible flirt."

"Eloise. Johannes. Gerritt. Petris. Catharina." The names came at Stella so fast she couldn't hope to keep track, but she did note that everyone was there from low to high and the baron made no distinction between them. They were practically running from room to room. She had to drink champagne. No wasn't a word the baron understood. She tried everything on offer and so did he. Stella would take a bite, but he would down an entire plate of meat and then move on to cakes. How he was so thin was a mystery and his energy was astonishing. The brief had said mid-fifties, but he moved like a man half that, almost childlike with his excitement and joy.

Stella went along, hoping they would run across Bikker and Anna at some point but enjoying the whole thing immensely. So much champagne. So many smiles. She had to keep her head and not be entranced by this man who exuded every quality she loved in her uncle. She had a job to do. She must focus on evaluation.

At one point in the courtyard, he saw another baron and pulled Stella off her feet in his rush to introduce them and then Cornelia was there.

"Here let me help you," she said as she helped Stella to her feet. The baron spun away, greeting people and kissing cheeks. His voice was high and almost frantic.

Cornelia brushed at her dress and said, "No harm done." But her friend was avoiding her eyes.

"Is everything all right?" Stella asked.

"Yes, of course. What could be wrong."

Stella looked across the room and saw two of the servants talking to the baron and then leading him away.

"What's going on?"

"Some trouble downstairs with a delivery," said Cornelia, now meeting her eyes without hesitation. "As if now is the time to demand payment."

"Oh, that will be sorted quickly enough," said Stella.

"Yes, but I should go and make sure they don't start in on next month's party prices. I don't want tonight ruined."

"There's another one next month?"

Cornelia laughed. "And it will be entirely different."

"I don't even know what to say. This is extraordinary."

She nodded, but Stella saw the wringing of the hands and the eyes darting around. Something was wrong.

"Don't let me keep you."

"I wouldn't want to abandon you," said Cornelia nervously as if she had to contain something.

Stella waved a hand over the room. "I know practically all of Amsterdam now." She came in close to the maid's ear. "Except Jan Bikker and his wife."

"Oh, really," she said. "You really must meet them."

They left the room, which took no notice of anything except the belly dancers coming in for a performance.

Cornelia suddenly stopped at the top of the stairs. "They're in the garden. There's a young woman near them, named Wilhelmina Rost. She's the daughter of a clockmaker. You have much in common."

"What does she—"

Cornelia was gone, hastily disappearing into the depths of the house, leaving Stella confused and more than a little bit worried.

Stella found Wilhelmina Rost easily enough. It didn't hurt that she was pretty and surrounded by men trying to get her attention. They all smiled and offered her drinks and treats, all of which she refused while skillfully making it seem like she'd actually accepted. It was quite a trick. Stella watched her for a moment, trying to learn the turn of phrase or exact look that made men thrilled to be told no, but it was impossible to capture.

The baron liked interesting and Wilhelmina was truly interesting with her long blond hair reaching to her waist, completely unadorned. She wore no jewelry, not even earrings, and her dress was a plain black satin. It was cut well and of expensive fabric, nothing that Stella would ever think to pick out, but it somehow made the wearer shine. That dress made her more not less, but none of that was why Stella noticed Wilhelmina Rost. It was because Anna Bikker was watching her with slitted eyes from under a bower laden with twisting vines. Occasionally, Anna would glance over at her husband, who was a few feet away, talking to a group of men and oblivious to Wilhelmina's charms and his wife's dislike.

Stella stepped to the side and walked the perimeter to admire a group of acrobats entertaining in the center of the courtyard. The fire maze had disappeared, leaving only a hint of smoke as evidence that it was ever there. Through the crowd and the entertainers, she watched Jan Bikker. He spoke to each man with friendly focus and an easy smile. She watched the hand gestures and how he checked his watch in a way that wasn't obvious or insulting to the men he was talking to. He was not the man she'd followed to and from his hotel or on errands, the unsmiling Bikker who strode the streets of Amsterdam not seeing anyone and rarely returning a greeting. This was a man of charm and sophistication. He got plenty of looks from the women in the courtyard and Stella had to admit he was handsome, every inch the Olympian. The charm transformed him. Before he'd been dour and Stella had thought him unattractive without any real physical reason.

"Excuse me," she said to a man at her elbow watching an acrobat climbing to the top of a human pyramid wearing a costume made entirely of silk-stocking material.

"Uh-huh?" He didn't look at Stella and she didn't need him to.

"Who are those men talking to Jan Bikker? I thought one was my cousin, but it's not."

He glanced over and then at her. "Oh, that's Hendrik Bruins."

"The grocer?"

The man burst out laughing. "He works for de Geer. A grocer? That's a good one."

The acrobat did a handstand at the top of the pyramid and then the splits. Stella was quite forgotten and she moved away. Jan Bikker chatting up someone who worked for the prime minister and suddenly so charming. Interesting.

Stella talked to several people about nothing important and then found herself at the edge of Wilhelmina's group. Anna Bikker had noticed her and her clothes. She couldn't slink away unnoticed, so she became Micheline once again, a businesswoman with a goal.

"Excuse me," she said to the center of attention. "Are you Wilhelmina Rost?"

Wilhelmina looked up and smiled. It wasn't just a trick of the light. She wore no lipstick, mascara, nothing. "Yes."

Stella decided a little lie was in order, especially since Anna was listening intently. "The baron sent me over. He said you're interesting."

She laughed. "Naturally." She waved a thin pale arm over her crowd of admirers and Stella. "We all are or we wouldn't be here. Who are you?"

"Micheline Dubois. It's my first time."

"I can tell by the shock on your face." Wilhelmina stood up and shook off a couple of restraining hands. "Go on now. The baron sent her. She must be interesting."

The men, ages twenty to at least fifty, wandered off casting back regretful looks and hoping to be summoned back, but Wilhelmina took Stella's arm and whispered, "Thank you. They can be so overwhelming, you know."

Stella did know, but Micheline did not. "I wouldn't really." But she smiled with genuine warmth and amusement in her voice, so Wilhelmina wasn't put off. She held her arm tighter. "You're just what I need."

"Am I?"

"You've got humor and that's in short supply."

"Here? It's all smiles and champagne."

Wilhelmina turned her away from Anna Bikker and they walked to a bar where a man was lighting drinks on fire. For what purpose, Stella couldn't guess.

"Two Gin Rickeys," said Wilhelmina.

"And what will you have?" The barman gave Stella a wink.

"A Manhattan, please."

He nodded and Wilhelmina was impressed. "Very American."

"Like your Gin Rickey."

She laughed again. "Here I was trying to impress you with my knowledge of the world and you know it better than I."

"I work for Americans and I go to New York sometimes."

Wilhelmina's eyes widened. "Have you been to the Stork Club? I was in New York two years ago, but we couldn't get a table."

Stella went through a quick calculation on whether Micheline would ever be in the most stylish club and decided to go for it. "Yes, actually I have."

"How did you get a table?"

"I didn't. The company I work for booked it and I was asked along."

Wilhelmina pummeled her with questions and then they got into antiques and art, jewelry and design. She was Stella's kind of person and even better, she would point out who was who. This time she could remember the names. Stella got everyone that Jan Bikker was talking to. All members of the ministry. Very nice.

"You said earlier that humor was in short supply," said Stella. "Everyone seems happy to be here."

"Fiddling while Rome burns," said Wilhelmina.

Stella lowered her voice. "Because of the Germans."

"Any day now and we're all acting like it won't happen."

"It sounds like it will."

"Without a doubt, but I won't be here to see it."

"No?"

"I'm leaving tomorrow for England."

"Really?"

Wilhelmina downed her second Gin Rickey and flipped her silky hair back over her shoulders. "I don't want to live under Hitler's boot heel and even if I did, my father wouldn't allow it. If the royal family can leave, so can I."

"They're really leaving?"

"Absolutely. My father knows everyone in government, but I also overheard it from them." She jerked her head to the right, indicating Bikker and his ministry friends.

"They're talking about it right out in the open?" Stella asked.

"They're trying to get a leg up with Bikker."

"On what?"

"Jobs. When the Germans take over, nobody will need them in government."

"He's offering them jobs?"

Wilhelmina glanced over her shoulder and sneered. "I don't know what he's doing. He's never come before and look at him smiling." She shivered.

"You don't like him?"

She looked to the side. "I can't really say that. I don't know him, but nobody knows him. Jan Bikker only cares about his hotels and sport."

Stella watched Bikker take a cigar out of a silver case and offer to one of the men who was extremely impressed and grateful. He glanced at Wilhelmina and a look of dislike flashed over his face. One second and it was gone.

"What about his wife?" Stella asked.

"Her?" Wilhelmina rolled her eyes. "Poor thing. She doesn't know what she's doing."

It was the first kind word anyone had given Anna Bikker and it warmed Stella to Wilhelmina even more. Kindness was a virtue she'd come to prize. There was so little of it going around those days.

"That's not good news for me," said Stella.

"No? You like Anna Bikker?" She was extremely doubtful and Stella could see why. Anna was now standing in a group of women, wives of the men her husband was talking to, but she was out of the circle. It was subtle, but it was there. They were in. She was out.

"I don't know her, but she was recommended to me."

"For what?"

"It's embarrassing," said Stella.

Wilhelmina ordered another Gin Rickey and settled on a bar stool expectantly. The girl could drink. Stella didn't know where she was putting it all. The Manhattan had gone straight to her head after not drinking a drop for months.

Stella accepted another Manhattan because what else could she do and told Wilhelmina a tale about a bunch of ugly jewelry she bought out of pity. Now she was stuck with it and the Americans didn't want jewelry at all.

"They were so sad and desperate. I couldn't say no, but it's ugly. Very ugly."

"No wonder people told you about Anna. She loves ugly. Look at that dress. Why would that ever happen to fabric I ask you."

"Those are mink tails on the back, right?" Stella asked.

"Indeed. That dress hurts me. It really does."

"Not everyone can have your style."

Wilhelmina smiled sweetly. "No, but everyone can *have* style. Madam Milla tried to dress her and she ruined it."

"She told me."

She touched Stella's sleeve. "This is beautiful and suits you perfectly. See? Style. What is that? It's like wearing a checkbook."

"I agree, but is she in the market for jewelry?"

"Always and Bikker gives her whatever she wants. God knows why. It would be kinder to rein her in." Wilhelmina gave Anna a critical look that Stella's target noticed and a grimace passed over her pretty overly done up face.

"Doesn't she like you?" Stella asked.

"No. I tried to help and that was insulting. Sequins aren't right for every occasion. It's a fact."

"Would you introduce me? I'm only in town for another day or two. She seems like my best opportunity."

Wilhelmina finished her drink and slipped off the stool. "Of course, I will. Poor Anna. She'll probably buy it all and look worse than ever, but she insists upon it, so you might as well make a profit."

They made their way across the lawn, past the men talking to Bikker and they all stopped to watch Wilhelmina's progress. The women in Anna's group weren't happy and scattered before they got there, leaving Anna alone with her chin stuck out and an empty drink in her hand.

"Anna," said Wilhelmina. "It's been such a long time."

"Has it?" Anna's voice was high and nervous.

"Yes. You weren't here for the baron's December party."

"We were skiing in Bavaria," she said.

"Of course. It must've been beautiful. I envy you. I can't ski at all. I took lessons, but I always fall down. I have no coordination. You should see me on ice. I end up black and blue."

Anna Bikker puffed up with pride at hearing Wilhelmina's failures and she simpered at them, "It takes natural grace and skill. Not everyone is born with it."

If Wilhelmina was offended, she showed no sign of it. "That is so true. I just had to give up. I didn't want to break a leg or my head. I hear you are very good."

"I am and I get better every season." Anna preened and held out a hand to show off a set of truly gaudy rings to them, but they didn't take the bait.

"I do wish I could ski. It's such a sociable sport. What about you, Micheline?" Wilhelmina threw up her hands. "Oh, my goodness. Too many Gin Rickeys. Anna, this is Micheline Dubois, a favorite of the baron's."

Anna's eyebrows shot up and she looked Stella up and down,

finding her lacking in every respect, despite her Madam Milla dress or maybe because of it.

"I doubt she skis," said Anna with a sniff.

Stella smiled. "Not well, but I do enjoy the Alpenspitze."

A waiter approached with more champagne and Wilhelmina replaced Anna's drink with a glass. "Not well is better than me, Micheline."

"My family has gone to Bavaria every year since I was a child," said Stella. "It is very beautiful, but none of us excel at the winter sports."

That was a trigger for Anna and she began to tell them how the French were never good at winter sports. They listened to her blathering on, neither bothering to correct her on Micheline's origins.

"I do wish I had your skill," said Stella. "I have such trouble with leaving the lift."

Wilhelmina kept a steady stream of champagne going down Anna's gullet and Stella kept on asking leading questions. Anna started slurring and they took her by the arms to lead her into the house. A man greeted them at the door in German. Anna was blank so Stella answered in passable German that they were taking Anna to have something to eat.

"Your German is very good," he said, taking a good look to see if he recognized her.

"I'm pleased you think so. I am working hard on it," she continued in German.

"Are you?"

She gave him a sweet smile that could be interpreted as sly and said, "Of course. I'm a businesswoman."

Wilhelmina lost patience and said in Dutch, "Come on now. Cake is calling."

The German moved out of the way and they took Anna inside to find the dining room.

"Who was that troll?" Wilhelmina asked Anna.

Anna sneered at her. "Watch your tongue."

"Why would I try to? Surely you can see that he resembled an old toad."

A.W. HARTOIN

"Old or not, he's German and he knows people. Important people," Anna slurred.

Wilhelmina got her an Aladdin's lamp cake and asked, "How do you know? He's new here. I've never seen him before."

"I met him in Berlin," said Anna with a smear of frosting above her lip.

"Of course," said Stella, "in December. A very good time to be in Berlin."

Wilhelmina's eyebrows jolted up, but she said, "You did say it was fun."

Anna wavered on her feet. "Did I?"

"The Christmas market in the Pariser Platz sounds lovely," said Stella.

"Yes, yes. We saw that, but we were too busy to attend. So many things to do." She went on to describe a Berlin that to Stella didn't really exist. To Anna, it was a place of plenty, warm and full of the holiday spirit. She was never cold or hungry. Nobody was. The Reich was doing it all perfectly as far as she was concerned.

"I do love Berlin," said Stella.

"When were *you* there?" Anna asked as if only special people got admittance to Berlin.

"November." Stella lowered her voice and glanced around. "I was on a buying trip. Very lucrative."

Anna's bleary eyes brightened. "Buying what?"

"I'm not sure you should say," said Wilhelmina. "She might not agree."

"Agree with what?" Anna snatched a glass of champagne off a tray as it passed by and nearly upset the whole thing. The waiter saved the situation, but Anna got stains down the front of her dress from her own glass. It was almost an improvement.

"Well," said Stella, "this is between us, but I buy from *those* people."

"What people?"

Stella gave her a meaningful look. "You know. *Them.*" She jerked her head at a man introduced to her earlier as a tea importer. He was

Jewish and Stella guessed that Anna would know all the Jews and she wasn't wrong.

"Oh. *Them.*" She wrinkled her nose. "Why do you do that? Disgusting. They're dirty, you know, and the smell is awful."

This description took Stella aback for just a second. Anna was having an affair with a Jewish man. How could she say it? Was she just playing a part? If she was, she played it well. "Business is business." She glanced over at Wilhelmina, who was not covering her feelings. The girl's eyes were icy cold and staring at Anna with undisguised hatred. Not good for Stella just when she was getting somewhere.

"Wilhelmina, do you know where the baron might be? I just realized he wanted to know about the jewelry I bought in Berlin and I forgot to tell him."

Wilhelmina took a breath and her expression softened slightly. "I can go find him if you like."

"I would, if you don't mind," said Stella.

"What jewelry?" Anna asked.

Wilhelmina gave Stella a wink and left, squeezing past a sword swallower and waving off several man who tried to get her attention.

Stella turned back to Anna and said, "I didn't tell you about the jewelry?"

"No, but I only buy the best." She held out her hand to be admired and Stella obliged this time. Then she told her about a collection of jewelry she'd bought from a family in Berlin, making it sound as hideous as she could.

"It sounds amazing, but who would buy a Jew's jewelry?" Anna sneered.

"That's the thing. It's not." She went on to tell a tale about a German from the noble line of Hohenzollern who'd lost his wife's jewelry to gambling. A Jew bought it and sold it to Stella. Just as she hoped, Anna was intrigued. The noble house of Hohenzollern was right up her alley.

"How do you know it's genuine?" Anna asked.

"I do all my checking." Stella smiled. "You know people in Berlin and so do I."

"Who do you know?"

Stella looked around and bent over close to Anna's ear. "Well, I met some people at Valkyrie. The club. Do you know it?"

"You got into Valkyrie. How?"

She told her that her company, the Americans, had come in for meetings and gotten a table through government contacts. Stella was invited to fill the table.

"You're very lucky. Even we didn't get in."

"Maybe next time," said Stella. "When do you go back?"

Anna gave a nasty smile to the Jewish importer. "Soon enough."

"When you do go to Berlin—"

The baron pushed through the crowd. "What is this about Berlin? We are in Amsterdam. The most beautiful city in the world."

"Yes, of course," said Anna. "Nobody likes Berlin."

"Have you been?" he asked.

"Not for years, but she has." Anna pointed at Stella like she was pointing at a thief.

"Oh, yes. So you said. Jewelry was it not?"

"I bought quite a bit," said Stella.

The baron nudged Anna. "It's stunning. You should get it. The statement would be worth making."

Anna nodded emphatically. "I think I will. If it's any good."

"I'm sure it will be." A man came up behind the baron and smiled at Stella from around the aristocrat's bony shoulder. Stella didn't skip a beat, although her heart did. Several beats in fact. Fouquet was one of her contacts in France. If Oliver brought him in to watch her work, she would kill him.

"Have we met?" she asked.

"You don't remember?" he asked. "In Copenhagen. I specialize in clocks."

She threw up her hands. "Monsieur Fouquet, I apologize."

"You know each other?" The baron was delighted and ordered another round of drinks to Stella's chagrin. The last thing she wanted was a drink.

"We met during the course of business," said Stella. "He was very helpful with my purchase of a certain clock. What are you doing here, Monsieur Fouquet?"

"Like you, I am in search of opportunities," said Monsieur Fouquet, smiling down into his drink. "I think you perhaps know of one."

"Do I?"

"Is this not the beautiful wife of Jan Bikker?" Fouquet kissed Anna's hand and went on to faun over her rings, dress, and general appearance. He was a handsome man, about forty with the beginnings of a paunch. More importantly, Frederic Fouquet had charm and ability, not to mention style. He'd been recruited two years before to watch social activities in Paris. Who was in and who was out and he was very good at it from what Stella could tell.

"Don't fall for it, my dear Anna," said the baron. "His clocks are very expensive."

"What do I care about that," said Anna. "If it is the thing to have, money doesn't matter."

Stella smiled and said, "'Anyone who lives within their means suffers from a lack of imagination.'" It just slipped out. She wasn't thinking. Just for that sentence she wasn't Micheline Dubois. She was Stella Bled Lawrence and it showed in the horror on her face.

Frederic quickly said, "You are so right. I have a lot of imagination and so do you, don't you?" he asked Anna. She blushed and agreed. She was absolutely full of it. "And Micheline, your Americans, they have the imagination, too?"

"Very much." Stella watched Jan Bikker pass through the room behind Frederic. He was careful to stay clear of the Jewish importer and behind him was the German she'd met at the door. Where were they going?

"We should discuss a new clock I have acquired," said Frederic.

"Look there, Anna." The baron grabbed Anna's arm and pulled her away to watch a female sword swallower. Stella took her place against the wall and Frederic joined her. The performer climbed on the dining room table and began her routine, getting gasps from the audience that would muffle any interactions.

"What are you doing here?" Stella asked.

"I was going to ask you the same," said Frederic. "You were to have left."

Stella sagged against the wall. That was at least a good sign. If Oliver was sending someone to watch her that carefully, she was essentially useless and might as well pack it in. "I was."

"Oh, and now you're here."

"Yes, but I'm about to sell my last pieces," she said.

"Then you will go."

"Hopefully."

Frederic came closer. "What happened? I saw your face."

She paused to gasp at the size of the sword to be swallowed next and then whispered, "What I said. A mistake."

"What was wrong with it?"

"A quote from Oscar Wilde."

They clapped for the performer and he glanced at her puzzled.

"An English author. I don't speak English that well, certainly not well enough to know obscure quotes."

The crowd cheered and another performer, a man, climbed on the table to compete for who could swallow the most swords at one time.

"No one noticed. I read in English and I didn't recognize it."

"You'd be surprised at what people notice," Stella said as Anna headed over to them.

He nodded and said loudly, "I notice many things. Like how I need to tell this beautiful lady about my clocks and—"

Stella elbowed him. "Anna cares only for jewelry. I have it on good authority."

"I know a discriminating eye when I see one."

"You know nothing about women," said Stella. "You are not married."

"Which is why I know so much." Frederic winked at Anna, who blushed at the attention. They fought over her for a few more minutes and then Stella let him win. He began talking clocks, German ones specifically, and they turned away, letting Stella escape so she could follow the path of Jan Bikker through the house. The crowd was such that she could get quite close and listen without being noticed. Bikker did look around to see if someone was listening, but with the noise and people in fantastic costumes he didn't notice Stella, who was small and blended.

He talked to people all through the party and Stella watched with amazement at his changing demeanor. He went from charming to nasty without any hesitation or thought. To the German guests he was smug and confident as they were. To some of the Dutch, he was worried and occasionally defiant, but to others he spoke of "the coming changes" and positioning. Jan Bikker was all things to all people and he knew just what they wanted to hear. She even saw him be polite to a Jew when a Dutch couple were watching. Stella didn't know who they were, but they were definitely watching how he behaved and he passed the test. They smiled and chatted with him about keeping their country strong in the face of adversity, which he wholly agreed with. A few minutes later, he was talking to the German Stella met at the door and they discussed Wilhelmina, keeping their faces pleasant. Their voices were not.

"She'll learn soon enough," said Bikker.

The German laughed. "I can't wait to see her change her tune."

"The Rosts are close to the *family*."

"She won't say anything until after."

"We'll see," said Bikker before he moved away, working the crowd. He was very good at getting people to talk but not, in her opinion, good enough to last long in this, the most dangerous game. People talked. They noticed. One minute he was resisting Germany. The next an invasion was an opportunity not to be missed. She had enough on him. The baron was a little less clear. She'd seen him steer certain people away from Jan Bikker and a few other people. He did it in a way that could be seen as accidental, but it wasn't. He was protecting them, but would he act in a more deliberate manner? That she couldn't say. He would have to be approached to know and that wasn't her job, but she wouldn't recommend it when she made her report. There was something about the baron, as much as she liked him, that worried her. There was always a servant at his elbow.

Cornelia or one of the others right there to whisper in his ear. What was that about?

Bikker moved out of the library and Stella followed through another door, stifling a yawn. It'd been hours and the party was still going. Stella was exhausted from chatting. Her accent was slipping, but people were drunk and noticed nothing.

Bikker led her into a music room where Madam Milla posed by a grand piano while men threw themselves at her feet. Anna was there, completely drunk and being cautioned by a matronly Dutch woman that she must not be so obvious. That didn't go over well and Stella expected her husband to step in, but he passed right through and went for the stairs.

She trailed him down and outside where he went into the neighbor's house. He got his coat and hat, expressed impatience at waiting even a moment for them and then stalked out of the house. Stella hurried to the window to see where he went. It was like someone gave him bad news and everything changed. But there was no telegram or message. Jan Bikker had just had enough and he left, striding down the street toward the bridge without a thought to his wife or the niceties of thanking the host. The man would not last long. Jan Bikker would find himself at the bottom of a canal before long. Not soon enough in her opinion, but that wasn't her problem.

Stella stood at the window, slumped against the frame, and watched, not thinking of the man her eyes followed, but of another tall man entirely. Nicky. Where was he? What was he doing?

Bikker left the bridge and turned right. He walked back toward the baron's house and Stella stepped back in the shadows, wishing the Dutch believed in curtains. It didn't matter. Jan Bikker didn't look any way but straight ahead. Yet another reason he'd end up in a canal.

Then he disappeared into the night, but Stella kept looking out the window. She could leave now. She could go.

"Ma'am?"

She looked up and saw a servant peering out to see what Stella saw. "Is everything all right with you here?"

"Oh, yes. I was…thinking of the past and what will soon happen," said Stella.

"It is very late. Perhaps you should go home."

Home.

"Is everyone leaving?"

The woman laughed. "No, no. They will stay to dawn. It is the way it is done. Didn't you see it on your invitation?"

"I did, but…"

"You can go home if you like."

Stella looked back out on the street. It was deserted. Totally deserted. No one was leaving. But Bikker left and he turned right. Right wasn't his home. That would be left. Where was he going? She didn't care, but she did care. One last bit of information for them.

"Will you get my things? Micheline Dubois. I must say goodbye to the baron," she said.

The woman nodded and went into the depths of the house. When she was gone, Stella hurried to the front door and ran out into the chilly early morning air. The breeze went right through her dress. It didn't matter. There he was, a tall man walking alone. One last thing.

The house was dark and it remained so. Jan Bikker went in and he didn't come out. Stella waited, shivering in the dark for a light to come on as some hint of where he was or what he was doing, but it didn't happen. She wrapped her arms around herself and checked her watch. Five minutes. She'd give it five.

Ten minutes later, she was still waiting. It was hard to give up, even when her feet were losing feeling. They'd lost it before. It wasn't a problem, but Jan Bikker was. What was he doing in there?

Another ten minutes and she gave in, turning away to disappear herself into the alley behind her.

CHAPTER 12

𝒜 sharp knock on Stella's door finally woke her, but she just rolled over, dragging a pillow over her head.

"Go away," she muttered.

"Madam Dubois!" called out a voice. "Micheline!"

Ludwik.

"Why?" she muttered.

"Micheline, I bring you your breakfast!"

She threw back the covers and squinted at the light streaming in through the window. She'd forgotten to pull the heavy curtains after she'd stumbled in just before dawn.

"Micheline?" Ludwik had started to sound worried and she heard the distinct rattle of keys.

"I'm coming!" Stella jumped out of bed, found her wig on the floor next to her handbag and coat, and jammed it on her head. She took a quick look to see if she got it on right and she did. Mostly.

Deep breath. You're dignified. A businesswoman. Successful.

She threw on her robe and unlocked the door. Ludwik didn't hesitate. He stalked into the room, carrying a tray. "I was terribly worried when you didn't appear downstairs this morning, but the night concierge said that you came in early. I brought you..." The neat and tidy man looked around and then picked his way across the room to put her tray on the foot of the bed.

"Thank you." She yawned. "What time is it?"

"You had a good time at the party?" The man was practically vibrating with excitement and all she wanted to do was push him out the door.

"It was amazing."

Ludwik clasped his hands together. "What did you do? What happened? There was fire? The smoke was smelled far and wide."

There was nothing for it but to settle in and tell the tale. She sat down on the bed and poured a cup of coffee. "There was fire. Very much fire. Do sit down. Looking up is hurting my neck." It wasn't, but that seemed like something a woman Micheline's age would say.

"Yes, yes, of course." Ludwik sat down and she told him everything he wanted to know. He was thrilled to bits about the baby camels and costumes. Horrified by the fire maze, not to mention the rope swing or whatever that thing was called.

"You met Wilhelmina Rost?" he asked. "She came to the hotel once. So very elegant and kind, too. How did you find her?"

"Exactly that. Lovely and…genuine I'd say."

"Genuine?"

"Well, I saw Anna Bikker as well."

"Ah, there is nothing genuine about her." He fiddled with his waistcoat.

Stella eyed him over a pastry, tore off a bit and waited for him to say what he wanted to say.

"Why do you look at me that way?" the concierge asked.

"Because you want to tell me something. I'm just waiting to hear what it is."

Ludwik glanced around like someone might be lurking in the shadows. "She comes here. Anna Bikker."

"I know," said Stella. "I saw her."

"You did? You didn't say so."

Careful. Don't look eager.

She shrugged. "It didn't come up."

"She comes quite often," said Ludwik.

Stella picked up her coffee cup and leaned back on her pillows. "I heard that."

His face turned red. "Where did you hear this? Not from a member of staff."

She laughed. "At the party. There aren't that many secrets in Amsterdam and I'm leaving. People tell me little things. Fun tidbits."

"What fun tidbits?"

"That Anna Bikker *loves* this hotel."

"Yes?" he said slowly as if he hadn't wanted to spill it a moment before. Now he was the careful concierge keeping things under wraps. Sweet, silly man.

Stella crossed her ankles. "Maybe I shouldn't be the one to say, if it isn't widely known in *this* hotel."

"I know everything that goes on," said Ludwik with his nose up.

"Do you know Willem Elek?"

He clapped his hands together. "You do know."

"And I'm not the only one," she said.

"Yes?"

"I heard it whispered a few times last night or this morning. I don't know. It's all a daze." She poured another cup and looked up at him. "You are friends with this Willem Elek?"

"I am. He is a charming young man," said Ludwik.

"What does he see in Anna Bikker? I can see Wilhelmina Rost. She is everything there is to have in a young lady."

He shook his head. "I haven't wanted to bring it up. It is so private."

"You should. Her husband was there last night. He could've heard."

"Jan Bikker was there?" Ludwik made a face. "You're sure?"

"Absolutely. He was pointed out. I'd had him described to me before, but he was very different than what I expected."

"What did you expect?"

"A cold man. No charm or interest in people."

"That is Jan Bikker. You are saying that he was…"

"Charming. He talked to many people. Not his wife. So, you should tell the young man that the husband may have found out."

Ludwik sat back and waved the thought away. "He already knows."

It was Stella's turn to be astonished and Ludwik laughed at her gaping mouth.

"I know, but it is true. He has been here a couple of times to meet a guest. She came in and he saw her. A friend of mine, a waiter, he said Jan Bikker asked him about Elek. He knows."

"And he doesn't care?" Stella asked.

"That was some time ago and she keeps on with it."

He can't know who Elek really is.

"So, you think Jan Bikker is cold, too?" Stella asked.

"I heard an American guest say it well. He is a cold fish. This was the guest he met here, so he would know."

"An American?"

"A famous American, I think. You know of the Bled family?"

Stella tilted her head to the side and thought for a moment. "Beer?"

"Yes, that's right. Bled Beer. They were here, looking to expand."

"Why were they meeting Jan Bikker?"

"It was only one Bled, the crazy one."

Uncle Josiah.

"There's a crazy one?" she asked.

"Very crazy, but truly charming. We love for him to stay, but it is always a disaster. Not the last time, but all the times before that."

"What happened the last time?"

"Nothing." Ludwik laughed and told her about her Uncle Josiah and his previous visits to the Hotel Krasnapolsky. Stella did her best to not be embarrassed or laugh. Both were appropriate, given the streaking down the halls and through the winter garden full of dinner guests. The affairs with maids, one of which quit and moved to Hollywood to be in the movies. She had a bit part in a Claudette Colbert movie, but the hotel wasn't mollified. She was a very good maid. And all that was just for starters. Uncle Josiah threw parties. He tore out the wall in one room because he thought he heard a ghost and there was the time he set up a chess tournament in the lobby without telling anyone. He moved thirty tables in at three in the morning and the tournament started at seven. They had odd little intellectuals from seven countries descend upon them with peculiar demands. They required certain pickles and special cushions.

"Chess?" That was new. Uncle Josiah didn't play chess that she knew of. It was too dull and slow.

"He won," said Ludwik.

"Who?"

"The crazy one. Josiah Bled. He won the tournament against an angry Russian. We had to give him all the caviar so he wouldn't throw the chairs."

"I don't know what to say," said Stella and she truly didn't. Her mother must not know or there would've been fireworks. Maybe a trip to South America again. "Why was this crazy person meeting Jan Bikker?"

"Oh, yes. You asked that already. He was wanting a deal to put the beer in the Bikker hotels."

"Did they do it?"

Ludwik laughed. "The crazy one didn't like him. He said something that didn't go well with the American."

"Like what?"

"I'm not sure, but it was something about the Jews. The crazy one listened then he stood up and walked away. He never came back. Jan Bikker was furious. Later, the Bled told me that he was a cold, unfeeling man."

"You sound like you like this crazy Bled man."

"It is impossible not to like him. He is as you say about Wilhelmina Rost. Genuine."

It was the nicest thing she'd ever heard about Uncle Josiah. Better than the other compliments he typically got like war hero or dashing bachelor. They always came with a touch of censure. Like he's a war hero, but…

"And nothing happened last time?" she asked. "That sounds unlikely."

"The crazy one was on his best behavior. There was an Austrian family with him when he stayed. They saw the sights and talked beer.

I think the Bleds might've been buying their brewery. Breweries buy other breweries, don't they?"

"Probably." Breweries did, but not Stella's family. Her father and his father before him preferred to grow their own brand, not take over others' work. "When was this?"

Ludwik raised a brow. "Why do you want to know?"

"Are you kidding? A famous American. I work for Americans. A little gossip goes a long way."

He tapped his temple. "Always to the business. Always thinking. This is why you are successful."

"I hope to remain so," said Stella. "When was it?"

"Let me think. A long time now. Before the war," he said. "Is that enough gossip for you?"

"Plenty."

"Will you stay in bed today?"

"No, I must get up and see people. I think my business is done. I want to say goodbye to Madam Milla. Thanks to her I was a great success. I couldn't have done it without the two of you. I'm very grateful."

Ludwik stood up and placed his hand on his heart. "It has been my pleasure." He hesitated and then said, "You will continue your kind works."

"I will do what I can," she said. "But kindness should be kept quiet, don't you think?"

"If it is to continue, yes." The concierge smiled and left her alone with her breakfast. Stella nearly settled down in the warm comfort of the bed and took her sweet time getting going. She was full of good coffee and pastry, warm and reasonably happy, but success wasn't what it once was. When she was warm she thought of those who were cold. When safe, she thought of friends that were frightened. She thought of Hanni, in prison or not, she would definitely be cold and hungry. She thought of the Dereczynski family and their cramped and cold attic. She couldn't do anything for Hanni, but she could try again for the Dereczynski family. Now that she could leave, there wouldn't be any harm in seeing if Truus had returned yet. When she was back in England, she could get her mother to write recommendations and the rest of it to get Józef and Weronika out. If she could've found out the name of Yannj's friendly American in Rotterdam it would be that much faster but writing to the States took forever and it was too late.

Those thoughts got her going. Action was the cure as the earl liked to say. She threw off the covers and got dressed as fast as possible with eating and finishing her coffee. Coffee could not go to waste. She knew how precious it would become once the Nazis took over.

After washing her old makeup off and reapplying it, she put on her coat, stuffed her Madam Milla dress in a laundry bag for cleaning, and packed up the jewelry to be returned. One o'clock. Not bad. She could do everything and be on the eight o'clock out of town. Success filled her mind. Failure seemed far away.

CHAPTER 13

Madam Milla's flat was just off Leidseplein and farther out of the center than Stella would've expected. It wasn't unfashionable but not posh either. The designer was, as always, full of surprises and so was her choice of homes, a normal street in a pretty brick building with arched windows and decorative brickwork. That wasn't particularly surprising. That she lived above her shop was. The first sign of success was typically moving away from the everyday work, but there Madam Milla was, living above her cutters and seamstresses, who were hard at work on a Saturday.

The dresses pinned to the mannequins were stunning and they appeared to be working on a fall collection with shades of brown, green, and gray. Stella pushed aside her longing and looked for someone to help her find the way to the flat, but everyone was hard at work. They didn't even glance up when the door opened.

"Excuse me," Stella called out and a tousled grey head popped up.

"Yes?" Paola asked and then her face lit up. "Madam Dubois."

"Micheline, please."

Paola took five pins out of her mouth and stuck them rather viciously into a dummy wearing a stunning jacket in silk brocade and mink. "Why do you come? Was your dress seen well?"

"Very well," said Stella. "In fact, I was a great success and I wanted to thank Madam Milla in person before I left Amsterdam."

Paola clapped her hands together. "Yes, yes. She said you are very good at the baron's party. He like you very much."

"I'm glad to hear that. Is she up yet?"

"She barely sleeps. I will take you." Madam Milla's squat little mother herded her through the back of the shop past tables of cutters working with gorgeous silks, velvets, and oddly, tulle to a narrow back stairs that wasn't what Stella pictured at all. No marble or glossy wood. Nothing that said the most fashionable person she'd ever come across lived there.

"Go up and it is the only door," said Paola before rushing away to continue her pinning.

"Thank you," Stella called after her and then went up the creaking stairs to find a black lacquered door that was more like it.

"Come in," called out Madam Milla in response to her knock.

"It's Micheline." Stella walked into a room that was completely open. No walls at all. It comprised almost the entire floor and Stella could see everything from the kitchen to the bedroom.

Madam Milla was lounging on a daybed, wearing a suit of extraordinary design. It was made of a plush black fabric with pads in the shoulders, decorative buttons that wrapped around her slender torso, and a kind of puffy bow that came out of the buttons on her hip, turning into a waterfall of striped fabric that trailed off the daybed to pool on the floor.

"Were you expecting someone?" Stella asked.

She smiled and took a puff on her long, black cigarette holder and blew out a perfect O. "I'm always expecting someone, even when no one is expected."

"It feels like there should be a camera and a director at the ready."

"Exactly." Madam Milla set aside a newspaper and swung her long legs to the floor. "Did you come about the news?"

"The news?"

She gave the paper to Stella and went to make tea. The headlines were grim. The Nazis were massing their troops on the border. The invasion was eminent, but they claimed to still be in talks with the Dutch government.

"How long?" Madam Milla asked.

"I have no idea," said Stella.

"You must know." She brought over a simple wood tray laden with a modern tea set done in the oriental style.

"I'm a small cog in a large machine."

"They were talking last night."

"About the invasion?"

Madam Milla smiled, her makeup stunning. No one would guess that she'd been up all night. Stella, on the other hand, looked more like the age she was supposed to be. "They are very confident. The Germans and the NSB," she said.

"I would be if I were them," said Stella.

"You won't tell me what you know."

"Honestly, I'm surprised they're not here now." She pointed to a map on the front page. "If this is accurate, any day now."

Madam Milla gave Stella a delicate little butter cookie and checked the tea. "You will go now."

"As soon as I can," she said. "You should consider getting out."

She puffed on her cigarette. "Where would I go? This is home."

"If they find out about you, they'll put you in a camp at the very least."

"I know. I've heard the rumors."

"They're not just rumors. It's true. It's all true and worse than you can imagine." Stella couldn't continue. For a second, she was in Brandenburg, looking into a little girl's crib and seeing what they had done to a child.

Madam Milla reached out and touched her knee with a gentle hand. "You have seen it?"

"I have."

"Tell me."

"I can't," said Stella. "But please listen, it's bad and they have no limits when it comes to what they want."

"What do they want?"

"Everything and the Jews annihilated."

Madam Milla's perfection cracked for a second showing her shock, but she quickly recovered. "That is ridiculous."

"Not to them. Get out while you still can."

"I'm not a Jew."

"There are rumors going around that you are," said Stella.

"I'm not," she said.

"But you're not Aryan either. There's no room for anything but."

She poured the tea and offered cream and sugar. "Is that what you came to tell me?"

"Yes, but I was hoping you could help me with one last thing before I go," said Stella.

"Of course."

Stella told her about following Jan Bikker and gave Madam Milla the address. The designer didn't know who lived there and had never heard of it before. She didn't know of any lover that Bikker might have. There weren't any rumors to that effect.

"What did you think of him?" Madam Milla asked. "I saw you in the same rooms."

"Was I obvious?" Stella asked with a start.

"Not at all. I had to remind myself of your interest. You are… almost invisible."

"Thank goodness. As for your question, I thought he was different than usual. No one said he could be charming."

"It was new," she said. "Did you notice who he talked to?"

"Everyone, but he avoided the Jews."

"He knows how to—" she blew a smoke ring "—work a room. People were talking to him."

"I know. Everyone thought he was on their side."

"Then you have enough?"

"I do."

"And the baron?" Madam Milla asked after blowing on her tea.

"Something's wrong there," Stella said. "Do you know what's going on?"

She frowned and shook her head. "Wrong? Nothing is wrong."

"His servants watch him very carefully."

She shrugged. "What do you expect of an aristocrat? They are born being pampered."

"It's more than that."

"What are you thinking?"

"Nothing really. It's just off."

"But you're still leaving?"

"I am," said Stella. "So, you've never heard any rumors about him? Nothing odd?"

Madam Milla lounged back on her daybed and looked at the ceiling. "There were rumors about a child, but that's nothing to do with what you're talking about."

"A love child?" Stella asked.

"Yes, but that was a while ago and no child has shown up in Amsterdam."

"Would the baron acknowledge an out-of-wedlock child?"

Madam Milla expected that he would. The Dutch were an open-minded society, especially where money and aristos were concerned. If the baron had offspring, it wouldn't be surprising if the child was acknowledged and could take the last name of the baron but not the title. Since the baron was far less conventional than the average citizen, Madam Milla was certain a child would be accepted, if they existed.

"What made people think he did have a child then?" Stella asked.

"He would go off to the country every once in a while and cut himself off socially. It was odd. You saw how social he is. When he travels, it's usually in pursuit of a woman."

Here we go.

"He'd just go off into the country for a vacation and people thought he had a baby to what? Visit?"

"Yes. That's exactly what they thought, but then the child never turned up."

"And he doesn't go to the country anymore?" Stella asked.

Madam Milla froze. "He does actually. Not often."

"He just runs off to the country? Does he tell people about where he's going?"

"No. He's just gone for a while and then he comes back."

"Like nothing happened?"

She nodded. "Like nothing happened."

Stella pursed her lips and then concentrated on her tea. That was familiar. Stella was a Bled after all and it wasn't unusual for Bleds to go to the "country" for a rest. In their case, "rest" meant private hospital. The Bled insanity reared its ugly head in every generation and was practically expected. For every Nicolai and Aleksej, you got a Josiah or worse. Stella's second cousin, Imelda, was taking a rest and it included a rubber room. She'd been biting again, but by way of consolation, Francesqua had written that Imelda was coherent this time and feeding herself. The bar was low for the crazy Bleds as Ludwik would have called them.

"What are you thinking?" Madam Milla asked.

"Just that people go to the country for other things, not just illegitimate children," said Stella. "But it doesn't matter."

"He's not ill. You saw him. A man could not be more energetic."

That was one way to put it and now that Stella thought back to the party, the baron was too energetic. Frantic would be another way to put it.

"You're right. He seemed healthy and happy."

Madam Milla smiled and relaxed. "He always is. I do think he just goes off to write a memoir or something. He would have a lot to say."

"I don't doubt it. He's lived a rare life." Stella checked her watch and drank the rest of her tea. "If you think of anything with that address before eight tonight, please message me at the hotel."

"I am very curious about that and I'll see what I can find." She raised an eyebrow at Stella. "How can I get in touch with you after you leave?"

"You can't," said Stella.

"But you will come back, won't you?"

"I can't say," she smiled, "but if you insist on staying, I'll find you."

Madam Milla got to her feet, a smooth elegant move that made her look more like a dancer than anything else. "I find that comforting with what is coming."

"I'm glad to hear it." Stella returned the jewelry and they went to the door, but as they walked a kind of change came over the designer. Something in the way she was moving, a stiffness that wasn't there seconds before. "What is it?" Stella asked when they got to the door.

Madam Milla looked down from her great height and said, "You're sure about what you said? About the invasion and what they will do."

Stella took her hand, warming it between hers. "Think of the worst thing you can imagine them doing."

"Yes?"

"They'll do it."

"Ludwik says you work for a company in New York."

"I do."

"It is called B.L. Imports?"

Stella hesitated but got her card out of her handbag. There were so many cards floating around now, one more couldn't make any difference. "If you ever need a buyer or a piece of art, call them for *help*."

"They will oblige me?" Madam Milla asked.

"I think they will."

CHAPTER 14

Oliver Fip was already in the café, sipping a coffee and looking slightly less miserable. His nose was still red and his eyes droopy, but he sat up straight and hadn't sneezed or coughed in the two minutes it took for her to sit down next to him.

"Fancy seeing you here," he said down into his cup.

"What a coincidence," said Stella and she extended her hand.

He kissed and stroked it like a lover while she did her best not to snarl at him. He was being so terribly French. More than French actually. He was being what other countries thought the French behaved like.

"I've missed you," he said as the same waitress came up and told Stella about the special, a potato soup.

She ordered it and a coffee, hoping that it would be better than the last time. "We just saw each other."

"It's been too long," said Oliver with feeling and his pale blue eyes lighting up with amusement.

"You're feeling better, I see."

"I am. It was touch and go there for a while. I had a high fever."

"You deserve it for pestering me."

"I prefer protecting you," he said.

"Prefer all you want. Let's get this done."

He speared a sausage off his plate and grease spurted out to his satisfaction. "Does that mean you're done?"

"I think so."

"Think?"

Stella told him succinctly what she knew and made a good case for both men being what was suspected of them, including her strong suspicions that the baron was unstable and shouldn't be called on to join the network.

"That's all circumstantial."

"You wanted me to get it in writing or ask them? Oh, by the way, Mr. Bikker, are you working for the Germans? I noticed you were lying about skiing in Bavaria. Oh, Baron, I think you're crazy. Can you confirm? How would that go over?"

"I see your point," he said. "Bikker will have to be watched."

"Sounds like a job for you."

He chuckled. "And I would do it well, but you think he will self-destruct before long?"

"The designer said they throw the suspected German spies into the canals. Bikker was not subtle in the least and *they* will be moving in any day now."

"Yes, and I think finally perhaps the people know it." He glanced around the café at the other patrons that were either reading papers or were in agitated conversations. Oliver was right. There wasn't any laughter or smiles anymore. Their faces were different. The set of their shoulders tense. What must it be like to know your country would be invaded and there was nothing you could do about it? She couldn't imagine thinking someone would invade Missouri or the United States. Her mother was safe. Millicent and Myrtle safe. There was so much comfort in that.

"They do," she said. "But they won't talk openly of it."

"What about last night?"

"Some discussed it, but mostly you would've thought all was right with the world."

"Self-indulgent fools," said Oliver.

"One last night of pleasure. I don't begrudge them that."

"They should be preparing."

"We are doing that," she said.

"Not we. You are gone."

The waitress brought the soup and coffee and to Stella's relief, both were good. She ate quickly and kept an eye on the clock.

"Going somewhere?" Oliver asked.

"To pack."

Oliver visibly relaxed and the tension he held in his angular face eased.

"You are ready to go then? No last private mission to keep you?"

"Nothing could keep me here," said Stella.

***

"I don't think today is a good day." Rena stood at the front door of Elizabeth Keesing's house and refused to budge.

"Don't worry. I won't stay long," said Stella. "I only want to say goodbye and tell her something."

"I will tell her," said Rena. "What is it?"

A strange feeling grew in Stella's chest, a nervous, worried feeling. She hadn't had that in a long time. "It's about the children, Ezra and Lonia."

"Good. Poor little things. We will help them. Tell me what you want or come back tomorrow."

"I'm leaving tonight."

The maid nodded furiously. "Good. Good. You go."

"Did something happen?" Stella asked.

"No, no. Nothing happens here." Rena tried to close the door and Stella slapped her hand against the wood.

"What is it?"

"Noth—"

"Rena!" called out Elizabeth. "Who is it?"

"No one!"

Stella went up on her tiptoes and called over Rena's head. "It's me! Micheline!"

"Let her in, Rena," said Elizabeth. "What are you—"

There was a muffled thump and Rena let out a screech as she spun around. The door flew open and Stella dashed in. Rena scrambled up the stairs to Elizabeth, who was halfway down, sitting in a heap and clinging to a spindle.

"I'm all right," said Elizabeth.

Stella closed the door and ran up the stairs behind Rena. "What happened?"

"All these people bothering her. She needs to rest."

"I need to be informed." Elizabeth sounded dignified, but she was the least dignified that Stella had ever seen her. She wore a nightgown that was slipping off her bony, emaciated shoulder, no socks or slippers, and her long hair was tangled and loose down to her waist.

"You have to stay in bed," said Rena.

"Says who?"

"The doctors. All of them."

"I hate being in bed. Why is that better than my chair by the stove? Answer me that," demanded Elizabeth.

"For one thing," said Stella, "you have to get there. Let's get you back into bed."

Elizabeth demanded to be taken downstairs. Stella would've ordinarily obeyed her, but in her current state, she felt justified in taking her back upstairs. They were able to carry her back upstairs without any help and got her into bed in a charming room with lilac wallpaper and a cheery fire in the grate.

"I don't know why you don't want to be in here," said Stella. "It's lovely and so warm."

"I can't see the garden and the tulips will fade soon."

Rena grabbed Stella's arm. "Thank you for your help. Go now."

"Rena, what in the world?" She reached out for Stella and took her hand. "I'm glad you're here. I was considering sending a message to the hotel or calling, but I wasn't sure if I should. Anyone could read it or listen in. You know how nosy operators are."

"I can tell her," said Rena, still tugging on Stella's arm. "You've got to sleep like the doctor said."

Elizabeth folded her hands in her lap and said, "I will stay in bed if you stop fussing and make some tea."

Rena didn't like it, but anything to keep Elizabeth in bed. The maid hustled out, giving Stella a sharp look before closing the door.

Stella sat on the edge of the bed and tucked Elizabeth in. "Why were you going to call me?"

"I've had a few visitors today."

"So I heard. Rena's pretty upset about that, but you like visits."

"They were about you."

"Me?"

"It's not good news, I'm afraid."

Stella wasn't so sure about that. The news wasn't as easy to interpret as Elizabeth thought. Jan Bikker had noticed Micheline Dubois at the baron's party and he'd begun making inquiries about her. Some of Elizabeth's connections had been called directly. Bikker asked where Micheline's loyalties lay. How did she feel about Germany? What was her business? Did she like the Jews?

"What did they say?" Stella asked with her heart in her throat.

"Don't worry. They were surprised but calm. You care deeply for Germany with many connections through your work."

"What about my buying from the Jews? It's out that I pay too much."

"And he knows that, but the two men he asked told him that you are trying to get their trust and the Americans don't care what you spend."

"But why would I do that? What would it get me in the end?"

Elizabeth sighed and twisted her tousled hair over her shoulder. "It was implied that you were keeping track of the Jews for later."

"A list?"

"Yes. You know how they love lists," said Elizabeth. "Presumably you will turn it over when it happens."

"What else did he want to know?" Stella asked.

"If you will stay in The Netherlands after."

"After the invasion?" Stella asked.

"That was the inference," said Elizabeth. "What happened at that party?"

"Nothing really. I confirmed the suspicions."

"About who? Bikker or the baron?"

"Both actually."

Elizabeth assumed an all-knowing posture. "Was I right?"

"Not about the baron."

"But he's nothing but a dilettante. He plays at life."

"Maybe, but at worst he won't choose a side. He'll go along to keep along."

"And at best?"

"He'd help us if asked, but we won't ask."

"You're sure?"

"As sure as I can be."

"Then why won't we ask?"

Stella told her about the feeling of something being off.

"But that's just a feeling. We have to use everything at our disposal. Everything to fight them. Nothing must be held back." Elizabeth's hands were balled up in fury. If she had been well, she would've been quite a weapon.

"What do you know about his trips to the country?"

Elizabeth blinked in astonishment. "You are thorough."

"I have to be," said Stella. "What do you know?"

"He has a child or two. Who knows? The way that man has behaved, he could have five or six."

"That's just rumors. Anything else?"

Elizabeth frowned. "Like what?"

"He's…an eccentric," said Stella, using her grandmother's term for the family streak of insanity. It sounded so much better than lunatic.

"He's nobility. Aren't they all?"

"No, they aren't." She told Elizabeth about the servants and how they hustled him away when he got loud.

"You think he's…ill?"

"I'm suspicious enough that I wouldn't make contact with him."

A.W. HARTOIN

"You'll report this."

"Yes, of course. I already have."

Elizabeth sagged down against her pillows. "Poor man. I had no idea."

"With enough money it's easy to cover. I could be wrong, but we can't take the chance."

"So he won't serve his country," she said.

"Not in this way," said Stella.

"I'm sad to hear it, but you are leaving now? You won't try to get any more information?"

"No. I'm done." That's what she said, but Stella had an inkling that she shouldn't leave. Jan Bikker asking questions about her and Germany. That could be bad or very useful, but her life was calling. Nicky waiting. "I'm leaving. It's been ordered."

Elizabeth took her hand. "Why did you come to see me? I wasn't expecting another visit."

Stella opened her handbag and gave Elizabeth a stack of bills she'd gotten at the bank earlier. "I said I'd pay for Ezra and Lonia. I meant it."

"What a dear woman you are. I always did like the Belgians."

"Has Truus come back yet?"

"Not yet. She hasn't been in contact, but as soon as she is I will tell her about the children. We will do everything we can."

Rena knocked on the door and brought in a tea tray. It had only one cup. Rena was many things. Subtle wasn't one of them. "You were just leaving?"

Stella chuckled. "I was." She stood up and then said, "I will see if I can help the Dereczynski parents, too."

"Can you?" Rena asked. "How?"

"I do know Americans. They have money and influence. When I get home, I can ask my company to sponsor the Dereczynskis."

Elizabeth clasped her hands together. "Would they? Is it possible?"

"I won't know until I try." Stella had kept Francesqua's list from Elizabeth and Rena. They could not connect Micheline to the Bleds, but this could be a new list. Micheline's list.

CHAPTER 15

Stella splurged and took a cab back to the hotel. It wasn't her normal practice when leaving a city. She liked walking along the most scenic route and planting it firmly in her mind so she could remember the beauty, not only the assignment and whatever difficulty it brought. Berlin taught her that she needed more than just the work to sustain her heart. It was hard to remember anything good about that city and when she thought of it, she sunk down low, closing in on despair. Stella could not sink. She couldn't afford it, so she began to find memories of beauty wherever she was to focus on when the bad memories came.

She looked out of the cab, forcing the image of a boat with a tall elegant mast into her memory. She thought of the bicyclists riding together and moving in concert like a school of fish, of the Magere Brug and its skinny, white-washed lines over the Amstel River, and, of course, the flocks of seagulls squawking or simply floating in the canals peacefully, something she didn't know that seagulls did. It would be enough to sustain her when she remembered Flore, sitting in her little house as the Nazis marched in or the Dereczynskis in their attic, awaiting help that might not happen. It would have to be enough.

A.W. HARTOIN

"Ma'am?" The driver twisted in his seat and looked at her with questioning eyes.

"Oh, yes," she said quickly. "I was lost in thought."

"You love our city, I think."

She smiled. "I think you're right, but I love the people most of all."

"That is the best compliment and I thank you."

She paid him with a nice tip as the hotel doorman ran to open her door.

"You had a good day?" Daan asked.

"I did." She pictured Flore and regretted not seeing her again before she left and then quickly replaced the image with the bridge, a good sturdy image.

He opened the doors and Stella headed for the elevator, bypassing the front desk by a wide margin. She didn't want to talk to anyone, but her effort wasn't rewarded.

"Micheline!" Ludwik hurried up and met her at the elevator. "Did you see Madam Milla?"

"I did and I think she was happy that I made a good impression. She really can dress anyone."

Ludwik looked down at his feet and then away from her. He was a straightforward sort of man normally, very Dutch in his open demeanor, and Stella's stomach got queasy. Eight o'clock wouldn't be soon enough. There had to be an earlier train to somewhere. Practically anywhere south would do.

"Is there something else?"

"Yes, yes. You send Madam Milla's dress down for cleaning."

"I did. Has something happened to it?" she asked.

"Oh, no. It is being pressed now." He pulled out a card. "The laundress found this in the pocket and wanted me to give it to you, in case it was needed."

Stella took it and frowned.

"You don't recognize it?" he asked.

"A man that specializes in clocks gave it to me, but he must've accidentally given me the wrong card." She smiled and rolled her eyes. "This is for someone else's shop in Paris."

212

They looked at it together.

"Bergère Antiques," said Ludwik. "Is that a good shop?"

I'm sure it is.

"I have no idea. Perhaps I'll go and see sometime. I'm always looking for a good buy."

"Of course." The concierge didn't excuse himself and they stood there awkwardly.

"Ludwik, is eve—"

"Here is the elevator," he announced.

The operator opened the door and they stepped back for the guests to exit.

"Michel, it is time for your break, yes?" Ludwik asked the operator.

"No, it is not quite time," said Michel, looking confused under the black brim of his hat.

"It has been a busy day," said Ludwik. "You may go now."

"I'm not certain that—"

"He agrees." The concierge pulled the operator off the elevator and steered Stella in. "I will take Madam Dubois to her floor."

With that Ludwik closed the door in Michel's face, cutting off two guests that were approaching. He put his hand on the elevator lever and very slowly got the car moving. Stella wasn't sure if that was because he didn't know how to operate the thing or if he was afraid to touch it.

The elevator made all sorts of clicks and clacks that it normally didn't make and Stella looked at the lever, wishing he'd go ahead and push it to the next position. It wasn't made to go that slow.

"What is going on?"

"I wanted to talk to you alone," he said. "It would be unseemly to come to your room."

"You did this morning," she said.

"Oh, yes. I did," Ludwik said all flustered. "I don't know. I have to tell you that Jan Bikker came looking for you and he was quite insistent."

Stella sagged against the wall. "Is that all? I thought at the very least the invasion had started."

"When are you leaving?"

"Tonight. I thought I'd get the eight o'clock, but—"

"You should go earlier."

"I can, but what did he want to know exactly?" Stella asked.

"Everything about you. Who you are. What you are doing here."

"That's fine. I want to sell to his wife if I can."

"Micheline, I told you that Jan Bikker is no friend to the Jews," he said.

She put the card into her handbag and closed it with a snap. "So what?"

"He knows you were buying from them." He slowed the elevator further and it groaned in protest.

"I told his wife that. It's not a surprise."

"And that you pay a lot to them. This is not good."

"What did you tell him?"

Ludwik stiffened up and said, "I lied." He said it like it was the first time ever in his life, but he was rather proud of himself. Ludwik told Jan Bikker that she was no friend to the Jews and he didn't know why she would pay more than she had to, since she was such a good businesswoman. A clerk at the desk overheard and parroted back the same information, although Ludwik doubted she knew a thing about it. Bikker's questions were about the same as what Elizabeth described. It sounded like he'd had some training. Ludwik said he would circle back and ask the same question a different way, but he felt sure that he fended him off well.

"What did he say about Germany?" she asked.

Ludwik's jaw tightened. "He made it plain that *they* are coming and he wanted to know if you would be staying here."

"What did you say?"

"That I didn't know your plans. Your reservation is open-ended."

She patted his arm. "It's fine. I wanted to sell his wife jewelry, but my company has been in touch. I'm to go to Bruges for an estate sale. We have a new client. I'll come back and talk to Anna Bikker."

"If he thinks you are friend to the Jews and the Nazis are coming, you will have problems," said Ludwik.

"We are all going to have problems with the Nazis."

"Not him. He doesn't care if they invade us." The concierge flushed with rage and she squeezed his arm.

"That's what I heard at the party last night. He was very friendly to the Germans and NSB members," said Stella.

"What kind of man is he to betray his country this way?"

"He's not a man to be trusted."

Ludwik shifted the lever and the elevator jerked to life, speeding up to Stella's floor. "I wanted to let you know what happened."

"Thank you for telling me."

"I was so flustered. He is a powerful man and if they come…"

When they come.

"He could make trouble," said Stella. "But you told the truth and it's fine."

Ludwik lit up. "The truth is you are a friend to the Jews. You are not making a list for the Germans."

Stella feigned astonishment. "A list?"

"He thinks you are keeping track of the Jews and making lists of them. He asked if I'd seen the lists."

"I have client lists and inventories. What does he think? That I leave them scattered around the hotel?" she asked.

He stopped the elevator at Stella's floor, but instead of opening the door, he patted the lever nervously. "He insisted on asking the maids about you."

"I'm surprised the hotel would go along with that," said Stella truthfully. Cooperation with the Nazis was common in the other occupied countries, but she hadn't expected it in The Netherlands. Germany wasn't even there yet and Jan Bikker was throwing his weight around.

"Mr. De Jong said to take him to the maids, so I had to," Ludwik said sadly.

"Don't worry about that. What did the maids say?"

"Nothing. You have ledgers that you record your purchases in. He asked if you noted who were Jews in the ledgers and the girls said they didn't know what your symbols meant."

"Was he happy with that?"

Ludwik frowned. "Yes. Very happy. I don't know why."

He wanted to find a secret list, so he found one.

"Happy is good, I suppose. I hope he doesn't bother you again," said Stella.

He opened the door with a broad smile for the guests waiting in the hall. "I hope your stay has been all you hoped for."

"It has."

And now it's over. Thank God.

The packing went quick. Stella took a bath and tried to make the wig as good as Madam Milla had, but predictably, she failed. She'd been thinking of tossing it out a train window to die a slow death in a fallow field, but with Jan Bikker asking after her, she'd have to keep the frizzy thing for future assignments. No doubt the SIS would want her to come back to explore the options once the Reich was in place. She'd seeded her preference for Germany a little too well. That Bikker and his wife bought it was a testament to her skills, but she wished she had gotten what she needed another way. Madam Milla was a huge plus, too, not to mention Ludwik and Cornelia. Park-Welles would be eager to use those connections and her feelings on the matter wouldn't be consulted. It was war after all.

Not that she minded Micheline. Stella enjoyed being someone that Cornelia and Flore liked. Strangely, she'd made a lot more friends as a fake person than she ever had as herself. The thought was distressing and she pushed it away for another time as she washed her hair and then used the clunky hairdryer that the maid brought up for her to use.

Her own long light brown hair lay in silky coils over her shoulders, exactly what she needed for when she became Charlotte Sedgewick again. Charlotte didn't make as many friends, but she did have good hair.

With a sigh, Stella coiled her locks up and tucked them under

Micheline's wig. She quickly reapplied the makeup to her face, neck, and hands and then checked her bags again. The train timetable she had said there were no useful trains out at six, so she'd have to wait until seven. The thought made her antsy. She wanted to go to the station directly, but if Bikker was watching that could be seen as odd, or worse, like she was running. She had to seem calm and untroubled by anything. Being the owner of a hotel himself, he'd know that his interest in her would be reported. The hotel's loyalty would be to Micheline, not him. He might be waiting to see what she'd do, so she swallowed the urge to leave and dressed in her favorite dull brown suit and comfortable shoes to go down to the café for a coffee and a bite to eat, just what someone would do if they hadn't anything to hide.

She grabbed her handbag and went out to the elevator. Michel arrived almost immediately and when he saw her waiting he looked wary.

"Ground floor, please," she said.

"Yes, ma'am." He closed the door and moved the lever into position. "Ma'am?"

She smiled at him. "I hope you're not upset about earlier. It's nothing to do with you."

The operator took a little breath and said, "I was a little concerned that you had cause for complaint."

"Not at all." After a tally of the options, Stella decided to be open the way a Dutchman might appreciate. "Ludwik was concerned for me after Jan Bikker came. He was asking about me apparently."

"That's what it was about?"

"Yes. Not a problem for you or the hotel."

Michel bit his lip and then slowed the elevator. "I would be very careful about that man."

"I only want to sell jewelry to his wife."

"He lied."

"Lied?"

Michel had heard from other staff what had gone on with Jan Bikker, his questions about the Jews and her work, but the elevator

A.W. HARTOIN

operator was a smoker, unlike Ludwik, and when he went outside for his pipe, he saw Bikker talking to Marga from the café. He was asking her the same questions but in a different way. He sounded like he didn't like Germany and that he didn't want them to come.

"I don't think it matters, Michel," said Stella. "He was different because Marga's just a waitress in the café. Ludwik is the head of concierge."

"He talked to her differently because Marga is a Jew."

"Oh, that."

"You knew?"

"A maid at the baron's told me," said Stella.

The elevator reached the ground floor, but Michel didn't open the door. "Bikker acted like you hate the Jews. He tried to scare her, but he's the one that does."

"She should know that."

"He offered her money and he was…warm with her. Nice. Jan Bikker isn't nice," said Michel. "I am worried for you."

"Money for what?" Stella kept her breathing quiet. It was a skill the earl had taught her. In through the nose. Out through the mouth.

"To get him into your room. He told her that you have a list of Jews that you are going to hurt."

"He's completely mad."

"I think he works for the Nazis. No, I am sure of it. The way he talked to Ludwik. The clerk, she said he was confusing, asking the same questions over and over again."

Stella put her hand on his. "It's all right. I'm not doing anything to anyone and I'm leaving. I have to go to Bruges for my company. Jan Bikker can ask anything he wants. I don't care."

Michel put his other rough hand on hers. "This is good news. You are a nice lady and they are coming. I think they are." His eyes were pleading as if he wanted her to deny it, but she couldn't.

"They are. We will all do the best we can."

Someone pounded on the door and yelled, "Are you all right in there? Michel! Michel!"

Michel reached for the door, but Stella said, "You'll get in trouble or we're behaving badly. Tell them I was dizzy. I fell. You had to help me."

He thought and then grinned. "My heart isn't so good. I took a turn. You helped me."

Michel slumped in the back of the elevator to put on a show. For an elevator operator, he was quite a good actor with his disheveled hair and pinched cheeks to make them flushed. "You're too much."

He winked and said, "Open the door."

She yanked open the door as if she could hardly manage it as a weak, middle-aged woman. Ludwik stood there, his own cheeks inflamed with beads of sweat on his broad forehead. "Micheline!"

"It's Michel. His heart!"

Ludwik and a doorman rushed in. Panic ensued. A doctor was called and a wheeled chair brought over for moving the mumbling Michel. Stella hurried out of the way and stood by, wringing her hands for effect. The doctor was just off the square and he arrived within two minutes and questioned Stella about Michel's turn. Then he went to examine Michel, who couldn't resist groaning. What a ham.

"Micheline, can I get you anything?" Ludwik asked.

"No, thank you. I was just going to the café for a coffee."

He turned her around and said loudly, "Such a thing to have happened. Let me walk you over."

The concierge walked her to the café and snapped his fingers at Marga and Ester behind the bar. "Madam Dubois needs a coffee. Quick, quick!"

Marga stared with those big eyes of hers and then spun around to go the other way. Ester merely stood there.

"Ester! What are you doing? Michel has had a heart attack in the elevator with Madam Dubois. Get her a coffee and perhaps a touch of whiskey."

Ester didn't move. The girl was a statue, but Dirk heard Ludwik and came running. He got Stella coffee and then went behind the bar to dig around, coming up with a dark brown bottle with a yellow label.

A.W. HARTOIN

"You've had a shock," said Dirk. "I recommend this."

"What is it?" Stella asked.

"Kahlúa!" said a man behind Stella in English. "I didn't think I'd find that in Amsterdam."

A jolt went through Stella, so hard and fast she had to grip the bar to keep herself steady. Could she walk out without turning around? Was there another way out? Yes, behind the bar.

Go. Now. Go.

"Mr. Bled! I cannot believe it," said Dirk in his heavily accented English. "What are you doing here in Amsterdam? It has been a long time."

"Too long, my friend. Too long," said Josiah Bled. "And you have Kahlúa. I'll be damned."

"I ordered it for our special guests."

Stella couldn't move. He was going to see her. He couldn't see her.

"And who is this special lady who rates such a delicacy?"

No. No. No.

"Madam Micheline Dubois," said Dirk.

And it happened. Josiah Bled came around Stella and looked down at his niece with the rakish grin he always wore when he was up to no good. She looked up at him, speechless, and he extended his hand.

"Josiah Bled of Bled Brewery," said Uncle Josiah. "Do you speak English? I definitely don't speak Dutch."

Stella took his hand and said, "Yes, of course. Micheline Dubois."

"Belgian?"

She nodded, dazed and nauseous.

"May I horn in on your Kahlúa? I just got in and it's been a bastard of a trip. You wouldn't believe what I had to do to get over the border. I'm an American, not some kind of anarchist agitator."

Ludwik gestured to Stella's usual table. "Micheline must sit. She's had a shock."

"Of course. Of course," said Uncle Josiah and he insisted on seating her himself since Ludwik had to attend to Michel in the lobby.

Her uncle was so attentive, Stella had no choice but to gesture to the chair opposite her and swallowed down the taste of bile in her mouth, gripping the edge of the table to keep herself from flopping off her chair.

"Mr. Bled is one of our most interesting guests, Micheline," said Dirk, bringing Stella's coffee. "If anyone can take your mind off Michel, it is him." He looked at Uncle Josiah. "Coffee and Kahlúa?"

"You read my mind, Dirk."

The manager dashed off and Stella heard him announce in the kitchen, "The Bled is back." Ester went in after him and they were alone in the café. Stella forced her eyes up to meet the ones that matched her own perfectly, but she couldn't let go of the table. Her hands simply wouldn't obey.

"Fancy meeting you here, sweetheart." Uncle Josiah ran a hand through his wavy hair and succeeded only in making it more tousled.

"What are you doing here?" she whispered.

"Looking for you." He poured a generous amount of Kahlúa in her cup. "Take a drink. You look like you need it."

She obediently picked up the cup and sipped. Then she coughed.

"Too much?" he asked.

"You are always too much," she said.

Uncle Josiah grinned in the way that made staid matrons think, oh maybe he's not so bad. But he was so bad. Definitely so bad.

"Not happy to see me?"

"Are you crazy?"

He lit a cigarette. "Certified 1920. By the imminent psychiatrist Dr. Thompson Smith. He killed himself in 1921, but that was not my fault. Don't let anyone tell you different."

"What?"

"He gambled. The man bet the farm, and I mean that literally, on one hand of cards. His wife left him and he shot himself in the head. The fact that I'm incurable had nothing to do with it and they couldn't prove it in court."

"Oh, my God," whispered Stella. "This is not happening."

Dirk bustled up with a tray laden with a whole pot of coffee, pastries of every variety, and a very large cup for Uncle Josiah. "What did I hear about a shooting?"

"A doctor of mine shot himself. I was telling Micheline about it to illustrate a point."

There was a point?

"Mr. Bled has very many stories," said Dirk.

"Josiah, please, we're old friends and this is Amsterdam," said Uncle Josiah.

"Josiah, it is a pleasure to welcome you back. Do you have plans tonight?"

"You know what? I don't. Is that little bar with the sassy waitress still in business?"

"*In 't Aepjen?*"

"That's the one," said Uncle Josiah.

"They've been there since 1519. They're going nowhere."

Uncle Josiah pointed at him. "You and me after you get off."

"And Ludwik. We must ask Ludwik."

This is a nightmare. It has to be.

Dirk poured Uncle Josiah a cup of coffee and a generous slug of Kahlúa before running off to tell what would be most of the staff about the night in store for them.

"Don't be mad, sweetheart. I have a reason." Uncle Josiah selected a huge pastry and bit off half of it in one go.

"Since when do you have reason?" Stella asked.

"We're being watched," he said.

Out of the corner of her eye, Stella saw the swinging door to the kitchen move. Ester. Wonderful.

Be Micheline. You are a professional. Oliver said so.

She assumed Micheline's usual posture of businesslike interest. After all, this was a rich American. Right up her alley. "I could kill you."

"Not my favorite girl. Never."

"How did you find me?" she asked.

"It wasn't that hard. You are in touch with Florence and Francesqua," he said.

"I don't tell them anything," said Stella. "I'm very careful."

"But I am observant."

He was. He really was and it was a problem. Stella had been sending what she bought back to the Bled Mansion via the New York importer. Uncle Josiah took a peek at what was coming in and who it belonged to. Then he looked at Francesqua's list. Who was getting letters? Where were they? What embassies were they applying to?

"I could've been anywhere," she said.

"No, you couldn't. The last shipment was full of items from families trying to get out of here, The Netherlands. They are applying to Rotterdam. Five children got out through that network you tapped into. That's centered here. Almost everything has been shipped either from here or Rotterdam."

She rolled her eyes. "And that's how you ended up here in this café today?"

"Nicky told me that you didn't come out when expected."

"How is he? Is he okay?" she asked.

"He was fine, worried about you but fine."

"Nicky writes to you?"

"I was in England and I couldn't find you, so I went to Nicky's base. He sent me to the earl. He and Albert said not to worry and they were calm," he said before taking a big slug of liquored up coffee. "I figured you were coming out of The Netherlands, but something held you up. Stands to reason you'd be working in the capital right before an invasion. You are who you are, sweetheart."

"But this particular hotel?"

"It's the family hotel. You know it. Where else would you go?"

She swallowed hard. A dead giveaway. A tell as it were. How could she have been so stupid?

"Why would you risk me? You were worried? Since when?"

"I'm not worried about you, my beloved girl. I would never do this if it weren't absolutely necessary. I swear to you on my life that I tried to avoid it, but there was no other way. I need you."

"Tell me what happened." Stella picked up a pastry and listened. Josiah told the story with big gestures and smiles. Anyone watching would've thought they were talking about the theater or something equally amusing, but Uncle Josiah's tale was anything but amusing.

The Bleds had always known other brewing families across Europe, large and small, it made no difference to the Bleds. One such family were the Wahles in Austria. They operated a tiny brewery in Hallstatt, specializing in unique heritage brews. They opened in 1909 and through Hans Gruber met Stella's grandparents, becoming fast friends. Stella had heard talk of the beauty of Lake Hallstatt and her grandmother's dear friends and their daughter-in-law, Klara. Her unemotional grandmother had once shocked the family by saying, "If I had a daughter, I would want her to be like Klara." Such affection was unheard of for Evangeline. She showed her love through action, not words.

The older Bleds visited the older Wahles several times before the war, but they had never come to the States and had never met Uncle Josiah or his brothers. Then The Great War started and all communications were cut off and when the fog was lifted, the surviving Wahles wrote to the Bleds to tell them the news. Their beloved friends the elder Wahles and their daughter had died during the Turnip Winter. Their son Felix had been conscripted and terribly injured in 1915 but had married a neighbor, Klara, who Evangeline would come to love. The Bleds sent money to many brewers throughout Europe to get them back on their feet. Stella's grandfather always said craft was important and they were obligated to make sure it didn't die with the war. So the Wahles' brewery survived, until now.

Felix and Klara had been open opponents of Hitler. They spoke out and used what means they had to support opposition leaders, a dangerous game for a Jewish family in a remote part of Austria. After Germany annexed Austria, they were targeted, only the quality of their brews saved them, but now, even that had run out. Their brewery and home were confiscated after Felix refused to take an oath to Hitler and he was declared an enemy of the state. Since then, they'd been trying to emigrate, but the Reich blocked them and every effort made by the Bleds to help them. Stella herself was an enemy of the state and the Wahles' connection to the Bleds did them no favors. Even help from others in the States didn't help. The Wahles were tainted by association.

"You want me to get them out?" Stella asked. "Because it's my fault."

Uncle Josiah made a move to reach out to her but managed to hold himself back. "It's not your fault. Our refusal to acknowledge the Reich or answer their many communications to us was also a problem, but even if you hadn't happened or the rest of it, Felix would still be an enemy of the state. He made that choice."

"It's no choice at all."

"He's a man of principle," said Uncle Josiah.

"We made it worse," said Stella.

He shrugged. "I tried to talk them into leaving years ago, but they didn't want to lose everything they worked for. They didn't think Hitler would last."

"When did you meet them?"

"That trip I took in '37. I stayed with them in Hallstatt."

There was something in his voice that caught Stella's attention, but she couldn't put her finger on it. Something different. Something not like Josiah Bled at all.

"I'm leaving," she said. "Today. Immediately."

"You can't," he said. "They need you."

"I can't go into Austria and spirit them out. They're people, not art. I can't hide them in a suitcase. Florence or—"

"They're here," he said, smiling and pouring another glug of Kahlúa in his cup.

"Thank goodness," she said with relief she didn't bother to conceal. "How did they do it?"

A frown passed over Uncle Josiah's face and then he went right back to smiling. "They got false documents and paid a smuggler to hide them in a shipment of their furniture."

"Inventive. What's the problem?"

"They were caught when their truck was searched."

Stella poured herself more coffee but no liquor. She had to keep her head.

"Where are they?"

"Westerbork, the refugee camp."

"Here in The Netherlands though," she said. "That's good. Surely, the Dutch have nothing against us. We have tight connections with brewers here and no enemies. Mother and Florence can get everything they need. The quotas aren't full."

Uncle Josiah looked out the window at the square, the lights were coming on as it turned to dusk and a light drizzle spattered against the windowpanes. "They aren't the Wahles. They didn't bring their real papers for fear they'd be caught in Germany and the papers would've identified them as enemies of the state trying to escape. They'd be sent straight to a camp."

"Then the false names. We can—"

"They weren't good forgeries. The authorities knew they were fake and now they're trying to find out who they really are." His voice shook. Stella had never heard her uncle's voice like that. Not when he'd been confronted by the police for various reasons or dressed down by his mother. Everyone else in the room quaked, but not Josiah. He didn't turn a hair when Stella made her first night landing in his Sopwith Camel. She'd panicked and they nearly crashed. Even then he'd been calm, yelling instructions that got through to her frantic mind. He was known to be a cool customer, despite being that crazy Bled. But now, she could see his pulse pounding in a vein in his neck and he couldn't quite keep his hands still. Would anyone else notice? No, probably not. But she did. She knew him.

"That's not ideal," she said, keeping an eye on that vein.

"I can't even go there to see them. We can't connect them to me, to us," he said. "I don't know what to do. The invasion can happen at any minute and once it does, they will be found out."

"What do you want me to do?"

"Help them. Use your connections here."

"Why didn't you ask the earl?" she asked. "Talk about connections."

"He's working on it, but he'd have to admit who they are. They're in this country illegally and fugitives. The earl can't overcome that."

She watched him. The vein pulsed. There was a blush high on his cheeks and he couldn't look at her. "What aren't you telling me?"

"Nothing. I need your help. You have connections here in Amsterdam."

The swinging door to the kitchen moved and Ester was peeking out again. Stella leaned back and laughed. "Naked?" she exclaimed. "So it's true?"

Uncle Josiah played along and chuckled, almost looking like himself and the door closed again. "I did it! I did it all!"

They laughed together for a moment and then Stella asked, "You have to tell me everything about them. What did they do?"

"I told you what they did. They are friends of the family. We have to help them."

"There are many friends of the family, but this time you show up?"

"Yes. They are close friends and they have children."

"How many?"

"Four."

"Under eighteen?" she asked.

He hesitated and then said, "Two are. Karl is fifteen and Hans is twelve. He was named for *our* Hans, Stella."

"Micheline," she said sharply, and he was momentarily chastened. "I might be able to do something for those two. How many in total?"

"Six and Felix is in bad health. His lungs. During the war. It's not good."

She ate her pastry and thought about it. Impossible situation. Impossible. "I can speak to my contacts about the younger two. They might have an idea of what to do. As far as Felix goes, they might be persuaded to let him out on compassionate grounds. That even happens in Dachau, if you grease the right wheels."

"That's not good enough," said Uncle Josiah. "It has to be all of them. We owe them."

The note of desperation was unmistakable. But why? There were so many families. Why this one in particular?

"I don't know what I can do. Maybe delay leaving for a day or two, but—"

"You can't leave."

"I have orders," she said.

"That you feel free to ignore when it suits you." The desperation had turned to anger. It was a first for Stella. Uncle Josiah could get angry. She'd seen it in the brewery when someone was injured because of a stupid mistake, but it'd never been directed at her before, no matter what she did.

"When I can do something. When there's a good reason," she said.

"There's a good reason," he said with a smile and clenched teeth.

"Tell me what it is. You want me to disobey orders, chance missing Nicky before it all goes to hell, and risk myself, my cover. Believe it or not, what I do is important for the war effort and the people on Mother's list. I have to keep doing it. If I don't, who will?"

Josiah looked at her with an expression she'd never seen before. He wasn't playing one of his many parts or trying to snow her. He was naked in his need.

"I love her."

CHAPTER 16

Stella stepped out of the front door of the Hotel Krasnapolsky and accepted an umbrella from the doorman, a young man she didn't know well.

"Are you sure you don't want a cab?" he asked, his face wreathed in concern.

She smiled up at him. "It's my last night in the city. I'd rather walk and really see it."

He looked out into the square with appreciative eyes. "We have a beautiful city. You will miss it?"

"Very much, but I must go to the station and check the schedules. There might be cancelations or delays with the situation as it is."

"You don't think the Nazis are interrupting the trains, do you?"

"No, but the government might need them for troop transport," she said. "I wouldn't want to arrive at the station with luggage and nowhere to go."

"It is prudent to check," he said.

"And it gives me a chance for one more walk." Stella gave him a tip and walked out into the drizzle. She would go to the station but not for the reason she told the doorman.

Stella hurried over a couple of blocks and then jumped on the tram to the station. It was jammed with people and their luggage. All the talk was about if they would be bombed and how badly. Some denied it would happen at all, but those voices were now few and far between. The evening papers had been less optimistic and there were instructions on how to withstand a bombing. Basements existed, but they weren't deep and the air raid shelters were above ground. Everyone seemed to think leaving the city was the only alternative and there was much talk of the London evacuations.

No one asked Stella anything and she was grateful. She was less optimistic than the papers and no one on that tram needed to hear how little hope she had. At the station stop, she jumped off with the others to join a queue of people heading into the station that was jam-packed. All she wanted to do was look at the schedule, not even buy a ticket, but it was a challenge between being short and so many heads in the way. With the help of a kindly man, she found the schedules for Westerbork, the town, not the camp, and Assen. Both towns had early milk trains, but she couldn't look too eager, so it was probably better not to get there at the crack of dawn, but that was taking a chance. There were already some cancelations and the trains out of the country were sold out until tomorrow. A good excuse or at least a start of one.

Stella thanked the helpful man and squeezed her way out of the station and just started walking. There was nowhere to go. She and Oliver had parted with an understanding that she'd leave immediately. There were no arrangements to meet again, so she wouldn't have to come clean about the situation. Her most immediate problem was staying. She'd made such a show of leaving at the hotel to change course was a problem. Instructions. New instructions. From New York.

She stopped suddenly and a couple ran into her, cursing her bad manners. She apologized and turned around, dashing back to the station and its crowds where she could be forgotten quickly.

The telegram office was hidden away in a corner, but plenty of people were waiting in a queue to contact family or ask for money.

Stella waited patiently, working on the telegram in her head. What to say to get a telegram back immediately? She couldn't give it away.

The harried clerk looked up at her with exhausted eyes. Behind him, the telegraph clicking sounded like a flock of woodpeckers. "Yes."

"Telegram to New York, New York," she said.

Usually that got some interest but not that night. The clerk wouldn't have cared if she said Timbuktu. "Address?"

She gave him the address of B.L. Imports and he wrote it with a dull pencil in large block letters. Then he slid the paper to her. "Hurry. I've got a line."

"Thank you." She took the pencil and wrote in her own block letters.

LEAD ON FINE FURNITURE SET.
    MAY SUIT NEW CLIENT. TIME TIGHT.
    ADVISE IMMEDIATELY.
    MICHELINE DUBOIS
    HOTEL KRASNAPOLSKY
    AMSTERDAM, THE NETHERLANDS

That should do it. Stella pushed the paper back to the clerk. He looked up from his cost chart and barely looked at the message. She paid him and asked, "How soon will it be sent? I'm in a rush."

"Who isn't?" He looked at her and sighed dramatically.

"What is going on there?" complained a woman behind her. "I have a train to catch."

Stella glanced back. "I just have to pay. One moment." Then she paid again and the clerk tucked the money away. In his pocket.

"It will go out immediately." He went in the back room and handed an operator her message instead of putting it on the pile. "Have a good day."

"Thank you and good evening." Stella moved away and the woman behind her rushed up to ask prices. How much for ten words to Brussels? How much for ten to Paris? How much for London? Norwich? Stella doubted that the woman had a train to catch. If she did, she didn't know where it was going.

Stella left the little office, almost getting run over by a bike messenger. They were doing a brisk business with all the telegrams flying around. If her little bribe worked as it should, she'd have an hour at most to kill. An hour in Amsterdam was easy to fill and she left the station to find a quaint café to waste it in.

"Did you enjoy your walk?" asked the doorman.

Stella smiled. "I did. Amsterdam is beautiful all the time, but I think I like it best in the rain. Very mysterious."

He took the umbrella from her and glanced out at the square. "Mysterious?"

"All those quiet canals and silent boats going by," she said. "Who knows what secrets they're hiding."

"I heard you were writing a book."

"I'm thinking about it, but I can't decide. A romantic novel or a tale of intrigue."

"Intrigue with a beautiful girl in distress." The doorman smiled and warmed to the subject. "She could be captured, held against her will, and your hero has to find her somewhere in the depths of Amsterdam."

She laughed and elbowed him. "Maybe you should be writing the book."

He ducked his head. "I have thought of it."

"Well, you will have plenty of material if *they* come," Stella said. "Lots of distress."

The doorman opened the door for her. "And villains."

"No shortage at all."

The young man was grim, but she could see his mind working and it made her smile as she entered the lobby. Uncle Josiah was off to the left, lounging against a pillar and charming the socks off the featherheaded Marga. She was blushing and twisting her long hair around a finger as she batted her eyes at Stella's uncle, who was never more endearing to her than he was at that moment. He played his part beautifully, once more enticing a beautiful young woman away from her duties and risking the wrath of Mr. De Jong who was trying and failing to conceal a frown as he looked on from the front desk. Anybody else would be thrown out after the trouble he'd caused and was still trying to cause for no other reason than he could.

Josiah Bled was always one to risk everything for practically nothing at all. He'd been arrested on four continents, thrown out of six countries, including his own, and had done jail time for breaking into Windsor Castle to steal a tea towel on a one quid bet. After drinking himself into a stupor during an economic meeting at the White House and throwing up in a spittoon that belonged to Andrew Jackson, Eleanor Roosevelt famously asked him, "Have you ever controlled yourself?" Uncle Josiah said, "I haven't ever found a reason to."

Now he had a reason and her name was Judith Wahle, the twenty-one-year-old daughter of Felix and Klara. He'd met her the first time he went to Hallstatt and had fallen for her "like a ton of bricks" as he put it. She was eighteen at the time and home after being told she couldn't study at the University of Heidelberg anymore because she was a Jew.

"That's the one thing I'd thank Hitler for before I shot him in the head," said Uncle Josiah. "If he wasn't such a racist bastard I'd never have met her."

The revelation had stunned Stella into silence, not that Uncle Josiah noticed. He was talking about Judith and the world did not exist. If Stella hadn't heard it from him, she wouldn't have believed it possible. Josiah the family ne'er-do-well in love? Her grandmother had given up on the idea long ago. She'd told Stella once, "We can only hope he won't ruin more than reputations."

He probably had. No Bled had been invited back to the White House, for instance, but none of that mattered now. Josiah loved Judith and he would do anything to save her. Anything. That was clear from the start. Stella's mission wasn't important. She didn't think he'd out her to save Judith, but it wasn't too far out of the realm. Judith and her family would die if the Reich got ahold of them. Josiah was convinced. He'd seen Dachau and nobody who'd seen that misery could forget it. The Committee for Jewish Refugees was running Westerbork so the Wahles should be safe for the moment, but that fact didn't soothe Uncle Josiah. Jewish control was temporary with the invasion imminent and to make matters worse, Stella had made the mistake of telling him about Ravensbrück, the camp for women, and he was properly terrified for Judith and her mother, Evangeline's beloved Klara.

When he finished describing Judith's many virtues, Stella finally got a word in edgewise. "Why didn't you tell us?"

"Felix and Klara wouldn't agree to let us marry," he said. "She was too young and I'm not Jewish."

"That doesn't mean you couldn't tell us about her," said Stella.

"No one would've taken me seriously."

"I wonder why." A smile crept onto her lips against her will.

"Don't do that," said Uncle Josiah. "You're my partner in crime. If I can't convince you, what hope is there?"

Not much, Stella had to admit. He had such a disastrous reputation and there had been others he'd been wild about, only to forget their very existence a few months later. "Do her parents believe you? I assume they *know* about you."

"Yes," he said. "I've won them over."

"How?" Stella asked. "My parents had a hard time with Nicky and he wasn't twenty years older and you know…crazy."

"Seventeen years."

Stella laughed for the benefit of whoever might be watching and then said, "Well, that makes all the difference."

"Three years is three years."

"You're Josiah Bled. I'm shocked Felix didn't chase you out of town with a shotgun. It wouldn't be the first time."

He looked her in the eyes, steady and open. "I said I'd convert."

"Really?"

"Stella, I love her. How can I explain it better?"

"You never do anything by halves, I'll give you that."

His eyes grew merry and he laughed. "Miss Dubois, you are a card. Come out with us tonight. We'll show you a good time."

Ester was peeking at them again and Stella yawned. "I'm afraid not, Mr. Bled. I have to get to the station and find a train to catch." She pushed back her chair and he got up to help her.

"Let me get your coat," said Uncle Josiah.

"Thank you."

Ester retreated into the kitchen and he helped her on with her coat. "You won't leave?"

"No, of course not," she said.

"What will you do?" he asked.

"I have no idea." She put out her hand and they shook. "Thank you for an amusing afternoon, Mr. Bled. You are one for the record books."

Dirk came in from the kitchen, sporting a huge grin. "He is, isn't he? You enjoyed your coffee, Micheline?"

"Yes. Mr. Bled is good for a laugh. I hope you have a lot of fun tonight."

The men wished her well and she headed out, hoping Uncle Josiah would behave himself while he waited for her to return.

Looking at him across the lobby with his rakish smile and Marga blushing furiously, it seemed like he had controlled himself, as much as Josiah Bled ever did. Marga was all for going out with him and his cronies and Ester was trying to horn in. It sounded like he was gathering quite a group for the night out. Typical Josiah.

Stella walked by them and went to the desk to smile at the night clerk, who was watching the group with longing. "Could you have a bellhop come to my room? I found a train."

The clerk looked surprised. "Was it hard?"

"Very. Everything is full. The invasion, you know."

"My father says it won't happen," she said.

Stella sighed. "I wish he would've told everyone at the station. It would've made my life easier."

"When would you like him to come up?"

Stella's palms began to sweat. No telegram. She checked her watch. "In an hour. I want to get there early."

The clerk said she'd send someone up for her luggage and smiled sweetly. "Anything else? Dinner perhaps while you wait."

"I don't think so. Mr. Bled fed me plenty of pastry. I can wait. Were there any messages for me?"

"No. Were you expecting some?"

"I was just checking," said Stella with a lump in her throat. She'd have to check out if New York didn't get a move on. "Thank you. I nearly forgot. How is Michel? Has he gone to the hospital?"

"He's fine, I think, but they sent him home." She leaned over the desk. "I think it was indigestion. He's a bit of a pig."

Stella laughed and said she was relieved before going to wait for the elevator, trying to think of what to do. A new hotel? She could switch to Charlotte Sedgewick if she had to, but it wasn't ideal. Her Micheline contacts like Elizabeth and Madam Milla would be lost to her.

The elevator doors opened and a new operator grinned at her. "I won't pass out, Micheline," said Max.

"Thank goodness. That was enough excitement for one day," she said, stepping on with a heavy heart.

"Michel told you about Jan Bikker?"

"He did."

"You should go. He's not a nice man."

"I am."

I have to. Dammit.

Ludwik came running toward the elevator just as Max started to close the door. "Micheline! Micheline!"

Max pulled the doors back and Stella stepped off. "What's wrong? Is it Michel?"

"No, no," said Ludwik. "You have a telegram." He said it loud enough for the whole lobby to hear and Stella was grateful. "It's from New York."

Thank you. Thank you. Thank you.

"Can you hold on for a moment, Max?" she asked.

"Of course," Max said, looking curiously at the telegram in Ludwik's hand.

She took it and said, "Let's see what they have to say."

"A raise?" Ludwik suggested and she smacked him with the envelope. "Just the thing. Cross your fingers," she said.

"Crossing."

Stella opened the telegram and read the message with a deepening frown.

NEW CLIENT. PURCHASE PREVIOUSLY MENTIONED FURNITURE SET. THOROUGH PROVENANCE DESIRED. MAY REQUIRE FURTHER PIECES IN SAME STYLE. ADVISE WHEN INITIAL PURCHASE COMPLETE.
JOSEPH O'CONNOR
B.L. IMPORTS

"Not a raise then?" Ludwik asked.

"No," said Stella with a sigh. "Is my room still available or have you booked it?"

"No, it's free. Are you staying?"

"I am. We have a new client and they want furniture."

Ludwik glanced at the telegram held so he could see the contents. "You have some already in mind?"

"I told them about a set I saw. It was very good, but not my personal client's style. It was an excellent buy though."

"A new client for you then."

"Perhaps." She smiled. "Now I get to unpack."

"Dinner in the dining room?"

"My room. I must dig through my books and see what else I can find for them. I have some ideas." Stella got back on the elevator and chatted with Max about the baron's party on her way up to her floor. He, like everyone else, was fascinated by extravagance.

"I don't think I could go through fire or swing on that rope," he said.

"Even for unlimited champagne?" Stella asked.

Max screwed up his mouth, opened the door for her, and then stepped back. "How much is unlimited?"

"I think people drank their body weight."

"Did they have good Jenever?"

Stella thought of Cornelia covertly having sips of her spiked coffee throughout the night and giving Stella a wink. "It's Amsterdam. What do you think?"

"I might risk it at that," said Max.

She shook her head at him with a laugh and went down to her room, stopping with her hand on the doorknob. She looked back at Max, but he'd already closed the elevator door. Too late. Or maybe it was a good thing. Stella's door was unlocked and slightly ajar. At least now she had a minute to think about what to do. If Max had noticed, the choice was gone and all might be revealed.

Stella took a breath and went in, reaching automatically for the light switch, but the light had been left on. She never wasted electricity. That alone would've tipped her off and, if by some miracle it didn't, the rest of the room would've. She'd left her suitcases together on the floor next to the bed. Now they were on the bed with her little briefcase on top with its clasp open.

"Marga."

No one else would've made such a mess of it. Certainly not Jan Bikker. Marga must've snuck up when Stella was in the café with Uncle Josiah. The girl really was as stupid as she seemed. Bikker would never pay her, unless it was with spite, and here she was trying to find names of other Jews for him, a man who fired her. Beyond stupid.

Stella opened the suitcases first and found her seals on the secret compartments were intact and nothing moved. The gorgeous sewing box was still on her dressing table and it was easily the most expensive item in her room, but Marga had stolen a ring out of the jewelry box she had for purchases. Luckily, the ring wasn't from Francesqua's list.

She'd bought it simply to fill out her inventory in case someone asked to see what she had. It was genuine but oversized and gaudy with a flawed pear-shaped diamond surrounded in equally flawed and cloudy emeralds. The jeweler had bought it as a favor to a friend who'd fallen on hard times years before and sold it to Stella at a substantial discount just to get rid of it. The ring was the worst piece in the box, but it was also the showiest and largest. If Marga had been paying attention, she'd have noticed it was the only piece without a tag with names on it. The ring's tag only said Apeldoorn and the jeweler's shop with a tiny note of special provenance.

Stella found the ring's tag in her trash bin on top of the crumpled tissues and some wig hair pulled out of her comb for realism. Stella's real stray hair got flushed.

"Nitwit." She sat on the bed and went through her briefcase. It looked like the whole thing had been dumped out and everything stuffed back inside without a care to how it looked originally. Marga had taken her copy of *Der Totale Krieg* out of her small suitcase and put it in the briefcase as if Stella wouldn't notice. The girl had jammed it in so quickly, the pages were crushed by being shoved onto one of the ledgers. The book would never be the same, but it was intact.

Stella spread the ledgers and notebooks out, looking through each one. No papers were missing. She seriously doubted that Marga knew what she was looking at. Stella's official ledgers were informative if you were an accountant. Dates, prices, places, and last names. Nothing to mark someone a Jew and the last names weren't necessarily Jewish. Berger could be Jewish or just German and she had names from nine countries. What did Marga know about Danish names? And the real lists were hidden in the compartment where Marga hadn't looked. What would the girl tell Bikker? There was a list? Both ledgers would have to be that list and they were thick. Park-Welles had them faked to look like Micheline Dubois had been working for B.L. Imports for years.

This was the last thing Stella needed and there was no way around it. Between the theft and Marga's bungling, Stella couldn't chance letting it go. She'd be in Amsterdam for a few more days and Jan

Bikker knew the girl from his hotel. If he had two brain cells to rub together, the man would know that girl could not search a room cleanly. It wasn't possible. She couldn't remember to bring a menu. Stella had to report the break-in or risk Bikker realizing she didn't because she had something to hide.

She kicked off her shoes and went to the window to look out onto the square. Everything was shiny and slick with the rain and lit up for Saturday night with couples and groups having a last hoorah before *they* came. She checked her watch. A few more minutes. Then below Stella's window, a group left the hotel under wide black umbrellas. It was quite a big group with seven umbrellas and even through the glass, Stella could hear hints of raucous laughter. She watched them walk into the square and was rewarded when an umbrella turned and tipped up, revealing Uncle Josiah's face searching for her. She waved and he saluted. The group looked back at her and there was Marga, silly Marga, waving with a flash of diamonds on her hand.

The umbrellas tipped back and the group headed toward a bar across the square. Uncle Josiah couldn't just go straight to his destination. He'd have to have a fortifying shot for the journey. That, at least, hadn't changed. Once the group had gone inside and were safely out of sight, Stella went to her telephone and dialed the front desk.

"This is Micheline Dubois. Someone has been in my room and robbed me."

CHAPTER 17

Stella's best option turned out to be a milk train to Assen the next morning. She could've waited an extra hour to take a faster, more comfortable train, but she had to get out of the Hotel Krasnapolsky. Her report of theft the night before had thrown the staff into such a tizzy that she almost regretted reporting it.

When she showed the night manager the tag in the trash bin, the poor man had palpitations and the doctor got called back to attend the sweating Mr. Hanson on Stella's floor. This time the drama was real and he was hauled off to the hospital for tests.

Mr. De Jong came in as Mr. Hanson was being hauled out. The poor manager was so tense Stella thought a prominent vein in the man's forehead would pop during his third apology. None of the anxiety was necessary. She loved the hotel and didn't blame them, but he couldn't be soothed until Stella said that she didn't want the police called and asked him to handle the situation in-house, which prompted an hour-long conversation about what would be done and by whom. Stella couldn't have cared less, but it was very important to the staff and absolutely everyone was questioned from the laundress to the bartender on duty. Stella denied having any suspicions about who the culprit was, but it didn't matter. Even the laundress working in the depths of the hotel at a steam press knew that Jan Bikker had been to the hotel and had been talking to Marga about Micheline Dubois.

The next morning when Stella went down for breakfast at the café, every staff member on duty came up to apologize. None of the people out with Uncle Josiah had come back, including him. That was unexpected. For Josiah Bled, coming back after dawn was usual. Most, like Ludwik and Daan, were off on Sunday, but Marga and Ester were supposed to be in the café. Neither had turned up and the night clerk had been persuaded to stay and help out. The poor girl was dead on her feet, but Stella tipped her heavily and that put a little spring in her step.

Stella had rushed through a croissant and coffee just to avoid any more apologies. Other guests had learned what happened and now she had to contend with them. It was too much and Stella took a cab to the station while still brushing crumbs from her suit.

The train was quiet, but nearly full of people trying to get away from the capital. The excitement at the station the night before had turned to silent apprehension and almost no one spoke the entire way to Assen, the closest stop to the Westerbork Central Refugee Camp.

Occasionally, a child would ask when they could go home, only to get the unsatisfactory answer of "I don't know" or "After it's over." Stella wondered if they meant after the invasion or after the war. The parents answering didn't look like they knew much of anything, except that they were exhausted. So was Stella, even with the clamor, it was hard to keep her eyes open.

After the train ground to a halt, she stepped off behind a mother and her five children, all silent with big eyes. They were going to their grandmother's and nobody looked happy about it, although Assen was a fine little town and certainly not a target for bombing. If it had industry, Stella didn't know what it was.

She hurried past them, off the platform and into the station where a sour-looking matron waited with crossed arms and a tapping foot. Stella hoped that wasn't the grandmother because it was going to be a long war if it was.

She went outside to look for a cab in the chilly morning sunshine but found the road empty except for a couple of delivery trucks. It was Sunday and she should've known. She rushed back into the ticket counter to ask the clerk for help, but he was as sour as the matron.

"Good morning," said Stella, stifling a yawn.

He just crossed his arms and didn't speak.

"Will there be any cabs this morning?" she asked.

The man looked her over, noting her frizzy hair and spending a long time peering at her face. He was handsome in a greasy way, but it wasn't about her looks or age for once. The clerk was giving her a familiar evaluation, although Stella hadn't experienced it much since being out of Nazi-held territory. "Where are you going?"

"Why does that matter?"

"I don't know if they will want to take you."

"That's between me and them," Stella said sharply.

"And me, since you want me to use my phone to call them."

"I will pay for the call, of course."

He lit a cigarette from the one already dangling from his lips and then grinned at her with tobacco-stained teeth. "Where are you going?"

"That is none of your concern," said Stella.

"You're going to that Jew camp. I can always tell."

Stella opened her handbag and took out her pocketbook. "Please call a cab."

He leaned forward and blew smoke through the hole in the partition. "You're a Jew, wanting to visit all your Jew friends."

"And what is that to you?"

The man stood up and yelled through the glass at the people behind Stella. "She's a Jew. Push her out of the way. We don't serve Jews."

Stella swallowed hard and tucked her pocketbook away before saying, "I am not a Jew, but you are a disgusting little worm and *they* will grind you into the dirt where you belong."

The cigarette dropped out of his mouth and she spun around to march out of the station. On her last visit to the camp, Stella had seen an old man with a couple of bicycles for rent around the corner of the station. Two bicycles were propped against the wall. The old man's wooden stool was empty, but he'd left a tin with a slot cut in the top. It had *Schenking* painted on the side and Stella stopped to stare in surprise. No one in the States would simply leave their rental bicycles out, unlocked, for a donation, even if they were a little rusty with broken baskets. They'd be gone, but in Europe donations were common. She'd seen it before with fruit and flowers, but not actual merchandise. The trust was truly amazing and she dropped a coin in the slot and took the smaller of the two bicycles, careful to keep her skirt out of the greasy chain. Not the ideal solution, but it was better than walking ten kilometers.

Stella rode out of Assen, the ride knocking the cobwebs away, and pedaled along the dirt road to Westerbork past tall, skinny trees, and fields full of lush life. It seemed like a fertile area, but the Dutch government had let the Jewish committee build the camp out in the middle of nowhere, presumably because nobody else wanted the land. How they managed to come up with the money required was a mystery. Her mother would say where there was a will there was a way, so the committee must have had tremendous will. One million guilders in three days was a feat Francesqua and her conies couldn't have matched and Stella's mother was quite the fundraiser. She'd put her considerable skills on getting two families into and then out of Westerbork. Neither task was easy. People had to prove they could support themselves and not be a burden. Not many people could do that, considering they were running for their lives. Francesqua's efforts were how Stella had ended up at Westerbork shortly after becoming Micheline Dubois. The first family were German Jews from Hamburg that literally walked from their home to the Dutch border where they begged for asylum. They had some connections and money, so they were let in when so many others were turned away. They wrote from Westerbork to a distant relative Simon Goldblatt, who happened to work at United Shipping and Steel. Simon appealed to Nicky's father who appealed to Francesqua who put them on her list. Stella bought their remaining valuables and delivered needed papers and the family was now living in New York. That's how people were saved, luck and contacts. That time it was easy. Stella's second trip to Westerbork was not.

She pedaled past the fields of purple lupins, blooming in gorgeous color in the bright sun. They'd just been sending up their stalks when she went to meet Egon and Olga Korbel, a pair of elderly Czech violinists, and their grandson, Pavel. They'd escaped Prague moments before the Gestapo came to arrest them. They traveled with help from friends out of Czechoslovakia all the way to The Netherlands where they ran out of funds and appealed to the committee for help. Stella's grandparents had been friends and that's how they landed on the list and a good thing, too.

Stella's legs were tired, despite the flat terrain, but the sight of the barbed wire fence up ahead spurred her on. Another kilometer or so and she'd arrive at the gate to figure something out. She was always figuring something out. Park-Welles would say that wasn't her job. Helping was not in the brief. What did he know about barbed wire, plank huts, acres of mud? Nothing. That's what.

The guards stood next to the gate, leaning on the camp sign and looking bored out of their minds. It wasn't much of a job. Westerbork didn't have an escape problem and if you had to be detained, Stella supposed this was the place to do it. She slowed down and looked past the strands of barbed wire to see if it looked any different since the last time. It was more crowded with lots of people walking around the rows of neat little houses built for individual families. The laughter of children came through the wire and straight into Stella's heart. She'd hoped she'd never have to come back.

The men looked surprised when she got closer and one waved. Stella didn't realize she was so recognizable, but he called out, "Madam Dubois! You are back!"

Stella rolled up to them and stopped, carefully holding up the hem of her skirt. "Hello. You remember me?"

"We don't have many Belgian ladies coming to visit prisoners," he said with a smile. "I did not think you would be back."

"Neither did I, but my company had other plans." She sighed and he helped her off the bicycle.

The other guard that Stella didn't recognize yawned and took her bicycle to lean it on one of the tall wooden poles, careful not to put it against the barbed wire. "You are a Jew?" he asked doubtfully.

"No," she said. "But I'm here to meet with a family."

"Madam Dubois is a businesswoman," said the first guard. "She works for Americans."

"Jews?"

"My boss is Joseph O'Connor so I don't think so."

"What do you do?"

"I buy antiques, jewelry, clocks, whatever our clients want and I was told a family here had a fine furniture set to sell."

Both guards frowned.

"Maybe not," said Stella. "But this is my job. I have to ask."

The first guard shrugged. "You're here. You may as well try."

"Thank you. I'd hate to bike all this way and not get in."

"Why didn't you take a cab?"

Stella sighed and stretched. "There weren't any there and the man at the station wouldn't call for me."

They nodded.

"Probably Frank. He is always causing trouble. The Jews don't do anything to anyone in here, but he has to complain. Always complaining." The first guard unlocked the gate and pulled it open for her. "How long will you be?"

"It depends on how long it takes to find them," Stella said. "I think they're new."

The other guard rolled his eyes. "It doesn't matter. We'll be here."

Stella walked in and turned to the right toward the administration building, picking her way through the mud and passing a group of children kicking a ball in a circle without a care for the dirty spray they were causing. A man in a small flower garden stopped weeding and chastised them as Stella hurried past to the main door. As she reached for the knob, a man came limping out while looking at a pile of papers in his hands and nearly bowled her over in his haste.

"Excuse me. Excuse me," he said and then squinted at her through smudged glasses. "You are new?"

"Visiting."

He brushed back a crop of unruly curls. "You have a pass from the committee?"

Stella handed over her old pass and he held it up like it might be counterfeit. Honestly, who would go to the trouble? It wasn't like Westerbork was one of the baron's parties. She wouldn't be there if it weren't for Uncle Josiah.

"This is old," he said, holding the pass closer to his left eye. His right eye's pupil was larger and he had a dent in his temple with a well-healed but recent wound in it.

"I know, but I've been here before." She held out her hand. "Micheline Dubois of B.L. Imports."

He looked at her hand for a moment before shaking it. "Dubois?"

"Yes."

"Where do I know that name?"

A woman with a mass of dark curly hair came out behind him and said, "From the Korbels."

"Elli," said Stella. "I'm glad you're here."

"What brings you back to the Drenthe heath?" Elli asked. "I didn't think I'd see you again."

"Business as always."

"You know her?" asked the man.

"Ulrich, this is Micheline Dubois, a woman of many talents." Elli gave Stella a friendly but appraising look, which was common for the student of Slavic languages. Elli specialized in Russian, which for all Stella's language talents, she found incomprehensible.

Stella brushed the dust from her skirt. "My talents are overrated."

"I doubt that." Elli gazed at her quietly. Those dark eyes always thinking. Of all the people Stella had met during her current mission, Elli was the only one who suspected she wasn't what she seemed and Stella had been glad to stay well away from Westerbork and the committee after the Korbel affair. The camp was run by Jewish volunteers and Elli was always around. Friendly and fun, she knew everyone. If Ludwik at the Hotel Krasnapolsky knew she was paying way too much to the Jews she bought from, Elli definitely knew.

"Right now, I wish I had a talent for going home, but I don't. I'm here and hoping you can help me," said Stella.

"Well, I have to go to the…" The man trailed off and wandered away with his papers.

The women watched him go and then Elli shook her head. "Ulrich's new and just out of the hospital."

"Should he be working?" Stella asked. "He seems muddled."

"They all must earn their keep and he was a bookkeeper at Daimler. The numbers will come back to him," said Elli, watching Ulrich bump into a building and then turn in a circle. "I hope."

"What happened to him?"

"Ulrich was in Dachau. You know all about Dachau, I imagine."

Inside, Stella quaked, but she didn't let it show. "I think I heard it's a prison camp. Was he injured there?"

She raised a brow. "Do you really want to know?"

"No, I suppose not," said Stella.

"I didn't think so. Not after the Korbels. You best keep to the job at hand."

Breathe. She doesn't know.

"What about the Korbels? I gave them a good deal."

Elli opened the door to the administration building and said, "Some would say so."

For a second, Stella considered not going in and Elli with those all-seeing eyes spotted the hesitation. She waited and Stella saw something, too. Uncle Josiah's eyes, his fear, and she went right in. No more hesitating.

They went through the small building packed with files and desks to a small office, equally packed with files and a rickety desk probably donated instead of being thrown on the trash heap. Elli had prettied it up with a huge bouquet of wildflowers and there were more decorations than the last time Stella had been in the office. A portrait of Baruch Spinoza took pride of place over the window, but there was also a portrait of Mendelssohn and a photo of an old man with wild grey hair and a huge mustache. Stella had no clue who he was.

"Who are you here for?" Elli sat down behind the desk and indicated a three-legged stool for Stella to perch on.

She sat down carefully and looked out the window behind Elli. Ulrich was back and wandering around in a circle in the muddy road. He was in Dachau where Abel died. They did that to him and it could never be undone.

Stella had to force her eyes away from the wounded Ulrich to dig in her handbag. She pulled out her telegram and a slip of paper with the Wahles' fake names. "The Cohen family."

"Cohen is a common name."

That's why they picked it.

She looked back at the slip. "Abraham Cohen. His wife is Rosa and four children."

Elli steepled her fingers. "Of course. I should've known. *The Cohens.*"

Stella gave her a blank look. "What does that mean?"

"Only that this *Cohen* family shows up at the border with fake documents and wads of cash. They won't tell anyone their real names or what they do or where they come from. They're scared to death and not for the usual reasons or at least, there's more than the usual reasons. And here you come, Micheline Dubois, the magician, ready to pull another rabbit out of her hat."

"I don't know what you're talking about," said Stella, using Nicky's cool demeanor that she'd learned so well. "Are they here or not?"

"They are, for the time being."

"Are they being deported?"

Elli glanced at the calendar. "In a week. The father bought a reprieve, but they don't have long."

"Bought?"

"Wads of cash, like I said. They appealed to the committee and offered to pay for two other families if they could stay while working out their difficulties."

"This is a problem?"

"No. I wish them well. I'd like to know how you know about them."

Stella handed over the telegram. "It wasn't my idea. I was supposed to be back home yesterday, but this came and here I am."

"How did you know about their furniture?"

Stella smiled slyly. "I have connections."

"I know you do."

"In my business that's a good thing."

"But it's not always right." Elli sat back and crossed her arms. "What are you going to do about the Cohens?"

"I'm going to buy their furniture if it's any good," said Stella.

"And?"

"*And* nothing."

"They are very afraid," said Elli.

"I don't blame them."

The committee volunteer clenched her teeth and then forced herself to relax. "Maybe they're afraid of you."

"Me? I've never met them in my life," said Stella. "If they don't want to sell, they don't have to."

"Don't they?"

"No, of course not."

"Like Pavel Korbel didn't have to sell," said Elli, her dark eyes flashing.

Oh, that's what we're talking about.

"Pavel's *grandparents* sold me their violins of their own free will," Stella said with a raise of one shoulder.

"Pavel had nothing to sell, yet you took."

The women stared at each other and Stella found herself at a loss for words. That Elli knew exactly what had happened with the Korbels and judged her harshly for it hadn't occurred to her. Those dark eyes bored into hers and she felt her resolve stiffen. It was right. She didn't care what Elli thought.

"Sometimes people don't know what is for the best," said Stella.

"People should be allowed to make their own decisions," said Elli.

"Not if they don't understand all the facts."

"No one can know all the facts."

"Yet some of us have a better comprehension without sentimentality."

Elli took a deep breath and asked, "You think I'm sentimental?"

"I wouldn't have thought so, but here we are," said Stella.

"Have you heard from the Korbels?"

"Why would I?"

"I thought you had an interest," said Elli.

"I had an interest in their violins."

"And Pavel."

Stella sighed. This was so difficult. Why did they have to do it? Why did she have to be made to think about it again? It was done. She wouldn't change it if she could.

"I'm sure Pavel is fine wherever he is," she said.

"Fine is a matter of perspective," said Elli. "He'll regret—"

"What?" Stella cut her off. "What does he regret?" She pointed out the window at Ulrich who was sitting in the mud crying and confused. Several people had rushed over to help him, but there was no help that could actually help. "Not ending up like that or worse?"

Elli looked out the window and said, "Not making his own choice."

"He made a choice from what I understand," said Stella.

"There was no choice. You made sure of that."

There was no point in arguing. For Elli, Pavel Korbel should've been allowed to go back to Czechoslovakia if he wanted to. Stella took that away from him. He was seventeen years old. He would've died. His grandparents were old and weak. Olga had looked at Stella with such misunderstanding. The old lady had left her glasses and bible on the mantelpiece when they left. She'd gone through their terrifying escape half blind and asked Stella to write to their son, Pavel's father, to send them to her. They'd been in Westerbork for three weeks when Stella got to them and it'd been over two months since anyone had heard from Pavel's parents and siblings. Letters, telegrams, everything had been tried. The only information was that they'd been arrested the same night that the grandparents and Pavel escaped. The whole family gone in the middle of the night and they hadn't come back.

Stella heard one of the other administrators whisper, "No one comes back. They can't understand."

Stella understood. The younger Korbels were gone, along with everything they owned, lost to the gaping maw that was the Reich, but Olga could not be made to believe it. She wanted her glasses. She wanted her family. She wanted her life. It hurt Stella so much to see her fine artist's hands groping around for things she couldn't have, that changed things for Stella. She decided to do what she shouldn't, to show connection and care however remote.

So, she went back to Amsterdam and got the old lady glasses. She sent them to Westerbork anonymously, along with a small Hebrew bible. It was a mistake. It gave her away. Elli knew all about Olga and her glasses. She'd seen Stella watching those hands reaching helplessly. And she knew about Pavel and his parents. The boy was determined to go back and find them. He was young and strong. He thought he could. He thought he had the strength to do the undoable and wanted to use some of the money from the violins to finance the trip. His grandparents needed that money. They needed him. Pavel was the only family they had left. Stella could replace glasses. She couldn't replace him, so she used the prostitute to message the earl in a roundabout way and got him to put an extra requirement on the Korbels visas to England. Along with having to guarantee that they had enough money to support themselves, they had to have a family member to take care of them so the state wouldn't have to put them in a home for care since they were elderly and infirm. Either Pavel went with his grandparents to England or nobody went.

It was a risk and she hadn't done it lightly. Pavel was so adamant, there was every chance he wouldn't do it, but in the end, Stella got word through Elizabeth that the committee had strong-armed him, saying that they needed the space for incoming families and the remaining Korbels got on a boat, all three of them.

"I don't know what you think I did," said Stella. "From what I understand, Pavel Korbel has a fine ear. Perhaps he will grow to be a great musician like his grandparents."

"And learn to live with the choice he didn't make? Is that what you think?"

"I think he will live. Isn't that the important thing?"

"Many things are important," said Elli. "Free will is important."

"And I'm sure you will exercise it," said Stella. "Probably to your own detriment."

"I don't know what you mean."

"It seems neither of us knows what the other means."

"Or we know exactly."

Stella looked at Elli and had the sad, inevitable feeling she'd had so many times before. Elli wouldn't survive. If she had a chance, she wouldn't take it. She would cling to ideals that weren't relevant anymore. The Nazis had made them irrelevant. Elli was as blind as Olga had been.

"Can I see the Cohens or not?"

Elli looked as though she wanted to say no, but her good sense won out. "I suppose so, if they want to see you."

"They will."

"Why are you always so sure?"

"Because I have been in Berlin." It just popped out. The truth. And it startled both her and Elli. "On business," she said quickly, but it was too late. Elli was fixed on her with total understanding. She saw the lines drawn on her face and hands. The wig. Everything. Stella was no longer slipping. She'd slipped. Over. Done.

"Berlin," whispered Elli.

"The Cohens. I haven't got all day."

Elli stood up. "I'll…I don't want you to…"

"I will buy their furniture," said Stella. "That's all."

"They're not Korbels."

"No."

Mollified, Elli went out and told someone to find the Cohen family and Stella could hear the short discussion about who they really were and why they were hiding in Westerbork. Did they have to? Why? Who were they really? Why do it? Why not tell the truth?

Why do it? Why? If you're a Jew, it's a good place, considering the alter-

A.W. HARTOIN

native. Hiding in Westerbork. Hiding. Hiding. The best worst place. Stella smiled. *Thank you, Elli.*

Stella recognized them instantly or rather she recognized Felix Wahle instantly and supposed the young woman with him to be his daughter, Judith. Uncle Josiah had described the family, in general, as being tall, charming, and intellectual. That was hardly helpful and his portrait of Judith even less so. Beautiful, wonderful, funny, and lovely could be anyone. Stella didn't know her hair or eye color. She did know that Felix was injured in the Great War, losing a leg and damaging his lungs irreparably. The man walking past the window fit that description, although Stella would've put him at sixty-eight instead of the forty-eight years he was supposed to be.

Felix Wahle hobbled past, painfully slow on what appeared to be a wooden leg and using two canes. He was tall but emaciated to the point of being skeletal with thin and greying brown hair and clothes that were made to fit a much larger man. Judith was nearly as tall as her father and walked by his side with an arm out behind him to catch him if he should fall. Stella hardly knew what to make of her. It wasn't that she wasn't attractive. She was, but not in the way Uncle Josiah's other interests had been. Stella knew all about those women. It was impossible not to know. Pictures of her playboy uncle were forever being splashed across the papers, always accompanied by a woman of a certain type. Leggy showgirls, buxom actresses, the occasional barmaid and even a society girl could fit the bill. Uncle Josiah's women were all eyelashes and lipstick without an original thought in their pretty little heads.

Once when he turned up for Grandfather's birthday party with a Vanderbilt cousin who'd just returned from five years in Europe, Stella's father asked if she spoke French or German. Uncle Josiah said, "I'm not even sure if she really speaks English." Stella met her and wasn't sure either. There certainly was a lot of cooing and exclaiming but no full sentences, only words like champagne and darling. Grandmother had informed Uncle Josiah that he was dating a toddler and to take her out of her sight immediately. He did and wasn't seen for a month. The Vanderbilt cousin ended up marrying a series of Wall Street tycoons and Uncle Josiah moved on to a gorgeous but idiotic barmaid who stole his wallet and watch.

Judith was nothing like that. Stella could tell even through glass. She wore pressed black trousers, a grey sweater over a white shirt, and a sensible pair of galoshes to deal with the mud. She had light brown hair, long and wavy, pinned back with a couple of bobby pins. No jewelry and definitely no eyelashes or lipstick. Judith didn't look like she'd just rolled out of bed, so Stella guessed this was her normal state, if it really was Judith. Stella had half convinced herself that it couldn't be when the pair passed the window and went out of sight.

"Do you recognize them?" Elli asked.

"I told you I've never met the Cohen family," said Stella.

"You were looking quite surprised."

"I'm surprised you made that man walk all the way over here."

Elli drew back and frowned. "I didn't make him. He insisted that he's not an invalid and could meet you like anyone else."

"I disagree on the invalid part, but it's too late now," said Stella. "What's wrong with him? Other than the leg."

"Something to do with the war. He might've been gassed."

"That would do it."

Voices in the hall announced the Wahles' arrival, but it was another ten minutes before they made it to the office. As soon as Felix appeared in the doorway, Elli jumped up and rolled her chair around the desk for him.

"No, no," he exclaimed in German. "Don't get up."

"I insist Herr Cohen," replied Elli also in German.

Judith helped to ease her father down into the seat. It looked almost as difficult as the walking and his hands trembled with the effort. He gave Judith his canes and clasped his hands together to control them. Judith stepped back and hooked the canes over her arm, looking at Stella curiously. She showed no signs of recognition or surprise. Neither did her father.

Felix fixed on Stella with lovely hazel eyes that were ringed with dark smudges and lines. "To what do I owe the pleasure, Miss… Dubois, is it?"

Stella held out her hand and he shook it with his ice cold one. "Micheline Dubois of B.L. Imports."

"Abraham Cohen and this is my daughter, Claudia," he said, and Judith nodded to her, a friendly smile on her wide mouth. Stella was careful not to look too closely, but what she saw continued to surprise her. Uncle Josiah's beloved was handsome rather than pretty with that wide mouth and jutting cheekbones. She had her father's lovely eyes, but overall she couldn't have been farther from a showgirl. Stella would've guessed she was at least five years older than she was and a professor of some sort, probably physics or math.

"Thank you for meeting me. I know this was unexpected."

"I'm happy to meet with you, although I can't imagine why you are here," said Felix. "Have we met before? I can't remember you."

"We haven't met, but I was told you have a set of bedroom furniture that you might be willing to sell."

"Who told you that?" Judith asked in a husky voice that was as unexpected as her appearance.

"Micheline has connections in the community," said Elli helpfully.

"We don't," said Felix frankly.

Elli leaned on a filing cabinet and crossed her arms. "I'm sure you do. Word gets around."

A volunteer peeked around the corner of the door and asked, "Can I get anyone some coffee or tea?"

Felix and Judith declined, so Stella and Elli did, too, but the man didn't leave. He leaned on the doorway and said, "What's this about furniture?"

"She thinks we have furniture to sell," said Judith.

"You don't?" Stella picked up the paper and telegram from Elli's desk. "My information was that you have a bedroom set."

The man laughed. "Here? In Westerbork?"

"I wasn't given the location."

Elli straightened up and looked at the man in the doorway. "Oh, that reminds me. Dr. Rosenberg has received some new furniture donations. Can you call the committee and find out when they can be picked up?"

"Now?" he asked.

"Would you?" she asked with a smile. "More families are coming in. We may have to double up."

The volunteer reluctantly left and Elli turned back to them. Stella had a feeling that Judith knew that she'd been getting rid of the man and his nosiness but wasn't so sure about Felix. He barely looked at the volunteer, lost in his own thoughts.

"Who did you say you worked for?" Felix asked.

"B.L. Imports," said Stella, switching her gaze to Judith, looking her hard in the eyes. "I work for a particular client. Dilbert Rutherford III of New York. We are an *American* company."

Understanding lit up in Judith's eye for a brief moment, but she covered it easily. "And you want to buy our furniture?"

"We have my parents' bedroom set," said Felix.

"I believe it's early Victorian, complete and unaltered," said Stella.

"Yes, I suppose so. This Rutherford person wants to buy our furniture?"

"I want to buy it for him. Of course, I will have to see it to tell if it is to his taste."

Felix nodded, thoroughly confused. "Of course."

"That man indicated that you don't have it here," said Stella.

"No," said Judith. "When we were…detained, it was confiscated and we had to pay to put it in a warehouse."

"It's still yours to sell?"

Elli colored. "The government didn't steal it, if that's what you're implying."

"I'm not implying anything," said Stella. "The government might have put a lien on the furniture as payment for something. Their stay here, for instance."

"Right. Of course."

Judith put a hand on her father's bony shoulder. "They haven't, have they?"

"No," said Felix. "But we sold everything else. It's all we have left."

His words hung in the air, filling up the small room with their sadness.

"I understand," said Stella. "Many of my sellers are in the same spot."

"We are not alone in our troubles." Felix leaned to the side and Judith had to prop him back up as the volunteer came back in.

"I called and we can pick up on Tuesday." He leaned on the doorframe. "So how is everything in here?"

Stella gritted her teeth, but Elli was thinking, as always. "Good, but I think Herr Cohen needs to get back to his hut."

Judith and Elli gently got Felix to his feet and out into the hall.

"We haven't talked about the location yet," he said breathlessly.

"How about I walk with you?" Stella asked. "We can talk about the location and price. I have a limit and a timeframe, you understand."

Felix nodded and started going down the hall with his canes. No one offered a wheelchair. It would've been refused. The old soldier shook off his daughter's helping hand and made his way with her keeping pace but not too close.

It took fifteen minutes to get outside and the volunteer followed. Stella wanted to kick him in the shin. He looked like he might follow all the way to the hut. Elli thought so, too, because she got ahead of him and said, "You know, I think there's some accounts for you to look at."

"Accounts? Me?" he asked in surprise.

"Ulrich has taken ill and he can't review them." Elli turned to Stella. "We'll leave you to it."

"Thank you for your help." Stella gave her a firmer than usual handshake and turned away to follow Felix, who was creeping across the street to a drier area.

She and Judith remained silent until they were out of earshot and then Judith said, "Americans?"

"Yes," said Stella.

"Who are you really?"

Felix's head jerked up. "What was that?"

Judith leaned in to say quietly, "She doesn't care about the furniture, Papa. She's here to help us."

"I thought that was strange, but Elli seemed to think it reasonable."

Stella moved to his other side and said, "I will buy the furniture. It's my job. I *am* Micheline Dubois of B.L. Imports, but apparently my company knows someone who knows you. They've been called upon to help, so here I am."

"I don't understand," he said so breathless he could hardly get the words out. "Someone knows an importer?"

"Papa, it's *him*. He's sent her to help us."

"How would he even know where we are?"

Judith swallowed hard and looked over her stooped father's back at Stella. "I telegrammed him during our last stop before the border."

Felix stopped, cursing quietly under his breath. "That was foolish, not to mention dangerous. A huge risk to us."

"It paid off, Papa. He found us and sent her."

"If the Nazis find out…"

"They haven't yet." Judith remained calm and collected.

"But…"

"But nothing. How else are we going to get out of here?"

"They're going to deport us. The connection could be made."

Stella touched his back lightly. No support. Just pay attention. "You're not getting deported. You're getting your *real* identities."

"We can't say who we—you know who we are?" he asked, looking up at her for the first time.

"The Wahles of Hallstatt," Stella whispered but instantly regretted it as the man swayed on his canes and Judith had to grab him by his waist to steady him.

"Let go. Let go," he demanded.

"I don't want you to fall," she said.

"If I fall, I fall. It's not the worst thing."

Judith's mouth went into a firm line, but she said nothing.

"So you really know," he said to Stella.

"Yes, but you aren't getting those names back. You'll have to accept something that might not be easy to accept."

"We can do whatever he wants us to do," said Judith.

"Within reason," said Felix.

"No, Papa. Anything he wants, we will do it."

"I haven't agreed, my dearest girl. This hasn't changed everything."

"It has," she said. "But we can talk about that later."

He grumbled about permission, but Judith was unmoved. She was going to marry Josiah Bled with or without her father's blessing. Stella had known the girl for five minutes and she knew that. Her father had known her her whole life and he didn't. The exchange reminded Stella of her discussions with her own father about Nicky. Aleksej Bled thought he had control. It took some convincing for him to realize he didn't.

"You said something about new names," said Felix when Judith wouldn't acquiesce.

"You are going to be the Milch family," said Stella.

"Milch isn't a Jewish name. We're Jewish."

"Not anymore."

"We can't—"

"Papa, please," said Judith. "Let her talk."

Stella explained as quickly as she could. Felix wasn't happy, but his daughter, in her quiet way, got him to at least listen. They were the Milch family, gentiles and Aryan. They said they were Jews because they thought they had a better chance at getting humanitarian help than if they were just run of the mill Austrians that had spoken up against Hitler. They were afraid to admit they were gentiles because they'd be kicked out of the camp. Arrest warrants were out for the head of the family, the ailing Ludwig Milch, and his wife Gisela. Ludwig would die in prison. Anybody who saw the man would believe that and it helped that it was actually true.

"But how are we connected to you and this company that you work for?" Judith asked.

"Herman Milch, who works for my client Dilbert Rutherford III. Mr. Milch appealed to his boss and Mr. Rutherford called on B.L. Imports because I'm here already and there you go."

"I don't suppose this Milch person is real?" Felix asked.

"He certainly is."

Stella knew Herman well. He was a local boy that Dilly's mother hired to be her son's companion when they were twelve, a kind of best friend whose real job was to make sure Dilly didn't get into too much trouble. Herman's official title was secretary, but he did a little of everything, including chauffeuring, haircuts, and gardening. Herman was a nice person but not a deep thinker. If someone asked him if Dilly sent some importer to help his distant cousins in The Netherlands, Herman would shrug and say, "Maybe." Herman took life as it came at him and was exceedingly calm. You had to be calm and not question the plausibility of things if you'd spent practically every day for the last ten years with a nutcase. Dilly, himself, was completely implausible, but it was a good, steady job as Herman told Stella the last time he saw her. At the time, he was wearing a loincloth and feathered headdress while putting out a teepee fire in Dilly's life-size Thanksgiving diorama, so Herman might've become a bit of a nutcase himself. Steady wasn't the word for his job, unless he was thinking steadily crazy.

"You'd like your cousin," said Stella. "He's unflappable, like you."

Felix chuckled as he pulled one of his canes out of the muck and Judith gave Stella a serene smile. "We'll need all the papers."

"We don't have the money for that," said Felix.

"I believe that's all been taken care of. You have a guardian angel."

Felix scoffed. "You wouldn't call him that if you knew him."

"Papa," said Judith. "He's my angel and you know it."

Angel? Uncle Josiah?

"This person would be an angel for all of you," said Stella. "You don't like him, Herr Milch?"

Felix smiled and made the deep smile lines on his cheeks activate for the first time. "Milch is growing on me. It is a good choice and yes, I like him. Everyone likes him, but an angel? That's going too far."

"Not if he saves us," said Judith.

"No," whispered Felix, "not if he saves us."

Stella and Judith waited while Felix struggled through a particularly muddy area and Stella took the chance to look at the camp. She'd never been so far inside before and she admired the planning and execution. The committee had fitted each little hut or house with the basics and from what she knew they were fed well and had workshops and a very good hospital. What would it become after the invasion? Another Dachau? Probably.

"Don't tell anyone about your *real* religion yet, Herr Milch. I will put this in motion and have your real papers to you immediately," she whispered to Judith and instantly wished she'd bit her tongue. As the words left her lips, she saw a woman's face in a window as they went between two of the houses. She'd withdrawn, but the window was open. She might've heard. Judith frowned slightly. She'd seen her, too.

"I'll need the name of your warehouse and written permission to see the furniture," said Stella.

"Of…" Felix couldn't finish. He was getting so tired; he could hard stay upright.

"I'll take care of that," said Judith. "How long before we get the money?"

"You will sell then?" Stella asked.

"Papa?"

Felix nodded and she said, "Yes, we will."

"Excellent. I will need to take your current identification with me today and I'll send a messenger with your money after I've seen the furniture."

"You won't come yourself?"

"I may, if you insist," said Stella.

"We won't insist, but it would be nice to see you again. We don't get visitors here."

Stella glanced over. "You will."

Judith looked straight ahead, seeing her future and freedom, lit with hope and love.

He's right. She is beautiful.

CHAPTER 18

The train station was quieter than before and the difficult clerk sat behind his partition, watching Stella walk across the room with her heels clacking against the tiles.

She reached him and he sneered as he reached up to pull the blind down to cut her off.

"Don't do that, Frank," Stella said.

"Huh?" He froze with his arm extended.

"Don't do that, Frank."

"How do you know my name?"

"Everyone knows about you," she said.

"Good," he spat, leaving a spray of spittle on the glass. "You Jews better know who you are up against."

"The Jews aren't up against *you*, Frank. If they were, they'd win."

"I don't sell to Jews."

"I'm not a Jew. I already told you that. See what I mean about winning. It's not much of a contest," said Stella. "I want a ticket to Amsterdam. Second class."

"I don't sell—"

"Anna Maria."

Frank's cigarette dropped out of his mouth and landed somewhere down below, smoldering unnoticed.

"What did you say?"

"Anna Maria."

A wisp of smoke rose up and he sniffed in confusion. "What in the—"

"You're on fire," said Stella, pointing down.

Frank looked, jumped up with a screech and then danced around, smacking at his crotch while Stella watched in amusement with a couple who'd come up behind her.

"What is he doing?" the lady asked.

"He set his pants on fire with his cigarette," said Stella.

The man rolled his eyes. "Idiot."

Frank stopped smacking himself and examined the burn mark on his zipper. "You made me do that."

"I did not make you set your crotch on fire. You dropped your cigarette and forgot about it," said Stella. "One ticket for Amsterdam, second class."

"I don't sell—"

"Anna Maria."

"Stop saying that."

"Anna Maria?" whispered the woman and the man's eyebrows jutted up.

"One ticket to Amsterdam, second class," said Stella. "How much?"

"I told you I don't—"

"Aletta."

The color drained out of Frank's face or rather a new color drained in. His pasty white was replaced by a pale puce. "Don't say… how did you…"

"The guards. They don't like you," said Stella.

"Well, I don't like you," he said.

"Fanny."

"Oh God."

"He's not going to help. You're not his type."

Frank started frantically plucking at his jacket. "What? I'm a good—"

"Isn't it number eight? Thou shall not commit a—"

"Here it is." Frank grabbed a ticket and shoved it under the partition. "Go to Amsterdam."

"This is first class," she said.

"A free bump to…go away."

"How much?"

"On the house," said Frank with sweat running down his temples.

"Your government doesn't give away train tickets," said Stella patiently. "How much?"

He gave her the price. It was probably wrong, but she paid it anyway. "Thank you and have a terrible day and a worse life."

The woman snagged Stella's sleeve as she turned to go. "What were those names?"

"Anna Maria, Aletta, and Fanny."

"Your train! Go catch your train!" yelled Frank.

"Who would've thought?" said the man. "He's such a *klojo*."

"There's only one name on my mind," said the woman.

"Don't cause trouble."

"He caused it."

Stella left them to it, but it didn't look good for Frank, the soon to be famous philander. He was already notorious among those in the know. When Stella came out of Westerbork, she found the guards talking to their captain. They told him about Frank refusing to help her call a cab and that prompted the captain to tell her what to say to Frank, a man who had sway over young, bored housewives. Stella had a feeling that the captain might have a bored housewife of his own, so it wasn't all for Stella's benefit. He'd been waiting to take a shot at Frank before Frank took a shot at his wife.

Satisfied, Stella got on her train a half hour later and sat in Micheline's proper class. She was alone in the car and no one came to tell her she wasn't supposed to be in second class, so she leaned on the glass and watched the flat countryside race by, thinking about her latest mistake. Revenge was sweet, even if it was stupid. She wouldn't have done that a month ago or on any other mission. Oliver was more right than she'd realized. Her patience was running thin. Watching Felix struggle took a good chunk out of what she had left.

He was such a sweet man, kind and intelligent, and Klara was just the same. Stella could see why her grandparents favored the family and indeed why Uncle Josiah had fallen in love. It wasn't just Judith, although she was plenty on her own, it was the whole family. Felix had shown her his medals from the war, so proud of the service that had cost him dearly. She watched the pain on his face as he talked about their brewery, lost to them forever and now run by a nitwit who knew nothing about beer and certainly had no passion for it. Their country had turned against them and taken what they had, what made them special and useful to their countrymen. Now their country was actively hunting them down and for nothing more than speaking the truth that everyone already knew. Stella wasn't sure if they knew what lie at the end of the Reich's ambitions and she certainly wasn't going to tell them. They agreed to everything she planned and it would work. She only had to convince Uncle Josiah to go along. He could be difficult at the most inopportune times, but she'd just have to persuade him that she knew what was best and not allow him to pull rank.

She closed her eyes and relaxed against the glass, letting the tiredness overtake her.

This time rank does not have its privileges.

An hour later, Rena opened Elizabeth's front door, glared at Stella, and then smacked her with a tea towel. "Why are you here? You are gone. Go. Go away."

"I'm not gone and for good reason," said Stella.

"There's no reason for you to come here again," said Rena, her face reddening. "You were to go."

"I had to stay."

"You tell me why."

"I'll tell Elizabeth."

Rena tried to shut the door and Stella stuck her foot in. Luckily she'd worn her damp boots to Westerbork and it just clunked against the good leather sole, causing no pain. "I need to see her."

"You need nothing so important." Rena's hands shook and her face was flushed.

"Is she worse?" Stella asked, hating herself for being there, but there was nowhere else to turn. She wasn't even supposed to be in Amsterdam anymore. "Please I have to—"

"Rena, what are you doing?" asked a man in a brusque Flemish accent. "The cold. You are letting the cold in."

"There's a friend here and I'm—"

A rotund man of about fifty with a short, pointed beard and round glasses yanked open the door and said, "Come in. Come in. What is this standing on the stoop? Why would you do this? We cannot have a chill in this house."

"No, no," said Rena. "She will disturb Elizabeth."

"Nonsense." The man grabbed Stella's arm and pulled her into the house. Rena gaped at him and he said, "Shut the door. What is the matter with you, Rena?"

"But Dr. Tulp, Elizabeth is so weak. She can't see anyone."

"Who are you?" Dr. Tulp asked Stella.

"Micheline Dubois," she said.

"A friend?"

"Yes."

He shook her hand and patted it, smiling kindly. His was a face formed with generosity in mind, all rounded cheeks and smile lines. "It is good to have friends at the sickbed. You have gossip and news?"

"I do, but what has happened?" Stella asked.

"Nothing that wasn't meant to happen," he said.

"She's worse," protested Rena.

He nodded. "She is, my dear woman, but keeping her friends away won't change her disease."

Rena glared and her mouth twitched with all the accusations she could levy. Stella didn't bring neighborhood gossip or news about a film star. She brought trouble. "But she'll tire her out. Get her excited."

He let go of Stella's hand and embraced Rena. It wasn't a typically Dutch thing to do and it startled the maid into silence. "You are a good woman and strong, but you cannot protect her from what is coming. Let her see her friends and occupy her mind with something other than her pain and darkness. This you can do for her."

Stella touched his sleeve. "Are you saying that…"

"She's dying." He nodded, sadly. "I cannot do anything for her and she knows this."

Rena stomped her foot. "You told her?"

"Elizabeth is a woman of keen intelligence. I did not have to tell her. She knew. She's known for some time."

Stella clutched at the collar of her coat and pictured the earl's face when she told him. The loss would be great. Elizabeth wasn't just a dear friend. She was an ally when allies were needed. "When?"

"Who can say?" The doctor got his coat and hat, hooking an umbrella over his arm before picking up his black doctor's bag. "She has spirit like few I've seen, a month, maybe two."

"Two months," whispered Rena, her eyes filling. "I didn't think…"

Dr. Tulp took her hand again, rubbing it briskly. "That would be on the long side."

"What can I do?"

"She is as comfortable as I can make her." He smiled at Stella, his face full of warmth and understanding. "You can send Micheline up to cheer her." He winked at Stella. "She looks like a woman full of interesting things to say."

Stella kept her face calm, but inside, she was startled. Maybe he was one of Elizabeth's contacts. Maybe he knew. "I will try to be entertaining."

Rena grumbled and the doctor tipped his hat to them. "I will be back this evening to check on Elizabeth."

"So soon?" Rena asked.

"Yes. The situation requires it." Dr. Tulp shooed Stella toward the stairs and left after reiterating the need for company in a time of sadness.

The door closed firmly and the women looked at each other. Stella wasn't entirely sure what Rena would do. Doctor's orders meant something to people, but Rena trusted her own instincts and they had served her well.

Stella took a breath, held it, and then said, "I'm going up."

"Take off those boots. You'll track the mud all over."

Rena turned on her heels and stomped down the hall without another word. That was almost worse than getting yelled at. It reminded Stella of her mother's quiet disappointment after she'd come back from a day at the brewery all dirty and reeking of toasted malt. Stella couldn't help that. She was who she was and this was not different. She was a Bled and going up those stairs to help her family was required if not desired.

Obediently, she took off her boots and tiptoed up so as to quiet the creaks. Rena, like Francesqua, didn't need reminding of her rebellion. She continued to tiptoe to Elizabeth's room although she didn't need to. There was a radio turned to the BBC and a distinctive upper crust voice saying, "Here is the afternoon news and Alvar Liddell reading it."

Stella knocked and the volume went down, quieting the talk of imminent invasion of France, Belgium, and The Netherlands. "Come in," called out Elizabeth.

"Sorry to bother you." Stella peeked around the edge of the door. "Can I come in?"

Elizabeth lay on the bed, looking exactly like she had when Stella left her the day before. She was wearing her nightgown and tucked up under mounds of blankets with a crackling fire in the grate. Her smile was the same, but her color no better.

"Oh, don't look like that," said Elizabeth. "Nothing's happened."

"I talked to Dr. Tulp." Stella came in and sat on the edge of the bed.

"Of course. I was wondering how you got past the Greek dragon I've employed."

"She's worried."

Elizabeth reached out with an icy cold hand and Stella took it in her warm one. "Worrying is unproductive, but she will do it. I'm very glad the good doctor was there to stop her from going overboard."

"I'm not sure I should be here."

"You wouldn't be if it wasn't important." She frowned. "Desperately important."

Stella swallowed hard. Desperately important. That was an excellent way to describe the situation. "Yes, it is."

"It kept you here, so it must be very bad. I know how much you wanted to leave."

"Did you?"

Elizabeth chuckled weakly. "I did. You had something calling you home. Someone, I suspect, but here you are. Still working."

"I'm going to trouble you."

She raised her palms. "What else have I got to do? Listen to the impending disaster that I cannot avert? I'd rather help you, if I can."

"You can. I hope you can."

"Is it about the Dereczynskis?" Elizabeth asked.

Stella drew back in horror. She'd forgotten all about Weronika, Józef, and their children. They'd disappeared like everyone else on Francesqua's list the minute Uncle Josiah had turned up. "No, not them."

"You look…ashamed."

"I am. It's just that I've got a new problem and I'd forgotten the old ones."

Elizabeth folded her hands in her lap. "Tell me."

Stella told her the story she'd concocted about Herman Milch and his German cousins. Elizabeth nodded as she told her that it was her job to get the family out of Westerbork before the invasion. She allowed herself to look and sound as frantic as she felt. Felix was in terrible shape. The hut the family had been given was nice, considering, but not nearly warm enough for him. She feared for his health and it felt good to say it out loud.

"He's in that bad a condition?" Elizabeth asked.

"Yes. To be honest, I think he should be in the hospital," said Stella. "I don't know why he isn't."

"Perhaps because they're not Jews and someone might *notice* if he's being cared for by strangers."

"Oh, right. I hadn't thought of that."

Elizabeth reached for her tea on the side table and gave Stella a sidelong look. "What aren't you telling me?"

"Nothing. I have to get them out of there. Someone's bound to figure it out and once the invasion happens…"

"Disaster for everyone there. I know, but there's something else," she said. "I can tell. What is it about this family? You've helped others. Why are they different?"

"If I don't do it, I could lose my job," said Stella.

Elizabeth waved the notion away. "You know people are more important than a job. Tell me what is really going on."

Stella searched around, trying to come up with something plausible. Elizabeth clearly wouldn't accept just any old excuse and she couldn't tell her about Uncle Josiah's love or his terror at Judith's predicament with the invasion days or even hours away. Or could she?

"Well, there is something else," she said with a sigh. "I wasn't going to mention it because it really isn't all that important."

"From the look of your face, I'd say it is," said Elizabeth.

"The girl. She has a fiancé."

"I'm not surprised from your description of her."

"He's American," said Stella.

"That is surprising. A friend of the American cousin?"

"Yes. That's how they met."

Elizabeth nodded. "A long distance love."

"Yes." Stella's mind was working so fast she could hardly answer. It had to be right and make sense if she was to make it work.

"What's the problem with this fiancé?"

"He's here."

Elizabeth drew back in surprise. "Here? In Amsterdam?"

"Yes. That's how I got this so-called job. He turned up at my hotel and told me the whole story. I confirmed with New York and now I have to figure something out immediately."

"He must be alarmed to come all this way."

"I'd call him terrified. He knows about the camps in Germany," said Stella.

"How? It's not in the newspapers, is it?"

"I don't know how he knows. I didn't ask," said Stella. "And he's looking at me and I have to do this for him, for them. If I don't…"

"You're afraid of what he'll do?"

"He won't hurt me on purpose. He's just so frantic. He would do anything to get them out."

"If he talks to the wrong person…"

"Exactly and I want to help. They are as deserving as the children we got out."

"Maybe I can telegram the earl."

"We can't do that. I've been ordered back. He doesn't know about this."

"He won't be happy. Your activities have been tolerated, but how long will they allow it?"

"I don't know," said Stella in all honesty. "If I can get it done quickly, it won't matter."

"If you don't, you won't be able to continue?"

"Probably not. It's my side interest and the interest of the company, but not what I'm here for really."

Elizabeth took a drink of tea and pondered Stella for a moment. "Why did you do it? Because of the fiancé?"

"Yes. He makes a good case and I do work for B.L. Imports technically."

"Are you saying that they're a real company?"

"Yes. Recruited by the earl. They know everything and I guess they decided to use what they have for the client when he asked."

"Does the client know about your generosity with the Jews?" Elizabeth asked.

"I doubt it. The company itself pays for the extra cost from donations."

DARK VICTORY

"So, Dilbert Rutherford III is a real person?"

"Oh, yes and I am buying for him. He's very pleased with my work," Stella lied easily. Elizabeth didn't need to know everything.

"Extraordinary." She clapped her hands together, looking more energized than Stella had ever seen her. "We have work to do."

"Then you know how to get the papers for them?" Stella asked.

"Yes, but we're going to do more than that."

Oh, no.

"We don't need more than that."

"Yes, we do," said Elizabeth. "You have to get them on a ship immediately. That can take weeks. We don't have weeks."

"Agreed. I have a lead on a friendly diplomat in Rotterdam. An American," said Stella. "I'm going to see if I can get the name."

"Why haven't you gotten it before?"

"The person couldn't remember it. They wrote to the States to find out," said Stella.

"That will take too long." Elizabeth frowned. "What are you going to do?"

"Have a telegram sent."

"That's dangerous."

"But fast." Stella leaned forward. "How long to get the papers?"

"I couldn't say. I haven't done it directly, but I still say we need more to get them out before *they* come."

"Like what?"

"How much does this American love the daughter?" Elizabeth asked.

"More than his own life, I'd say," said Stella.

"He should marry her now."

"Now?"

"Immediately. She'd be the wife of an American. That diplomat will be all the more willing to help. What is their religion?"

What do I say? What do I say?

"I...I didn't ask the family."

Elizabeth eyed her critically.

273

"They just said that they're not Jews. Probably Protestant. Most Germans are."

"What about him?"

Best to go with the truth.

"He had a rosary so, I assume, Catholic."

Elizabeth clasped her hands together. "That's perfect."

"Is it?"

"The girl will become Catholic and they will be married."

What will Felix say? The conversion was the other way around.

"I don't know if they'll agree to that," said Stella.

"If they want to get out of this country, they will," said Elizabeth, looking more suspicious.

"Of course, you're right. I just don't know them very well. I'm sure he'll be happy to marry her as soon as possible."

Elizabeth relaxed. "Good because I have a friend."

"How good a friend?" Stella asked.

"Very good. He's one of my contacts and he's been helping you for months," said Elizabeth with satisfied smile.

"Does he know a priest?"

"He is a priest."

CHAPTER 19

Despite wanting nothing more than to take a nap, Stella left the Hotel Krasnapolsky after changing her muddy boots to clean pumps and touching up her makeup and wig. No matter where she chose to go next, being presentable was absolutely necessary. The baron wasn't likely to be picky, but one never knew. If he caught her talking to Cornelia, it would be easier to talk her way out if she didn't have mud up to her ankles. There was no mud in Amsterdam and while he might be crazy, the baron was also observant.

As for the other option, Father Schoffelmeer was an unknown. Elizabeth adored him, she also described him as fussy and an all-around crank. Elizabeth had given her a letter of introduction to help her along, but his help wasn't guaranteed by any means. The thought of lying to a priest made Stella queasy enough to find herself on the way to the baron's house without giving it too much thought. The Father could wait until after she'd secured Cornelia's help and she strolled through the back streets she'd come to know so well, doing her best not to rush because Micheline didn't rush. She had patience and wasn't up to anything at all. Stella Bled Lawrence, on the other hand, was in a tight spot and wanted to run to the baron's house and pound on the door.

It looked like she wasn't the only one with a pounding heart and clenched teeth. Sunday was usually quiet with no one in a rush to do anything, but that day lots of people were out. Some had suitcases. Others just worried faces. Nobody was particularly interested in her. Everyone kept glancing up at the sky, furtive glances full of fear as if bombers were expected at any moment. Stella doubted the first sign of the invasion would be a bomber over Amsterdam, but it would happen fast and the thought made her feet move.

She turned the corner onto the baron's canal road and got the strangest feeling, a prickly kind of heat on the back of her neck. She stopped to look in a shop window and there he was. A man, like so many others, wearing an overcoat and fedora pulled low, stopped at the shop next door. It could be a coincidence, but Stella had been trained to notice and she'd noticed him outside the Hotel Krasnapolsky. His right pocket had a tear at the edge and it made him distinctive. Other than that, he was typical, short blond hair, very tall with the bone structure that tagged him as most likely Dutch. Stella turned away from the window and weighed her options, continue to the baron's or try to lose him. Losing him might tip him off that she knew he was there and show a professionalism that didn't work for her. He wasn't one of their people. She'd spotted Oliver before he'd met up with her in Rotterdam and he didn't follow her. There was no need. He'd just planted himself in the vicinity to check up, see if she were well and active. She was and he disappeared. This man wanted to know what she was up to. It was best to let him find out or at least, think he found out.

Cornelia it was. Stella walked away from the shop with a casual stride, no hurry, and looked up occasionally like everyone else seemed to do every few minutes. She reached the baron's house after a few blocks and turned down into the servant stairwell to knock on the wide lower door. It took a few minutes and she got nervous. Flore was an option, but it would be hard to explain why she wanted to telegram Yannj in the States right then and there. The old lady was so inquisitive and getting her out to send a telegram might be a challenge in itself. She'd probably never sent one in her life and was bound to talk about it.

Stella knocked again and the door finally opened. A young woman about Stella's real age looked out with wide eyes and stifling a yawn. "Yes?"

"Is Cornelia in?" Stella asked quickly. Too quickly.

The girl woke up and said, "Do you have a message? Has something happened?"

"With the invasion?"

The girl frowned. "With the baron."

"What about the baron?"

She clamped a hand over her mouth and tried to close the door, but Stella pushed it back. "It's all right. I'm a friend of Cornelia's. I was at the party on Friday. Don't you recognize me?"

The girl squinted at Stella, but nothing dawned on her. Micheline Dubois was hardly a showstopper on a night of showstopping.

Stella made herself laugh. "I don't blame you. It was quite a night. I have nightmares about the rope line."

She tried to close the door again and Stella said, "I won't mention anything to Cornelia. You have my word."

"Really?" the maid said through spread fingers.

Stella pushed her hand down. "Really. I just wanted to take Cornelia for a coffee, if she's not busy."

"She's not busy. There's nothing to do." She clamped her hand over her mouth again and Stella almost rolled her eyes.

"It's fine. Go get Cornelia." Stella wheeled the girl around and gave her a gentle push into the house. The girl dashed down the hall, calling for Cornelia and sounding like she was about to pee her pants. She was a lovely little thing, but the baron's secret wouldn't last long with her.

"Micheline!" Cornelia came down the hall and bounced off the wall, overcorrected and bounced off the other one. "What doing here?"

"Someone has been at the jenever early today," said Stella with a laugh.

Cornelia fluttered her fingers above her chest. "Who me?"

Stella rolled her eyes dramatically and said, "Let me take you for some coffee. I think you need it."

"I don't need coffee. We're to be invaded by the Huns, the nasty, disgusting Boche!"

"Let's get some coffee."

"No!" exclaimed Cornelia.

The girl was nodding emphatically and several other servants joined her. There was a consensus.

"Well," said Stella. "I want some coffee. You can have—"

"More Jenever." Cornelia grabbed Stella's arm. "I got the bottle you sent. It was so good. I drank it all."

"I see that."

"Wait a minute. You said…what did you say?"

"I have no idea," said Stella. "Let's go to the café."

"You were leaving. You sent the Jenever because you were going…somewhere."

"Home. I was going home."

Stella got in the hall and behind Cornelia to push her over the threshold. The baron's valet gave her Cornelia's coat and whispered, "Thank you."

"Don't mention it," said Stella.

"Don't mention what?" asked Cornelia. "Is it a secret?"

"There's no secret," said Stella. "We're going to the café."

"To get more Jenever?"

"Sure."

The other servants shook their heads frantically and Stella wrinkled her nose, shaking her head. She knew what to do. Years of wrangling Uncle Josiah had given her ample practice. Happy drunks were all the same. It was the mean ones you had to worry about. Cornelia was decidedly happy, despite her concern that they were about to be bombed to smithereens like London.

Stella got her up on the street and put her coat on. "London hasn't been bombed."

"All gone. It's all gone."

"You're thinking of Warsaw."

"Is that in...somewhere?" Cornelia weaved, nearly stepping into the road in front of a truck. She'd have been flattened if Stella hadn't pulled her back.

"Get yourself together," said Stella, yawning. "The baron wouldn't like this."

Cornelia raised a scraggly eyebrow and asked, "What do you know? What did that girl tell you?"

"I know that he wouldn't want his favorite maid to get run over by a truck."

She looked into the road, surprised to see vehicles there. "I should get some coffee."

"At last, we agree." Stella hooked her arm through Cornelia's and they headed down the canal toward the café.

"I can have just a little Jenever." She held up her fingers to show the small amount. It wasn't that small.

"Naturally."

"You understand me."

"I think I do."

They found the café half empty, which was unusual for a Sunday afternoon, and the people at the tables were hunched over, whispering.

"They've got secrets, too," whispered Cornelia.

"We've all got a secret," said Stella and the waiter raised his brows at them. "We're all terrified at what's coming."

"I'm not terrified," said Cornelia. "I'm mad."

"Be mad while having coffee." Stella called for two coffees and the waiter asked, "Large?"

"Very."

She moved Cornelia through a multitude of empty tables to an isolated corner, trying to decide if her drunkenness was a good thing or a bad thing. Presumably she'd be easier to convince, but she might yell, too.

The waiter brought their coffees in record time. "Might I suggest some toast?"

"Yes, please," said Stella.

"Who wants toast? Toast is for children and old ladies."

The waiter screwed up his mouth at the pair of them. He was twenty at most and from the look on his smooth young face you'd have thought they were grandmothers. Before becoming Micheline, Stella hadn't realized women aged so much faster than men. A man at Cornelia's age was in the prime of his life while she was over the hill and unimportant. Being unmarried made it all the worse.

"I have a nice brioche," he suggested, less dismissive than he might have been.

"Toast is good for indigestion," said Stella.

"I want some Jenever," said Cornelia.

"Toast and a bottle of Jenever."

The waiter pursed his lips. "I don't know about—"

"Trust me," said Stella with a hard look.

The waiter dithered back and forth, but in the end, he went to the bar and got a small bottle half full. Stella watched him walk back dragging his feet and wondered if he ever tried to deny a man of any age liquor, substituting his judgment for theirs. Somehow she doubted it.

"Thank you," she said sarcastically.

"Um…you're welcome."

She'd confused him and it felt good.

"Don't forget the toast."

He nodded. "Yes, ma'am."

Cornelia tried to grab the Jenever bottle out of Stella's hand and almost upset her coffee.

"Stop that," said Stella. "You are such a nuisance today."

Cornelia drew back and burped. "You don't mean it."

"I do. Look at yourself, all red-eyed and burping in public. What would the baron think?"

"He's in the country." She reached for the bottle again.

"I'll do it." Stella unscrewed the cap and said, "Look at that. A spider."

Cornelia looked and she poured in just the right amount to get the flavor of the liquor but not enough to sustain the high. She'd gotten Uncle Josiah sobered up against his will that way quite a few times. The trick was to ease the drunk into it. Never rush the unwilling or they'd do a runner. She'd made that mistake and had to hunt Uncle Josiah down in the seedy riverfront bars of St. Louis five hours before Uncle Nicolai's wedding. It was a nightmare.

"Here you go," she said, tapping Cornelia's cup.

The maid peered down into the blackness and Stella thought for a second that she'd go nose down in the brew, but she only wavered before picking up the cup. "I need some Jenever."

"It's already in there," said Stella, screwing on the cap and putting the bottle on the other chair.

Cornelia took a sniff. "Oh, yeah. That's the stuff." She took a good drink and relaxed. "It's been a long day."

"Has it? I thought the baron was in the country."

"Who told you that?"

"You did five seconds ago."

"Oh, well. Yes, he is."

"Is he ill?"

"Who said that?" demanded Cornelia.

"Nobody. I'm asking," said Stella with a sigh. This wasn't going to be fast and she needed fast. Maybe Flore would've been better after all. The old lady was sober at the very least.

"He's gone for a rest. The party wore him out."

"It was an extravaganza. I've heard of parties like that after the last war before the depression, but I never thought I'd see one."

They talked of the party and the guests while Cornelia sobered up. It was a long road, but about forty minutes later her eyes focused and she asked, "Did you sell that jewelry to that Bikker woman?"

"I tried, but it was going to take some doing." Stella leaned over to Cornelia conspiratorially and said, "She's not the brightest bulb and I wanted to get home, so I shipped it off to America. I'm sure they'll find some gaudy women with new money to buy it."

"So why are you still here?" Cornelia asked.

"I'm glad you asked," said Stella. "I could use some help."

"Is there a finder's fee involved? I could use the money."

"I'm sorry about the jewelry, but that's why I thought of you," said Stella smoothly although she'd forgotten all about the finder's fee that Cornelia was so keen on. "My company contacted me for a special buy, so to speak."

"Really?" Cornelia gripped her cup, eyes alight. "More jewelry?"

"Something more important. Can I count on your discretion?"

"Absolutely."

"Even from the baron?"

The maid sucked in her lips and weighed her options. "It must be a very special buy."

"With a fee to match," said Stella.

"What do I have to do?"

"Send a telegram."

Cornelia tilted her head to the side, lost her balance, and then nearly tipped herself off the chair. Stella grabbed her, yanking her upright with a laugh. "You should really cut down on the Jenever."

"I can't think of a better time to drink than now, can you?"

"As long as you send my telegram, I agree."

"How could a telegram be so important to you?" asked Cornelia before burping.

"It's not to me personally. It's important to my company." Stella explained about the new-minted Milch family and the need to get them out of the country.

"So, who am I telegramming? I don't know anyone in government. I could ask the baron to help though."

"He's in the country," said Stella.

"Oh, right." Cornelia glanced around, looking for a safe place to land. "He's having a little holiday, a rest."

"Of course. I want you to telegram Yannj. Can you do that?"

"Yannj? Why in the world?"

Stella reminded Cornelia about the American diplomat in Rotterdam that was so helpful and the maid agreed eagerly. "That's all you need?"

"That's it," said Stella. "Can you do it tonight?"

"Certainly, but how does that get me a finder's fee?"

"They're selling me their furniture, a bedroom set. You'll get the fee for that." Stella explained what to say in the telegram and had Cornelia, who was still listing to the left, repeat it several times.

"No names. No you. I understand. I'm drunk, not stupid," she said.

"It's the drunk I'm worried about."

Out of the corner of Stella's eye, she saw him come in, the man with the torn pocket, and loiter around the door. The waiter approached him and then waved his arm over the room, indicating that he could take a seat wherever he liked. The man took off his coat and hat and Stella got a good look. It was definitely the same man. It couldn't be a coincidence. The only difference was in his expression. It'd been mild and disinterested before as befitted the job he was doing. Now he looked crabby and cold with an inflamed nose as he came into the tables, weaving his way through multiple empty tables to plant himself as close to them as he could without butting up against their table.

Got tired of waiting outside? Ah. Such a shame. Idiot.

"This is important for my job," said Stella. "I could get a promotion."

"Really?" Cornelia asked. "It matters that much?"

Stella shrugged. "To somebody."

"Your client will be happy if you get it done."

"I think so. I've heard he gives bonuses. I could use a bonus and a holiday."

Cornelia drained her cup and dabbed at the corners of her mouth, very dignified like she hadn't just been about to fall off her chair. "You deserve a holiday. How long have you been traveling?"

"Months and I'm worn out," said Stella, finishing her own coffee.

"You look it."

"Thanks."

Cornelia laughed. "I didn't mean it that way, but you're tired. Who wouldn't be? You haven't been home in a long time."

"I'd like to sleep in my own bed for a change. I can hardly remember what it feels like."

"Get this thing done and you can go home, right?" Cornelia asked.

"Yes. I just hope they don't find anything else for me to buy or any more clients," said Stella.

"You better hurry then. You keep trying to leave and it never works out for you."

"Maybe I should stop reading their telegrams."

Cornelia threw up her hands. "Oh, sir, I had no idea there was another client."

Stella threw up her own hands. "Too bad. I went home."

The women laughed together and the waiter came over. "More coffee, ladies?"

They looked at each other and Cornelia said, "No, I should get back. Who knows what they'll get up to if I'm gone too long."

Stella insisted on paying the bill and the waiter helped them on with their coats. Torn Pocket sat uneasily at his table, picking at the pastry he'd ordered and glancing at his watch.

The waiter opened the door for them and wished them a good afternoon. Stella put on her hat, tweaking the brim while stealing a glance into the café. Torn Pocket was getting up.

"Micheline," said Cornelia as she buttoned her top button. "Did you see that man at the table next to us?"

"I did. Why?"

"He got awfully close."

Stella looked up in surprise. "I thought so, too."

"I think he was trying to listen to our conversation," said Cornelia.

"Do you? Why?"

"Because I know him. He works for Jan Bikker. He does security for his hotels."

Well, how do you like that.

"That's concerning," said Stella.

"And he came to see the baron."

Stella hooked her arm through Cornelia's and they walked toward the corner. "What did the baron say?"

"Nothing. He was already in the country. Kraan—he's the butler—

answered the door. I heard them talking. His name is Mussert and he was asking about you."

They stopped at the corner and hugged. Torn Pocket came out of the café and dawdled by the door, fiddling with his coat and hat. He might be security, but he was not a professional.

"What did Kraan say about me?"

Cornelia chuckled. "He said he didn't know you."

"I guess that makes sense. I've only been to the baron's that once and today, of course."

"Oh, he knows who you are. He's a servant. It's his business to know who the baron's guests are, but he wouldn't tell that klojo a thing about the baron's friends."

"Or yours?" Stella asked.

"Or mine."

They exchanged cheek kisses.

"Should I send the name to your hotel?" Cornelia asked.

"I'll come to the house when I need the name," said Stella.

"He's watching us."

"I know."

The women parted ways, going in opposite directions. Cornelia went home to the baron's to get Yannj's address and Stella toward Father Schoffelmeer's church. She wasn't entirely sure where Torn Pocket would go. He could be suspicious of Cornelia and think she was more important, so Stella stopped to dig in her handbag for a small tin of mints. Torn Pocket stopped half a block from her and looked in the window of a tailor shop that had gone out of business.

Honestly. A shuttered shop? You're pathetic.

Stella popped a mint in her mouth and checked the time. It was an unnecessary delay and she was so worn out, but she enjoyed tormenting him. He deserved it. He'd ruined her plans. Clearly, he thought she was some dumb, middle-aged woman who couldn't possibly notice what a stealthy man like himself was up to and it galled her. She had half a mind to stomp right up and tell him how lousy he was at the job he was probably being paid way too much to do, but she couldn't. She had to let him think he was good and cement the idea that she was no one special, just a woman doing a job she didn't want to do.

She tucked her handbag in the crook of her arm and walked down the street, turning twice. Then she peered up at a street sign, looked around to backtrack but turned the wrong way on the right street. Stella led Mussert aka Torn Pocket around the back streets of Amsterdam for an hour, feigning confusion, and pulling out a small map, time and time again to no avail. She hoped he'd get sick of her stupidity and give up so she could make her way to Father Schoffelmeer, but unskilled or not, he just kept following. He was getting irritated though. Her glimpses of his face showed her his nose running and grim expression. And he was getting closer, no longer bothering to keep even a remotely reasonable distance. Once when she spun around to change direction, she'd run right into him. After she apologized, she'd hurried off with her map and there he was right behind.

After an hour of this song and dance, she began to get worried that his frustration would boil over and he'd march up to give her a good crack on the head to put himself out of his misery. He had that kind of face and it had been an hour, plenty of time to convince him that she was a dizzy broad up to nothing much, so Stella went into a bar and asked directions, even bringing the barman outside so he could literally point her in the right direction. There was Mussert, standing on the corner blowing his nose into a sopping handkerchief and looking like he would cheerfully strangle kittens if he could just be done with her.

It was time.

She thanked the barman and tipped him before finding her way back to the Hotel Krasnapolsky. The priest would have to wait. Maybe it was better at that. She could find him at the rectory in the evening after his day was done. He wouldn't be happy, but it couldn't be helped.

When she got back, Daan rushed over to open the door for her and said, "Chilly evening."

"It is. I'm glad to be back."

"Business on Sunday?"

"No, just a coffee with a friend. I do love your cafés."

"They are the best in the country."

She went inside and found Uncle Josiah at the front desk. He leaned on the polished wood with ankles crossed, looking every bit the pointless playboy he was thought to be and had been most of his life. The clerk smiled up at him and batted her eyelashes. She bought it. Of course, she did. Josiah could flirt with the best of them. Clark Gable had nothing on him and he could do it all day. He probably had, waiting for a glimpse of her.

Stella went to walk past the desk to the elevator and Uncle Josiah looked up, quickly changing his demeanor. She gave him the smallest shake of her head, but he moved for her. Rather than having to snub him, she called out to Ludwik who was sitting in a room behind reception with the door open.

The concierge jerked awake and looked out the door. "Oh, Micheline."

"I don't mean to bother you," she said.

He stifled a yawn. "It's no bother. I wasn't…"

Awake.

"…doing anything. What can I help you with?"

"Just some tea. It's cold out there." She rubbed her shoulders for effect and Uncle Josiah got the message, going back to the clerk who was saying something about a restaurant with fabulous Oysters Rockefeller. "They're American, aren't they?"

"The oysters?" Uncle Josiah grinned at her and she giggled.

"I'll bring the tea right up," said Ludwik. "Let me walk you to the elevator."

Stella was afraid he had more news about Bikker nosing around, but he just wanted to know if she was doing all right.

"I'm fine," she said. "Why do you ask?"

"You just look so tired."

She laughed. "You should talk."

Ludwik ducked his head. "It was a long night."

A.W. HARTOIN

"So I gather," she said. "Have you found out who was in my room yet?"

The concierge's face got serious. "We have a good idea, but we will be questioning a few more people before we're sure."

"That's fine. I just don't want it to happen again."

"Of course not. I'll have your tea brought up immediately."

The elevator arrived and she rode up to her floor, chitchatting with a man she didn't know very well about the invasion like it was a new film coming out. The operator wasn't terribly concerned. He had faith in the government and oddly in the Nazis. They wouldn't be so cowardly as to attack a neutral country. The world wouldn't stand for it. He seemed to forget that the world was standing for just about anything those days, but she didn't bring it up.

"Have a nice evening, ma'am," he said with a sweet smile.

"I'm sure I will." Stella went to her room, tossing her hat and coat on a chair before checking to see if anyone else had been in there rooting around, but everything was as she left it. It was still early, only five, so she ran a bath and tea came before it was even full.

She thanked the young waiter, tipping him well, and then poured her tea.

"Let's see, shall we?" Stella kicked off her shoes and went to the window with her cup to look out at the square. Sure enough, there he was, miserable as all get out, huddled by a cab and going nowhere.

Stella sipped her piping hot tea and he shivered while staring at the front door as if that were the only door. Idiot.

CHAPTER 20

Stella hadn't planned on sleeping. She'd taken her bath and crawled into bed to drink the rest of her tea, but she hadn't gotten that far. The tea was on the side table and Stella was under the covers, still wearing her robe with a towel twisted around her head.

Someone had knocked, but she could only vaguely remember it. She must've told them to go away. So tired. Even opening her eyes was such effort. She grabbed her watch and groaned. Two. It was too late to go see the priest. Priests didn't stay up until all hours, did they? She closed her eyes and fell back asleep before answering the question.

Knock. Knock. Knock.

"Micheline!"

"For crying out loud," she grumbled and pulled a pillow over her towel-wrapped head.

A key rattled in the lock.

Oh, my God!

Stella sat bolt upright and spotted her wig lying on the floor. She grabbed it and stuffed it under the blankets. "Who is it?" Her voice came out hoarse and low.

The doorknob turned and Stella quickly checked the towel in the mirror on the dressing table. In place. Hair hidden.

"I'm not decent," she called out and jumped back in bed.

"Micheline?"

The door opened and Ludwik peeked in through the crack. "Are you all right in there?"

She smoothed the covers. "Come in, Ludwik. I fell asleep."

Ludwik crept into the darkened room like she might scream or accuse him of something. "Micheline, how are you?"

"Fine. Why do you keep asking that?" She frowned as she said it. Her voice sounded terrible and her throat scratchy. She must've been snoring. So embarrassing.

"It's just that you didn't come down," he said.

"I'm sorry if I was snoring." She cleared her throat and took a big gulp of cold tea, thankful for the gloom so he couldn't see her makeup-free face.

"I don't know if you were snoring. You are well, yes?"

"Yes. I'm incredibly tired but fine. Kind of you to check on me."

"Would you like a tray?"

"Now?"

Ludwik tilted his head, not unlike Cornelia, except he didn't try to topple over. "You should eat if you are unwell."

"I'm not unwell." She cleared her throat again. "I only need a good night's sleep."

His head tilted further. "Micheline, it's nearly two."

"In the morning?"

"The afternoon. We were worried. You are always an early riser."

She looked at the window and bright light was shining between the heavy shades. "It's tomorrow?"

He smiled. "It's today. You slept a long time. Should I call a doctor?"

"I don't need a doctor," said Stella. "I guess I was tired."

She was still tired. Dog tired as the men at the brewery would've said. What was wrong with her? She felt fine, except her eyes wanted to close.

"Maybe you should stay in bed," Ludwik suggested.

"I wish I could, but I've got furniture to see. People are waiting."

He began to wring his hands and said, "I have to tell you that we found the culprit."

"Culprit?" She swung her feet from under the covers, holding her towel in place.

"The person who broke into your room."

"Oh, that." She yawned. "I'd forgotten."

Ludwik stuck a finger in the pocket of his waistcoat and fished out the ring. He placed it on her dressing table, where it managed to look gaudier than ever, even in the dim light.

"That's a relief. My company. The insurance. It would've been difficult."

"We are very sorry and we want you to know that it's been taken care of."

Stella widened her eyes and said, "Who was it?"

He made a face. "That is difficult."

"Why?"

Ludwik told her and it was difficult. The hotel believed Marga was the one who'd gotten a key from housekeeping and gone into her room. She'd been seen in the head of housekeeping's office and on Stella's floor. Marga denied it, so the politie were called and they searched the flat she shared with Ester. The ring was found in Ester's belongings. The girl was hysterical, decrying her innocence. Marga, on the other hand, didn't look at all surprised but did a good deal of crying, which didn't surprise anyone. Marga was always a crier.

"Marga put the ring in Ester's things, so she would be blamed?" Stella asked. "What kind of girl is she?"

"The stupid kind," he said. "We have fired them both and you will have to decide whether or not to press charges."

This was the last thing Stella needed. Her mind was foggy and she should've been out the door six hours ago, maybe seven. Uncle Josiah would be going out of his mind.

"I don't want to press charges. It would be unkind with what is going to happen," she said.

"You mean with them coming."

"Yes, and nobody knows what is going to happen. There's no need to make it worse."

"You know that Ester and Marga are Jews?" asked Ludwik surprised.

"I had heard that," said Stella.

"They shouldn't have made an enemy of you." He hesitated and then said, "I've heard things about how you do business."

"I know. Madam Milla told me, but you shouldn't believe all you hear."

"Some things you should believe and be thankful for."

"Ludwik, are you Jewish?" she asked.

He retreated to the door as if pushed by a stiff wind. "My grandmother was."

One fourth. Will they hate him for that much?

"No one needs to know that."

"I've heard things about Germany. When they come, there will be questions?"

"Yes. Don't tell anyone. You will be all right," said Stella. "This isn't Poland."

"If it was Poland?"

"You don't want to know." She stood up, holding her robe tightly closed, and Ludwik opened the door to leave. "About Ester," she said.

"What about her?" he asked.

"You don't think Ester had anything to do with coming in here and stealing from me, do you?"

Ludwik shook his head sadly. "No, I don't. Jan Bikker was talking to Marga. He tried to get her to help him get in your room, but Ester avoided him. He scares her."

She's the smart one.

"I know. Michel told me before his attack," said Stella. "Do you think Marga will tell the truth to save Ester's job?"

"No. I had hoped to protect them when *they* came, but now I can't."

"Don't fire Ester. It's not her fault."

"She was caught with the ring, Micheline," said Ludwik. "It's done."

"Then undo it."

"It's not up to me."

"Who is it up to?" Stella asked.

"Mr. De Jong, the manager, but he won't be receptive. This is a stain on the hotel," said Ludwik, wringing his hands harder.

"There's no stain as far as I'm concerned," said Stella assuming the full dignity of Micheline Dubois despite feeling like she wanted to curl up in her mother's lap and be coddled for the whole day. "Is he in?"

"I'm afraid not. He has a cold."

"Who can I speak to then?" she asked.

"Mr. Elek is in charge, but he won't change Mr. De Jong's decision," said Ludwik.

I bet he will.

"Let me talk to him," said Stella. "I'm a good guest and it was my ring. That should count for something."

"I don't know. Maybe."

There's no maybe about it.

Stella stepped on the elevator and Michel gave her a hard look. "You look worse than me and I had a heart attack yesterday."

"Oh, you did not, you old faker," she said with a yawn.

He chuckled and closed the door. "I got time off and my wife made my favorite soup. I should have heart attacks more often."

"Don't push it." Stella leaned on the wall and closed her eyes.

"Are you sure you should be up?"

"I have things to do."

"With your eyes closed?"

"My company isn't picky," she said.

He stopped the elevator on the ground floor and said softly, "I wish you could've gone home."

She touched his sleeve. "You are the sweetest man, but I'll be fine. Everything will be fine. Which way to Mr. De Jong's office?"

He gave her directions and asked, "Are you complaining about the incident with the ring?"

"In a manner of speaking."

"He's out sick," said Michel. "You'll have to wait."

"No waiting. I'll be talking to Mr. Elek."

"He's more difficult than Mr. De Jong. A real stickler for the rules."

Her eyebrows went up under the frizz of her wig. "Oh, really?"

"What are you thinking, Micheline?"

"Only that Ester needs her job," said Stella. "Wish me luck."

"Um…good luck. You're going to need it."

She winked at him. "No, I'm not."

Stella left the operator looking confused and walked past the front desk. Uncle Josiah wasn't there flirting with the clerk, another pretty girl or anywhere in the lobby thankfully. She'd deal with him later. One problem at a time.

She went through the bowels of the Hotel Krasnapolsky, encountering no one on the way, which was unusual, but the hotel had emptied out as the invasion grew nearer with people only staying a day or so on their way through to what they hoped was safety. Stella suspected that the staff was, like Ludwik, catching up on sleep. There wouldn't be much of that in the coming weeks and she half expected to find Mr. Elek stretched out on his former secretary's desk catching a few Zs, but the middle office was empty as before with both Mr. De Jong's and Mr. Elek's doors closed.

"Mr. Elek," she called out and knocked on his door.

"Come in!"

She opened the door to find an office so neat it was a wonder anyone worked in there let alone a man. Stella's experience with men and offices was extensive. Her father, an exacting man if there ever was one, left a terrible mess in his office daily. It took two secretaries to clean up after him and it was the same with Uncle Nicolai and the rest of the Bled executive staff. The family took away Uncle Josiah's office, but that was mainly because it wasn't used for brewery business at all, rather things that ought not be discussed in polite company. It was a mess though and the earl was no better. Aggie, his wife, cleaned up after him. Park-Welles was neat as a pin, but she hardly considered him a man. He was more robot than anything.

Stella went to stand in front of the desk, but Mr. Elek didn't look up immediately. He stayed hunched over a huge ledger with rows of neat figures written in a copperplate hand with a Hamann Manus calculator sitting on the desk next to him. The brewery accountant had a similar machine and he'd tried to teach Stella to use it, but the thing was full of levers and pointers and such an unwieldy thing she couldn't comprehend it any more than Russian and the poor accountant had to tell her father she was unteachable. Stella had to scrub wort kettles for a month as a punishment and the accountant was given a better parking space for putting up with her. Rather unfair in Stella's opinion, but she had no say in the matter.

"Did you—" Mr. Elek looked up and jerked in surprise. "Oh, I thought you were someone else." He jumped up to offer her a chair. "Please sit down. The chef was coming and I had the figures to do."

Stella sat down and smiled. Discombobulated. That was helpful. "It's quite all right. I only wanted to speak with you about our situation."

He swallowed hard and then sat down to look at her with that handsome face of his. "Our situation?"

What in the world do you see in Anna?

"The theft in my room," she said pleasantly and watched him shift in his seat. "I don't think the outcome is quite what I had in mind."

"You were told…what happened?" he asked.

"I was."

"Madame Dubois—"

"Micheline," she said.

He nodded and smiled. "Micheline, we believe we found the culprit and she has been dismissed. You're welcome to speak to our witnesses, if you like."

"Culprit?"

His forehead creased and he became adorable rather than merely handsome. Not many perfect-looking men could do that. Nicky couldn't. "Yes. What are you getting at?"

"You think that Marga Kübler broke into my room and stole a ring," she said.

"We do and we have quite a bit of evidence to that effect, including the ring. Do you wish to press charges?"

"No, I don't," said Stella, settling into her chair comfortably while he got more and more uncomfortable. "My point is that you have fired two people when only one committed the crime."

Mr. Elek blew out a breath and loosened up. "The ring was found in Ester's things."

"Put there by Marga, undoubtedly because she thought no one would look in her friend's things."

He nodded. "Probably."

"So, you admit Ester had nothing to do with it?"

"That's what we think, but she can't prove it."

"Mr. Elek—"

"Please, call me Willem." He smiled at her with genuine warmth and Stella thought that Anna must be plum out of her mind to choose Jan Bikker over the man behind that desk.

"Willem, it's very hard to prove one's innocence, don't you think?"

"I suppose it is, but we can't have a reputation for keeping staff that steal from our guests," he said.

"You can have a reputation for being fair and doing what is right, especially at this time."

He frowned, making himself adorable once again. "At this time?"

Stella lowered her eyelids to half-mast just the way her grandmother did when she was about to convince you that you were a terrible person who had done nothing but disappoint her. It worked on everyone but Uncle Josiah. He thought it was funny. "Ester is a Jew. Where else do you think she'll get a job with the Nazis coming any day now?"

"Oh, I…didn't know that was common knowledge," said Willem, back to being flustered.

"A lot of things aren't common knowledge, but that doesn't mean they aren't *known*."

The man squirmed exactly the way Stella's father did when Grandmother confronted him on not going to mass or being indifferent to her charitable efforts. "What do you…I don't know what…"

"Willem, you have a chance to do the right thing here. I would like you to do it."

"I can't change Mr. De Jong's decision," he said.

Stella crossed her arms and then her legs. "I think you can and you should."

"Why do you care so much about this girl? Do you even know her?"

"I know she's young and vulnerable. Ester's worst crime is having a terrible friend and I believe she deserves a second chance and a safe haven," said Stella. "I'd hate to think I was the cause of her ruin when I could do something to stop it so here I am."

"We didn't ruin her," he said.

"What do you think is going to happen when *they* come? Everything will just go on as they have? Let me assure you that is not going to happen and I think *you* of all people know that."

"Me? Why would I know anything about it?" Willem couldn't keep his hands still. They fluttered around the desk, touching everything and picking up nothing.

"Think of the opportunity you have here in this hotel, Willem. Think of who you could help as you have been helped."

He stared at her, his face colorless. She could see his mind working and questioning. Did she know? How? What should he do? She'd done the same thing plenty, but hopefully she was better at covering it.

"I can't…"

"The fact that you are sitting behind that desk says you can. If properly motivated, that is," she said. "Am I properly motivating you, *Willem* Elek?"

His mouth moved, but he didn't speak.

"Never choose wrong when you can choose right. Let's choose right."

"By doing what?"

Stella stood up, looked out at the empty office, and then closed the door. "Ester Isaksohn could become Martina Strik, for instance."

"How would I—"

"Or Anna Bikker," said Stella, leaning on the door. "That's a nice name."

"Are you…"

"No. I'm asking you not to fire an innocent girl days before an invasion by the Nazis of all people. I think you can help her and I want you to do it."

"And if I don't?"

Channeling her grandmother, Stella said, "I will be gravely disappointed but not as disappointed as you will be in yourself." She opened the door and stepped out before saying. "Willem, do the right thing. It's not something you'll regret."

He slumped back in his chair the way her father did and sighed. "Micheline, you are not a regular businesswoman, just out to make money."

"Let's just keep that under our hats, shall we? I wouldn't want to get a reputation for being soft. How could I ever drive another hard bargain?"

Willem smiled and returned to adorable. "No one would accuse you of not driving a hard bargain."

"I do the right thing whenever possible," she said.

"I had heard that."

"Good. I'm glad to hear it." That wasn't exactly true. Stella was starting to think there wasn't anyone who didn't know about her. She said goodbye and closed the door on a young man who now had something more important to do than just accounts.

"Micheline!" Dirk rushed over to her from behind the bar. "We were very worried about you."

"I'm sorry to get everyone upset," Stella said. "I overslept."

The café manager looked her over and then insisted on feeling her forehead. "You are a touch warm."

"I'm a touch exhausted. I would love some coffee."

"Yes, yes, of course." Dirk led her to her usual table and rushed off to get a coffee and an omelet. He said she needed eggs for the strength. Stella wasn't aware that eggs had strength-giving properties, but there was no talking Dirk out of it, so she agreed. As long as it came with coffee, she'd have eaten practically anything.

While she waited, she gazed out at the square, yawning and hopefully not looking terribly interested as her eyes roamed around looking for Mussert with the torn pocket, but the square was mostly empty. A few people rushed here and there, looking up at the sky and then hunching over to rush off.

Dirk came back with a large cup and her own pretty little pot. "Newspaper?" he offered.

"Is the news all bad?"

"Are you German?"

"Definitely not."

"Then it's bad."

She held out her hand. "I guess I'd better be informed."

He handed her the paper and asked, "Will you get to go home soon to be with your family?"

"I hope so," she said. "I'm praying for no more telegrams."

He laughed and went to greet a couple who came in for tea. She poured a cup of coffee and gave herself an obscene amount of cream before opening the paper. The headlines were all bad with everything from questioning whether Queen Wilhelmina should leave the country and where she would go if she did to suspending football for fear of attack. She sipped her coffee and felt the warmth spread through her hoping that it would wake her up, but it only made her feel anxious.

"Micheline Dubois! You caused all kinds of fuss today."

Oh, no.

Stella lowered the paper to find Uncle Josiah leaning on the chair opposite with casual indifference. His eyes were anything but.

"Did I?"

"The whole staff was thinking you'd had a fit in your room or gone apoplectic," said Uncle Josiah with a laugh.

"I overslept. That's all."

His fingers drummed on the chair and she reluctantly asked him to sit down. She really hadn't had enough coffee yet.

"Don't mind if I do." He sat down and Dirk came over with Stella's omelet.

"Can I get you some coffee, Josiah?" Dirk asked.

"And a little hair of the dog, if you don't mind. It was a late night."

Dirk laughed. "I heard." And he went off to find whatever would ease the hangover that Uncle Josiah didn't have. Stella knew him too well to think he'd been drinking like he normally would.

He leaned back in his chair and stretched out his long legs, crossing them at the ankles and put his hands behind his head. "What do you think you're doing?"

"Hello, sweetheart," said Stella sarcastically. "How are you? I was worried you like the hotel staff. People that *aren't blood related*."

"People that don't know that you're half the age you appear to be," he said, smiling broadly.

"Not half. How old do you think I am?"

"Forty?"

I'm getting too good at this makeup.

"I am not forty, Mr. Bled," said Stella as Dirk came up with a cup and a bottle of Jameson's. The café manager's eyes went wide and he quickly said, "Micheline is very tired."

Uncle Josiah laughed and said, "I didn't mean to offend you. I'm not seeing straight. Too much of that good Jenever that you turned me on to, Dirk."

"I'm glad you liked it." Dirk looked up and then rushed off to greet more customers. He was alone in the café since Marga and Ester had been fired.

"I repeat," said Uncle Josiah once Dirk was out of earshot. "What do you think you're doing?"

"Having coffee and an omelet, although I can't tell you why I'm having an omelet. I've never been less hungry in my life."

"Don't change the subject. I'm serious."

"Seriously crazy if you think I'm not doing my best." Stella forked a bite of omelet and ate it with gusto.

Uncle Josiah sat up straight and poured a small amount of whiskey in his cup. "I know that, sweetheart, but I've been going out of my mind."

"I'm sure."

"I came to your room, but you didn't answer."

"That was you? Are you crazy?"

"We've established that I am. Certified. Have you seen them? How are they? How is she? What did she say? Can you do it?"

Stella yawned and said, "Please calm yourself. Everything's fine."

"Is it? You've told me nothing."

"I'm figuring it out."

"How? By lying in bed?" he asked.

"Do you want to do this? 'Cause I'll hand it over and good luck to you," said Stella while smiling at her furious uncle who could barely contain himself.

"I can't do it."

"Then leave me alone. I will figure it out."

"Sweetheart…is she all right?"

His eyes pleaded with her and her heart twisted a little. She wished her grandmother could see him now. She would wonder who this person was, wearing a Josiah Bled suit and worrying about people's welfare. "She's fine, but I don't think the father is in great shape."

"He hasn't been for a long time," he said, and she gave him a look. "Oh, I see. So, it's really not good."

"Correct."

"Have you gotten anywhere?"

"I have, but you can't press me. This isn't easily done and it isn't fast."

"Then why were you wasting time on some thieving waitress?"

"I was choosing to do right when it was easier to do wrong."

He grimaced. "Don't be using Florence against me. Our situation is desperate."

"So is the waitress,'" she said.

He made a grumbling noise in his throat.

"You would've done the same, if you weren't out of your mind."

"I doubt it."

"I don't," she said before letting out a huge yawn. "But it's sorted now."

He poured himself some of her coffee with a grin at her complaints and Dirk came up to replace the pot with a fresh one. "Do you need anything else, Micheline?"

"I'll just have a little more coffee and be on my way," she said. "I've got furniture to see and friends to meet."

"Don't tire yourself out," said Dirk.

She started to open her handbag, but Uncle Josiah said, "Put it on my tab. She's good company," he grinned, "for a Belgian."

"Josiah." Dirk laughed. "He's joking, Micheline."

"I am not. Remind me to tell you about the time I was arrested in Antwerp."

"Is there any city you haven't been arrested in, Mr. Bled?" Stella asked.

"I'll have to get back to you on that, Micheline Dubois, but I can reiterate that you are good company."

Stella finished her coffee and stood up. "On that cheering note, I'm off. Have a lovely day, gentlemen, and Mr. Bled—"

"Josiah," he said quickly.

"Josiah, try not to get into trouble. It sounds like you find it wherever you go."

"That's about the size of it." He grinned at her and then turned to Dirk. "Now about Antwerp."

CHAPTER 21

Stella knew the Basilica of St. Nicholas and had loved it from afar. It was close to the main train station and she'd often found reason to walk by to admire the big building shoehorned in between small insignificant ones. Its architecture and symmetry appealed to her in a time when nothing was so neat and tidy as two towers flanking a rose window with a beautiful dome behind. She'd never been inside, of course. Micheline Dubois was created a Protestant and had no reason to go there, except now she did.

She'd left Uncle Josiah jawing with Dirk in the café and had gone up to get her coat and hat. But instead of going out the front where Mussert might be waiting, she went out the service entrance that was nearly a half a block away from the square and went the long way around. No one followed her and if they had somehow managed to escape her notice, she'd lost them by jumping in a cab on a whim.

Unfortunately, there was no other choice but to have the driver drop her right in front of the basilica out in the open. Other churches in other cities had back and side entrances. Sometimes they were locked, but you could usually find one that wasn't. Uncle Josiah had taught her that. Grandmother would keep a beady eye on the main doors, waiting for Uncle Josiah to show up for mass. Nine times out of ten, he didn't, but occasionally, just to keep his mother on her toes, he'd turn up in the pews and she wouldn't know how he got there. There was a back out-of-the-way door that was never locked and he'd just tell Grandmother that she was losing it. He'd been there the whole time.

St. Nicholas wasn't like that. It butted up to a canal in the back and there wasn't an inch of space on either side. She'd have to go in the front and the thought made her queasy. Micheline wasn't well-known in Amsterdam, but she was known and it was taking a chance that had the potential to sink her.

The cab driver stopped and she paid him, stepping out onto the cobbled street. Across the way was the train station, busy by the sound of it, but Prins Hendrikkade was practically empty, making her all the more noticeable. Forcing herself to be calm, she stood on the sidewalk and checked her watch. Casual. No hurry. Then she walked over to the wrought iron fence and swung open the gate. Space was at a premium in Amsterdam, so she stepped from the gate right onto the steps up to the front doors of the basilica. They were nice doors, polished wood with six panels and iron grills at the top, nothing like the huge ornate doors of Venice. There were no knobs or door handles, so she was lucky that the third set on the right had been left open.

Stella walked inside and a rush of comfort came over her. The smell. The chill in the air. The gloom. The feeling of family that always accompanied the faint scent of incense. She went through the vestibule and opened the interior doors to see a magnificent interior that wasn't particularly old but still beautiful in a combination of styles, mostly baroque and renaissance, her favorites. She indulged herself by walking down the nave to admire the rose window and the paintings. It was all dark and mysterious in jewel tones, made more beautiful by those knelt in prayer. There were quite a few parishioners for a weekday afternoon, but she could see the appeal. It felt safe in St. Nicholas' and almost nowhere else did.

She looped around and went back down a side aisle to see the chapel devoted to Mary and then she found a small door tucked away.

It wasn't marked and she was hesitant to knock, but there had to be an office or meeting room somewhere.

"Hello?" a woman said behind her.

Stella turned and nearly gasped in surprise. The woman was a nun in full habit, but she'd rarely seen this type of garb. American Carmelite nuns wore the bandeau and veil, but this nun had something more like a large bonnet with a veil over the top. The habit itself was the same, but it seemed larger and stiffer, like the woman wearing it.

"Did I startle you? I'm sorry," she said in a warm musical voice, nothing like her thin-lipped exterior.

"Yes, but I was thinking, worrying actually, so it's not your fault." Stella decided to be honest. That was best with nuns.

"This is the place to be if you are worried. You are one of the faithful?"

Please forgive me.

"I am a faithful Protestant. I've come to see Father Schoffelmeer. Is he in?"

Stella thought the nun frowned, but it was hard to tell her face was so far back in the bonnet. "He is. May I recommend you see Father Brandsma? He is visiting."

"Well, I…"

"Did I hear my name?"

The woman turned and there was a man wearing the brown robes of a simple friar.

"Father Brandsma, this lady would like to speak with someone," said the nun.

"Very good," he said pleasantly. "This is not my parish, but I am happy to speak with you."

Stella didn't know what to say. It was a bit of a stroke of luck. She knew of Brandsma. He was virulently anti-Nazi and well-known for it. Several of Stella's contacts had suggested reaching out to him, but she'd held off after hearing how outspoken he was. His was the kind of passion that wouldn't end well and she thought it was better to let the earl think it over rather than act on her own.

"I was to speak with Father Schoffelmeer," said Stella.

Brandsma definitely frowned. He had a high forehead under a crop of thick greying hair that was swept back and hid nothing. "I can help you."

"Is there something wrong?" Stella asked.

They both shook their heads, a little too much. "No, no," they said in unison.

"Father Schoffelmeer isn't at his best at the moment," said Father Brandsma.

"He's ill?" Stella asked.

"He's indisposed."

What does that mean?

"Well, a friend of his sent me to speak to him, so perhaps I should just wait."

Father Brandsma's eyebrows went up a fraction of an inch and Stella thought she saw something in his eyes, a kind of understanding. "We wouldn't want to disappoint his friend. If you were sent in search of Father Schoffelmeer, I will take you to him."

"Father, I don't know if you should," said the nun. "He's…"

"It will be fine, Sister Teresia." He reached out for Stella's arm and she went willingly, even though the nun looked as though she was going toward a firing squad.

"The Sister is a little nervous, my dear," he said, opening the little door and ushering her through into a kind of wardrobe and then into some offices. None of the doors were labeled, but he stopped at one and turned to her. "May I ask who the friend is?"

Should she tell him or not? It was hard to say, but a friendship would be known, although it didn't sound like friends were Father Schoffelmeer's usual thing. "Her name is Elizabeth Keesing."

"I know this name. The lady is very ill, I understand."

"Yes, very ill."

He placed his hands in the prayer position. "Is she in need of the last rites?"

"Not yet."

"She told you about Father Schoffelmeer?"

"Told me what?" Sweat started to run down her sides. Why was this so difficult? She just wanted to see a priest.

"He is not always an easy man."

She blew out a breath. "Oh, that. She told me. He's crabby apparently."

The priest chuckled. "You could put it that way. Are you sure I can't help you?"

Stella bit her lip and then said, "You might be able to, but I must do as Elizabeth requests first."

He nodded.

"I can hear you out there!" yelled a gruff voice from inside.

Father Brandsma winced. "Can I—"

"Are you coming in or do I have to drag you in?" yelled the voice.

Father Brandsma opened the door and the voice practically shouted, "Oh, it's you. Go away. I don't want any, Titus."

"I know that, Max, and I'm not here for myself. You have a visitor."

"I don't want that either."

"Be that as it may." The priest waved Stella in, whispering, "Be patient."

"I heard that," bellowed the voice.

Stella swallowed hard and steeled herself for anything from thrown objects to spitting, but she didn't need to worry. Father Schoffelmeer sat on an armchair in a small library with his feet up on a hassock. Books covered the walls top to bottom and other than a little lamp on a tiny side table and an electric heater in brown Bakelite, the room was empty.

"Who are you?" Father Schoffelmeer demanded.

"Please," said Father Brandsma. "She's come from your friend, Elizabeth."

"Friend? I have no friends. She hasn't visited in weeks and here I am, day after day. I might as well be dead for all she cares." The priest glared at Stella and she was at a loss. She'd known plenty of priests and a couple had been quite frustrated with her. Stella wasn't good at learning her catechisms, but none had yelled or complained about dying from neglect.

Father Brandsma took Stella's arm and brought her in to stand by the heater. "The Father exaggerates. We are looking after him."

The priest scowled. He had what should've been a jolly face, rounded with pink cheeks and a ring of fluffy white hair on his mostly bald head. "I asked for tea three hours ago. Do you see any tea? Do you?"

"It was thirteen minutes ago and I'm sure it's coming."

"Everyone is always sure. The doctors are sure. The papers are sure. The Holy Father is sure."

Father Brandsma sighed. "You just have to rest."

"I've been resting." He whipped off the blanket over his feet and revealed his big toes and ankles swollen to epic proportions. "Does that look better to you?"

"Oh, my goodness," Stella burst out. "She didn't tell me you were sick."

His face softened slightly. "What did the good Elizabeth tell you?"

Father Brandsma still stood by her side and the door was open, so Stella said, "That you were helpful and kind."

He pointed at her. "Liar!"

She stomped her foot. "I was trying to be nice, but I can see there's no point in it. She said you were crabby and difficult. Happy?"

To her surprise, he didn't throw the book in his lap or launch a torrent of anger at her, he tilted his chin down and his lower lip poked out. "She said that?"

"She did indeed, but she sent me anyway because she also said that under it all you are kind and a thinker."

Elizabeth didn't say the thinker part, but Stella took a chance based on his book, *The Social Contract* by Rousseau. He fingered the spine of the well-thumbed book that had multiple bookmarks stuck in the pages and turned into a fat cat, very well pleased with himself. "She did, did she?"

"Yes, and you should know that she's very ill," said Stella with her own glare.

The lip poked out again. "You've seen her recently?"

"I have and the doctor was there."

Suspicious, he asked, "Who's the doctor?"

"Dr. Tulp."

"What did he say?"

Father Brandsma touched her arm and said, "I'll leave you now." He turned to go and Sister Teresia glided in with a tray. "Here you are, Father."

"Speculoos?" asked Father Schoffelmeer.

"The doctor said you can't have sugar."

"I like sugar."

"We know." The Sister put a cup and small pot on the tiny side table and tucked the tray under her arm. "What is happening here? Your poor feet."

She covered his feet, chided him about his well-being, and then glided out.

"That'll teach you," said Father Brandsma cheerfully.

"No, it won't," said Father Schoffelmeer.

Father Brandsma sighed, but Stella laughed. She was so tired she wouldn't have thought it possible. He was just so funny, sitting there with blankets up to his chin, unable to walk, and basically threatening everyone with his bluster.

"What's so funny?" he demanded.

"You." She wiped her eyes. "Oh, I did need that. Thank you."

"You are not welcome. Why are you laughing at a sick old man?" He pointed at Father Brandsma. "Take her away."

The priest crossed his arms. "I want to hear this."

"I don't."

"Too bad." Father Brandsma looked at Stella and asked, "Why do you think he's funny? No one else does."

"He reminds me of my grandfather. He gets so cranky when he's ill, but he's so adorable, we love him to bits." She went over and planted a kiss on the crabby priest's forehead. "So there. You won't get rid of me. I like you."

Completely undone, Father Schoffelmeer sputtered and fiddled with his book. "Ridiculous. I've never been adorable in my life."

"I will leave you now." Father Brandsma stepped out the door. "I can see you're safe."

He closed the door and Father Schoffelmeer burst out, "Safe from what? Me. I never heard anything so insulting in all my life. I'm a man of God."

Stella turned away and examined the books on the shelves. It was quite a collection. He was a thinker. "Do you want to hear what I've come to say?"

"I already know," he said. "Some child is in desperate straits and I'm to pull the strings to help, but I can't. Truus is out of the country. There's nothing I can do at the moment."

"It's not that."

"No? Fundraising with the Jewish committee for that abomination Westerbork?"

"No."

"Food drive for the Romani?"

Stella crossed her arms. "Shall I just tell you or would you like to play guessing games all day?"

"My you're saucy for an older woman," he said.

"Experience has led me to be so."

He sniffed and said, "First, tell me what Tulp said."

"She's dying."

"I know that."

"Soon. She has a month or two, maybe less."

The priest folded his hands in his lap on top of his book. "So, she's taken a turn for the worse."

"Yes, and she won't recover. Rena is devastated," said Stella.

He didn't speak for a moment and then pulled his rosary out from under his blanket to run the beads through his fingers, a soothing gesture Stella's grandmother did from time to time. "Is that what you came to say?"

"Do you know who I am?" Stella asked. "I wasn't introduced and you didn't ask."

"Micheline Dubois. Elizabeth told me you were brisk and efficient."

"That describes a lot of people in Amsterdam."

"She also told me about the hair," he said.

"Ah, the feature I can't escape."

He chuckled and rubbed his bald pate. "We all have our troubles."

"Indeed, and it's troubles I come about," she said.

"So many to choose from."

"I pick my battles." Stella told him about the Milch family in Westerbork and the scowl came back, but he listened patiently to her plan before speaking.

"Do you have their papers?"

"I have their fake papers."

He held out a hand and Stella got them out of the hidden compartment in her handbag for him. The priest looked them over twice. "The photos are accurate?"

"They are."

"Are the ages and birthdates correct?"

"Yes." They weren't, but he didn't need to know that.

Father Schoffelmeer used a finger to pry up Felix's picture and glanced under it. "I will have to call in several favors to get it done so quickly. Are you certain they can't just keep these identities for a while?"

"The camp committee knows they're fake and so does the government."

"Oh, right. You said." He stared down at the face of Hans. "Truus could possibly take out the youngest two."

"My company wants them all out."

"Because of this client of yours?"

"Yes. I gather he's very insistent. We don't want to lose his business and honestly, it's the right thing to do anyway," Stella said.

"Very clever to say they are Jews."

"I thought so, but now they're stuck. Can you do it?"

"You have money to pay for the new papers?" he asked.

"I do. Money isn't an object to my client."

"So I've heard." Father Schoffelmeer leaned his head back and closed his eyes. "I'm so tired and it hasn't even begun yet."

"It will shortly. We must hurry."

He nodded, keeping his eyes closed. "I don't know how we will do it."

Stella's heart twisted. He was her only plan. "Get the papers for them?"

"Help all the people who are going to need help. Our own people."

"Catholics? Why would they need protection?" Stella had heard things secondhand. Priests sent to Dachau for preaching against fascism and Catholics that wouldn't comply with the Nazis' rules were punished, but nothing like the Jews. They weren't killed and she never imagined they would be.

"I was thinking of our converts, the Catholic Jews."

"Do you have many?"

"Several hundred and I fear for their safety," he said, seeming to shrink down under his blanket with the weight of it all.

"I hadn't thought of that."

"No one has, but we must protect them. There are priests and nuns in their number. I fear they will not fare well when *they* come."

I can't handle anymore. I have to do this. Just this thing right now.

"Will you help the Milch family, all of them?" she asked.

He opened his eyes. "Your company, will they continue to help after you're gone?"

"I will find a way to continue," she said.

"It wasn't planned to continue?"

She had to be honest. The thinking man looking at her would know if she lied. "No, but I will put it to them."

"You, yourself, won't be back?"

"It depends on what happens," said Stella.

"Yes, so much depends on that."

"What do you think the church will do when they come? There are supporters here already, probably in your church, too."

The priest stiffened and his eyes turned icy. "They will be excommunicated."

Stella's mouth dropped open. She hadn't thought of that. "That's severe, isn't it?"

"The situation must be made clear. Our faith and fascism are not compatible."

This was true, but she doubted anything could stop Hitler's followers from doing his bidding.

"Are you all right?" Father Schoffelmeer asked.

Stella swayed and had to grab a shelf. "I'm very tired."

He squinted up at her. "You don't look well, even in this light. You should go home."

"So everyone keeps telling me."

The priest moved his legs off the hassock and tried to stand. "I will send a message to my friend. He will make the papers."

"How soon?"

"A day or two."

"So long?"

He chuckled. "This is not his profession. He learned to help me."

She tried to push him back into his chair. "You can't get up on those feet."

"If you can go on, I can go on."

"It's not the same."

"I'm not a weak old man!" he bellowed.

"You are an ill one." She pushed him back and kissed his forehead again. "How about Father Brandsma?"

The priest scowled. "I don't know him well enough and he is always giving his opinion."

At least I got that right.

"How about Sister Teresia?" Stella asked.

He pulled the blanket back up to his chin. "She is sympathetic to your cause. She is one of them that I spoke of."

"One of them?"

"A converted Jew," he said. "Send her in with paper and envelopes but don't you come back. I need my rest. You are very tiring."

"But I'm so efficient." She smiled down at him.

"Yes, yes, but troublesome is more like it. Asking for favors and from Americans, too, all fat, dumb, and happy without a care for what happens to the rest of us."

"My company cares."

"Yes, yes. Go away now."

Stella tucked in his feet and hurried out, but she had to stop once she got out in the nave. Her vision was swimming and she wanted nothing more than to lie down in a pew and go to sleep.

"How was he?" Father Brandsma came up, looking at her with concern as she leaned on a black pillar.

"Fine, just fine."

"*You* don't look well though."

"I'm fine, too, just tired. Thank you for your help." She turned to go, but he laid a hand on her arm.

"Is there something I could do?" the priest asked. "I would like to be helpful. I heard that Elizabeth Keesing has done much good for the…community."

Stella looked in his eyes to gauge his knowledge but couldn't discern more than kind intentions. "I don't think so. Father Schoffelmeer has it well in hand."

"Does he?"

"I think so."

The priest took her hand and said, "I will help, if needed."

Stella decided to trust this kind priest and asked him to tell the nun to bring in papers and envelopes for Father Schoffelmeer.

"I will tell her," he said with a gentle hand on her arm. "Are you feeling all right?"

Stella nodded, unable to say more. She had to go, if she didn't she might just lie down on the floor. Movement was her only option to stop it happening.

She hurried out of the nave and through the vestibule to rush out the door into a cold drizzle that she hadn't prepared for. No umbrella and a practically useless hat. The street was still empty, so no cab to help her.

"I can walk. I can do it," she said, and she almost believed it.

An hour later, Stella arrived at the warehouse where the Wahles' furniture was stored. She hadn't walked long. Fifteen minutes at most to the tram, but it was enough to soak her flimsy hat and shoes. By the time she found her way to Prinsengracht, she had a tickle in her throat and felt unreasonably cold, but it was May. It wasn't that cold out, but she'd have put on Anna Bikker's hideous fur coat if she could've.

The warehouse was right on the canal in a business section close to the Westerkirk. The company itself was a silk importer, but somehow the committee had convinced them to store the Wahles' furniture under Felix's assumed name of Abraham Cohen instead of having it sent to some anonymous government warehouse where it might never have been seen again. It must've cost the Wahles a considerable amount, but the furniture was Felix's parents and he was desperate to save something of them for his children.

The narrow building had three windows across and a door on the right. It was both the company office and warehouse. Since it was still light out, Stella expected someone to be there, but the door was locked. She banged on it for five minutes, but no one came to answer her. She leaned her forehead against the wood and coughed into her fist. She couldn't go back and tell Uncle Josiah there was hardly any progress because she slept the day away. He might do something rash and they couldn't have that.

She pounded on the door again, but no one came. Maybe a neighbor would know where to find the owners. She turned around and saw a man and two girls walking down the street under a large black umbrella. He had a businesslike air to him and she heard him say to the younger girl in German, "It will only take a minute. I will ask Miep and we can go."

"You always say a minute and it is never a minute," said the younger girl also in German. The girl was about eleven with large eyes and a crop of dark hair that couldn't be controlled by the barrette trying to hold it in place. Her expression was one of extreme annoyance, making her look stubborn and difficult, despite her pretty face and blue coat with its Peter Pan collar.

The other girl took her hand and said, "I can take you."

"I want Pim to go."

The father shook his head as they passed and said, "You are quite the demanding little chatterbox."

Stella smiled in spite of how she was feeling. Their accents said they were from Berlin and reminded her of Hanni and Irma and days of friendship before it all went bad. The family moved on and she went after them as fast as she could, coughing with the effort it took to catch them. "Excuse me!"

The man turned around and smiled. "Yes?"

She'd feared he'd be annoyed with somewhere to be and a complaining daughter, but his thin face with its narrow mustache and deep-set eyes showed nothing but curiosity.

"Can you tell me anything about that company?" Stella pointed at the warehouse. "I'm supposed to meet with the office manager, but no one is there."

"Ah, yes," he said, extending his umbrella over her. "They leave early. You must be here before three or they will be gone. Sometimes they do not come at all. It is a family business and they don't have outside staff."

"Their name is Fischer?" she asked.

"Pim." The girl tugged her father's hand.

"One minute, Anne."

"You always say one minute and it is never a minute."

The older girl who looked like a sister said, "You already said that."

"I did not."

"You did."

"Girls, please." The man looked at Stella and said, "The Fischers live in the Jodenbuurt, but I don't have the address." With the mention of the Jodenbuurt, his eyes became guarded and then his face blurred. Stella bumped into the lamppost and then he and the older girl had her by the arms.

"Ma'am, are you all right?" he asked.

She coughed and nodded. "I'm fine."

"I'm sorry about the address."

"It's quite all right. I should've arranged a specific time."

"Come with me to my office," he said. "I will call you a cab."

She shook her head. "It's not necessary. I will take a tram."

"On Westermarkt?"

"Yes."

"We will walk with you," he said, placing his hand on his dapper coat. "I am Otto Frank and these troublesome girls are my daughters, Margot and Annelies."

The younger daughter crossed her arms and gave a coquettish toss of her head. "I am called Anne."

"Well, I am called Micheline Dubois."

"Are you Belgian?"

"I am. You have a good ear."

"I'm very good at lessons."

"I can tell," said Stella.

The father smiled at his younger daughter in an unmistakable way, his favorite. "You must not brag, Anne?"

"I'm not bragging. It's true."

Margot said shyly, "I do well, too."

"Then I admire you both," said Stella. "I wasn't a good student until I was much older than you, but then I did well. I'm in business."

The father herded the now-chatty girls down the street toward the Westerkerk. "We must get along. She's not well and this drizzle isn't helping."

Stella settled in beside Mr. Frank as the girls, mainly Anne, pelted her with questions.

"Slow down," their father said.

"I'm a buyer for an American company in New York," said Stella. "I buy antiques, paintings, and jewelry. Anything my clients want really."

"Do you travel all over?" Margot asked shyly.

"I do, but it's tiring. I'm ready to go home. The silk company was almost my last stop before I can."

They chatted about Amsterdam and Stella learned that they were from Berlin. Otto said they had moved for a business opportunity, but she was pretty sure that they were Jewish. It was the strain around his eyes when he said it.

"I do love New York," he said. "I went there to intern at Macy's."

"Really? I've been there. What a lovely store."

"It is and that was a wonderful time in my life." He stopped in front of a warehouse and shop with the name Opekta on the door. "Here we are. You don't want me to walk with you the rest of the way?"

"No, I feel much better and I will go straight back to my hotel." Normally, that would be a lie, but this time it was true. Stella couldn't possibly go hunting around the Jodenbuurt. She might fall over and lose her wig.

"Here take my umbrella." He tried to give her the enormous umbrella.

"I couldn't possibly." She turned to the girls. "Thank you for walking with me."

The girls grinned at her and Anne went running to the office, bursting in to yell, "Miep! Miep!"

Stella said goodbye to Otto and Margot and headed off at a good clip, mostly for their benefit. She didn't want Otto to think he had to run after her and she was past the Westerkerk and to the tram stop in good time. Her hat was dripping when she got on and started the ride to the square.

The cough was rattling her chest by the time she walked into the lobby and Ludwik was there to greet her with a beaming smile. That is, he was beaming until her cough nearly knocked her over.

"You are ill." He helped her off with her coat and hat, tossing them to the front desk clerk with an order to have them dried out and cleaned. "Let me help you to your room."

"That's not necessary. It's just a little cough."

"Nonsense." The look he gave her brooked no excuses and they went to the elevator where Michel was waiting with a curious look on his face.

Once on the elevator and the door closed, Ludwik and Michel both said, "How did you do it?"

"What? Get entirely soaked because I forgot an umbrella? It's a talent of mine," said Stella, leaning on the wall.

"Not that, although you are much too old to forget your umbrella." *Not really.*

"My mother would be very disappointed," said Stella.

"How did you get Ester's job back?" Michel asked and Ludwik gave him a jab with his elbow. "Oh, right, but it's not Paulina yet. How did you get *her* job back?"

Stella grinned. "I appealed to Mr. Elek's better nature."

The men drew back and made faces.

"He's a stickler, that Elek," said Michel. "He wanted to dock my pay for having a heart attack."

Ludwik rolled his eyes. "Heart attack, my foot. Now Micheline, how did you really do it?"

"I'll never tell," she said with a wink.

Michel stopped the elevator on her floor and she left the men disappointed, walking down to her room using the last vestiges of her energy.

"I'll send up tea and soup," called out Ludwik.

Stella nodded and went inside, collapsing on the bed in a fit of coughing. What a time to get sick.

CHAPTER 22

⚜

The next few days were a blur. The next morning, Stella to see the Wahles furniture and it was beautiful, especially the bed with its detailed carvings, so glossy and in mint condition. She'd sent a messenger out to Westerbork with an offer, which was accepted and then a messenger with a bank draft, keeping her distance so she wouldn't look too terribly interested in the family. After that the arrangements were easily made. The Wahles' furniture was packed up with her other purchases including the lovely sewing box, and they were all sent to New York by the usual route.

After that, she went to Elizabeth's to check on her, but Rena could not be moved and she wasn't allowed in, which was for the best since her cough was worse. The hotel wanted to call a doctor, but there was no way Stella could be examined. She refused and kept going to St. Nicholas' to check on the papers and to the baron's house to see if Yannj had sent a telegram back. She hadn't. Not a peep. She made the rounds every day and Bikker's man, Mussert, had turned up a couple of times like when she went to the drugstore for some truly disgusting syrup that didn't help her cough one bit, but she was able to give him the slip and then go back to the baron's and back to St. Nicholas's again. Since then Mussert hadn't shown up again.

By Thursday night, it was all she could do not to plop down in a pew and pray. She'd never been so tired and the cough was just getting worse. The invasion was inching closer and the Wahles were still in Westerbork and she was still in Amsterdam. It'd been five days since she'd met Oliver in the café to report in. She had a week leeway. Maybe a couple more days at most. They'd probably think she'd been delayed with all the Dutch moving around and plenty of people trying to leave the country and packing the trains. That could be believed, but longer? No. Park-Welles would expect her back. If she wasn't, he'd send someone to find her, if he hadn't already and she had no idea what to say if someone turned up. She just hoped it wouldn't be Mr. Bast. She'd hate to disappoint him.

The good news was that the Wahles' new papers were supposed to be done in the morning. It'd taken much longer than expected since Father Schoffelmeer's friend was out of town taking his family to safety in the Zeeland area where he thought the Nazis were unlikely to attack. Stella didn't know about that and she'd annoyed Father Schoffelmeer so much by asking every day that he had taken to throwing books at her. The latest was *The Sound and The Fury*, which was appropriate given the yelling that accompanied it.

After her daily rounds, she coughed her way through the hotel lobby, hoping to avoid Uncle Josiah's intense eyes lighting on her with hope, only to have it dashed again. He claimed to be meeting Jenever makers because Bled Beer was considering moving into the liquor market. People seemed to believe him, mainly because it was Josiah Bled saying it. Nobody else in the world would be doing that with the Nazis ready to swoop down at any minute but since it was Uncle Josiah, the plan was met with shrugs or a muttered, "Crazy Bled."

But that day he wasn't in the lobby flirting or drinking or playing cards and she scooted by to the elevator, so tired she almost bumped into walls on her way.

"Micheline! Madam Dubois!"

So close.

The front desk clerk chased her down and said, "Sorry to bother you." She waited until Stella stopped coughing before continuing. "I just wanted to tell you that a woman came by asking for you."

Stella lowered her handkerchief. "Who was it?"

"She didn't leave her name and…she was a little angry. I thought you should know," said the clerk.

"What did she look like?"

"Curly hair. Rather stern."

Rena.

"Thank you and can you send some tea up? I'm so tired," said Stella.

"Yes, of course," she said. "It's all right, isn't it?" She glanced at the café where the soon-to-be Paulina was waiting tables. "I was worried considering."

Stella patted her arm. "It's fine. Nothing to do with that."

She nodded and hurried back to the desk. Stella got on the elevator with Michel, who talked enough for the both of them. Then she walked back to her room, weaving back and forth. People probably thought she was a drunk, but the exhaustion was too much. She couldn't hold it together much longer and collapsed on the bed without even taking off her coat.

Knock. Knock. Knock.

Stella forced her eyes open. "Who is it?"

"Ester!"

"Come in!" Stella sat up and shrugged off her coat.

Ester came in with a tray and shyly looked at Stella with a ducked head. "You ordered tea, ma'am?"

"Just put it on the bed," Stella said with a smile. "I didn't know you brought the room service."

Ester stepped back and clasped her hands. "I don't usually, but I asked to do it this time."

"Why is that?"

"I wanted to thank you for getting my job back."

Stella kicked off her shoes and propped up her pillows. "I don't know what you mean."

"Yes, you do. I know it was you. I'm so grateful. I don't know why

Marga did it, but she was always like that. Doing things. It wasn't my fault."

"I know that and I'm glad you're safe here," said Stella.

"I am. Oh, I am. They've given me a room in the attic."

"That doesn't sound too nice," said Stella, wrinkling her nose.

"It's very nice. I have a sink and everything."

Stella poured a cup of tea. "I'm glad you're happy about it."

"It's so I don't have to go out," said Ester, twisting her long curls around her fingers.

"Oh?"

"When *they* take over, I'll stop serving in the café and start cleaning or whatever they need. Ludwik will pretend to fire me and I'll sort of go away, but I'll still be here as Paulina."

"That's a good idea," said Stella, thinking that this young woman was looking at spending the foreseeable future living only inside a hotel and was thrilled. She was much smarter than Stella had originally given her credit for. "Can I ask what happened to your friend?"

"You won't believe it."

"Try me."

It was hard to believe. Marga Kübler went to work in Jan Bikker's house as a maid. Stella could hardly keep her face straight. That man was wilier than she ever imagined.

"He's saying he gave her the job *because* she's a Jew and Jews need work, but that's why he fired us."

"Maybe he's turned over a new leaf in light of what's coming," said Stella.

"He hasn't turned over anything. He's lying. He just wants people to think he's not for *them*, but he is. I knew when I worked in his hotel. He wants the Nazis to take us over and make us German. But we're never going to be German." Ester glared at Stella in fury. "It doesn't matter what they do."

"I quite agree."

The fury went out of Ester and she ducked her head again. "I didn't mean to go on like that. It's just she's over there working for that horrible man. She wouldn't tell the truth about your ring and she was my friend. I don't understand it."

"Ester, I think you understand it very well."

She wiped a tear off her cheek. "That's not why I brought your tea though."

"No?"

"Henriette told you a woman came to see you today while you were out?"

"Yes, she did."

"Well, I know who it was," said Ester proudly. "Ludwik and Mr. De Jong asked, but I didn't tell anyone. I don't want you to have any trouble."

"Who was it?"

"Elli Gelber."

Stella sat back on the bed and thumped her head on the headboard. "Elli? Are you sure?"

"Of course, I'm sure. The committee helped my family when we first came here." The tiniest wrinkle appeared between Ester's eyes.

"You don't like her."

"She thinks I'm stupid and naive." The wrinkle got deeper.

"Naive I could believe," said Stella. "Certainly not stupid."

"Thank you. Tell her that, will you?" Ester asked.

Stella tried to speak, but a coughing fit made her double over and then Ester helped her under the covers. "You need a doctor?"

"No doctors," Stella managed to get out between chest-burning hacks.

"Well, I guess you won't be going to see Elli tonight." Ester poured her another cup of steaming tea and Stella held it under her nose breathing deep. It helped for some reason.

"I can't see her anyway," she said. "I don't know her address."

"She lives in the Jodenbuurt over the Van Thyn bookshop. My mother made me clean her flat as a thank you."

"It didn't go well?" Stella asked.

"She said I didn't dust her books well enough and I had to listen to a lecture on Dutch culture," said Ester. "I refused to go back. She said she was going to work on my accent and I was going to have to do her ironing. She irons everything. Everything."

"I don't blame you one bit. Elli is..."

"A know-it-all. Now that I think of it, you shouldn't go at all. She'll lecture you and say you're doing it wrong."

"Henriette did say she was crabby," said Stella.

"I think she's mad at you."

"I must've said the wrong thing to a client."

Ester topped off Stella's cup and said, "It's none of her business, but she thinks everything is her business because she's on the committee and went to university."

Stella nodded and settled deeper into her pillows. "I got that impression. Thank you for telling me."

"You're welcome." Ester straightened her covers and went for the door.

"Oh, Paulina."

Ester turned and smiled. "Yes."

"You picked that up fast," said Stella.

"I'll be Paulina soon enough, so I better. Can I get you something?"

"Could you tell the desk that I don't want to be disturbed? I need to sleep," said Stella.

"No dinner?"

"I'm not hungry."

Ester left and Stella started coughing so hard she had to set down her cup before she spilled it all over the place. More than anything she longed to pluck off her wig and go to sleep, but an angry Elli wasn't a good sign and she'd taken the trouble to come to her hotel. She'd have to be pretty upset to do that. The Korbel situation was done and dusted, so it had to be the Wahles. Stella couldn't imagine what could've happened. She'd done nothing other than buy the furniture for a princely sum. Surely, even Elli couldn't object to that.

Still, it was worrisome. She got out of bed and went to the window. A heavy evening fog had risen off the canals and socked in the square so that she could barely make out the building on the other side. Not an ideal night for her to go out, but she couldn't ignore the visit. She might regret it. Regret was something she couldn't stand, so she drank her tea for fortification and put her shoes back on.

I hope this is worth it.

No one was pleased to see Stella coughing her head off on the tram. Everyone gave her the widest berth possible and the ride was more comfortable than usual. Instead of getting squashed between men with their briefcases and women with their shopping, Stella got to cling to a pole all by herself. The cough was almost worth it.

She got off near the *Jodenbuurt* and walked over as fast as her chest would allow. Luckily, she'd passed by the Van Thyn shop before and knew where it was, just a block from the Portuguese synagogue. It was closed when she got there, but the owner had pity on her with all the coughing and let her in. There was a back way up to Elli's flat outside, but he told her to go up the inside stairs to a narrow door on the second floor that had no name on it. Stella knocked politely and then pounded on the door until her knuckles hurt. If she didn't get in, she'd have to sit on the step. Climbing the stairs and knocking had taken it out of her.

She grabbed the knob to lower herself down, when the door yanked open, pulling Stella inside. She stumbled into a small living room so filled with books there wasn't an inch of space on the walls or chairs.

"What in the world are you doing here?" Elli demanded.

Stella held up a finger and proceeded to cough so hard she could taste blood. Elli watched her in distaste while she rung out her wet hair with a threadbare towel.

"I—" Stella couldn't stop coughing and Elli threw up her hands.

"Fine. I suppose you want to sit." She cleared a wooden chair of books on philosophy and Eastern religions and pointed at it impatiently.

Stella sat and coughed for a while longer. When Elli got bored of watching her, she left the room to get dressed in a heavy flannel nightgown and woolen socks that were so big and thick they must've been made for a man.

"I'm sorry," Stella gasped.

"You should be," said Elli. "You're going to get me sick."

She coughed into her handkerchief and muttered, "Sorry," again.

"How did you know where I live? I don't advertise it."

"A friend told me."

"Which friend?" Elli demanded.

"It doesn't matter. You came to my hotel. The clerk said you were angry. What happened?"

Elli cleared a spot on her settee and sat down, crossing her arms and legs. "And you came out tonight in this weather to find out?"

"Yes, of course," said Stella. "It must be important to bring you to the hotel."

"It doesn't matter. Go home and go to bed. You need a doctor."

"I need to know what happened." Stella crossed her own arms but then had another coughing fit.

Elli shook her head, but then said, "I found out you lied to me."

Which time?

"What do you mean?"

"You know perfectly well what I mean," she said with color blooming on her cheeks.

Stella had another coughing fit. "Please just tell me so I can leave."

"You know we have to work very hard for donations and we have to turn away almost sixty percent of people asking for our help. That you would lie to us and—"

"Elli, please. I didn't take away any money from the committee. I don't know what you think I did, but—"

"We know who the Cohens are." Elli clenched her hands into fists. "How could you?"

It was an eventuality Stella had not considered when she came up with the plan to turn the Wahles from the Cohens into the Milch family. She'd thought it made sense. Gentiles desperate to get out of Germany the only way they knew how and hiding their true identities to boot. That would've been all well and good, if Stella could've shown up with their new papers and visas to get them out with a tidy payment to offset any cost, but that wasn't going to happen now. Some woman at the camp, a fellow refugee, had overheard just enough of their conversation to put it together that the Wahles were gentiles posing as Jews and taking up valuable resources. The woman wasn't able to get her family visas and her sons had been caught stealing medication at the camp hospital. Now that family was in danger of being turned out of Westerbork, which meant they'd be deported. The woman turned in the Wahles in an effort to save her family. Stella couldn't really blame her, but it was a huge problem. The committee was enraged and rightfully so and the Wahles had stuck to Stella's story. Stella couldn't tell Elli they were really Jews without revealing who they were. The government didn't care. They were trying to negotiate themselves out of being invaded. Offering up some enemies of the state would be a good show of faith.

"I don't know what to say," said Stella.

"There's nothing for you to say now. They're gone."

Stella clung to the arm of her chair. Gone. Back to Germany. The room went misty until Elli gave her a good shake. "What's wrong with you?"

"I...think I was going to pass out."

"Obviously." Elli pointed at the door. "Now get out before you do."

"When did it happen?" Stella asked, her eyes filling with tears. What would Uncle Josiah do? He trusted her to take care of Judith and look what happened.

"What?" Elli tried to yank Stella out of her chair, but she stubbornly refused to use her legs.

"When did you send them back to Germany?"

"Oh. They haven't actually left yet. I meant gone in the sense that we have washed our hands of them."

"So," Stella took a breath that resulted in terrible coughing. "They're still in Westerbork?"

"For the moment."

"Until?"

"The first train tomorrow. The government has been informed and they're sending an officer to take them to the border."

Stella grabbed her arm. "When is he coming?"

Elli wrenched her arm away. "I told you in the morning."

"Can I pay you to delay?"

"They offered to pay everything you gave them for that furniture, but we don't want them. Do you know how many families we've turned down since they've been in that hut? Do you?"

Stella shook her head. She had no idea and she couldn't care about that at the moment. She'd think about it later.

"They're not even Jews, Micheline! We hardly have anything and they took that."

"They are enemies of Germany. They spoke out against Hitler and the Reich. They supported the opposition and the Reich took everything they have. If you think they're not desperate, you're wrong. They'll end up in Dachau and you've seen Abraham, he'll die."

"Don't you mean Ludwig?"

"The name doesn't matter. The death will be the same," said Stella.

Elli drew back and said quietly, "Be that as it may…"

"We're on the same side. I swear to you that we are."

"You shouldn't have done it. You're interfering in people's lives again."

"I didn't make this choice," said Stella. "I was sent by my company to help them. It's my job and I do it happily. I help people. I think you know that."

"Like the Korbels?"

"I did help them and I want to help the Milch family. Please, what can I do?"

Elli sat back down, her hands in fists. "Nothing. It's over."

"It can't be. You don't want them in Dachau, do you?"

"I don't want anyone in Dachau, but there's nothing I can do about it," she said. "They lied about their identities and we pulled so many strings to keep them in the country and now this. It's hopeless."

Stella had another coughing fit where her eyesight got blurry again. When she caught her breath, she said hoarsely, "There's always a way. Always."

"I see you believe that, but not this time."

"Their identification papers will be here tomorrow and everything they need to get visas to the States."

"They won't get them instantly. You'd have to know someone to get them through the queue. It takes months."

"I do know someone," Stella fibbed. "At the American consulate in Rotterdam. He can do it."

Elli's fists relaxed. "Why would he do that? What's in it for him?"

"The daughter, she has an American fiancé."

"Really?" Elli was full of doubt but still intrigued.

"Yes, absolutely, and he's here in Amsterdam," said Stella. "He'll marry her as soon as we get her out of Westerbork. She'll be an American wife."

"Who's going to marry them? We're about to be invaded."

"Father Schoffelmeer at St. Nicholas. I spoke to him. He agreed. He's happy to do it." Stella held her breath, hoping Elli didn't know the old crank. He wasn't happy to do anything. She shouldn't have said that, but it just popped out. She planned on turning up at the basilica with Uncle Josiah and Judith and bullying him into it. Technically, there were steps to marriage in the church, but Stella knew well enough that they were flexible when the right person asked, such as her mother had when she got Stella's wedding to Nicky done in record time. The devout Francesqua had considerable pull, but Stella had death on the line. That ought to be a powerful motivator.

"Well, that would get them out of the country faster, but it won't help with the deportation. It's too soon," said Elli and Stella could see her bright mind was working on the problem.

"What would?"

"Who do you know that can help?"

"My company."

"That's not good enough," said Elli. "They have no standing here and they're part of the lie."

"The American," said Stella.

"What does the government care about some American?"

Should I say he's a Bled? Would the whole thing unravel? Would I be recognized?

"Well, the right American could—"

"What? Do nothing? They sit over there and watch the Nazis advance on us. They don't lift a finger to help us," spat Elli, her hands in fists again.

So no.

"Who then? Tell me who would make a difference?"

"Someone important. Do you know the archbishop?"

"I have no idea who that is," said Stella.

"What about that Father Schoffelmeer? He would know."

Stella shook her head. The priest would know, but she seriously doubted that old crab would be able to talk an archbishop into anything on a moment's notice. The church probably barely tolerated him.

"I don't think so. He's rather difficult."

"Who else do you know? Anyone in government?" Elli asked.

The baron's party flashed through Stella's mind. She met a few officials, but none she could call on.

Wait a minute.

"I do know someone," said Stella.

"Not another useless American?"

"Baron Joost Van Heeckeren."

Elli's mouth dropped. "You don't."

"I do. I was at his party last Friday," said Stella.

"How in the world did that happen?" Elli indicated Stella's apparently unintriguing self and said, "I mean you're not exactly part of his world."

"I'm friends with his maid," Stella said with sniff. She wasn't really Micheline Dubois, but it still stung. Why shouldn't Micheline be invited to a party? Was she really so unappealing?

"His maid? You cannot be serious."

"I'm completely serious. Would he be enough?"

"He's...I don't know. Could you get him to go there and speak for them himself first thing?"

Stella gasped and then had a coughing fit that ended in high-pitched wheezing.

"You have to go home and go to bed," said Elli. "You shouldn't be out at all."

Stella waved that away. "He's gone."

"The baron?"

"In the country for a rest."

"Oh, the famous rests," said Elli, wryly. "I've heard about those."

"You have?"

"He has Jewish doctors. He's a friend to us and word gets around," said Elli. "Can you get him back?"

"My friend might be able to. He has great affection for her."

"Oh, he does, does he?"

"It's not like that. She's about as attractive as you think I am," said Stella.

That stunned and embarrassed Elli into silence.

"I know you feel betrayed," said Stella. "I'm not saying you're wrong, but the Milch family was desperate to escape. In that, they're no different from any of the other families you've helped. Will you please help me?"

Elli found her voice and said, "By doing what? It's not up to me."

"Delaying in the morning."

"I don't think I can. It would take a miracle."

Stella smiled. "A miracle it is."

Stella didn't go home to bed and it was a mistake. She knew that by the time she got to the baron's house. Her breathing had turned into a raspy whistle and she was shaking so hard she couldn't pick out the coins for the cab driver. He had to get his fare out of her pocketbook himself.

"Ma'am," he said with a worried frown. "Are you sure you—"

"I know, but I have business to attend to."

He nodded with admiration. Business was the ultimate answer. She got out and tried to make it to the steps without coughing. She failed and nearly fell down the stairs with the violence of the spasm.

The door opened without her having to knock and Cornelia stood there in shock. "Micheline?"

"I—"

"Oh, my. What have you done to yourself?" Cornelia brought her inside and one of the other maids rushed over.

"What happened?" the maid asked. "She wasn't so bad this morning."

Stella couldn't answer she was coughing so hard. They didn't require an answer anyway. They hurried her off to Cornelia's room, took her shoes, and tucked her up under a pile of blankets with a hot water bottle. Once she was warmed up and had a cup of horrid fennel tea with honey forced down her throat, she could finally string together a sentence.

"What are you doing here?" Cornelia asked after she forced the rest of the staff out the door and closed it. "Did something happen with that family?"

Stella told her the situation and the maid took her tuxedo cat off her little flowered armchair and plopped him on the bed. The big tom was very inconvenienced but went back to sleep purring like a buzzsaw next to Stella's feet.

"I wouldn't ask if I could think of any other way," said Stella.

Cornelia settled into her chair. "The baron's in the country. You know that."

"I do, but how is he? Could he come back?"

She leaned forward to pet her cat, who yawned and purred louder. "He's fine. Of course, he is."

Stella breathed the fennel steam in and looked at Cornelia over the rim of the cup silently.

"What are you getting at?" Cornelia asked.

"I don't want to offend you. I really don't and I have great affection for the baron. He's a lovely person, but I know that he's a special person, too."

"Of course, he is. He's kind to everyone and he throws the most fabulous parties."

"That's not what I mean. He's special in another way. I have family like the baron. I don't judge. I love them just the same."

"I don't know what you're talking about," said Cornelia, bristling.

"Yes, you do. He's having a rest at a hospital, isn't he?"

The maid stood up with a jolt. "He certainly is not. He's perfectly well."

"Most of the time," said Stella.

"What do you know about it?"

"Plenty. I have a cousin who's having a rest right now. We hope she'll be better soon. Maybe she will this time. Maybe she won't."

Cornelia paced back and forth in her cozy little room, wringing her hands, and Stella could practically hear her heart pounding.

"My cousin is sweet when she's well and we take turns with her. She can't live alone. She has to be watched all the time, so she goes from house to house, so no one gets overwhelmed by the worry. Two months with my parents. A couple with my aunt and uncle. Cousins. Her parents and siblings, too, of course. If we didn't do it, she'd have to be in a hospital all the time and that's not good for anyone."

"She's a lunatic?" Cornelia asked. "And you tell people that?"

"No, we don't, but I'm telling you that she gets ill. I trust you."

"The baron isn't a lunatic."

"Neither is my cousin. She has her ups and downs. We don't know why. The doctors can't tell us. They wanted to do something awful to her brain. They said it would…settle her permanently."

Cornelia shivered.

"Exactly. My family insisted on seeing other patients that had been 'settled' and decided that we'd care for her ourselves, except for the times we couldn't."

"I don't know why you're telling me this," said Cornelia.

"Because I know the baron has an illness."

"Who told you?"

"Nobody had to tell me. I could tell," said Stella. "You should know that I'm not the only one who has figured it out."

Cornelia went back to her armchair and pulled her cat into her lap where she held him to her chest. "He wouldn't like that."

"I'm sure, but no one I know has thought the less of him for it."

"For being a lunatic."

"For being ill," said Stella. "And it's not all the time, is it?"

"No. It comes and goes. The parties are a problem, but he loves them. He's always looking for excitement, the next thrill. I worry about him."

"How is he right now?"

"I can't have them bring him home just to suit you," she said sharply.

"Believe me, I know, but how long does he usually stay after a party?"

"A week or maybe two, if it's…" It was hard for Cornelia to give up any information. She'd taken on the baron's illness as if it were her own. The shame was hers, too, and a kind of guilt for not being able to help him. Stella knew that combination. It went hand in hand with the illnesses that regular people scorned as if it were a character flaw that a person could will away if they weren't so damn weak.

"So he might be better now?" Stella asked.

"He might, but I don't want to upset him. It could throw him off."

"Does he hurt himself?"

"Oh, no. He just gets…"

"Frantic?"

Cornelia nodded with tears in her eyes. "He tries so hard to stop, but he can't stop."

"My cousin does that. Sometimes she hurts herself."

"That's terrible." She took Stella's hand and the shared understanding was something new for her. Imelda wasn't something the Bleds discussed. The family dealt with the situation and moved on. No one talked about it. No one was sad. It was a fact. Imelda was ill. Her burden was the greatest burden, not theirs.

Stella had a coughing fit that broke the spell and then she said,

"Sometimes she's sad, so sad she can't stop crying. I think that's worse."

Cornelia nodded. She didn't confirm the sadness. She didn't need to.

"Was he sad or frantic?"

"Frantic."

"That stops faster for my cousin."

She nodded and wiped her eyes. "He's such a lovely person. No one can know. He'd rather die."

"I understand. Would he help the family, if he were able?"

"What would he have to do?"

"Go with me to the camp and vouch for them. Say they're family friends. Ask a personal favor. Whatever it takes."

"And they'll have the paperwork they need for the visas?" Cornelia asked.

"It'll be here in the morning," said Stella. "If we could get the name of that diplomat in Rotterdam, that would help."

The maid jumped up and went to her dresser. "I forgot. It came an hour ago." She held up a telegram. "I was going to bring it to you in the morning."

"Yannj?"

"Yes, and it has the name."

Stella bent over her cup and thanked God. Cornelia sat beside her and rubbed her back. "You've worked yourself into a tizzy over this, haven't you?"

"I've tried very hard to help them and I think this might do the trick. Who is it?"

"Zebulon Wilcox III." Cornelia handed over the telegram. Yannj apologized for the delay. She had moved and it had taken some time for the telegram to find her. She gave her new address and everything she had on the diplomat, including his name, his wife's name, and where his office was in the consulate. They were still in touch and Yannj had sent him a telegram saying she had a friend in need of immediate help. He'd returned the telegram with a phone number, telling her to hurry her friend because they might be evacuated at any time.

"Oh, Cornelia. She's as good as gold," said Stella.

"She is. The best person. Truly."

"Will you see about the baron?"

Cornelia screwed up her mouth and then nodded. "I will if you lay down and rest. That cough is getting worse. You shouldn't have come out."

"I had to."

"It means that much to you?" Cornelia asked.

"Yes, it does."

"It's not just your job, is it?"

"No, it's not just that."

Cornelia gave her the big tom cat and pushed her down into the covers. "Let me see what I can do."

"I'll go with you," said Stella before going into another coughing fit.

"And have you spread your disease around the house?" Cornelia asked. "I don't think so."

"But—"

"If you don't stay there, I won't lift a finger."

Stella scooted down and scratched the cat's big noggin.

"That's what I thought," said Cornelia. "Now close your eyes and try not to cough. Your throat needs the rest."

She left and Stella did try, but it was hopeless. When she breathed, she could hear the rumbling in her chest. It sounded like popcorn and she could hardly go five minutes without doubling over, but the longer she was in the warm room, the better it got, so she settled down and closed her eyes. Her mind wandered away from her chest and the baron and Judith and Uncle Josiah and went to a more pleasant place. Bickford House and her room with a crackling fire in the grate and Nicky sitting in the needlepoint chair with his feet up on a stool, smiling at her and putting aside a newspaper to chat.

The door creaked and her heavy eyes struggled to open. A warm hand patted hers and Cornelia said, "I spoke to the doctor. He's better."

"Will he come?" Stella murmured.

"I think so. He'll call back and I will persuade him."

Stella started to push the cat off her lap, but Cornelia stopped her. "Just rest. It will be a little while. He was asleep."

She lay back and heard the door creak again. She should get up. Park-Welles would say she should. Leaving herself vulnerable to discovery was exactly the wrong thing to do, but she wasn't trained on illness. It wasn't discussed. She was young and healthy.

Get up. Go.

She didn't get up and the only place she went was to sleep, listening to the sound of pleasant purring and feeling relief in her chest along with the rumbling. The baron would come and it would work.

CHAPTER 23

"Wake up!"

"Huh?" Stella opened her eyes and then closed them again.

"Wake up! Micheline! Now!" Cornelia's voice was high and panicked. That would've been enough to get Stella's attention, but the cat was grabbed out of her arms with a squawk and someone shook her into a coughing fit.

"What? What?" Stella asked, looking up at the maid's terrified face.

"It's happening." She flipped back the covers and yanked Stella's feet over the side of the bed.

The baron ran in. "Isn't she up yet?"

"How did you get here so fast?" Stella asked.

"It wasn't fast. It was a nightmare," he said. "Get up. We must go into the cellars."

She couldn't think straight. "Why?"

"Did you give her Jenever?" the baron asked.

"Just a little," said Cornelia.

When did that happen?

"A little is too much," he said, patting Stella's back as she coughed and then he lifted her out of the bed by her armpits. "Come on. It's not far."

"Where are we going?"

"The wine cellars. It's not deep but it's the best we've got."

"Got for what?"

The baron turned Stella around and she tripped on her own feet. She would've fallen over, but he held her fast by the shoulders. Looking in his clear eyes, no one would suspect he was in a hospital just hours before.

"It's begun," he said. "All our efforts have failed."

Stella's chest got tighter. She wouldn't have thought it possible; it hurt so bad already. "The invasion."

"Yes." He dragged her into the hall.

"What time is it?"

"Three."

"In the morning?"

"Well, it isn't afternoon," he said, trying to drag her along to a set of steps where Cornelia was waving for her to come.

"I have to go," she said.

"You're not going anywhere. We're under attack."

She wrenched herself out of his hands. "I can't be gone."

"Gone from where?" The baron chased her back to Cornelia's bedroom.

"The hotel. They'll worry." She grabbed her coat and hat.

"It's just a hotel."

Uncle Josiah. My kit.

"I have to go." Stella shoved her feet into her shoes and tried to push past him.

He held her back. "You can't go out there. You could get blown to smithereens."

"They won't bomb Amsterdam," she said. "Just the ports."

"We're a port."

"Not like Rotterdam or The Hague."

"The Hague isn't really a port," he protested.

"The queen and the army are there," said Stella.

The baron looked down at her, still holding her fast. "You've thought about this."

Oh, no!

"You haven't?" Stella asked.

"No, not like that." He was looking at her and thinking. The Baron Van Heeckeren might be crazy, but he was no fool.

Distract. Distract. Distract.

"Will you help me get the Milches out of Westerbork?"

He squeezed her shoulders. "I will, but you won't."

"Won't what?"

"Come to the camp. You have to rest and see a doctor. I can hear your chest from here," he said.

Cornelia ran in. "What are you doing? I can hear them. More are coming!"

The baron squeezed her shoulders again and Stella said, "I promise. I'll bring you the papers and let you do it for me."

"I can—"

"*I* will bring you the papers." She couldn't let him go to St. Nicholas. He would know what Father Schoffelmeer was doing for them. All would be revealed.

"Agreed," the baron said reluctantly.

"It must be early before the first train."

"I doubt that is a worry now. There probably won't be any trains."

"They'll try to keep them running for as long as possible so people can flee."

"You seem to know a lot about invasions." His eyes grew sharper, searching her face and she yanked back.

"I'll be back early. By seven, if I can."

"Don't let her go," cried Cornelia.

The baron released Stella's shoulders. "She knows what she's doing."

"She can't possibly. Micheline! Don't."

Stella grabbed her friend and kissed her cheeks. "It will be fine, my dear friend. I promise." Then she ran down the hall, coughing so hard she bumped into the walls on her way out of the baron's house.

Not everyone was as prudent as Cornelia and the baron. Plenty of people were on the street, their faces turned upward toward the sound of propellers. The moon was the thinnest sliver of a crescent and barely illuminated the large carrier-type aircraft with the distinctive black crosses on the underside of the wings as they passed over. Paratroopers.

Stella rushed through the streets, listening to the panic in the people who'd gathered outside or were looking out their windows. Some thought the Reich was on its way to bomb England, but that idea was dashed by the time Stella got to Dam Square. The sound of concussions came from the Southwest, putting an end to the idea of a peaceful fly over.

A woman grabbed Stella as she rushed to the doors of the Hotel Krasnapolsky. "What is that? What is that?"

"They're bombing Schiphol," said Stella automatically. She couldn't seem to keep her mouth shut and the woman stared at her in horror.

"What did you say?" a man asked.

"She said they're bombing the airport," said the woman.

The man turned in that direction as if he could see that far and nodded. "I thought they'd bomb The Hague first."

"The Hague," screeched the woman, digging her fingers into Stella's arm. "My daughter is there."

The man shrugged. "Maybe they will only use the Wehrmacht."

"What kind of planes are those?" asked someone else.

"Bombers."

"They carry troops."

"Well, they can't land, if they bombed the airport," said the woman with relief.

"They'll just jump out," said the man.

"Jump out of planes?"

Stella peeled the woman's fingers off her arm and ran for the door but got stopped three more times. Everyone was asking everyone what was happening as if someone might have the answer. Stella stopped being polite and shoved people off her to run smack dab into a disheveled Daan.

"Micheline! What are you doing out here?"

"I...wanted to see what was happening," she said. "The planes. Do you see the planes?"

He squinted up at another squadron going over. "It's really happening. I didn't think it would, not truly."

"Excuse me." She pushed past him and he called out after her. "They were looking for you."

She didn't stop to ask who they were and it didn't matter. The lobby was full of panicked guests. Ludwik and Mr. Elek were trying to herd them down to what they were calling a cellar, but it couldn't be very deep, not like St. Louis cellars. Probably a third was above ground, not much protection and Stella couldn't see the point. She avoided the men and ran to the back stairs. Some people were coming down in their dressing gowns or wearing coats over their pajamas. Children were crying. Some of the wives were, too. The men looked pale and shocked.

"Do you hear that?" a young mother asked.

"I hear it," her husband said.

"Hear what?" their little boy asked.

"They're bombing us, stupid," said their older child.

"Shut up, Jan!" The father grabbed his son by the scruff of the neck and carried him down the rest of the flight past Stella as he apologized for his son's wailing and kicking.

Once Stella got past that family, it was easier and she made it to her floor, which was empty and her room, which was not.

Uncle Josiah sat on her bed, shoes on her duvet with his arms crossed. "Well, there you are," he said. "If I didn't know better, I'd have thought you had a little number on the side."

Stella closed the door and bent over coughing.

He got up and took her hat and coat off while trying to avoid a few strategic smacks. "Don't hit me. I'm helping."

"Helping? You don't help. It's not in the Josiah Bled handbook."

"I got a new handbook," he said with a grin. "It's called Judith."

"It's called idiot," she said. "What if you were caught in here?"

"They already looked for you and you weren't here, sweetheart. They're not coming back. We're being invaded, haven't you heard?"

"I have. They're bombing Schiphol," said Stella.

He nodded. "And every other airport."

She locked the door and yanked off her wig, doubling over to cough with her knees going weak.

"My God." Uncle Josiah felt her forehead. "You're burning up. Why did you go out? Is it Judith? Please tell me it's good news."

Stella stripped off her suit, not worrying about modesty, and got into bed wearing only her slip. "It's good news." She told him what happened and he went to the window to look out before speaking.

"If I have to storm the gate and kill the guards, I'm getting them out of there," he said quietly.

"You won't have to," she said.

"You trust the baron?"

"I do."

"Why?"

"Let's just say I've done my research." Stella pulled the covers up to her chin and closed her eyes.

Uncle Josiah got a cold washcloth from the bathroom and put it on her forehead. The cold was a jolt and she began shivering along with her coughing.

"I'll go get the papers," he said. "You can't possibly."

"We're not revealing you to the baron or Cornelia."

"Who's Cornelia?"

"Never mind. Get out of here and let me sleep for a couple of hours," said Stella.

She waited for the door to open, but it didn't. Of course, it didn't. When did Josiah Bled ever do what he was told? "Will you please buzz off?"

He didn't and Stella opened her eyes to see her uncle smiling at her fondly.

"What?"

"You're going to bed," he said.

"What else would I do?" she asked.

"Scream. Run around. Cry."

"Not likely."

"That's my girl." He came over and kissed her forehead. "You might be Aleksej's daughter, but you take after me."

"My mother's thrilled," said Stella with a smile.

"Francesqua understands who you are now."

"Then she knows more than I do."

"Go to sleep."

"I will if you get out of here."

"You'll leave first thing?" he asked.

"So much for sympathy," said Stella.

"Sweetheart—"

"Yes, first thing. I will be at the baron's by seven. Happy?"

"I won't be happy until Judith is safe," said Uncle Josiah and he slipped out the door.

The basilica was crowded. Nearly every pew was overflowing with praying people dressed in black. The mourning for their collective loss had begun. The sound of Latin bounced off the walls and there seemed to be a mass going on. That wasn't usual for a Saturday morning, but it was called for. Stella slipped around the back with a handkerchief clamped over her mouth to muffle her coughing, but she still got some disapproving looks.

She went through the little door and found Father Schoffelmeer in his library, listening to the radio with a man Stella didn't recognize. He glanced up and scowled. "Brandsma thought you might not come," he said. "He didn't see the steel in you."

"There's no steel, only my job," she said.

He snorted. "I'm no fool, woman. I know who I'm dealing with. You'd have dogged me until I dropped unless I gave you what you wanted."

"And have you got what I want?"

He waved at the man, who nodded.

"This is my friend. You can call him Johannes," said the priest.

"I will call him nothing," said Stella and a smile passed over "Johannes'" face. He got a sheaf of papers out of his jacket and Stella had to admit they were good. Very good. Park-Welles couldn't have done better.

All six sets of identity papers were as official as official could be with the correct photos, stamps, and the dates Stella had named. The birth certificates looked original and correct for their time period. The Wahles weren't Jewish. They weren't Austrian. They were Germans from Hamburg. The accent might be tricky, but she doubted anyone had that good an ear, especially with paratroopers attacking The Hague and panzers heading for Maastricht.

The required paperwork for American visas was just as good with a medical doctor's written letters for each of them, stating that they were healthy and fit. There was even a tax document with two stamps in purple ink and a one and a half schilling paper stamp glued to the top and Felix had a discharge paper from the German army. Even better, all the papers had been worked. Folded and unfolded. Stuffed in envelopes and taken out multiple times. There was a coffee ring on Felix's Polizei certificate, like some pencil pushing bureaucrat had casually put his cup down on it.

"These are truly amazing," said Stella.

The man nodded and stayed silent. She assumed it was to hide his accent, so she didn't press and asked Father Schoffelmeer the price. He named it and she paid.

"You could've haggled," he complained just to have something to complain about.

"I don't haggle over lives, Father."

The man rewarded her with another smile, shook her hand and the Father's before leaving without saying a single word.

"He's nervous," said the priest.

"I don't blame him."

"And you're sick."

"You don't miss a trick," said Stella.

"There's that steel again."

She nodded and tucked the papers in her handbag. "Thank you."

"Have you been listening?" He inclined his head toward the radio.

"Not particularly."

"They say Chamberlain will resign today."

"About time."

"Who do you think will replace him?" he asked.

"You're very talkative today," she said.

"I want your informed opinion."

Look at you being all pleasant and rooting around for my identity.

"What makes you think I'm informed? I'm a businesswoman working for Americans." Stella coughed into her handkerchief and had to lean on the door to steady herself.

"That's the last thing you are," he said with a sneer.

So much for pleasant.

"Funny. If someone told me you were a priest, I would've said the same thing," Stella said.

"Why of all the ungrateful—"

"I'm very grateful to you, Father, and—" she tapped her handbag "—so are they."

"And that's to be my reward? Insolence and unheard thanks from people I'll never meet," he said with a hint of a pout.

"You'll get to hear it," said Stella. "Don't worry about that."

The old man stiffened. "Huh?"

"I'll be back."

"What? No!"

"Yes." She pointed at a plate of pork knuckle someone had seen fit to feed him for breakfast. "And don't eat that. It's bad for you."

"I'll eat what I want!" he yelled as she went out the door and ran right into Sister Teresia, who was nearly bowled over. "Oh, I'm so sorry, Sister."

The prim nun straightened her veil. "I heard Father Schoffelmeer yelling. What happened?"

"I told him not to eat pork knuckle," said Stella.

"Father doesn't get pork knuckle. He has gout."

"Well, he has pork knuckle right now."

Father Schoffelmeer bellowed from his library. "Don't tell her that. She makes the Gestapo look like our neighborhood knitting circle."

The Sister sucked in her thin lips and hurried into the library to harangue the father and defend Stella. "She was only looking after your welfare!"

"I have no welfare without pork!"

Stella hurried out of the basilica in case anyone else wanted to appear and question her. She hoped to avoid Father Brandsma, but there he was outside the doors with a missal in his hands and a serene smile on his face.

"Madam Dubois, I didn't think I'd be meeting you again."

"It's not that big of a city, Father," she said with a discreet check of her watch.

"You're not staying for the mass?" he asked.

After a coughing fit, she said, "No, I can't. What are you doing out here?"

"Waiting for you."

I shouldn't have teased Father Schoffelmeer. I'm sorry. Please make him go away.

"Why?" Stella asked.

"You're very ill and out in the weather," he said. "You shouldn't be. I dare say you wouldn't be if there wasn't something very important on your mind."

She didn't speak and merely coughed violently, hoping he'd have pity and leave her alone.

"Something with Father Schoffelmeer, I think, and his friends."

Stella tilted her head and said in a dubious voice, "Father Schoffelmeer has friends other than Elizabeth?"

Several people came rushing through the gate and the priest guided Stella to the side as he nodded to them with an understanding smile. "My friend knows many people, as I do."

Stella clutched his arm and stumbled down the stairs. He managed to prevent her from falling and held her as she coughed and shook. "You must go back to your hotel, my dear."

She shook her head. She couldn't do more.

"There comes a time when one has to decide whether to save oneself or to save another," he said.

"I can't..." She ended by wheezing.

"I am not done, Micheline," said Father Brandsma. "Where is the greater purpose? Where is the greater need? You are seriously ill. Dangerously ill, I believe."

She tried to speak, gasping like a fish.

"Can those you save do what you can do in the fight?"

He knows.

Stella shook her head and whispered, "No, but they are worth saving."

"All God's children are, but in this case, we should not sacrifice you to get there when there is another choice."

"You can't mean..."

"It will take more than you to save them, my child," he said. "I can take this burden from you. I have the weight of the church and the confidence of the Archbishop De Jong. You can get well and do what no one else can."

"I don't need you to do that." She doubled over coughing and then he pulled her upright to see a formation of German planes flying overhead. Stella watched them pass with a growing sense of dread. So many. How long could the Dutch hold out? Then she lowered her eyes to the train station across the way. So close, but she still couldn't get out. Her eyes fell on a man walking past. Slowly. Too slowly. Torn pocket. Mussert. He'd followed her and she hadn't even checked to see if he were there so she could lose him. She doubled over. She couldn't have done it anyway. She couldn't do it now.

Please let this be right.

"All right," she whispered. There was no choice. She couldn't bring Mussert to the baron's and connect him to the priest. "I was followed."

"I know. He's walked by four times already." Father Brandsma turned her around and she hadn't the strength to say no. They went up the stairs back into the basilica and stepped into the dim interior.

"We have a phone now. An extravagance, but a necessary one. I will call for a cab."

A.W. HARTOIN

Stella shook her head. "No, let me lead him away from you."

"You can't walk all the way back to your hotel."

"No, but I can walk to the station. I'll be able to get a cab and so will he." She coughed so hard blood stained her handkerchief. The priest hesitated, watching with a grave expression, but then he said, "I will bow to your will. Give me the papers. I will take them to their destination as soon as you are gone and he follows."

"Who told you about me?" she asked.

"I heard tell of a woman who was helping the Jews, giving money and papers, and then you came to see Father Schoffelmeer. You were correct. He has few friends, but they are all righteous." He leaned over to her and whispered, "He will do well when they come. Who would suspect him?"

She smiled into her handkerchief and surreptitiously gave him the papers. The priest hid them under his cassock. "I will be right back." He rushed away and came back with a long scarf knitted in crimson. "A parishioner made this for me. My favorite color."

"I can't take that," said Stella.

"We need a reason for you to come back in." He wrapped the long scarf around her neck and tucked it up over her ears. "There. If anyone asks, you were donating for a mass for a friend in need."

"Elizabeth."

"Yes. Perfect. Elizabeth." He took her hands and said, "We will pray for her and for you."

"And for them?"

"May God hear our prayers." He pressed her hands between his in prayer position. "'Let us then with confidence draw her to the throne of grace, that we may receive mercy and find grace to help in time of need.'"

"That's a good one," said Stella.

"And one you know, I think," said Father Brandsma.

"I am a good Protestant."

"Of course, you are."

"You won't have to go far." Stella had been trying to think of a way to keep the priest from knowing about the baron, having him give the papers to Cornelia or something. But the prayer changed her mind. "Baron Van Heeckeren is going to take the papers to Westerbork to get a family out, so they won't be deported."

He tilted his head to the side. "I know of the baron. He is not a godly man."

"But he is a kind one. Take him the papers. He is expecting me."

"We will go together." He smiled down on her, his face beaming with faith. "How can they resist both church and nobility?"

She tapped his chest. "And papers."

"Go now and into bed. I will send word when it is done. Where do we take this family?"

Stella started for the door and then stopped. "I hadn't thought."

"We will decide."

"But—"

"We will decide."

She bowed to his pressure. It was right and she could barely think anyway. If she had, she wouldn't have done any of it, but instead, she left the basilica walking as fast as her chest would allow with the Father's warm scarf up over her nose.

There he was. Mussert walking past once again. He didn't have skills, but he was persistent. Stella used all her remaining strength to walk to the station. It had to be less than a quarter mile, but it felt like ten. Stella decided she much preferred frozen feet to what was happening to her chest. It didn't care about her will and it had sapped her strength like nothing else ever had. She had just enough left to get to the front of the station, but she was wrong. There weren't any cabs, only panicked people trying to get in and get tickets. The trains would be packed. Thank goodness the baron had a car.

She went to the tram stop and clung to a light pole. A tram rolled up and to her relief everyone flooded off and almost no one got on, except her and Mussert, who was right behind her.

"Are you all right, ma'am?" asked the driver, leaning away as she got on.

She nodded while coughing into the scarf and her handkerchief before staggering to her seat. Mussert, subtle as always, sat opposite her, but she couldn't have cared less. She couldn't get a full breath in, even a shallow breath burned and crackled.

Thankfully the ride was short and she got off to walk across the square. Mussert was hard on her heels. A few times she thought he might grab her. It was just a sense, a feeling of threat, but he didn't. Perhaps her illness kept him at bay. When she got within fifty feet of the hotel, Daan saw her. The doorman came running across the street onto the square's cobbles to grab her. "Micheline! What are you doing out?"

"My friend. I had to get a mass for her."

He half carried her to the street and waited for some cars to pass. "Why Micheline? You are so sick."

Mussert was right there. She could see him out of the corner of her eye.

"She's dying," Stella said. "She wanted a mass."

"You need a doctor."

She nodded and he took her across the street into the hotel. Once inside, she glanced back. Mussert was gone. Satisfied, she hoped, but more importantly, well away from Father Brandsma and the baron.

CHAPTER 24

Her room was abuzz with activity. Stella wanted to tell them to go away and leave her in peace but speaking was so hard. Ludwik ordered hot water bottles, a hot plate and kettle for steam, soup, and aspirin.

"Did you eat this morning?" he asked.

She shook her head and whispered, "Not hungry."

"You must eat. My mother had pneumonia. The doctor said she must eat and drink."

"I don't hav—" Coughing racked her body and she couldn't finish. Pneumonia? She didn't have pneumonia. She wasn't old and weak. It was just a terrible cold.

"The doctor will decide what you have." He turned to the maid hovering behind him. "Go to Mr. De Jong. We must have the doctor here immediately."

Stella grabbed his arm. "No," she croaked. "Please."

He looked down confused and touched her forehead. "She's burning up."

"Is she delirious?" the maid asked.

Stella forced herself upright. "No."

A.W. HARTOIN

Ludwik looked at her sweaty flushed face and turned to the maid. "Check on the aspirin and the rest of it."

"What about the doctor?"

"I think Madam Dubois has another plan."

The girl frowned and hurried off to do his bidding. Ludwik closed the door behind her and then came to sit on the edge of the bed. "Why don't you want a doctor? We have a good one on call."

She couldn't have a doctor. He would examine her. Touch her. Know she wasn't who she pretended to be. Doctors weren't supposed to tell others about their patient's private details, but she wasn't fool enough to think she could keep a random doctor from telling everyone he knew that she was a fraud. She could be arrested. No one thought the Dutch could hold off the Reich. When they got ahold of her…

"I don't want a doctor." She squinted at him. Things were blurry around the edges.

"You have to have help. This is crazy."

She shook her head and the blurry edges got wider. If she passed out, he would get a doctor. No doubt about it. Uncle Josiah. He could stop him, but in truth, she did need a doctor. Did people die of pneumonia? Young people?

"Milla," she whispered.

He leaned as close as he dared. "Who?"

"Madam Milla."

"The designer? She's not a doctor. What in the world did she tell you?"

"Call Madam Milla?"

"She's very busy. I was lucky to get her the last time. There's no way she'll come in the middle of the business day."

Stella pointed a weak arm at the window. Planes were flying over. Could be German or Dutch. She didn't know. "Invasion."

"Well, I suppose there aren't a lot of dress fittings today." He looked out at the blue sky. "Half the city is panicking. The other half is trying to leave."

She grabbed his hand. "Call her."

DARK VICTORY

"Then you'll have a doctor?"

"When she comes."

Ludwik slumped. "If you insist, I'll try."

She nodded and he went to the door to find Uncle Josiah standing outside. For a split second, Stella saw his distress, which was immediately replaced with a jovial smile. "I heard a certain lady was ill. Anything I can do?"

"How kind of you, Josiah, but I'm going to call…a friend for her right now," said Ludwik.

"I brought a radio. Nothing's worse than silence when you're sick." He produced a small radio in a brown Bakelite case from behind his back.

"Excellent idea." Ludwik stepped out of the way. "Bring it in. The plug is by the bed. I must make that call."

The concierge left and Uncle Josiah closed the door behind him, listening with his ear pressed against the wood for a moment before turning to her. "All clear." His expression changed and he rushed to her side. "What happened? It wasn't this bad before."

Stella shrugged, but it triggered a bout of coughing and gasping.

"You do have pneumonia. You don't need a friend. You need a doctor."

"She'll help. She knows."

"A contact?" Uncle Josiah asked.

Stella shook her head.

"But she knows? How?"

She tried to answer and nothing came out but a wheeze.

"Never mind it doesn't matter." Uncle Josiah stood up and began pacing. "I didn't think you were that sick. I should've done something. I made you go out. That's what happened, isn't it? No, don't answer. I should've just gone to that camp and blasted them out or paid everyone in sight off."

Stella pointed at the radio, hoping to distract him from his rant. There was no point. It was done. He cleared a spot on her side table and plugged the cord in. It took some fiddling for him to find the BBC on the dial, but then an announcer came through clearly and said, "It has been reported to me that Lord Chamberlain has requested an audience with the king. This request has been granted."

"Finally," said Uncle Josiah. "Now we're gettin' somewhere."

The announcer went on to say that it was believed that Lord Halifax would be offered the position of prime minister.

"That guy? He's another Chamberlain. We need Winnie. Goddammit. They're about to overrun this country. What are those fools thinking, Hitler will stop at the channel? Jesus Christ!" He looked down at Stella and ducked his head. "I'm sorry, sweetheart. I get carried away and here you are sick as a dog and all because of me."

"Judith," she whispered. "Aren't you going to ask?"

He touched her forehead. "Goddamn, you're hot."

"I did it."

Uncle Josiah turned away, his hand over his mouth.

"We'll know—" She began coughing again and he turned back with his eyes full.

"I was afraid to ask after what you've gone through to help us," he said.

She pointed at her ledger and fountain pen. He brought them to her and she wrote out that Father Brandsma and the baron were going to Westerbork with the papers to get them out.

"A priest and an aristocrat. You don't mess around, sweetheart. I'm sorry I ever doubted you."

"You doubted me?" she wrote.

He grinned at her. "Maybe just a little. I watched you get potty-trained and learn to walk. Sometimes I forget you're a full-grown woman."

"You have to marry her," Stella wrote.

"I will. Don't worry about that."

"Now! As soon as possible."

"Sweetheart, I haven't converted yet. I can't do that overnight," said Uncle Josiah.

She tapped the pen hard on the paper. "In basilica. Father Schoffelmeer. Today."

"Felix will never allow that and I won't ask. Their religion is very important to them."

Stella's breathing got worse and she tapped the ledger again. It had to happen. She wrote, "There's a waiting list. She needs to be an American wife."

"But you have a contact at the consulate."

"Take no chances. He may be gone. He may be unwilling to help if they don't have an American claim. It could take months. People are on the list for years." The writing took it out of Stella and she dropped the pen. Uncle Josiah looked down at what she had written and said, "You have the name of this man who holds our future in his hands?"

She nodded and closed her eyes.

"Stella, write the name," he whispered, but she didn't. She couldn't. So tired.

"All right, my girl. Rest." Uncle Josiah ripped the page out of Stella's ledger and then tore it into bits before flushing it. "I'll explain it to Felix. I'll make him understand."

Stella nodded, but she thought of Pavel Korbel. He couldn't be made to understand that going back to Czechoslovakia would be the death of him. Sometimes people didn't want to understand. She didn't know if Felix was another Pavel who would have to be made to save himself or if he would be guided by Josiah, a man he didn't really want marrying his daughter in the first place.

There was a sharp knock on the door and Ludwik came back in with a smile pasted on his face. "She's coming. I don't know why she is, but she's coming."

The maid came in behind him and they began packing the hot water bottles around Stella's icy feet.

"She's burning up, but she's shivering" said Ludwik. "I don't know what to do."

"I saw it in the war. We've got to keep her warm. Give me that aspirin." Uncle Josiah gave Stella two aspirin with some horrid fennel tea and then forced three bites of a thin potato soup down her throat.

"I didn't know you were such a caregiver," said a bemused Ludwik.

He grinned up at his friend and pulled out a flask to pour a good amount in Stella's tea. "I'm full of surprises. Never lost a patient. Whiskey is essential."

Stella drank the tea, more because she didn't want him harassing her than anything else. The combination of licorice flavor, honey, and whiskey was abominable and she resolved never to get sick again if it meant drinking that concoction. In the end, she feigned sleep just so they would leave her alone.

"Well, I'll leave you to it," said Uncle Josiah. "Maybe I'll come back later to see how the patient is doing."

"You're staying?" Ludwik asked.

"Where am I going to go? They're bombing the airports and I tried to get a call put in to the States but no dice. Besides, this is where the excitement is. Maybe I'll get the chance to take a couple of potshots at a Hun or two before I go."

"You…you think there will be fighting in the streets?" Ludwik asked with a quaver in his voice. "Here in Amsterdam?"

Stella took a peek and saw Uncle Josiah pound the concierge on the back. "I was joking. Between you and me, your government will surrender before long. I give it another day or two at most."

"But we're holding them at The Hague."

"Yes, they are, but Hitler hasn't put his back into it yet. Just about now he's getting the picture that you all aren't exactly anxious to become part of the Reich. You're not Austria."

"No, we're not," said Ludwik stoutly. "We will fight them, even if there is a surrender."

"That I believe." Uncle Josiah pounded his back again and went to open the door. "Let me buy you a drink, my friend."

"I'm on duty."

"We're being invaded. If a man ever deserved a drink, it's a Dutchman on this day."

Ludwik laughed, but said, "I can't leave her alone in her condition."

"You won't be." Madam Milla swished through the door, wearing wide-legged trousers, a draped red sweater, a mink stole that reached her knees, and a pair of cat's eye sunglasses.

Uncle Josiah whistled up at her. He wasn't a short man, but she towered over him in suede platform heels. "Look who the cat drug in. Madam Milla, in the flesh."

"Josiah Bled, what are you doing in Amsterdam?" She posed with an arm out, holding her cigarette holder, cigarette unlit.

"Getting a drink."

"Naturally."

"How do you know our little patient?" Uncle Josiah asked.

"I dressed her for the Baron Van Heeckeren's latest party," she said.

"Go figure. I've been trying to get you to *dress* me for years. What's Micheline got that I haven't got?"

"Sense and sobriety," said Madam Milla.

"You got me there."

"Really. What are you doing here? You've heard we're about to be overrun by the jackboots or were you too drunk to notice?"

He laughed and said, "I might've heard something of that nature, but it doesn't bother me. The Reich's wanted Bled Beer in their corner for years. Killing me wouldn't help their cause."

"Will you go to their corner?"

"Hell, no! But they don't know that. It's a carrot. We keep dangling it."

That wasn't true anymore, but Uncle Josiah sold it well.

"Some people have all the luck," said Madam Milla.

"You know it." Uncle Josiah winked at her and turned to Ludwik. "Getting burned by the most beautiful woman in Amsterdam makes me even more thirsty. What do you say, Ludwik? Drinks on me."

Ludwik threw up his hands. "Why not? What are they going to do? Fire me?"

"I doubt it." Uncle Josiah pointed at Madam Milla. "She won't have a doctor, but she's about on death's door. See what you can do, will ya?"

"That's why I'm here."

"I have every confidence."

"You should," said Madam Milla.

Ludwik looked completely confused and allowed Uncle Josiah to

A.W. HARTOIN

push him out of the room. "Let's leave the ladies to it." He winked at Stella behind Ludwik's back and closed the door.

"I thought they'd never leave," said Madam Milla.

Stella nodded and went into a coughing fit.

"He wasn't kidding when he said you were sick." She touched Stella's forehead and drew back in horror. "Well, you have to have a doctor. That is a certainty."

"But…" Stella wheezed.

"I know I'm not here just for looking at. I have a discreet doctor. He's liable to be understanding of your unusual situation."

Stella pointed at Madam Milla and raised her eyebrows.

"Yes, he knows, and he hasn't said a peep."

She relaxed back onto the pillows. Thank goodness.

"I'll call him. You can pay, right? Discretion doesn't come cheap," said Madam Milla.

Stella nodded and the designer picked up the phone. It might've taken quite a while, but it only seemed like minutes before a bearded little man and his large black bag were at her bedside.

"Dr. Tulp," she whispered.

"Micheline Dubois!"

"You know each other?" Madam Milla asked.

"We have a mutual acquaintance, a patient of mine," he said with a frown as he touched Stella's forehead. "Where did you pick this up?"

Oliver Fip, the bastard.

Stella shrugged and he stuck a thermometer in her mouth. He looked at her with dismay, his hands fiddling with the buttons on his jacket. Stella and Madam Milla exchanged a look.

"How long have you been sick?" he asked.

"A few days," Stella whispered with the thermometer still in her mouth.

"Last Sunday? Were you sick last Sunday?"

She thought about it. She'd been very tired when she went to Westerbork and then she'd got caught in the rain. "Maybe."

"Do you know the proverb 'Pride goes before destruction, and a haughty spirit before a fall'?"

She nodded and pointed to herself.

"No, not you. Me, but I have learned my lesson."

"What are you talking about?" asked Madam Milla.

"Nothing. Not to worry," said Dr. Tulp, but his face belied his reassurance. "Let's see what we've got." He read the thermometer and then cleaned it with a swab and rubbing alcohol. "I will have to examine you."

Stella went stiff quite involuntarily.

"You told her that I am discreet?" he asked Madam Milla.

"I have, but some secrets are hard to reveal," she said, "for more than the usual reasons even."

He frowned and told Stella, "I must listen to your chest to make a decision on the correct course. Will you trust me?"

Stella nodded, although she was so afraid of being revealed, her chest hurt even more. Madam Milla unbuttoned her blouse and Dr. Tulp went through the usual checking of her lungs, front and back. He took her pulse and got very close to check her eyes with a light. "All right. Milla, can you get her into pajamas?"

Stella's eyes widened and he patted her hand and then held it up. "I should've seen it before. I am a trained professional." A light went on behind his eyes. "Then again, I suppose you are, too."

"What do you mean?" she managed to gasp out.

"You are *not* a middle-aged woman or dumpy." He leaned in. "You are good with the makeup." He glanced up at Madam Milla. "Not quite as good as some people, but very good. I'd say you're twenty years old?"

Stella smiled.

"I finally got something right."

"What does that mean?" Madam Milla asked.

"Nothing. Just my professional pride has taken a blow," said the doctor as he opened his bag.

"You couldn't have known she was going to get sick on Sunday."

"No, but I should've considered it."

Stella rolled that around in her mind, but she couldn't really focus. Sunday seemed like a year ago. So much had happened.

"Well, young lady, you are in luck," said Dr. Tulp.

"Luck? Does she look lucky to you?" Madam Milla went to the window to look down on the traffic jam with its frantic honking below. "Do any of us?"

"Lucky in one sense, not all senses. Micheline, I think you had bronchitis. Do you know what that is?"

She nodded.

"You didn't rest."

She shook her head.

"Because you didn't rest, it got worse and took a turn. You now have pneumonia," he said.

"Where's the lucky in that?" Madam Milla asked.

"She's lucky I know a man in England."

Stella was lucky, extremely so. Dr. Tulp followed all the latest developments and he had heard about a drug being developed at May & Baker. He wrote to Dr. Lionel Whitby about his discovery and the two men struck up a friendship. As a result, Dr. Tulp had a sample of a brand-new drug, M&B 693.

"It doesn't have a proper name," he said.

"What is it?" Madam Milla asked skeptically.

"It's a sulfonamide and it kills infections like the one Micheline has."

"Safe?" whispered Stella.

"I wouldn't give it to you otherwise. Besides, you seem like a girl who isn't afraid of risk," said Dr. Tulp.

"True enough," said Madam Milla. "Take it, Micheline."

Stella nodded and he gave her the first of many tablets.

"When will she be better?" Madam Milla asked.

"With her youth and usual vigor, she should start feeling better within twenty-four hours, but," he tapped Stella's arm, "you must take the whole course and rest. And on that note, take this."

He gave her another pill and she swallowed it dutifully.

"That will put you to sleep for a good long while," he said. "If I know you and I think I do, sleeping's the only thing to keep you down."

The doctor went on to put a poultice on her chest and take her temperature again. By the time he was done she couldn't keep her eyes open.

"You'll stay with her?" was the last thing she heard before darkness.

Someone shook her, but she couldn't wake up. Everything was fuzzy. Maybe her eyes were open. Maybe they weren't.

"Sit her up."

Stella was upright, but she didn't like it. She groaned and they took the opportunity to put foul-tasting tablets in her mouth.

"Drink this and swallow."

She tried to spit the pills out, but they forced some tea in her mouth and she swallowed automatically.

"Good. Now go back to sleep."

Aren't I asleep?

She had to go to the bathroom. That's what woke her up in the end. Stella opened her eyes to find her room well lit and the heavy curtains drawn. Madam Milla was still there, sitting elegantly in her chair with her long legs draped over one arm. She had a large book and was making broad sweeping gestures across the pages.

"How long have I been asleep?" Stella asked.

Madam Milla jumped and then smiled. "About ten hours."

"You've been here ten hours?"

"It's as good a place as any to wait for destruction of one's country and the room service is excellent," she said.

Stella had a huge coughing fit and Madam Milla tossed her book on the bed to get her a glass of water. "You have to keep drinking. Doctor's orders."

"I need the bathroom."

Madam Milla helped her get up and moving. It would've been

impossible to make it on her own and she held Stella upright on the toilet. She should've been embarrassed, horrified really, but she found she didn't care.

The designer, who managed to look elegant and not horrified herself, got her back in bed with a glass of water. Then she checked her reflection in the mirror. There was a wrinkle on her trousers and that was more concerning than Stella on the toilet.

Stella listened to the never-ending bad news on the radio and worked herself up to ask in a hoarse voice, "Have we surrendered?"

"We? Are you Dutch now?"

"I'm more Dutch than German."

"Some will decide they are the other way round when *they* are in charge."

"People like Jan Bikker."

"He's already decided, I'm sure." Milla touched up her lipstick, which looked perfect to Stella. Then she came to the bed with the lipstick, Tabu by Dana in a gold-plated tube. "Here, let me. It will make you feel better."

Madam Milla painted her lips a glamorous deep velvety red and had Stella roll her lips. "There. Much better. You needed some normal color."

"I don't think that's a normal color for lips."

"When I got here, your lips were grayish blue."

"What do they look like now?"

"Gorgeous. You have a very nice natural shape. You. Not Micheline."

"But I am Micheline," croaked Stella and she downed some more water.

"And I am Milla. Both of us, just what we appear to be," said Madam Milla, touching Stella's forehead. "Your fever is coming back up. It's time for some aspirin again."

She took her aspirin and the music on the BBC cut off. The women looked at each other and Madam Milla took her hand. Stella didn't know if the gesture was for her or herself.

Prime Minister Neville Chamberlain was announced and Stella looked at her watch. Eleven fifteen. Late for a speech.

"'Early this morning without warning or excuse Hitler added another to the horrible crimes that already disgrace his name,'" said Chamberlain in a voice that seemed more sure and stronger than Stella had heard him before. The man was quite ill, but his voice didn't betray what the earl had told her about him.

They listened together as the prime minister resigned and announced his replacement. Winston Churchill. Stella almost cried with relief. No more appeasement or half-hearted efforts. Winnie was a fighter and he'd been preparing for this fight his whole life.

"Is this good?" Madam Milla asked.

She nodded. "Very."

"You would know?"

"I would. It won't get better for a long time, but with him we have a chance."

"*We* again," she said.

"It's us and them," said Stella and she went into a coughing fit so harsh that she could taste blood again.

Madam Milla pushed her down under the covers. "You've been talking too much. Go back to sleep."

The tiredness overwhelmed Stella, rising in a wave to push her down into blackness again, but she held it off to take her friend's hand. "You should go."

"I'll stay the night. You can't be left alone."

"I mean out of the country. Get to America."

"You already told me that," said Madam Milla.

Something horrid bubbled up in Stella's chest and she hacked into a handkerchief while her friend waited patiently. "It's worth saying again."

"It's not worth making your voice sound like that."

"It is," said Stella. "You'll need papers."

"I'd need the right papers. Those aren't easy to come by."

"Father Schoffelmeer."

Madam Milla straightened her trousers and arranged her sweater into perfect folds. "At St. Nicholas?"

"You know him?"

"The Jews do and I know them. He's crabby but kind," said Madam Milla. "You shouldn't be telling me this."

"I should. You're here. You didn't have to be."

Madam Milla looked away, giving Stella a view of her perfect profile. "I have few friends and even fewer that know me."

"Please leave, Milla. They will kill you if they find out."

"I can't. I asked. She won't go."

"Who?" Stella whispered and the darkness threatened.

"My mother," said Milla. "This is her country now. She's too old to change."

"Make her."

She stood up and took her book to the chair. "I can't make that decision for my mother and I won't leave her."

"Milla."

"Who do I have, if I don't have her?" Milla asked, her face transformed, no longer elegant, only sad and lonely.

Stella drifted away.

CHAPTER 25

*D*r. Tulp had Stella sitting up before she was fully conscious. He bent her forward and told her to take a deep breath. She couldn't. Then she was back against the pillows, having her heart listened to and her temperature taken.

"Better," he said. "I told you twenty-four hours."

"What time is it?" Stella asked.

"Eight. Let's get you up."

"Up?"

"Up," said the doctor and he tossed off her covers. "I want you to take a little walk."

Stella looked at Milla, who was still lounging on the chair and sketching. "Don't look at me," she said. "I haven't had a cigarette in twenty-four hours thanks to you."

"Good," said Dr. Tulp. "Nasty habit. It will kill you."

"It will have to wait in line."

Stella teetered on the edge of the bed and asked, "What's happened? Did they take The Hague?"

"They did not," said Dr. Tulp. "We surprised them."

"But Rotterdam isn't looking good," said Milla.

"They've only captured a few river crossings, not the city itself, and the French are coming."

"We're blowing up the bridges. How can they get in if they don't have bridges to cross?"

"The Nazis don't have them either."

"They're coming across the border like locusts," said Milla.

"You are a pessimist," said Dr. Tulp.

"I'm a realist. They're not the most patient people in the world. If we don't surrender, they'll start bombing us like Poland."

With the doctor distracted, Stella crept back under her blankets and closed her eyes. It didn't last.

"Oh, no, little lady." The covers were once again stripped away and Stella upright. "Milla, help me," ordered the doctor.

Between the two of them, they got Stella to her feet and walked her around the room to the window and then to the door and back again.

"Why are we doing this?" Milla asked.

"It's good to move and get the blood pumping, especially with the lungs full of fluid," said Dr. Tulp.

"Are you sure?"

Stella had started coughing to an alarming extent and her head swam, but the doctor didn't give up. They did another lap before getting her back in bed, where she gagged and spewed up a foul substance.

"Excellent," he said. "Better to get it up and out. This is why we walk."

Stella lay panting on the bed with what little breath she had, wanting to make a rude gesture but she hadn't the strength to do even that.

"If you say so," said Milla.

"I do. Time for your pills, Micheline." He got her propped back up and forced more fennel tea down her throat with his medicine and some aspirin. Then he packed his bag and said, "I'll be back tonight. Pills every eight hours without fail."

"When?" Stella croaked.

"When what?" he asked. "When will you be better? You're better now, but I'd say a week before you're fighting fit."

She spewed a little more and asked, "When can I leave?"

"Leave? You're not leaving. Nobody's leaving. The rail is only for troops and they're blowing up the bridges that the Germans haven't taken already. You'll stay here in bed."

"I can't do that," said Stella. "I have to go. I'm supposed to go."

The doctor got a cool cloth and put it on her forehead. "I know. I heard."

Her eyes got heavy, but she asked, "Heard what?"

"Nothing," he said. "I know you have to go."

There was something in his voice, a heaviness she hadn't heard before and it got her to open her eyes again. "Has something happened?"

He was quiet as he dried his hands on a towel and snapped his bag shut. "I'm only tired and I, too, have to go." He ordered Milla to make sure she took her pills in eight hours and then left without meeting Stella's eyes again.

"What was that about?" Milla asked.

"I don't know." Stella just wanted to sleep. Curiosity was banished for the time being.

"I'm going to get you some soup."

"Coffee," said Stella.

"Tea is better."

"Tea is disgusting."

Milla stood up and gave herself the once over. How she managed to stay fresh and pristine for twenty-four hours was a mystery to Stella who couldn't manage it for a quarter of that time. "How do I look?" she asked.

"Fabulous," said Stella.

"You're not looking."

"I don't have to. You're always fabulous."

"I knew there was a reason why I liked you," said Milla.

Stella heard the door open and a joyful voice cry out, "Madam Milla! You are still here. Perfect. You deserve this for all your efforts."

"Champagne?" Milla asked and Stella opened her eyes to see Ludwik come in with a champagne bottle and two glasses.

"Did we win?"

"Win?" Ludwik popped the cork with a practiced twist and poured two glasses to the brim.

"The war, Ludwik," said Milla. "We're being attacked."

"No but we must celebrate when there is something to celebrate, even on a dark day such as this." He gave a glass of champagne to Milla and then brought one to Stella. It was pink, her favorite, but she couldn't imagine drinking it.

"It's eight o'clock in the morning," she said.

"We celebrate when the news happens. We might not be around to do it later." He tapped the bottom of Stella's glass. "Drink up."

Milla came over and took the glass. "She can't have champagne. She has pneumonia."

"Josiah said she should have it. He absolutely insisted," said Ludwik.

"You still haven't told us what happened," said Milla, using her long arms to keep Stella's glass away from Ludwik.

"Haven't I?" He leaned over to Stella. "I've had a few glasses myself."

"I can tell."

"Josiah Bled only buys the best, you know," said Ludwik.

If Stella could've gotten out of bed and shaken him, she would have. Instead, she kept her voice calm and asked, "Why are we having champagne?"

The concierge threw up his hands. "It was all a lie and well told, too. He's not here to meet Jenever people or to have contracts."

Milla sipped her champagne and wrapped a long arm around her torso. "You don't say."

"I don't." He paused. "Or maybe I do. Do I?"

"Ludwik!" Stella burst out and then began coughing so hard she fell over.

He rushed to pull her roughly upright and behind him, Uncle Josiah swaggered in, carrying an open champagne bottle and no glass.

"So, you've heard the good news." He took a big swig and smacked his lips, grinning at everyone and no one at all. Typical Uncle Josiah, but Stella wasn't sure what to make of his performance. Drunk could mean anything.

"Actually, we haven't," said Milla. "Ludwik is drunk."

"I am not drunk. I'm happy. I needed good news. This is good news." He pointed at Milla, fell across Stella's bed, and started laughing. "I love champagne."

"So do I." Uncle Josiah took another swig. "I'm going to drink it all day. I should drink it every day."

Stella raised an eyebrow. "I think you already do."

"I don't. Contrary to popular opinion, I am not a drunk. I am a social drinker. I'm just extremely social."

"And engaged!" cried Ludwik, jumping up to grab the champagne bottle off Stella's dressing table.

"And engaged!" Uncle Josiah raised his champagne and the two men clinked their bottles before taking huge swigs. Behind them, Stella saw Milla's face fall, a look of pure agony transformed her beautiful features into someone Stella hardly recognized. For a moment, she thought the elegant and always poised designer would burst into tears.

"Oh," Stella whispered and Milla transformed back. She struck a pose and resumed her stance of fashionable disinterest. If Stella hadn't been looking right at her, she never would've known. Uncle Josiah wasn't so he didn't. He turned to Milla and said, "Congratulate me, gorgeous! I'm getting married today."

Milla raised her glass without batting an eye and said, "Congratulations." Then she downed the champagne in one go.

Uncle Josiah sauntered over and smacked Milla on the shoulder. "You should dress her for the big moment."

"Josiah!" Stella burst out, but he paid her no mind.

"She's beautiful," he said. "She doesn't have any clothes with her."

"Yes, she is beautiful, but very quiet," said Ludwik. "I didn't think you'd marry a quiet girl."

"She's here?" Stella found herself shaking with relief, but she was able to cover it with coughing.

"She is," said Uncle Josiah with a wink at Stella. "The whole family is here. They need clothes. Nothing's open, but Milla—"

"How did they get here?" Stella asked quickly, meeting Milla's distraught eyes. "My doctor says the trains are only for the troops."

"They drove, but it took a very long time with roadblocks and avoiding certain areas." Uncle Josiah turned back to Milla. He could be relentless when he chose. "Can you get together—"

"Milla has to go," interrupted Stella. "Right now. She has to go."

"What now?" he asked. "But my beautiful bride, her name is…"

Say the right name. Say the right name.

"Alice, by the way. Alice needs a dress," he said, and Stella blew out a ragged phlegmy breath.

"Alice will have to make do," said Stella with a look at Milla, who immediately went to the dressing table, set down her champagne glass, and picked up her hat and coat. "I was just leaving."

"But Milla," said Uncle Josiah, "you're the best designer in Amsterdam or anywhere and we've known each other for years. This is just a small favor, but I will pay you."

"She has to go," said Stella. "She's literally been up twenty-four hours nursing me through the worst. You can't expect her to start working after that, during an invasion, can you?"

"I…I guess not. I was just hoping that—"

"Milla," Stella said, holding out her hand. "I can't thank you enough."

Milla came to the bed and took her hand, mouthing, "Thank you."

"I couldn't have gotten through it without you," said Stella. "I owe you and I will do anything to help you. You only need to ask."

"I was happy to help," said Milla and she slung her handbag over her shoulder. "And I hope you can go home soon."

"You have my card?"

"I do. I won't lose that."

"Good," said Stella.

"Well, I'm off." Milla looked at the men. "Don't drink yourselves to death. We're going to need fighting men." With that she left with a swish of hips and a whisper of perfume.

"What did she mean by that?" Ludwik asked. "Am I supposed to fight? I've never held a gun in my life. I have flat feet."

"You're not fighting today." Uncle Josiah looked out the window. "Or maybe you will. Who knows? I'm getting married."

"Today? I can't fight today. Maybe later."

"We're being invaded today," Stella pointed out. "You will probably have to do something at some point."

Ludwik went pale as if his having a part to play in the fight had never occurred to him. Maybe it hadn't. He had many skills, none of them seemed suited to war.

Uncle Josiah patted him on the back. "Don't worry, my friend. You have a job to do already."

"I do?" Ludwik looked like he might throw up all his champagne.

"We need tickets out of your fair country and you're just the man to get them."

"I am?"

"You are an excellent concierge and you do know agents with all the lines, don't you?" Josiah asked.

Ludwik stood up straight. "I do. I can make some calls, if the lines aren't down."

"Or telegrams. Whatever it takes. I'll make it worth your while."

"I could…buy a gun," said Ludwik.

"Let's put a pin in that for now." Uncle Josiah clapped an arm over Ludwik's shoulder and led him to the door. "Now that I think of it, you might make a valuable quartermaster."

"What's that?"

"They get supplies, organize things for the army."

"Do they have guns?"

"They don't need 'em," Josiah said, opening the door.

"I could do that," said Ludwik. "I organize every day."

Josiah eased Ludwik out the door and said, "Good. Now go organize some tickets."

"First class?"

"Any class. We'll take the decking, the luggage hold, whatever you can find."

Ludwik gave him an off-kilter salute and wandered off. Josiah closed the door behind the concierge and said, "I thought he'd never leave."

"They're safe?" Stella asked.

"Well…"

"They're out of Westerbork?"

"Yes," he said, taking another swig of champagne. "Thanks to you."

"Thanks to the baron and Father Brandsma," Stella said.

"I don't know how they did it."

"No?"

"No."

According to Uncle Josiah the trip to Westerbork had been nothing short of a miracle. Normally, the drive would've taken about three hours. It took seven. Every road was clogged with the fleeing Dutch and troops trying to get wherever they were supposed to go. There were accidents to get around and more than one road was bombed into smithereens for no apparent reason, but the baron and Father Brandsma made it to the gate of Camp Westerbork at two in the afternoon. The guards were gone and the baron talked his way in before the priest took over, soothing and cajoling the committee members that were there into letting the Milches a.k.a. the Wahles go. No one was happy with the supposed gentiles and it wasn't easy, but they crammed the Wahles into the baron's enormous black Mercedes by four. Uncle Josiah said they did encounter some German troops moving across the road at some point near Arnhem, but they were ignored, possibly because of the Mercedes. Even so, the trip back took even longer. They ran out of gas and couldn't find a pump. The baron had to find a farmer who could be bribed into giving up the petrol in his tractor. Even so, they ran out of gas on the outskirts of Amsterdam and had to walk the rest of the way. Felix couldn't do it and they found a wheelbarrow somewhere and put him in it. They arrived at the Hotel Krasnapolsky almost exactly twenty-four hours after they left Amsterdam.

"Are they all right?" Stella asked, picturing poor Felix trying to walk in Westerbork.

"They're exhausted but very grateful," said Uncle Josiah. "That was the worst night of my life. You're in here with pneumonia and I couldn't be with you. Judith was out there. Somewhere. I had no word. I didn't know where they were or if the baron even made it to Westerbork." He sat down abruptly on Milla's chair. "Christ. I thought I would go crazy."

"But you talked them into it? The wedding, I mean," said Stella.

Uncle Josiah ran his fingers through his thick wavy hair and chuckled. "That was the one easy thing."

"It was easy? You're kidding?"

"Nope. That night of hell convinced Felix that me marrying Judith any way I could was the wisest course of action. If Father Brandsma hadn't already proposed the idea, I think he would've come up with it himself."

"That's a relief."

"Relief doesn't cover it." He waited until she stopped coughing to quietly ask, "I don't suppose you can come?"

Stella thought it over, but it was impossible. She could hardly keep her eyes open and her chest hurt with every breath. "I'd like to more than anything."

"I guess no one will be there. Not even Milla. I thought she would come. She loves a wedding."

"How do you know her?" Stella asked, watching him closely to see if he knew, but his eyes were clear and guileless.

"Oh, we met years ago. I was here for a meeting with Heineken, collaboration, distribution, total pain in my neck."

"And a total failure as I recall." Stella laughed and then coughed.

"It was, but a good time. I always have a good time," he said. "Anyway, Florence had just lost her mind and agreed to marry my brother, so I thought I'd get her a dress or something. You know how she loves European fashion. Someone suggested Madam Milla. She knew just what to give her. Every time I'm in town I get something. You know your going away dress for after your wedding?"

"Milla?"

"That's why it was your favorite thing in your trousseau, right?" He chuckled and took a swig of champagne.

"It was gorgeous. I wondered how that dress happened. I thought Mother picked everything out."

"Not that. Me and Milla. She's amazing. What a woman."

Stella smiled. "I bet."

He pointed the bottle at her. "And immune to my charms, I'll have you know."

Not hardly.

Stella briefly considered telling him, but it wasn't her secret to let loose and it would do no good for anybody. Josiah had a big heart and it would hurt for her and on his happiest day, too.

"A good thing," said Stella. "She doesn't need you mucking up her life."

"She needs someone to muck it up. It's so neat and tidy. She's never been married or even engaged."

"She's married to her work."

"I guess so." He jolted out of his seat. "I have to go."

"When's the wedding?"

"This afternoon. I was going to say this morning as soon as possible, but they're exhausted. Felix has to sleep or he won't make it to the basilica."

"Do you have rings?" she asked.

"Going to find some right now. Ludwik made a call. Good man. Can't handle his champagne, but a good man none the less." Uncle Josiah came over and kissed her forehead. "Get some rest, sweetheart. I'll find a way to come see you later."

He started to go, but she grabbed his hand. "I think you should wait to leave."

He looked out the window. "Don't worry nothing will happen here. They'd be crazy to bomb Amsterdam. It'd be like bombing Paris. Even Hitler wouldn't do that."

"I meant that you shouldn't try to leave the country until after the surrender," she said.

"The plan was to get out as soon as possible. Ludwik will find passage. I have every confidence in him."

"The plan was to get out before the invasion. It's too dangerous now. Think of how hard it was for them to get out of Westerbork. The ports are prime targets. After the surrender, you can use the confusion—"

He kissed her on the forehead again. "I know. I know. I've been through a war before, remember?"

"Not this war."

"It's all the same, sweetheart," said Uncle Josiah. "Winning is the only thing that matters in the end."

"Not the only thing," said Stella.

He smiled indulgently at her and said, "I'll talk to Felix."

"Don't talk to him. Tell him."

"My, aren't we bossy?"

"I'm not bossy. I'm right."

He laughed and shook his head. "They grow up so fast."

"Wait," she pleaded through coughing, but he went out the door and said loudly, "Get some rest, Madam Dubois and no more champagne for you." Then he gave her a wink and closed the door.

Stella saw the smoke in the distance over the buildings across the square. The bombs had hit quickly and in rapid succession. She didn't know how many there were, at least two. They rattled her out of sleep and instilled terror in her already taut chest but not for herself. There was no formation of bombers come to wipe them out. The sky was clear.

She dragged herself out of bed to the window to see. Down in the square, people were running and screaming. Some pointed in exactly the direction Stella didn't want toward the basilica, but the city was large. It could be anywhere in that direction. It didn't have to be the place where Uncle Josiah was getting married. If it was, she was the one who sent him there.

"What are you doing out of bed?" Ester ran into Stella's room like her hair was on fire and grabbed her robe and slippers. "Come on. Come on."

"Where are we going?" Stella asked.

"Downstairs. We have to shelter."

Stella staggered back to the bed and said, "I don't think so."

"What do you mean? You don't want to get blown up," said Ester.

"Do you see any other planes?"

Ester looked, standing on her tiptoes. "No. Not yet. But they're coming with tanks. I heard it on the radio."

Stella reached out to her and Ester helped her lay down. It was amazing how hard everything was, even lying down. "I heard it, too."

"You're not scared?"

"I'm terrified." She went into a huge coughing fit that ended disgustingly and Ester nearly ran right back out.

"But you won't go downstairs?" the girl asked.

"I'll take my chances."

Ester crossed her arms. "Well, I think you're crazy."

"You wouldn't be the first," said Stella with a smile. "I think it's time for my pills."

"Let me get you some water."

Stella took her pills and asked Ester as she was leaving, "Can you find out where it hit? That Josiah Bled said he was getting married at St. Nicholas and that's the direction the smoke is coming from." Stella said it calmly, but she was just about to throw up her pills.

"Don't worry about that." Dr. Tulp walked in and excused a very relieved Ester. "It was on the Herengracht and nowhere near the basilica."

"I'll tell everyone." Ester ran out and the doctor closed the door.

"Were many people hurt?" Stella asked.

"Yes." His voice shook and he pulled up the chair.

She watched him for a moment. "Shouldn't you be there?"

"There are other doctors and I wouldn't be any use." He held out his hands and they shook badly. "I couldn't suture. All I can do is give you your pills."

Stella held up the bottle. "I just took them."

"All right. I came because I knew you would be calm. No one else is calm and I need calm."

Stella wasn't calm, quite the opposite, but it did no good to show it. "You were in the war?"

He nodded. "I volunteered for the Red Cross. I can't…it stays with you."

"Yes." She thought of Abel and the boxcar, Rosa in Venice, and the dying children in Brandenburg. "It certainly does."

"Maybe you're not twenty. Right now, you seem a hundred and five."

"Thank you very much."

"I didn't mean it as an insult," said the doctor.

"It's not a compliment," she said with a smile.

"That's what I like about you, very cool and collected."

Her smile grew. "Now that is a compliment."

"So, I know I can talk to you about the Milch family."

"Who?"

"I put it together, Micheline. Elizabeth said you were desperate to help some people in Westerbork for your company and here they turn up out of the blue with no luggage and scared to death. That crazy Josiah Bled is your client, isn't he?"

"No."

He frowned. "I could almost swear you're telling the truth."

"That's because I am."

"Well, all right, if you say so," he said.

"I do."

"Okay."

"Is there something you wanted to tell me?" Stella asked.

He opened his bag and took out the thermometer to stick it in her mouth. "I was going to tell you, but now I'm not sure if you're the one to tell."

"Try me and we'll see," she murmured around the rod.

"The father. I examined him. He's very weak."

She nodded, wondering where this was going.

"I think he's got cancer."

Stella raised her palms.

"Experience. His breathing. The pain. It probably is a result of the gassing during the war. I can't know without a picture of his lungs." He checked the thermometer. "You still have a low fever."

"Why are you telling me this about the father?" Stella asked.

"Because he knows and the rest of them don't. He shut me up when I tried to ask him about it."

"What did you want me to do?"

"I don't know them. I thought you did," he said.

"Sorry. I don't," she said.

"But you bought their furniture?"

"I did do that, but it doesn't mean that I know them. I don't."

He cleaned the thermometer and put it away. "You know Josiah Bled though, don't you?"

"What makes you say that?"

"He's very concerned about you," said Dr. Tulp. "He tries to hide it, but he can't."

Stella folded her hands across her stomach and said nothing.

"He married the daughter and you were worried they got blown up."

"As anyone would be. What's your point? I'm very tired."

The doctor got out another pill bottle. "They're intent upon leaving from what I hear."

"So am I," said Stella.

"But you aren't, not for a few days. You have no one to help you do it."

"Yes," she said slowly.

"Ludwig Milch does and he shouldn't do it. He's too weak to travel. If he were my father, I'd stay put." He popped open the bottle and took out a tablet. "Take this. You'll sleep again."

"It's five o'clock in the afternoon," said Stella.

"Another night's sleep is essential to your recovery."

Under his beady-eyed glare, she took the pill. "Don't you want me to tell Josiah Bled about his new father-in-law? I'll be asleep."

"You can tell him in the morning. He's not going anywhere on his wedding night." The doctor packed his bag and went for the door.

"Why don't you just tell him or them or whatever?" Stella asked with a yawn.

"Because I don't know these people. I don't know their priorities. Officially, they're the Milch family from Hamburg, not Jews out of Westerbork, running from God knows what. Would the family stay if they knew? And if they did, what would happen? I don't know. Their father has a better chance if he isn't moved. That's what I know. As for the rest of it, I can't make that decision without the facts. I was hoping you could."

"Swell," said Stella.

"Some American put it best. War is hell," he said, opening the door.

General Sherman. Dorthea hated him.

"Which American?"

"Who knows? Americans never stop talking," said the doctor. "I'll be back in the morning."

He left and Stella slid down under the covers. Sherman might've been a son of a bitch, but he was right. War was all kinds of hell.

CHAPTER 26

Ludwik bustled into Stella's room the next morning, put a tray on her bed, and yanked the curtains open. "Good morning."

"Is it?" Stella blinked at the bright blue sky. No smoke. That was good, but the radio was announcing all manner of horrors. "What time is it?"

"Eight. Time for your pills, I'm told."

"Who told you?"

"Dr. Tulp." Ludwik pulled a thermometer out of his pocket. "I'm to take your temperature, too."

"Isn't he coming?" Stella asked.

"He called. Something about a patient," he said. "I think it might have something to do with the bombing. He just didn't want to say."

"How many were lost?"

"Over forty people and many more injured."

Forty people gone just like that. No warning. No reason. Dead.

"I'm sorry to upset you," said Ludwik gently.

"It's worse elsewhere," she said.

"They're trying to get through to France, I think." He put the thermometer in her mouth. "You're worried about your family?"

Stella nodded. Uncle Josiah would be married by now. He could've left for Rotterdam. They could be in the middle of a battle, not looking at the clear skies over Amsterdam.

"I will pray for them," said Ludwik. "I do have some good news though."

She raised her eyebrows and he tapped the pot on her tray. "Dr. Tulp said you could have coffee. He thinks you might eat more if you don't have the fennel tea."

She smiled and he poured a cup of beautiful black coffee and added some lovely steamed milk to the cup. "I have eggs and ham. You need the strength to get to your family when the time comes?" It wasn't a question, but that's the way he said it, so she nodded.

He took the thermometer out and frowned. "It is higher. Why is it higher?"

"I need some aspirin," said Stella, reaching for the bottle.

He got it for her and she took all her pills with coffee. That alone had the power to make her feel better.

"So, did you find tickets for Josiah Bled?" Stella wasn't sure what she was hoping for. Tickets. No tickets. Only that he hadn't left yet.

Ludwik beamed at her. "I did, but it wasn't easy I can tell you. So many tickets at one time are hard to come by."

Feigning ignorance, she asked, "How many are there?"

"Eight."

Eight? Oh, no.

"His fiancé has a big family," she said.

"There are six of them," said Ludwik.

"Who's the eighth ticket?"

"I don't know. A friend in Rotterdam."

Stella's chest tightened and coughing erupted out of her. Rotterdam? Not Rotterdam.

"Maybe the coffee wasn't such a good idea." He gave her a couple of fresh handkerchiefs.

"It's fine," Stella whispered. "My chest is trying to clear. So, they're taking a ship out of Rotterdam?"

"It's the earliest one I could get tickets on for the whole group to New York."

"Was there another choice?"

"IJmuiden, but that was to England and they don't want to go to England," said Ludwik.

"Why not?" Stella asked.

Ludwik took the cloche off her ham and eggs. "Josiah is anxious to introduce his bride to the Bled family. I gather she will be a surprise."

"Anyone who's met him would be surprised."

Ludwik had a good laugh and there was a knock on the door. "Maybe the doctor was able to come after all." He opened the door and to his surprise Josiah and Judith stood there.

"Are we interrupting?" he asked.

"Not at all," said Ludwik. "I was just checking on Micheline."

"Can we come in?"

Ludwik glanced at Stella, who was coughing again but nodded in spite of it.

"Come in," said Ludwik. "But don't stay too long. Dr. Tulp says she needs to rest."

The concierge left and the couple came in. Judith wore a new dress in a fashionable plaid with a wide skirt and three-quarter sleeves. Not exactly an outfit to escape in, but Stella figured Uncle Josiah picked it out. He had a good eye, thanks to Milla, and she looked well in it. Other than the dress, Judith was unchanged with her long hair loose and undressed and no makeup. Her eyes, while tired, were happy and she cast loving looks at Uncle Josiah every second or two.

"Madam Dubois," he said. "I wanted to introduce you to my new bride before we left. Micheline, this is my beloved Alice. Alice. Micheline."

The women shook hands and smiled at each other while Josiah gazed at Judith with abject admiration. He loved her. Stella hadn't quite believed it until she saw it. He looked at Judith the way Nicky looked at her. It seemed unlikely. They weren't an obvious match. She was serene while he was jumping out of his skin with joy, but opposites attracted or so they said.

"I'm pleased to meet you, Alice," said Stella. "I hear you're going to Rotterdam."

Uncle Josiah flashed a warning look at Stella and any thought she had of appealing to Judith's good sense died an instant death. Her uncle was not having it. He looked exactly like her father when Aleksej made a decision. Stella didn't know Uncle Josiah had that look in him. She barely believed he could make a decision.

"We are. The concierge got us tickets," said Judith. "We're very lucky."

"You deserve all the luck."

Judith came forward and took something out of the pocket of her dress, a long velvet box. "We know that it is due to you. You were our luck. My parents held this back just in case we needed it to sell later and now they'd like you to have it."

"Let me see." Stella took the box and found a gorgeous necklace in diamonds with natural pearls for accents in the Art Deco style. Florence would go mad for it. She adored Art Deco. "It's stunning. You'll get a good price in New York."

"We're not selling it," said Judith. "We're giving it to you."

"I can't accept it." She closed the box and tried to hand it over, but Judith stepped back.

"You must. It's all we have to thank you. My parents are aware that you took terrible chances to help us. Father Brandsma said you were being followed. It's very dangerous what you did. Please take it."

"I…"

Uncle Josiah gave her the look again and she said, "It's too much, but thank you. I will treasure it."

"I'm glad. Now I must go. My father, he isn't well and we need to get him downstairs," said Judith.

"You have a car?"

The young bride squeezed Uncle Josiah's arm. "Josiah bought one. A Volvo and all for one trip. As I said, we are very lucky. There are no trains."

"I think you are both lucky," said Stella. "Congratulations."

Judith went for the door and then glanced back at Josiah.

"Give me a minute. We need to discuss buying your parents' bedroom suite back," he said.

"They will be so happy." Judith nodded at Stella and left the room.

"Rotterdam," said Stella.

Uncle Josiah stuck his hands in his pockets and went to the window to gaze out at the square. "We're going anyway. We have to get the visas."

"But you don't have to get on a ship out of that port."

"Stella."

"You know it's a target. The radio says it about twenty times a day."

"It's decided," he said, not looking back at her.

"Then change your mind," she said. "I have a bad feeling about it."

He spun around and raised his voice. "And they have a bad feeling about being in this country a minute longer than necessary. Klara is distraught. She hasn't slept in days. Felix is falling apart. Judith seems fine but don't let that fool you. She's terrified. They all are. I am."

"You could go to IJmuiden. There's a ship there. It probably won't be bombed. It's not much of a target."

"We can't."

"Why not?"

"We have enough gas to get to Rotterdam and that's it."

Stella balled up her fists. "You can get gas there."

"Can you guarantee that? I can't," said Uncle Josiah.

"I know you," she said. "You can do anything if you set your mind to it."

"Well, I'm not doing that. We'll leave out of Rotterdam. That's it."

"Why? You can wait until after the surrender."

"I told Felix about that, but he wouldn't go for it. The Nazis will be in charge and he won't take the chance of being discovered."

"You have the papers. You can—"

"No," he barked at her. "I'm not going against my father-in-law less than twenty-four hours after joining his family. I'm not doing it."

"He's sick. He's not thinking clearly. You can wait. You should wait."

"Stella, he's the head of the family," Uncle Josiah said.

"Since when has that ever mattered to you?" she asked. "You joined the army without your parents' permission and went to war."

"This is different. I'm married and my wife is Jewish. This is their lives we're talking about. It's their choice, not mine, and it sure as hell isn't yours."

Stella sat back and a tear slipped down her cheek. She could get herself out of bed and drag herself down the hall to tell Judith her father had cancer and he shouldn't be moved, but was that right? Elli would say no. It was Felix's life, his cancer, his family.

"Don't look at me like that," said Uncle Josiah. "I understand everything you're saying. I've heard the same reports, but have you thought of this? Why would they bomb Rotterdam's port? It is one of the major reasons for taking this country. They want it to launch an attack on Britain."

"I know," she whispered. "I just—"

"Have a feeling, I know, but sweetheart, I thought of all of it. Ludwik found us a hotel in the center of Rotterdam, a block from our consulate. They're not going to bomb us or the actual city for the same reason you don't think they'll bomb Paris. It's beautiful. Historic."

She wasn't convinced, but she only had one card left. The name. Without Zebulon Wilcox, they'd have a harder time getting on that ship.

Uncle Josiah sat on her bed and took her hand. "We'll stay at the hotel until the last minute. Does that help?"

"I don't want you to do it," she said simply.

"You can't stop me."

I can.

"Stella, we have eight tickets," he said. "I want you to come."

"I can't," she said. "There's no reason for it. My cover would be revealed."

"I don't think I care."

"I do."

He squeezed her hand. "I'm your uncle and I'm thinking of what's best for you."

"I'm not leaving. I'd be done with the SIS," she said.

"I could take you out of this bed. You couldn't stop me. Nobody would if I told them who you were."

"And I could withhold the name of the diplomat in Rotterdam."

Uncle Josiah's face fell. "You wouldn't."

"Same to you," she said.

They looked at each other with the same blue eyes, each as strong as the other.

"What will I tell your mother?" he asked.

"Don't tell her anything. You never saw me," said Stella.

"I'm telling Judith as soon as we're out of here."

"So?"

He smiled and kissed her hand. "I forget you don't know her. Judith isn't a natural liar. Concealing that she'd seen you indefinitely will be difficult for her."

"Then don't tell her," said Stella. "She doesn't need to know right now. When I'm back in England, I'll send word and you can let it loose then."

Uncle Josiah put a hand to her forehead. "You're still hot. When can you leave on your own?"

"Two days. Maybe three. Once the trains are going, I'll get on one."

"Don't wait until it's too late."

She smiled at him and picked up her coffee. "You forget. It's never too late for me. Being here is what I do."

"Will you give me the name?" Uncle Josiah asked.

"Will you leave me here?"

Her uncle sighed. "There's going to be hell to pay, but yes, I will, against my better judgement. I have feelings, too, you know."

"Your feelings are all about Judith. You can barely see straight."

"Very true."

"Zebulon Wilcox III." She gave him all the diplomat's particulars. "It's going to work. He's waiting for you to contact him."

Uncle Josiah kissed her forehead. "I don't doubt you anymore."

You do or you wouldn't be going.

"I love you," she said because nothing else would do.

"And I love you, sweetheart," he replied. "Wish us luck."

You're going to need it.

Her uncle went out the door and she could do nothing or at least, she would do nothing. Stella wiped a tear off her cheek and picked up the sleeping pills Dr. Tulp had left her. If she couldn't stop him, she could sleep through it. Two pills ought to do it. She washed them down with coffee and forced herself to eat the breakfast Ludwik brought. He was right. She needed her strength. She needed to get the hell out of there.

CHAPTER 27

Stella woke at eleven thirty or so the radio announcer said. He didn't say what day it was or maybe she missed it. Everything was vague and indistinct. She'd taken the sleeping pills and they'd made everything easy. She didn't have to be conscious while the Dutch waited for French troops that might not arrive or listen to reports on the battle over Willemsbrug outside Rotterdam. She only had to get the aftermath. The French had arrived. It wouldn't be enough, but they had come. The Dutch had retaken the bridge over all odds, but the situation was in tatters. Ludwik and Dr. Tulp kept her informed, occasionally prying her out of bed to walk.

The doctor had taken the sleeping pill bottle away at some point, not realizing she wasn't an amateur. She'd hidden a stash of the pills in with her pills from Park-Welles. The only bright light was Uncle Josiah. Ludwik had woken her up to say that he'd telegrammed of their safe arrival in Rotterdam. Stella had taken one sleeping pill instead of two. Then later, at a time she couldn't pinpoint, Ludwik had said that they had their visas and would leave on the fourteenth as planned. She'd taken half a pill.

Light was streaming through the cracks in the heavy curtains and Stella pushed herself upright to switch off the radio and reach for the telephone. Before she picked up the receiver she stopped. No coughing. She took a tentative breath and smiled. Not perfect, but the crackling pain was gone. Dr. Tulp's British pills were a miracle.

She cleared her throat and spoke in a still husky voice when Henriette answered the front desk phone. "It's Micheline Dubois. What day is it?"

"What day is it?" Henriette asked, sounding confused and stuffy.

Stella closed her eyes and prayed. "Is it the fifteenth?"

"No, it is May fourteenth, Micheline. How are you feeling?"

"Better." She stifled a yawn and took great pleasure in the lack of pain. "What time is it?"

"Almost noon. You've had no breakfast. Ludwik said you wouldn't wake up."

"Yes, well, can you send a tray now? I'm so much better."

Henriette said she would, but there was something in the young woman's voice, a tight constriction that helped wake up Stella. "Are you ill?" she asked. "Did you get my pneumonia?"

"No, no, I'm fine," said the clerk. "I will send up your tray directly."

She hung up, even more constricted than before and Stella got out of bed to check her strength. She was still lightheaded and her limbs felt soft and loose as over-cooked pasta, but she went to the window without having to grab the bed or wardrobe for support.

The square below her window was mostly empty with only a few people rushing by. It looked like the whole city was hunkered down and bracing for the worst. They hadn't been overrun by German troops and there was no smoke in the sky. All good signs, but something had happened. She could turn the radio back on, but she found she didn't want to face it. The Nazis would get through. The Manstein plan would work. The only question was could the French hold. The Dutch could not. That they'd done so well against overwhelming odds was impressive, but people were dying and she couldn't help but think it wasn't worth it.

"Micheline?" Ludwik peeked in the door. "Oh, you're up."

Stella jumped and checked her wig. That was fast. Too fast. She wasn't prepared, but it didn't matter. Ludwik wasn't really looking at her. He hurried to the bed to set down her tray, keeping his eyes down.

"What's wrong?" Stella asked. "Did…did I do something?"

The concierge jerked upright to look at her for the first time. His eyes were swollen and he had dark smudges underneath. "No, no. You're fine. And up. I'm glad you're better."

"I am and I think I will be leaving you in peace today, if the doctor says I can."

"In peace," he whispered.

It's happened.

Stella went over to him, laying a light hand on his arm. "I'm sorry I said that. It was a poor choice of words. Have we surrendered?"

"You don't know?"

"I've been sleeping," she said.

"Dr. Tulp has been very concerned about that since he took those pills away," said Ludwik. "You were still sleeping. He couldn't understand it."

"Did we surrender?"

"No, but she's gone. She left." The prim and proper concierge dropped down on the bed and buried his face in his hands.

Stella sat next to him and rubbed his back the way her mother would've done. "Who? The queen?"

He nodded. "And the government."

They left us.

Her chest got tight and she whispered, "But we're still fighting?"

"The high command hasn't given up, but the radio says they are negotiating a surrender." He patted her leg. "Your people are fighting on."

It took Stella a moment to remember which people he was talking about. She didn't really have people anymore, at least not one particular set.

"Will Belgium hold?" she asked.

"Longer than us," he said, pulling out a handkerchief and wiping his eyes. "What's going to happen, Micheline?"

"I'm sure I don't know."

"But you've been to the east. What's it like there? What will they do to us?"

"This isn't Poland. They've decided the Dutch are Aryan."

"Not me," he said.

"Aryan enough," said Stella.

"Enough for what?"

She couldn't tell him about the ideas for extermination that were flowing around the Reich. They'd made no secret about their views in speeches and newspapers, but still, no one comprehended their intent. If she hadn't heard Oscar von Drechsel's plan in Berlin, she wouldn't have believed such ideas were possible, much less detailed plans to eradicate an entire people for absolutely no reason other than hate and fear.

"To keep them from singling you out," she said.

"I'm going to have to fight," he said. "I can't fight. Look at me."

"Most won't fight."

"You will."

She chuckled. "Will I? A woman of a certain age?"

"You're already fighting and I admire you for it," he said. "Let's get you back in bed."

The concierge insisted Stella get back in bed and he served her coffee and a good hearty breakfast that she was actually hungry for.

"You do look better." His eyes searched her face. "Much better."

She looked down at her coffee. Her makeup was probably non-existent. She couldn't remember the last time she'd applied it. She couldn't even remember the last time she cared.

"Do I remember something about Josiah Bled and visas?"

Ludwik got distracted and retold her about Uncle Josiah's telegram.

"When does his ship set sail?" she asked.

"This evening, I think. I'd have to check." He frowned slightly. "You're very interested. Not nursing a broken heart, I hope."

She smiled up at him. "Don't worry about that. I'm not sure if that lovely girl knows what she's taken on, but I wish them well."

"We all do. It was such a surprise. I never thought he'd get married."

"The entire world will be surprised. I do hope they get away safely."

His face fell again. "Once we surrender, it will be fine, don't you think?"

"As fine as it gets."

Ludwik straightened his jacket and said, "Dr. Tulp will be by soon."

"He didn't come this morning?"

"You really don't remember much, do you?"

"I don't."

"He called and asked me to give you your pills and have you eat," said Ludwik.

"Did I?"

"You took the pills, but you wouldn't eat."

She apologized and he went to the door. "You really think you'll leave today?"

"Are the trains running?"

"Some, but not all."

"We'll see then."

Ludwik looked somewhat cheered before he left. He'd gotten attached to her and she to him. Stella wished she could do something for the kind concierge but being only one fourth Jewish would probably protect him from the worst of it anyway.

Stella pushed the thought of the Reich's cold approach to lineage away and concentrated on eating everything on her plate. The food situation was about to take a dive. The Dutch would soon find themselves as hungry as the Germans after they'd swept over the countryside, taking everything for their army.

It was harder to eat it all than she thought. Her stomach seemed to have shrunk and she was trying to make herself finish her roll when there was a soft knock on the door.

"Come—" She didn't get the whole phrase out before a man slipped in the door and a bite of roll fell out of her mouth onto her lap.

"What on Earth are you doing here?"

Uncle Josiah whipped off his hat and unwound a scarf from his face. "You recognized me? I can't believe it."

"Of course, I did. I'd know you in a blackout." She pushed the tray away. "What are you doing here?"

"I came back for you," he said with a roguish grin.

"How? Why?"

"I got you a visa. That Wilcox fellow is a very accommodating guy."

Stella threw back the covers and got out of bed. "I don't need a visa. Get out of here before someone catches you."

"I don't care if they do catch me. I'm getting you out of here," said Uncle Josiah.

"We agreed. This is my job. I'm not leaving."

"I changed my mind."

"You told her," she said.

He ducked his head. "I might've said something."

She punched him in the shoulder. "Where is she? You didn't bring her back after everything I went through to get them out of here?"

"Of course not. They're at the Hotel Weimar near the consulate. We sail at seven. Plenty of time to get you out of here," he said.

"I'm not going. Are you insane?"

He grabbed her by the shoulders. "For the first time, I'm seeing clearly. You're my family. I have to get you out of here. You're sick."

She shook off his hands and said, "I'm better. See? No coughing."

"So much the better." Uncle Josiah glanced around. "Where are your suitcases?"

"If you think you can force me to go back to the States, you are crazier than I ever thought. I'm not going to leave Nicky in England while I turn tail and run home. I can get out of here and see him, if I hurry."

"I didn't say you were getting on my ship," said Uncle Josiah. "I might be crazy, but I'm not delusional. Zeb got you a berth on a small ship going to England. You're not a passenger. You're crew. It's illegal, but you don't mind about that."

Stella's mind could hardly comprehend her luck. "Are you serious?"

"I am. It's leaving tonight late under cover of darkness to run the blockade." He paused and then said, "It will be dangerous."

She laughed. "When do we leave?"

"I have a car and enough gas to get us back. I don't know how you found Zeb Wilcox, but he's a prince."

"Does he know who I am?"

"No, only that you are a friend to the Bled family," said Uncle Josiah. "When can you be ready?"

"How long will it take to get there?"

"It took me four hours. I'm getting good at this."

"So, we have time," she said.

"For what?" he asked.

Stella hated to say it, but she couldn't think of a lie quick enough. "A bath."

He grinned and said, "I was going to say…"

"Shut up and get out." She pushed him toward the door and he put his disguise back on.

"All right. All right. I'll go get something to eat around the corner. How long?"

"Forty-five minutes."

Stella prepared for a protest, but he simply pulled his scarf up over his nose and checked his watch. "I'll be back at one fifteen."

"I'll be ready."

He grabbed her, pressing her head to his chest. "I'm glad I came."

She hugged him, luxuriating in the touch of family and whispered, "I'll have to thank Judith."

"We both will," he said, taking a quick peek out the door. "Don't waste any time. It's going to take longer to get back. I'm not taking any chances of missing our boats."

Stella nodded and he was gone.

Stella turned on the taps in the bathtub and yanked her suitcases from under the bed. Charlotte's papers came out of the secret compartment and were quickly hidden in her handbag to be handy when needed. Then she threw her ledgers in her briefcase and resisted the urge to cram her clothes in her suitcases. If someone were to search her, nothing said escaping like unfolded clothes, so she neatly folded everything and picked out a stolid, plain dress to wear and set it aside.

She left her makeup out and took off the wig to try and fix it, but days in bed had rendered it in need of more than a couple minutes of fussing, so it would just have to wait.

Glancing around for odds and ends, she spotted Judith's gift. The box had fallen off her dressing table and popped open, spilling the gorgeous diamond and pearl necklace on the floor in a sparkly heap. It was a good thing Uncle Josiah didn't see that. She'd never hear the end of it.

Stella put the necklace back in its box and tucked it in her handbag just as someone knocked on the door. She shoved the wig back on her head and opened the door to find Dr. Tulp standing there, red-eyed and shocked.

"Micheline, you're up?"

"Oh, doctor!" She'd forgotten all about him coming and was briefly as stunned as he was.

"May I come in?" he asked.

"Well…I…yes, of course." Stella stepped back and the doctor walked in to frown.

"Are you going somewhere?"

"I hope so," she said. "I'm much better."

"I see that, but I will have to examine you," he said. "Is that running water?"

"Oh, I forgot." She ran in the bathroom and turned off the taps. "I was going to take a bath."

"Good. You'll need a bath."

She was going to the bed and stopped short. "For what?"

He didn't answer but instead moved her to the bed and sat her down to take her temperature and check her chest. "Very good. Yes, I'm quite pleased."

"Then I can go?" she asked as if she might be talked out of it.

"You can." He fiddled with his stethoscope and his mouth twitched.

"Is everything all right?"

"Yes, yes, it is."

"Are you upset about the queen?"

The doctor looked blank for a second and then said absently, "Oh, yes. She's gone to England with the ministers."

Well, that's not it.

"Have you had to treat many patients?" she asked.

"They are coming in from other areas, but that has not been my primary focus." He didn't elaborate and she sat on the bed, glancing over at her watch and hoping he'd get to the point.

"So…are we done?" Stella finally asked. "I have to take a bath."

"I need to tell you something," he said.

Dread washed over her. She didn't know what it was, but she wasn't leaving. That much was plain from the set of his eyes. "Yes?"

"I don't want to delay you, but I really have to tell you that she's back. Elizabeth insisted you be told."

It was Stella's turn to be blank. "She who?"

"Truus. She's come back from wherever she was."

Maybe I can still make it.

"Did Elizabeth want me to do something or is it already done?" Stella asked.

"Rena told me this morning that you know some children that need to get out. You'd paid for their passage," he said.

"I did. Will she take them?"

He nodded and sealed her fate. Geertruida Wijsmuller-Meijer had come back to Amsterdam, returning the night before. That morning the garrison commander of Amsterdam had called her. There was a ship in IJmuiden that would take a group of refugee children from the Burgerweeshuis. She only had to arrange transport and get them there. The ship would sail that night, hopefully getting out before the surrender, if there was one.

"She'll take Lonia and Ezra?" Stella asked.

"If you can get them to the Burgerweeshuis by the time she leaves," said Dr. Tulp.

"When is that?"

"Four o'clock. Micheline, she won't wait and there won't be any more transports."

Stella sank back on the bed. Four o'clock. Way too late. "Could you take them or Rena?"

"No, absolutely not." The doctor looked surprised at the harshness of his own voice. "I'm sorry. It's been a long day."

"Is Rena—"

"She's fine but very tired. She has her own children, you know."

"Yes, I know that." Stella wanted to beg the doctor to do it, but his red eyes and exhausted manner stopped her.

"I don't know them," he said. "I could go, but what parent would give their children to a strange man? I would not. If you want them on that transport, it will have to be you, Micheline."

Stella turned away and put a hand over her mouth. Nicky went from a day away to a week, if there were trains, if she could get on one. Then there was the question of passage over the channel.

"I'll do it," she whispered.

"I know you want to get to your family."

She nodded. "What time is the ship leaving?"

"Eight, I believe," said the doctor. "People are clamoring to get tickets. I don't know how they managed it."

"What's the ship?"

"The SS Bodegraven. Why do you ask?"

"Just wondering. I think that was the ship Josiah Bled was going to get on if they were leaving from IJmuiden ," said Stella.

"I think you're right. Small world, isn't it?"

"Very small."

"But you'll do it?" he asked.

She took a breath and blinked away her tears. No use crying over spilt milk. She'd get out and to England if she had to swim the channel. Stella turned back to the doctor. "I hope the children will be safe in England. Have you heard anything? Are they attacking Britain yet? I stopped listening to the radio."

"It was thought that they would, but we have slowed them down and of course, your country as well has put up much resistance."

My country is sitting on its hands.

"Hopefully, Churchill will make a difference," she said.

"Isn't he a drunk?" the doctor asked.

Stella concealed a smile. It was amazing how far nasty rumors could spread. "Let's hope not. Is there anything else?"

"No. Just be at Burgerweeshuis by four and then you can go, if you think it necessary."

"It's necessary. Are you going to see Elizabeth today?"

The doctor packed his bag and went to the door. "I did this morning."

"How is she?" Stella asked.

"Eager for your children to get on that transport. You know how she feels about children." He held out his hand. "If I don't see you again."

Stella took his hand and pressed it to her cheek. "You saved me. I won't forget it."

The doctor embraced her and then hurried out the door. Stella almost turned on the radio but in the end, she didn't want to be distracted. Four o'clock wasn't so far away and she had to do battle one last time with Uncle Josiah. He wouldn't take this well and she didn't blame him. She wasn't taking it well.

She got in the lukewarm bath and washed the clinging scent of long illness off her skin and out of her hair. By the time she got out, she was so tired she felt like she'd taken one of the sleeping pills. She briefly considered pepping herself up with an energy pill, but she didn't want to be frantic when she saw Weronika and Józef. It was no easy thing to persuade parents to let their children go. Truus would've been ideal. She was made for the job with her warmth and reputation, but Stella would just have to make do.

With packing no longer immediately necessary, she made up for lost time and dried her long hair thoroughly and worked on her wig.

Once she'd put on her makeup and got dressed, it looked like nothing had happened. She was thinner, but certainly well enough to be trusted with small children. She hoped anyway. Stella hadn't had a lot of experience with children other than Myrtle and Millicent.

Knock. Knock.

Right on time. Stella straightened her shoulders and opened the door. Uncle Josiah nearly bowled her over and went directly to the bed. "You're not packed."

"I'm not going," she said.

He rounded on her like her father when she'd accidentally ruined an entire batch of wort. "You are going, if I have to drag you out of here by the hair."

"I'm sorry you came back, but it can't be helped. I made a promise and it's time to keep it."

"You promised me, Stella. Me. Your family."

"I know."

"What about Nicky?" he asked. "The Brits might start flying in support of the Dutch and the Belgians. They will certainly support the French."

Stella got a hat out of the wardrobe to give herself something to do. "I know that."

"We're talking about the battle for Britain. That's what we're talking about here." He grabbed the hat off her head and threw it across the room.

She went across to the window and picked up her hat. "I know what's happening better than you."

"You don't even have the radio on. They're talking about surrender or fighting to the death. How are you going to get out, if you don't go with me?"

"I'll figure it out," she said. "I'm very good at figuring things out."

He grabbed her by the shoulders. "Why do it? So, you promised the earl, so what?"

"It's not him or the service." She told him about promising Weronika to get the children out and the last transport in IJmuiden. And Elizabeth. She was dying and while she was dying she was still looking after other people. She wouldn't stop until the last breath left her body. "I can't let her down. You don't know how many people she's helped on Mother's list and she'll keep on helping. She'd be dreadfully upset if Ezra and Lonia didn't get out. You know how bad it will get."

"She doesn't even know them," he said.

"I know them," she said. "Are they any less important than Judith?"

"Don't do that."

Stella went to her uncle and hugged him fiercely. "Go to your wife and get on that ship. I'll be fine. I know what I'm doing."

"I don't."

"So what's new?" she asked, and he gave out a chuckle.

"Promise that nothing else will delay you. You will get to France or wherever you're supposed to go and leave."

Stella tilted down her chin and promised. She didn't know what she was saying.

CHAPTER 28

Uncle Josiah was gone and no one in the hotel knew he'd been there. She'd seen him barrel away in his Volvo with the back seat filled with gas cans and prayed he'd be careful. One little fender bender and he'd go up like a firework.

After watching him round a corner, Stella hurried across the square. It wasn't empty anymore. People were coming in from the provinces, hoping to avoid the bombing or running from it with only scant belongings in their arms. The military was there and the police out in force. There was talk of barricades to block the Nazis from entering the city as if that were possible. No one wailed or was frantic. When Stella found a tram that was working, she marveled at the stoic faces around her, but their voices weren't so stoic.

"He killed himself," whispered a woman.

"Surely not. It must've been an accident. He was a professor," said her friend.

"It wasn't an accident and it's happening all over the city," said a man.

"Why would they do it?"

"They're Jews. Why do you think?"

The conversation went on and Stella blocked it out. It was too distressing. Weronika wouldn't do that, or would she? It seemed a choice the foreign Jews were making. Stella moved away from the conversation and clung to the pole by the exit until the tram stopped near the Jodenbuurt.

"I heard there are tanks outside the city," said a man, pushing past her roughly.

"They're not going to bring tanks into Amsterdam," said a woman.

"Why not? They mean to crush us."

"It's stupid."

Stella got past the couple. Tanks?

Please don't let that be true.

Eiger Menswear was closed, but the lights were on and it was the middle of the day on a Tuesday. The lettering on the window said they were supposed to be open, although not many were shopping in the *Jodenbuurt* that day.

Stella cupped her hands around her eyes and peered inside. No customers and no one behind the register, but the neat racks of clothing weren't so neat. Some suits had been tossed on the floor and a collection of hats had been taken off the rack and left on the counter. The owner, while not friendly in the least, had been neat and businesslike.

She pounded on the door for a third time and then backed up to look at the attic window. Closed. She could yell, but nobody would hear her. Maybe there was a back way in, but it wasn't obvious with no alleys. She'd have to loop the block and see if she could find an entrance.

Turning around to decide which way to go, Stella saw a couple glance at the shop and then cross the street, averting their eyes. She waited and it happened again. The people that were out sure weren't coming anywhere near Eiger Menswear. She turned back to the door and tried the knob. Locked, of course.

She shouldn't do it, not in broad daylight, but she was short on time and she didn't fancy going around to the back to find another locked door, if there even was one. Stella huddled up to the door and pulled her tiny set of lock picks out of the secret compartment in the side of her handbag. Two seconds and the lock clicked. She opened the door and wasn't five steps in before she smelled it. Feces and blood.

Oh, God no.

She rushed around the counter and found the till open and emptied. The smell was worse at the back and she followed it through to the storage area. It, too, had been gone through with boxes opened and rummaged through. She didn't know what they were looking for, but they weren't stealing wholesale. Plenty of nice suits had been tossed aside and some good quality sewing machines were left, not to mention a large safe unopened.

Stella turned back around and was going for the narrow stairs when she noticed a door next to them. It was ajar and she could hear a little buzzing.

"Hello," she said, knowing nobody in that room was going to answer. "It is Micheline Dubois. I've come to see the Dereczynski family on business."

She held her breath and reached for the door.

Not them. Not them.

Inside was a minuscule bathroom with a tiny sink, toilet, and a body. The owner lay slumped down on the toilet with what was left of his head propped against the wall. A revolver lay at his feet with a note. It might've said something about a will, but Stella couldn't worry about that.

She closed the door and ran up the stairs, having to stop at each room with her lungs burning and her cough kicking up again. At the small attic door, she bent over gasping and knocking at the same time. No answer and she almost sat down and cried. If they weren't there, she had nowhere else to look. They might've left Amsterdam and she'd have given up Nicky for nothing at all.

Once she'd caught her breath and calmed her panic, she shifted on the narrow stair to peek through the hole where the knob should've been. From what she could see, everything was still there from the hotplate to a small sweater hanging on the back of a chair. Stella could smell cabbage but no blood. They could just be out and she checked her watch. Two fifteen. She could wait. She had to wait. How long to get to the Burgerweeshuis? Twenty minutes by foot, but she'd have the children. They wouldn't be fast. Myrtle and Millicent were like dragging lead weights, especially when they didn't want to go. A cab. A tram. She had time, if they would just come back.

She leaned against the wall and closed her eyes. The tiredness overwhelmed her again and what seemed like a minute later, someone shook her.

"Micheline?"

"Mama, she is dead," said a plaintive little voice in Polish.

"She's not dead," said Lonia. "I can see her breathing."

Stella opened her eyes to find Weronika, Ezra, and Lonia crammed into the staircase and peering at her with worry.

"I'm not dead. I was waiting for you." She checked her watch. "Oh, my God."

"What is it?" Weronika asked. "Have they come?"

"No," said Stella, struggling to her feet. "I don't know. Where have you been?"

"There has been an accident. I was looking for a new place for us."

Ezra tugged on his mother's skirt. "What accident?"

"Poopy accident." Lonia pinched her nose.

Stella met Weronika's eyes. "I heard about that accident. Hasn't *anyone* else?"

"They have, but with the situation, he is not a priority."

"When did it happen?"

"Early this morning," said Weronika. "Józef heard it and he called, but no one came."

Lonia smacked her mother's hand. "Heard what?"

"Nothing, darling."

Stella reached out to her. "Can I come in?"

The mother told her to open the door and she led the way into the small flat. The children went running to their room and Weronika offered to make tea.

"I don't have time for that. It's almost three fifteen."

"You got them a transport," said Weronika and tears flowed down her cheeks like someone had turned on a tap.

"I did with Tante Truus, but we have to go now," said Stella.

"Now? They can't go now. I haven't…I haven't talked to them and Józef isn't here."

"There are buses leaving at four from the Burgerweeshuis. They're going to IJmuiden where they'll get on a ship to England." Stella took her hand and found it shaky and cold. "It's the last one."

"She could…I heard of children getting out through France and Switzerland," said Weronika.

"That was before. Once the Reich is in control, it will be different."

"I can't. Józef would never forgive me. We will wait." Weronika pulled her hand out of Stella's and stood shaking like it was five degrees. "Thank you for coming."

"Don't do this. It's their last chance."

"There will be other chances."

"Maybe, but there will be thousands trying to get them and I won't be here anymore," said Stella.

"Where are you going?" Weronika's shaking got worse and tears flowed again.

"Home to Belgium. I have to find my family and see if they are okay."

"When will you leave?"

"Today as soon as I take the children to Tante Truus," said Stella.

"You aren't taking them. I can't. Józef…"

Stella came close and whispered, "Your landlord has killed himself because they are coming. This is not an idle threat."

Weronika tried to speak but choked on the words, ending up shaking her head.

"I understand this is hard."

She jerked her head up and her streaming eyes bored into Stella's. "You don't have children." She grabbed at the front of her dress, tearing at the fabric and popping off a button. "They are my heart, my life."

"That's why they should go. Protect your heart. This is what you can do and it is the hardest thing, but you know about Tante Truus. You know she saves children."

"It's so far and you're not going?" Weronika asked.

"No, but all the children from the orphanage are. There will be bigger ones and the voyage is short. Once they are in England the children's society will take over," said Stella.

"Józef is usually home at five. I don't know where he is working today. Somewhere on the docks, but if you can wait."

"I can't wait. It's now or never."

A little voice came from behind them. "Am I going to see Masło now?"

Weronika ran over and swept Lonia up in her arms, sobbing until she crumpled to the floor. Little Ezra ran in and shook a finger at Stella saying, "Stop making Mama cry."

His mother grabbed him, too, clutching at her babies in a wild searching way that struck at Stella's heart. She touched them all over, kissing and looking so as to memorize every ounce of their small forms. She was going to let them go and it was breaking her.

"I won't go, Mama," said Lonia. "England is awful and wet. I will stay here with you."

Ezra wailed and buried his head in his mother's neck. "I'm not going."

"Weronika, you have to decide. I only have a little time to get there," said Stella.

"No, I won't go." Lonia stomped her foot and her mother pushed her back.

Weronika savagely wiped the tears off her cheeks. "You will go. Micheline will take you to the nice woman. Tante Truus. You remember, we talked about Tante Truus."

"I don't want to."

"You have to or you might not get to see Masło for a long time."

Lonia swallowed hard. "I want you and Papa to go."

"We can't go, darling. It's only for children," said Weronika.

"Special for children?" Lonia looked up at Stella.

"Yes," she said. "You will go with a lot of other children on a huge boat to England. It's an adventure and you will have to be brave and strong to do it. Not everyone can."

Lonia puffed up. "I'm very strong."

Weronika hugged her again. "You are my strongest girl."

"What about me?" complained Ezra.

She told him that he was the strongest boy and that they could do it and make their papa proud. Slowly, the mother eased them into the bedroom and packed two suitcases. Then she dressed them warmly in their winter coats and asked, "Lonia, do you remember what Micheline told you last time? How do you find Masło?"

Lonia dutifully repeated everything she was supposed to remember and then Weronika had her memorize her parents' full names and birth dates, where she and Ezra were born, and their address in Poland. Then she looked up at Stella and said, "I heard that was good for them finding us later."

Stella nodded, overwhelmed by the idea of a six-year-old's memory being key to finding her parents. "You should write it, too."

Weronika went back into the bedroom and brought back an envelope. "I did, but things get lost."

Stella took the envelope and tucked it in her handbag. "We have to go now."

Weronika hugged her children and told them to be good.

"You can come to the busses," said Stella. "No one will mind."

"They might think they aren't orphans and not let them get on."

"I don't think the children are necessarily orphans. Their parents just aren't here," said Stella, "and I'll need you to take them out for me."

"Out where?"

"Out of here," she said. "I don't want to be seen leaving with them."

"Why?" Lonia asked. "Don't you like us?"

"I like you very much, but there are other people who wouldn't like it and I want us to avoid them," said Stella.

Weronika agreed to take the children out the back. There was a way, but she said Stella wouldn't have found it. The door to the alley looked like any other door. "Where should we meet?"

"The Waterlooplein?" Stella asked.

"At the market. There's a stall on the corner with children's clothes."

They agreed on the spot, but Stella was reluctant to leave, fearing Weronika would change her mind. There was nothing she could do about it, if the mother couldn't bear it, so she went down the stairs. It might've been her imagination, but the smell seemed worse or maybe it was just because she knew now where it originated. She put a handkerchief over her nose and went through the shop as fast as possible, catching two men coming in with bags and a defiant look in their eyes.

"Excuse me," said Stella.

One of the men grabbed her arm. "Where do you think you're going?"

"Out of this stench. When are the politie coming?"

The men hesitated and one said, "Someone called them?"

"That's what I heard," she said.

He let her arm go and she scooted out the door before he could think better of it. Then she hurried down the street and that's when she saw him. She should've seen him earlier. Mussert of the torn pocket. The bastard must've taken up residence outside the hotel. She'd totally forgotten about him and would've assumed he'd have forgotten about her, too, but there he was, lounging on a corner, obvious as ever.

She hurried by him and he followed, only ten feet behind. She couldn't imagine what was the point of this, but it didn't matter. Stella got herself into the market at Waterlooplein. Thankfully, all the sellers were there, trying to make one last buck before the Nazis came and stole it all. She weaved through stalls and around tables. Mussert stayed doggedly on her heels, but he didn't follow her into the larger stalls. Stella smiled. If she could lose Cyril Welk in a market, she could lose a man who didn't really care the way Cyril did.

Cyril had a passion. Mussert had a job and it was time for him to lose it.

Stella ducked into a woman's clothing stall. It was crammed with the most godawful items, third and fourth-hand dresses, skirts, and shoes, but crammed was called for. She went through the different racks, going in circles. An advantage to being short showed up in a big way. Mussert looked over the racks and Stella looked under them. He made a circuit through the racks and then another. Stella dodged him easily. The lady running the booth caught her and Stella quickly gave her a coin whispering, "He won't leave me alone."

The old lady grimaced and picked up a broom. She headed Mussert off and started asking why a man was in her booth. She didn't have clothes for him. Was he some kind of oddball who bought women's clothes or worse, stole them? Mussert protested and she smacked him with the broom. Stella peeked between two racks and watched him get driven back toward the exit and she went out the back, just like old times in Paris.

Walking as fast as she could, Stella got to the booth Weronika described a little late and the family was leaving.

"I'm here." Stella bent over coughing. She couldn't hold it anymore.

"What happened?" Weronika said, clutching the children to her hips.

"There was a man, but I lost him."

"Where? What man?"

"It doesn't—" She spotted Mussert coming through some booths and ramming people aside in his rage. "He's coming. We have to go."

They ducked behind a booth full of books and Weronika peeked around the corner. "Which one is he?"

"Don't do that," said Stella, checking her watch. Twenty minutes. She'd just have to make a break for it, if Mussert saw and told Bikker so be it. "Never mind. We just have to go or we'll never make it."

Weronika peeked out again. "Who is he?"

"He works for Jan Bikker. He isn't a kind man."

Ezra began to sniffle. "A bad man is coming?"

"He won't get you," said Stella.

"I'll make sure of it." The mother dropped down and hugged her children. "Go. I will stop him."

"Mama," pleaded Lonia.

"Go. I can do this for you."

"But Mama—"

"Go now to England and we will come as soon as we can." Weronika stood up and threw back her shoulders. "Good luck." With that, she marched out into the market and got in Mussert's way. "Pieter, it's you!" she cried.

Stella grabbed the suitcases and said, "Lonia, get your brother. We're going."

They went as fast as Ezra's legs could carry him until they were past the square. Then Stella gave Lonia the small suitcase and picked up Ezra. They weren't going to make it if they walked and the tram was too far and would take too long. A cab. She looked out at the traffic. There were cabs, but they all had passengers.

"Come on," she said.

"Where are we going?" Lonia asked.

"To the corner so we can get a cab."

"I don't have any money."

Stella couldn't help but smile. "Don't worry. I do."

They got to the corner and three full cabs went by. Then there was another. He saw them and scowled, driving right by, but someone made a wrong turn and tried to correct in the middle of the intersection.

"That's our cab." Stella ran for it, dodging around cars and a mule cart. "Come on, Lonia."

"But he didn't stop!"

"He's stopped now!" Stella wrenched open the door and shoved Ezra in.

"Hey! Get out of here," the driver yelled.

Stella responded by boosting Lonia in. "To the Burgerweeshuis."

"I don't want any dirty Jews in my cab," he bellowed. "Get out. I'm going to lunch."

She shoved a fist full of money in his face. "We'll pay double."

"I don't drive Je—"

Stella yanked open his door and shoved her face in his. "Do I look like a Jew?"

"I...I..."

"Good. Now take us to the Burgerweeshuis on the double." She slammed his door and hurtled herself in the back with the children and the luggage.

"I don't know who you think you are, but I'm taking you to the politie station," said the driver as he eased around the now stalled car still in the middle of the road.

"How about you take me to the Baron Joost Van Heeckeren's house? You can explain why his agent didn't do as he asked." A little name dropping never hurt.

"Baron Van what?"

"Heeckeren! The one with the parties and the money and the women. He has friends, you know. Friends in important places." She put her card in his face.

"New York?"

"That's right. That's my company and I work for the baron. Are you going to drive us or not?" Stella demanded. "What's your name? How long have you been in the city?"

The driver threw up his hands. "All right. All right."

The cab lurched forward and the children shrieked. The driver began muttering about never getting lunch and the Nazis and the panic. His wife was in a quiet tirade. His son left to fight. He grumbled about anything and everything as they drove across the Amstel River, zipping in and out of traffic without an inch to spare. They were making good time, despite the traffic. Stella kept looking at her watch and the children watched her. Ezra sucked two fingers, despite Lonia trying to pull them out of his mouth and chiding him. Ten minutes. Five minutes.

"Is Papa coming?" Ezra asked around his fingers in his mouth.

"Papa can't come," said Lonia.

"Who will take care of us?"

The driver glanced in the rearview and said, "Dirty Poles. They invade our country." He yanked the car to a side street and slammed the brakes, throwing the children to the floor and Stella against the back of his seat. "Get out."

"We're not there!"

"It is right over there." He pointed in a vague direction and got out to shove the keys in his coat pocket.

"You have to take us!"

"No, I don't!" He yanked open Stella's door and grabbed her arm.

"Let go!"

"Pay me!"

"Where is it?" Stella got out and spun around. The driver rolled his eyes and pointed across the main road. "Follow the sign and pay me now."

Stella would rather have slapped him, but she didn't have the time. She shoved some coins at him, grabbed the suitcases, and then the children. Carrying Ezra, she ran for it right into the street, nearly causing an accident, but they got to the other side and she saw a sign for the Burgerweeshuis.

"Come on, Lonia," she said between coughs.

"Are you sick?"

"I was. Come on."

They ran down the narrow shopping street and took a right past stone reliefs with figures and poetry about orphans to the fifteenth century gate, huge with more orphans and a dove symbolizing the Holy Spirit or so Elizabeth had told her. The right door was open and Stella went through into the large courtyard, but it was empty. Not a single bus. Five after four.

"Where are they?" Lonia asked in Polish.

"Gone," a young voice answered, also in Polish.

Stella turned and saw two older children with suitcases, a girl and boy about twelve and fourteen, both wearing the saddest expressions she'd ever seen in her life.

"When did they leave?" she asked them. "Did we just miss them?"

They shook their heads and their shoulders dropped as if weight had been added. "They weren't here."

"What? Tante Truus—" Stella had to stop and cough until the blood was back.

"We came before they were supposed to leave, but the doorman said the buses were on the Lijnbaansgracht."

Stella's legs buckled and she almost dropped Ezra before she caught herself. The Lijnbaansgracht wasn't close. They'd never have made it. "I...I was told to come here."

"So were we," said the boy, his sad eyes fixing on Ezra, who was now snuffling into Stella's shoulder, "I want Mama."

"Why are you still here?" Stella asked the boy.

"Our mother wanted us to go and now we've missed our chance," said the girl. "We'll never get out now."

"She'll be so upset," said the boy. "She cried and cried when we got word, but she will cry more now."

Lonia tugged on Stella's jacket. "I don't get to see Masło?"

All manner of curses went through Stella's mind and she said, "No, you're going." She shoved Ezra into the boy's arms. "Go to the street. I'm getting a car. I'll take you."

"You?" the girl asked. "Who are you?"

"Micheline Dubois. Go to the street. I will be right back. Don't forget the luggage." Stella ran out of the courtyard and down the street. She hadn't run that fast since Berlin, faster even since there was no snow to contend with.

She retraced her steps right back to the cab and it was still there. A café was across the street, packed with people, and that's where the surly driver would be, him and his grumbling stomach.

All right, Park-Welles, let's give it a go.

Stella tilted her hat down low over her eyes and once again thanked her mother for making her short in a country of the very tall. She squeezed in easily and no one paid her any mind. Not being young and pretty was always useful, if disheartening. Men saw her and looked away, instantly assessing her as not worth their time. She wanted to kick them, but instead worked her way through the crowd until she saw the driver. He had a beer in one hand and a chunk of bread in the other. He guzzled the beer and yelled something about bombs and the goddamn Reich. Stella was behind him to the left. There was the bulge in his pocket. The keys.

"Soup!" yelled a man at the bar and he held up a heavy bowl with a handle.

"Me!" yelled the driver and he went forward, shoving the bread in his mouth.

A distraction. Park-Welles had drilled that into her. Distract and reach. She'd practiced and had gotten pretty good. Good enough to take her skills into Piccadilly to lift wallets. It was quite good fun, especially when she gave the wallets back to their astonished owners. The keys she would not be giving back.

He reached out over the heads of some other patrons and in her hand went. Keys and cash. She took it all. No time to pick and choose. And then she was away and out the door with shouts of "Shut up" and "Turn up the radio" ringing in her ears. She didn't know what was going on and she didn't care. She had a car and it had gas. She'd checked out of habit.

Peeling off down the street and getting back to the Burgerweehuis took only a couple of minutes. She jammed on the brakes in front of the astonished children and cranked back on the brake, making a terrible grinding noise before jumping out.

"Come on, Lonia!" She grabbed their suitcases and tossed them in the back of the cab and then Weronika's children scrambled in after them with big eyes but no questions. The other two had plenty.

"Where did you get it?" the boy asked.

"A friend," said Stella. "Are you coming?"

"What friend?"

"Do you want to come? I'll take you."

"How do you know where to go?" the girl asked.

Stella didn't, but she thought she could worry about that later. Getting going was the important thing. "We're going to IJmuiden to the SS Bodegraven."

"Can you drive?"

"You saw me drive."

The older children's faces were a riot of emotion. They wanted to go, but they were afraid. She was a stranger, after all, so she had to play on the one thing that would work. Disappointing Mother.

"If you don't come with us, you'll have to go home right now and tell your mother that you missed Tante Truus and then you didn't go with me," said Stella, crossing her arms. "My mother wouldn't be happy with me if I did that and she won't be happy if I leave you here either."

"How old is your mother?" the boy asked with a grimace.

Stella threw up her hands. "Does that matter? The Nazis are coming."

The pair exchanged a look and shuffled their feet. Stella was losing the fight, but she wasn't going to argue all day. They had to get there before Truus was on the boat or she couldn't get Lonia and Ezra on.

"All right. It's your choice," she said.

Lonia stuck her little hand out the door. "Come on, Wolfgang. Come on, Gisela. Don't be scared. My mama says Micheline is the best person and she will help us."

That did it. Testimony from a child and the big ones climbed in the back seat. They were going to IJmuiden with a total stranger. Stella only hoped they wouldn't regret it.

CHAPTER 29

The trouble began before they even cleared Amsterdam. Uncle Josiah might've mentioned roadblocks, but she didn't remember anything specific, much less how he got through them.

Wolfgang leaned over the front seat. "They've got guns."

"Yes, they do." Stella gripped the steering wheel and watched the Dutch soldiers approach the cars ahead. She couldn't see what was going on, but from the expressions on the weary soldiers faces, there was probably a lot of yelling and it wasn't working. Cars were being turned around. A couple got through and when they did, papers were read and handed back. Papers. She needed papers.

"Truus would've gone this way," she said.

"What?" Wolfgang and Gisela asked together.

"There've been no buses coming back. Tante Truus had buses. She got through. How'd she get through? How'd she get through?"

"She had papers?" Gisela asked. "But we don't have any papers?"

"The garrison commander called her," said Stella. "Do you have any paper?"

"I have my school notebooks," said Wolfgang.

"Let me see one."

The boy got a notebook out of his suitcase while his sister groused about leaving her dolls behind when he packed stupid schoolwork that no one was going to make him do.

"Let me see." Stella leafed through to a blank sheet in the back. Not great, but better than nothing. She ripped out a paper and got out her fountain pen.

"Hey!" Wolfgang protested.

"Quiet!" Stella wrote a note to herself as Charlotte Sedgewick from Truus and naming the garrison commander and the ship. Being British was essential. They inched forward in the line and she folded and then crumpled the page like it had been through a bit of a war itself.

Here goes everything.

Stella whipped off her wig and shook out her hair. The children gasped, all except Ezra who was too busy sucking his fingers.

"Who are you?" Wolfgang demanded. "Are you a spy?"

Very astute.

"I'm Charlotte Sedgwick and I was in disguise so I could help Tante Truus."

"You're…not German, are you?" Gisela asked.

Stella slipped into her best upper-class British accent and said, "Certainly not. I'm a British citizen and my job is to get Jewish children out of the Reich's power." She exchanged her Micheline papers for Charlotte's and grabbed her handkerchief to scrub the makeup off her face, neck, and hands.

Wolfgang watched with fascination and asked, "Why did you have to be so old and ugly?"

"I was neither, thank you very much," she retorted.

"But…"

"I blend better when I look older and less myself," she said. "Gisela, do you have any lipstick?"

"She's twelve!" exclaimed Wolfgang.

Three more cars got turned around and they were almost to the soldiers.

"She's a girl," said Stella. "Gisela?"

"I…I took Mama's lipstick, her favorite," the girl said, tearfully. "I stole it."

"Why, Gisela?" Wolfgang asked. "Mama won't like it. She'll be mad."

"She always wears it. It looks like her."

"Can I borrow it?" Stella asked. "I'll only use a little."

"Why?" the girl asked.

"It will help us. Trust me."

"You lied to us," said Wolfgang. "I don't trust you. I want to get out."

"You are getting out, out of this country, like your mother wants," said Stella. "Gisela, the lipstick."

Gisela opened her little suitcase and handed Stella the precious lipstick, a very nice one indeed in a silver engraved tube. Stella applied it heavily and rolled her lips. A little touchup and it was back, her cupid's bow. Then she dabbed a little on her finger and rouged her cheeks. It was too bad she hadn't any mascara or shadow but combined with the long loose waves of hair cascading over her shoulders Stella once again became the girl who made the elusive Nicky Lawrence fall head over heels and entranced Nazis in Berlin. Would it work on the Dutch? She didn't know. She'd never tried it, but young and pretty tended to win out.

Gisela stood up and leaned over the front seat to get a look. "Why'd you put it on your cheeks? Mama doesn't do that."

Stella handed her the precious lipstick and shifted in her seat to beam at the children. "It gives me rosy, happy cheeks."

Lonia, who had been looking quite frightened, smiled and clapped her hands. "You're so pretty, like my mama."

"And mine," said Gisela.

Stella tweaked her chin. "I can tell you have a pretty mama."

The girl smiled in return and Stella turned her attention to Wolfgang. He was the fly in the ointment, if there was to be one. "Well, how do I look?"

"I…well…"

"Good enough for soldiers?" she asked.

He nodded and blushed before saying, "It's our turn."

Stella drove forward and said, "My name is Charlotte and I'm taking you to Tante Truus. I want you all to be loud about it. You want on the ship. You want Tante Truus."

The children agreed as the soldier tapped on her window. Stella rolled it down and beamed up at him. "We are going to IJmuiden to meet Geertruida Wijsmuller-Meijer," said Stella in strongly-accented Dutch.

"You are…"

"English." Stella stuck out her hand for him to shake, smiling and batting her eyes for good measure. "Charlotte Sedgwick. Do you want to see my papers?"

The soldier looked down at her and paused. Stella didn't know if he was just so exhausted he couldn't think what to do or was transfixed by her face. Either way worked for her.

"What's the hold up?" Another soldier, a gruff older man with blood on his uniform and bandages on his neck and hands.

"She's English," said the first soldier.

The older soldier scoffed. "We've heard that before." Then he looked down at Stella with her not-remotely Dutch face and raised his brows. "You're English?"

"I am. Charlotte Sedgwick."

"Then you can speak English," he said, dripping with doubt.

Stella beamed at him and said in perfect English, "Of course. I worked for the Barbier family in France and I've been trying to get home. You know how hard it is. I've been traveling for days and days. Then I met Tante Truus. My employer, who knows her, said she could use my help, so here I am, taking these children to IJmuiden."

The men looked at her blankly and she said in Dutch, "Did you understand me?"

Embarrassed, they shuffled their feet and she repeated the entire thing in Dutch, still smiling, and handed her Charlotte papers to the older soldier. He scrutinized her papers, but he wasn't really doubting her. She could tell.

"I have a note," she said helpfully.

"A note?"

"From Truus." She unfolded it and handed it out the window. The soldiers exchanged a look and the younger one said, "She just went through with a bunch of children."

"This Geertruida person did?" asked the older one. "Who let her?"

"The commander."

"Navy?"

"Yes, sir," said the younger with a glance at Stella, which earned him a glowing smile.

The older one leaned down and looked at the children. "Where are you going?"

Ezra unexpectedly yelled, making the others jump, "Tante Truus!" Stella didn't know three-year-olds could be so obnoxious and useful at the same time.

The others chimed in pelting the soldiers with questions about how long it would take to get there and why did they have to stop when their ship was waiting.

"You will let us go, won't you?" Stella asked, giving him the big eyes. "I just want to go home. There's no reason for me to stay here. Please."

The soldier relented and gave back her papers. "Fine, but are there any more of you?"

She grinned up at him. "There's nobody like me. I don't even have a sister."

He chuckled and said, "That's a shame."

His attitude had changed so completely that inspiration struck and Stella held out her fake Truus note and said, "Would you please write something so I can get through? There are going to be other roadblocks, aren't there?"

"Yes, but—"

"Please, it will save so much time for everyone. I'd hate to waste anyone's time with *them* coming," Stella said with a plaintive plea in her voice.

"Oh, all right, but I bet you were nothing but trouble to your father." He pulled out a pencil and wrote a quick note for her.

"I am his favorite, if that's what you mean," she said.

He chuckled again. "I bet you are. Move along, Miss Sedgwick, and good luck."

Stella thanked him sweetly and hit the gas.

"You did it," said Wolfgang in amazement.

"Soldiers like pretty girls and papers. It's a fact," she said.

"We're going to the ship?" Lonia asked.

Stella smiled in the rearview. "Absolutely. You all did very well, especially you, Ezra."

"I'm a good boy," he announced and went back to sucking his fingers.

Definitely a good boy.

The note worked and it was scrutinized by soldiers at five more roadblocks and sometimes they got stopped for no reason at all other than they were driving. Stella would've thought with all the hassle that the roads would've been empty, but they weren't. They were joined by cars, trucks, wagons and even the occasional donkey cart. People were walking to the port, pulling handcarts with their belongings piled high behind them.

Stella didn't know what was going on, but the faces she saw were certainly grim. She asked what the news was at a couple of roadblocks, but the men just looked away and waved her through. That was good but unsettling. Maybe they had surrendered and couldn't bring themselves to say it.

"Are we there yet?" Lonia asked. "I'm hungry."

"Almost," said Stella automatically as she'd heard Florence do with Myrtle and Millicent. Luckily, Lonia was less persistent than her little cousins, who could not be fobbed off so easily, especially after nearly three hours in the cab. Stella never would've imagined it would take so long. It should've taken an hour and a half. Three was a nightmare. The children were hungry and they had to pee. Both Lonia and Ezra broke down and cried at several points, causing

Wolfgang to threaten to walk, which he did. They were going that slow.

"Is that it?" Gisela asked, pointing past Stella at a city in the distance.

"Yes, thank goodness." Stella had gotten so tired, she'd considered having Wolfgang drive, but when she went in that direction, the boy's eyes had turned into saucers and she thought better of it.

Lonia stood up and threw her arms around Stella's neck. "Will they have ice cream?"

"Who?"

"The ship."

The older kids laughed and teased her, saying there wouldn't be any ice cream until England. England had lots of ice cream. Stella didn't know where they got that from. She'd had it at the Savoy, but it wasn't common, especially with the rationing, but she saw no need to disillusion them. They had a crossing to face, after all, and it was better to think of ice cream at the end of it.

"I want to get there now," whined Lonia.

"What flavors do you like?" Stella asked and they discussed the varieties as they inched toward IJmuiden. When they actually got in the city, the traffic was worse and they were low on gas. The needle was on E and the engine was beginning to sputter. They'd never make it to the dock; even if they had enough gas, it would take too long to get there.

"What are you doing?" Wolfgang asked.

"Parking. We're out of gas."

"Not yet."

She looked back at him sternly and the boy could take a hint. "Walking will be faster anyway."

"Yes, exactly," said Stella. "Everyone out."

Wolfgang took charge and got the others going and then took Ezra over to have a pee in the alley while the girls expressed disgust and just a little bit of envy. They weren't peeing in any alley though and simply crossed their legs. Stella stowed her Micheline wig under the seat along with the handkerchief smudged with makeup. Then she got out and locked the cab. She'd be back for it, if she could find some gas.

"Everyone ready to find the ship?" she asked cheerfully, and the kids smiled and cheered.

"Mama's going to be so proud of us," said Gisela.

Wolfgang picked up Ezra and a suitcase. "She already was."

"Our mama's proud of us, too," said Lonia, taking Stella's hand.

"I know she is. You'll write her from England and tell her all about your adventures."

The children started drafting their letters as they joined the people heading to the docks. Darkness had fallen, but the streetlamps were lit. It seemed so bizarre with planes going overhead. Any one of them could've obliterated them. There was no blackout. The Dutch hadn't planned for that. They didn't think they'd need it. Now the small city of IJmuiden was lit up and sparkly with a nice You're Welcome to Bomb Us signal.

Stop thinking about that.

"Where do you think you'd like to live in England?" she asked to distract herself as much as the children and that started a discussion of town versus city. Farm versus shop.

The suitcase was heavy and Lonia's hand grew sweaty the closer they got to the dock. The little girl got quiet and kept glancing up at Stella. They worked through the crowd and Stella found a couple who seemed to know where they were going. They followed them to the docks, moving in a surge of people. With every block, Stella got more and more nervous. So many people and all so desperate and afraid. They came from all walks of life, rich, poor, Jews, gentiles, Dutch, Belgians, and beyond. Not everyone would get on a ship. Very few would and she hated to think about what would happen to them. Would it be like Poland? Brutal and unrelenting. Or Austria? Quiet and cruel.

Wolfgang pointed. "I see a mast."

They came out from between two buildings so old that they leaned toward each other like lovers longing to touch and saw IJmuiden's small port laid out before them. It looked untouched by the battles raging around the country but was unbelievably crowded.

"Look for the Bodegraven," said Stella.

"What does it look like?" Wolfgang asked, ever the practical one.

"I have no idea." She grinned at him. "A ship."

He laughed and called out, "Bodegraven! Where are you, Bodegraven?"

A man turned around and asked, "Is that your ship?"

"Yes," said Stella. "It's the children's ship."

"Do they have tickets? How did they get them?"

"I don't know. I'm just bringing them."

His face fell. "We have to get out. We are…desperate."

Stella looked at the man and his wife and felt the heavy weight of their fear in her chest. It was worse than pneumonia. It was worse than most anything.

"I know. We all are." She hustled the children past them and started asking people where the Bodegraven was. On the fifth try, she got a direction and they squeezed through a crowd worse than any before. The smell of rank sweat and fear filled their noses. Suitcases knocked into the children. Lonia got a bloody nose and Stella had to pick her up to get her out of the crush.

"There it is!" She pointed a bloodstained handkerchief at a long ship with a black hull, two masts, and one steam funnel. Not an elegant way to travel, but it would definitely do.

With new energy, Stella shoved her way through the crowd, using her elbows and the suitcase. She was quite merciless, but she didn't regret it. Steam was coming out of the funnel. Something was happening.

Ships officers and dock workers had cordoned off the gangplank and Stella almost tipped over the rope in her rush to get there. A starchy uniformed man shoved her back. "Where do you think you're going?"

"The ship. The children have passage."

"And I suppose you do, too, like all of these people yelling at us," he said, turning away.

"No, I don't. I'm just bringing them." Stella dropped the suitcase and grabbed his arm.

"Hey!"

"They're going with the children from the Burgerweehuis in Amsterdam. They're Tante Truus children."

"We already have seventy-four fracking orphans to look after. That's enough." He yanked his arm away, but she snatched it back again.

"Now you have seventy-eight. It's all arranged. They're part of the group," said Stella, trying to think of what would work. Money? Smiles? Begging? All that was happening around her to no avail.

"We're leaving."

"Then we're just in time."

"You don't have—"

Stella dropped Lonia and got out the note. "They have permission. Look here from the garrison commander and Truus sent me."

"She's a huge pain in the ass. All those kids, crying."

"Another officer signed it." She pointed at the note from the soldier. "He told us to come. He sent us."

He peered at the note and then spat on the ground. "They're too little."

Stella grabbed Wolfgang. "He'll take care of the little ones. He's big. Fourteen and Gisela, she's twelve. Lonia's no trouble." Stella pushed Lonia forward and squeezed her shoulders. "You'll be good, won't you, sweetheart?"

"I'll be very good," she said on cue.

"Ack, Poles?"

"Yes, and you know what happens to Poles," said Stella. "Please, I beg you."

"Maybe the big ones."

"Sir," said Wolfgang puffed up. "I will take care of them. You won't hear a peep and Ezra here he's so smart, you'll be pleased to have him."

"Ah, Jesus," he said. "Let me see that letter."

He read it again and the ship's horn blasted, causing a surge in the people behind them, pressing forward in desperation. "We're leaving right now. We have to go or we won't be going at all."

"Yes, yes. Fine," said Stella.

"They're ready?"

"Yes, absolutely."

"You can't go on to settle them," he said.

"I don't need to."

"But Micheline," wailed Lonia.

His eyebrows shot up. "Who's Micheline?"

Stella bent over to her. "Shush! Micheline can't come."

Lonia's eyes flew open. "I'm sorry. I love Micheline."

Stella hugged her. "I know you do and she loves you, too."

"Are they coming?" the officer asked.

Stella pushed Lonia under the rope and then helped Wolfgang and Gisela, too. Wolfgang held Ezra out to Stella and she kissed his plump cheeks. "Be good and write as soon as you can."

"Lonia," Stella called out as she pulled out Weronika's letter. "Here. Give this to Tante Truus."

Lonia took the letter, grinned at Stella, and then led the way to the gangplank. A sailor stood there anxiously fiddling with a rope and looking at the sky. Lonia tugged on his uniform and when he looked down, she saluted him, garnering her a rare smile on such a day. Then she dashed up the shifting bridge to the ship. At the top, a matronly woman appeared. Underneath her big floppy hat, her round face held another smile. She opened her arms and Lonia ran right into them. Tante Truus. Love personified. Lonia waved wildly at Stella and then disappeared. Gisela was next and her tentative nature showed. She walked carefully and held tight to the ropes. Gisela got a wonderful smile but no hug. Truus knew who she was before she spoke, so she gave the young girl a handshake and a pat on the back. Gisela turned for a last wave when Wolfgang was halfway up. He had a hard time with Ezra and the two suitcases he had, one in his hand and the other under his arm. Truus came down the gangplank and relieved him of Ezra and he made his way quickly after that. Truus kissed his fat cheeks and turned him toward Stella for a last wave. The chubby little guy waved at everyone and then sucked his fingers. Wolfgang took him from Truus and the officers ran up the gangplank. There was shouting, but Stella couldn't make it out. A murmur went through the crowd and Truus had a tense discussion with one of the officers on the ship. She shook her head and then waved to the children before coming back down as quickly as her rotund form would allow. As soon as her feet hit the wood, the dockworkers sprang into action. The moorings were thrown off, anchor up, and bells clanged wildly.

"They could've taken more," said a woman bitterly.

"What's happening?"

"They weren't due to leave yet. Why can't we get on?"

The crowd on the dock yelled and begged, but it was too late. The big ship belched smoke and began moving from the dock. People began to cry and Stella was one of them. She probably could've gotten on and gotten out. It was like watching Nicky sail away with the children waving furiously at them from the deck. She was happy for them and brokenhearted all the same.

A woman sobbed behind her and a man said, "Don't worry, darling. There'll be other ships."

"No there won't," said a man sadly.

"What do you mean?"

"We've surrendered."

A gasp went through the crowd, followed by denials and curses. Stella wiped her eyes and looked up to see Truus' eyes searching the crowd, looking for her. Stella could've spoken to her. She could be trusted more than anyone else probably, but Stella didn't want to speak to her or anyone. She melted back into the crowd and the life she had chosen.

CHAPTER 30

The crowd didn't disperse. They stayed on the dock for lack of anything better to do. Stella felt their hopelessness. It matched her own. The trains weren't running and she had no gas, but she had to get back. Her kit was in Amsterdam and Francesqua's list and the rest of it.

She let herself get jostled around with no sense of purpose. The children had taken it with them. It was a victory and she had to remember that. Plenty of people were on the dock with their children. They didn't get away. Who knew what would happen now that the worst was just beginning.

Get yourself together. You'll get back. It's just a matter of time.

Stella took a breath and started thinking. Gas. Uncle Josiah got it. So could she. The crowd got thinner as she stepped off the dock and then a wave of screams and panic came over them, rippling in a heart-pounding crush. Bombers, a whole squadron could be heard in the distance and then seen. They were low and formed in a V. The crowd dropped down and Stella with them. The sound got louder. They were there and then gone, disappearing over the ocean.

"Thank God!" cried a woman.

"They could come back," said a man.

"No, they won't. They've gone to bomb the Brits."

"That's what they thought in Rotterdam."

Stella got to her feet with the rest and she heard it again and again. Rotterdam. She grabbed a man's sleeve and asked, "What happened in Rotterdam?"

"Haven't you heard?" he asked.

She grabbed him with both hands. "What happened in Rotterdam?"

"Sweetheart, calm down."

A woman put an arm around her shoulders. "Do you have family there?"

She nodded. She couldn't speak.

"I'm sorry. It was bombed."

Bombed.

Stella was on the ground, but the crowd picked her up. Their panic had turned to concern.

"Who's there? Where were they?"

"Hotel," she whispered. "They were getting on a ship."

"Jesus."

"Oh, dear."

"What hotel?"

"What ship?"

She couldn't answer. She couldn't think. Uncle Josiah. Uncle Josiah.

A woman turned Stella to face her. Instead of saying anything, she gave her a stinging slap. "Where were they?"

"I…near the consulate," said Stella.

"Oh, the center." More whispering. The center was bad.

"When was it? When did it happen?"

"This afternoon," someone said, and Stella started running. They called after her, but she didn't stop. Gas. The cab. Now.

She found it unmolested where she left it, but there were no gas stations around. There were cars. Plenty of cars. She looked in the trunk. Nothing useful and then went running through the streets, looking for a hose. She found one three blocks over and she stole it. Another thing she didn't regret.

The hose was old, but long, which was the most important thing. She searched through the cars near the cab and found one with a nearly full tank.

Thank you.

She used the last drops of gas the cab had to move it next to the car. Then she threaded the hose into the tank. Park-Welles never taught her that. She heard about it on one of Florence's radio programs. The villain was going around stealing gasoline in the dead of night. Stella couldn't remember why and it wasn't terribly clear then, but she learned enough to suck that gas out of the tank and not poison herself, unlike the villain. He drank a tank and died. "Good riddance," said Florence and they'd laughed themselves silly with their Tom Collinses in hand. Her mother called those shows rubbish. Stella couldn't wait to tell her how wrong she was, because she was going to get to Uncle Josiah.

"What are you doing?" a man yelled and ran over to yank at the hose.

No matter. She was done. "I have to get to Rotterdam."

The man's furious face changed. "You have family there?"

She swallowed hard and wiped the hint of gasoline from her lips. "I do. I have to get there."

"It is bad and you are so young." He took her by the shoulders and said, "Don't go. You don't want to see it."

She pulled back. "I have to. They need me."

His face said there was a good chance they didn't, not anymore, but he said, "Where were they? In the north?"

Her hopes soared. "In the center, near the American consulate."

"My dear, the center, it is destroyed."

The word stayed in her ears, playing over and over again. "All of it?"

"A good deal and on fire. The ships, everything."

She shoved the hose into his hands. "When?"

"This afternoon."

"When?" Stella screamed. "Three? Four?"

He stared her. "Earlier."

She pushed him aside and jumped in the cab. He pounded on her window. "You will get hurt. There's nothing you—"

Stella didn't hear the rest. She was driving pell-mell out of IJmuiden. Later, she wouldn't remember leaving the city or how she got to The Hague, through roadblocks and past tanks and Nazi troops swarming into the city. There were only flashes that remained. Dutch troops with their arms up. An SS pointing a rifle at her. Screaming at him. Driving through a field. Smoke. Fire in the sky. Rotterdam.

She got stopped for good in the outskirts next to a little blue house. The streets were too clogged to go further in. People were streaming in and out. She locked the cab and turned to see the flames glowing to the south. A woman grabbed her arm and pleaded, "Where is the hospital? Where is it?"

"I don't know. What hospital?"

"Bergweg! Bergweg!"

Stella shook her off. "I don't know. Where is the American consulate?"

"It's gone. It's all gone! Where's Bergweg hospital?"

"I don't know!" Stella grabbed a man passing. He had a bloodied face and a limp child in his arms. "The hospital? Are you going to the hospital?"

He stared blankly at her and then gave a slight nod. The woman had gone on to another person begging for directions. Stella chased her down and put her on the man with the child. "He's going to the hospital. Follow him."

"Thank you! Thank you!" She ran to catch up and Stella joined the people heading into the city, but they were moving too slow. She ran past them with no clear destination in mind. Uncle Josiah said a hotel. White? That wasn't right. Whitman? No. Those were American names. The consulate. That was all she could think as she ran to the flames. The smoke got thicker and thicker and then she hit the first rubble, blasted buildings, skeletons with flame fingers reaching out of remaining windows. The Red Cross volunteers were carrying people out on stretchers, struggling over remnants of buildings and even bodies.

She heard shooting in the distance and an explosion up ahead, but she kept going, asking everyone where the consulate was. Had anyone seen a handsome American? No one knew. No one cared. She kept moving. Bodies in a row. A child being dragged away by a nurse from a dead mother. She couldn't get anyone to listen. The Dutch were frantic. She didn't know they had it in them. The Germans were moving through in their stiff calm way, following orders and seeing nothing they hadn't been ordered to see.

Do it. They won't care.

She ran up to a group of Wehrmacht, searching for the right insignia. Park-Welles' demand that she memorize the Nazi ranks had been previously useless, but now she knew an Oberst when she saw one. He stood stiff and unyielding on a corner watching as his men tried to clear a road of debris so his vehicle could pass. He didn't notice her walking up. Stella had the feeling he wouldn't have paid her any mind if she had a gaping head wound or was spewing blood from a missing limb. She'd met him before in several incarnations, and they were always the same man, but she was about to surprise him.

She launched herself at his pressed immaculate sleeve and pleaded in German with a very strong American accent, "Can you help me? I'm trying to find the American consulate."

He sneered and tried to swat her away. "Let go of me, you fool."

"I'm an American," she said. "I have to find the consulate."

When she said American, something clicked. He wasn't at war with America. He didn't want to be at war with America.

"You are American?" he asked in the harsh tones of a man educated in Berlin and the army.

"I am. Please, I just need directions," she said, making sure her blue eyes were wide and very obvious.

He didn't melt or even defrost, but he did say in his clipped tones, "It is gone. Completely destroyed."

"They blew up our consulate? Why? We're not at war." She made herself sound silly as if bombs could pick one building and leave next door alone.

A flicker of distaste went over his stern face, but Stella didn't think it was about her. "It was not a target."

"My family was in a hotel nearby. We were trying to get home."

"Where were you?"

The tears came easily enough. God knew she had plenty waiting. "Amsterdam. I was late. I couldn't find a ride here and now…"

The Oberst regarded her with a little less coldness. "How many were in your family?"

She swallowed and more tears spilled down her cheeks. She hated to say it. She didn't want it to be the number. "Seven."

"Seven Americans." He gritted his teeth. "What hotel?"

Stella gave into the panic she was feeling. "I don't remember. I can't remember."

That cracked his cold reserve and he took her arm to lead her back from a surge of people carrying the wounded on cobbled together stretchers. "I have been here before the war. Americans like certain hotels. This is usual."

She nodded.

He began naming hotels. None were right and then he said, "Hotel Weimar?"

She clutched his arm, quite involuntarily. "That's it. Where do I go?"

"I believe it will be destroyed."

"But where?"

He pointed and she ran, dodging stretchers and Wehrmacht, crying women and firefighters covered in soot. But she didn't find the Hotel Weimar. It wasn't there to find.

In the distance, Stella could make out four stories of a partially collapsed building that had flames licking up the remaining section. One person said it was a bank. Another the hotel. It was hard to make out with all the smoke, but someone else confirmed. That wreck was once the Hotel Weimar.

She ran over a bridge that was partially intact, ignoring the bodies in the water, and joined people alongside the quay digging in the rubble beside the smoking hulk.

"I'm looking for an American. Have you seen an American?" she asked everyone until she found a man, wearing a Red Cross armband. He threw a huge chunk of stone masonry and nearly hit her. Stella screeched and jumped out of the way, tumbling down onto the jagged remains of the Hotel Weimar.

"I'm sorry." He came to her and helped her up. "I didn't see you."

"I can hardly see anything." Her lungs were burning again and her eyes streaming from the smoke.

"Come with me," he said. "I need help. I think there are survivors."

"I'm looking for an American man. Tall, handsome, blue eyes."

He pushed her back. "I don't have time for that."

"He was a guest at this hotel. He was just married. His wife was here and her whole family," Stella pleaded. "Please, I have to find them."

The man grabbed another chunk and heaved it off the pile before looking at her, squinting and trying to see with only the flames from the hotel to light up her face. "I saw him. Eyes like yours?"

"Yes. Is he alive?"

"He is."

Stella sank down, all the fight going out of her, and the man started digging again. "Be useful," he said. "Start digging."

"Where is he?"

"Others matter, too! Look around, girl! Dig! Help us!"

"I will, but where is he?" Stella yelled back, getting to her feet and finding her hands bloody from the rubble. They didn't hurt. She didn't feel anything.

The man pointed and went back to digging and cursing her selfishness. She was selfish. She had to find him. Know he was safe and then Judith and then Felix and the others. When that happened, she would dig.

Stella picked her way past more volunteers and firefighters who wanted her to go back, but she pushed past them to a road filled with rubble and thick with smoke. Fire was on both sides of the street, but the horror was beyond. Total destruction. Fires and collapsed buildings. She could make out what looked like the remains of a church tower, backlit with flames. Central Rotterdam was flattened. The ships in the port were on fire or sinking.

"You were looking for an American?" A woman appeared at her side. She wore the uniform of a Red Cross nurse, blackened with soot and stained with blood.

"Yes." Stella had to drag her eyes from the hell before her. "Where is he?"

The nurse took her arm and pulled her away. "This way. He's digging."

He wasn't digging. Not anymore. Josiah Bled sat in the rubble, thirty feet from a raging fire and cradling a body. Stella stood with the nurse and she couldn't think what to do. The body. It was Judith.

"Get him back to work. We need his strength," said the nurse.

"She's dead."

"Yes, and more will be if we don't hurry." She gave Stella a little push to get her stumbling over the rubble.

"Uncle Josiah?"

He didn't look up. He pressed Judith's body to his chest, rocking back and forth. Stella crept up and knelt by his outstretched feet, touching his ankle.

"Uncle Josiah," she said. "It's me, Stella."

Josiah Bled looked up with a face that was almost unrecognizable. If he saw her, she couldn't tell. Then he looked back down and stroked Judith's bloody hair. Her face was concealed on his chest, but her left arm was broken in several places and the rest Stella couldn't bear to look at.

"Never mind him." The nurse took Stella under the arms and hoisted her to her feet. "Help me. I need you."

"I can't leave him."

"He's in shock. It doesn't matter," she said. "There are others."

And so they dug, forming a line with firemen and ordinary people, to lift away the rubble to find the dead and living. Hours went by and then daylight, which made it all the worse. Then Stella could see what she missed in the night. The full destruction, the dead and the wounded. The fires were still raging and she'd coughed her throat raw. Her hands were torn up and so were her knees from falling, always falling. But it still didn't hurt, because everything did. Uncle Josiah hadn't only found Judith. He'd found them all. Felix, Klara and the boys. All dead, killed in the initial bombardment. They hadn't been in the hotel. She could see that in the harsh light of day. They were in the street going somewhere. Maybe running back to the hotel or to an air raid shelter. The bombs had dropped and a building hit them with the blast, a bakery by the look of it. There were cake pans and specialty molds in the street along with ruptured bags of flour, coating everything white in stark contrast with the soot.

"I don't think there's anyone else alive here," said a fireman. His face was streaked with tears and his hands shaky, but he took her hands in his gloved ones. "You should go to the hospital and see to these. You don't want an infection."

"It doesn't matter," she said, looking at Uncle Josiah. He hadn't moved other than to rock and beside him was Klara's body. Stella had missed it in the dark. She may have stepped on the dead woman's hand and the thought made her want to vomit. She would have if she hadn't already three times before.

"How many are there?" the fireman asked.

"Seven, counting him," she said. "What do we do now?"

"Take them to the Bergweg hospital for identification and then to Crooswijk," he said.

"We know who they are," said Uncle Josiah, speaking for the first time.

"Then straight to Crooswijk." The fireman gestured to a man who was coming by with a handcart. It was monstrous. There were two bodies on it already. "Can you take another?"

The man with the cart looked at Judith and her mother. "I can take them. They're not big."

"No," Uncle Josiah hissed, but he didn't look up.

"I don't think we want them buried here," Stella said.

"You don't have a choice. It's warm and we don't have the space… anywhere else. We're talking about hundreds of people, young lady."

"No," said Uncle Josiah. "She goes to the hospital. I want her at the hospital."

"Sir—" The fireman was going to say something else, but Uncle Josiah looked up with an expression of complete madness. It looked like he'd scratched at his own face, leaving bloody gouges in his forehead and cheeks.

Stella drew the fireman away and said, "He's my uncle. They were married three days ago. Please, can they go to the hospital? I fear for his mind."

The fireman looked back at Uncle Josiah, who was rocking again, and he put a hand on Stella's shoulder. "We don't know who they are. They'll go to Bergweg."

"Sir! Sir!" A priest came climbing over the wreckage. His face and hands were burnt and peeling. "Help! Please! There are girls in our vault. I can't get to them. I need help."

The priest tumbled forward over what looked like part of an oven and they caught him just as he was going down.

"Where is this?" the fireman asked.

"My church. The girls. Three maids. Someone said they hid down in the vault. I can't get to them. Please. Please."

The fireman directed some of his men to go further into the center to help with the digging. Then he and Stella carried Klara, her grandmother's dear friend, out of the debris and laid her on the cart. It wasn't careful or gentle as Stella would've wanted. It was quick and that was what the day demanded.

Stella put a hand out to try and take Judith, but Uncle Josiah showed her his face again. "No."

So they took Hans, the youngest at twelve, and put him with his mother. The handcart went off to the hospital and they pulled out the rest of the Wahle family placing them on carts as they became available until only Judith was left. Stella knelt next to her uncle and leaned over to kiss the hand cradling Judith's head to his chest. "We have to take her to the hospital."

"The hospital?"

"Yes."

"I don't want her to go to the other place."

She brushed the matted curls off his forehead and wondered if he knew she was dead. "I know. That's why she's going to the hospital."

"I'll carry her," he said.

Stella looked up at the firefighter and he shook his head.

"It's too far, but we'll walk with her."

Josiah swallowed hard and nodded. The firefighter gestured to a Red Cross nurse, who was helping a battered woman and child past. "I'll help them. You help her."

The nurse nearly objected, but she saw what was happening and relented.

"My name is Maria," she said in Dutch with a Spanish accent.

"He doesn't speak Dutch," said Stella. "You can talk to me."

"He is American?"

"Yes."

"I speak English," she said.

Gently, she told Josiah that they would take Judith from him and take her to a handcart. "You must let go, so we can do this."

His hands relaxed, but Judith's body didn't move. In a horrible moment, Stella thought she was stiff, but she wasn't. Her blood had seeped into Josiah's clothes and onto his body, attaching her to his very skin. They had to peel her away, making a scratching, tearing sound that Stella would hear late at night for the rest of her life.

Once they got her free, Uncle Josiah got up stiffly. Stella thought he would object, but he let them carry Judith to the handcart and they laid her with Felix.

"To the cemetery?" asked the burly man handling the cart.

"No, to the hospital," said Stella.

"Don't you know who—"

"No," Stella cut the man off and the nurse nodded, briefly touching Stella's hand before going off in the direction the priest had gone.

Uncle Josiah didn't move from the spot he'd been in. He stood there and stared at nothing until Stella went over and took his arm, leading him through the rubble to the handcart. He reached out to touch Judith but then pulled his hand back.

The burly man looked at Stella and said, "I can't wait."

She nodded and he went ahead with the cart, pushing it over rubble and broken glass. Stella and Uncle Josiah walked behind him, but Stella wasn't sure her uncle would make it very far. He walked like his joints were welded and he couldn't quite get them to bend. Stella kept one arm around his waist and held his hand. She wasn't entirely sure he knew she was there.

They got past the bombed area and a truck waited. Bodies were stacked in the back like cordwood.

"No," Uncle Josiah whispered.

"We have to get her to the hospital," Stella said. "This is the way. Klara and her brothers are there. She won't be alone."

"Alone."

Stella helped put Judith's body on the pile after Felix and then some others on top of her. She could feel this thing she was doing hurt her uncle. She knew without looking, but it had to be done. More stretchers and carts came until the truck was full. Then it left, crunching over concrete chunks and a rocking chair that must've been blown out of a window somewhere. The truck took the Wahles away and left Uncle Josiah behind with arms loose at his sides, standing in the street, lost.

Sheets were for those that died at the hospital, but Stella got them anyway. She and a volunteer named Hendrick went through the bodies, getting the identification and jewelry off them and putting it in a little bag. Hendrick took pictures of each of the Wahles and wrote down the names that Stella gave him. He questioned why they didn't go directly to the cemetery, but one look from Stella quieted him on the subject.

"Will you put them on the next truck?" Hendrick asked with a glance at Uncle Josiah who stood by during the whole thing like a statue.

Stella said yes, mostly to get him to move on. They were in the garden of the hospital where all the dead were and there was plenty for him to do.

"She should be covered," said Uncle Josiah.

"I'll go get sheets."

"He said no."

"I say yes." Stella went inside and stole some sheets off a cart. It was wrong, of course, but she didn't care. She did care a bit that they weren't white hospital sheets, but flowered ones from someone's house, but she wrapped the bodies in them anyway. Then she went to stand with Josiah, taking his hand. They'd have to be buried. The day was warm and the smell was already starting, but she didn't know how to broach the subject.

"I know," he said. "But not yet."

Stella took his hand and pressed it to her chest. "I don't know what to say."

"She's dead. There's nothing to say. There never will be anything to say."

"There will be someday," said Stella. "You told me so."

He stared down at his wife's body wrapped in a faded daffodil print and asked, "What did I tell you?"

"After Abel, you said, 'whatever causes night in our souls may leave stars.'"

"That was Victor Hugo," said Uncle Josiah.

"And you," she said. "It helped."

"You didn't love him."

The more time went on, the less sure Stella was of that. "He loved me."

"Yes, but you didn't kill him," he said. "I brought her to this."

"No. You brought her to love. This is the Reich's doing. Don't take what they own."

"I could've made them go to IJmuiden. You knew. You told me," he said in a ravaged voice.

"I didn't know and what you said made sense. I didn't think they'd do this. They gained nothing by it. The queen was gone. The surrender imminent."

A shiver went through him and Stella wrapped an arm around his waist.

"I thought I was so lucky," he said.

"You were."

"But not for long."

"No, not for long," said Stella. "But you had her love. That's something to remember and cherish."

"'For she had eyes and chose me'"

Othello. Why did it have to be a tragedy?

"Maybe there's a way to take them home," said Stella.

"I am taking them," he said.

She looked up at him, but his eyes were on the shroud. "Well, not for some time. Later, when it's all over. There's space at Prie Dieu. Grandmother will have a new section cleared."

"I'm taking them to *their* home," he said, turning to her with a new ferocity in his eyes. "They should never had been forced to leave it. I'm taking them back."

"To Hallstatt? You can't."

"I will."

"Don't you want them close? The family will—"

Uncle Josiah turned her to face him, laying his hands heavy on her shoulders. "Don't tell anyone about this."

"We have to tell the family," said Stella.

He shook his head, his eyes becoming familiar again, the uncle she knew, but different, changed. "We don't."

"They would want to know. Grandmother would—"

"I won't be a tragedy."

"It is a tragedy."

He shook her with tears coming for the first time. "Then it belongs to me, Stella. Nobody else."

"They will know something happened," she said. "You can't conceal this."

"I can and I will," said Uncle Josiah. "And so will you."

"But—"

"We will never talk about it. I never want to talk about it."

"You might change your mind."

"I won't. Promise me."

Stella promised. She didn't want to, but she did. She would keep it from the family and from Nicky. She would never tell and the name of Rotterdam never passed between the two of them again.

"You should leave now," he said.

"What? I'm not leaving."

"Why are you even here?" he asked but didn't give her a chance to answer. "Of course. The children. You went to IJmuiden with them."

"I did."

His eyes went back to the shroud. "And it worked?"

"They got on the ship," she said.

"Good. I knew you would do it." Then he looked back at her face as if seeing it for the first time. "You're not Micheline."

"No, I needed to be someone else."

"Can you be her again?"

Stella looked down at her hands. They were empty. She hadn't brought her handbag with her. She patted her pocket and the keys were still in there. "I guess. I have to find the cab back. Everything is in there."

"Then do that. Go back to Amsterdam and do what you do," he said.

"What are you going to do?"

"I will get them into the morgue and help until I can arrange to bring them back to Austria." Uncle Josiah sounded very sure and there really was no question. He would do it and she couldn't stop him. No one had ever stopped Josiah Bled.

"I don't think I should leave," said Stella.

The sound of German voices echoed around the courtyard and they turned to see a trio of Wehrmacht walking in to see the damage they had wrought.

"You're Stella Bled Lawrence," said Uncle Josiah. "You have to go. Once they find out who I am, it won't be hard to connect us."

"I hate to leave you," she said.

"I know, sweetheart. I know."

CHAPTER 31

Stella found the cab right where she left it with her wig and handbag still inside. There was a little gas left in the tank, not enough to get to Amsterdam, but that didn't matter since there was a flat tire. She had no idea when that happened. A spare hung off the back of the cab and looked all right, but Stella had been taught a lot of things, how to change a tire wasn't one of them. Hailing a cab was considered beyond the pale by Francesqua Bled. Uncle Josiah probably knew how, but she wasn't going back to ask.

She craned her neck back to look at the beautiful blue sky. It was eight o'clock in the morning. She hadn't been awake for twenty-four hours yet, but it felt more like thirty-six. Her energy pills were tucked away in her handbag, but she needed rest so she could think. Energy wouldn't help with that, if she didn't have a plan, so she opened the cab and crawled in the back. A couple of hours should do it.

But it wasn't a couple of hours and a hard rapping on the window knocked her out of her deep sleep at what felt like five minutes later. Stella rolled over in the tight backseat and looked up at a sight that sent a jolt of fear through her.

The cab was surrounded by Wehrmacht, a whole lot of Wehrmacht frowning and saying something about what she thought she was doing. Germans did like rules and sleeping in the back of a cab in broad daylight had to be against one or maybe a dozen, knowing them. But she wasn't Micheline at the moment and had no shot of becoming her again if she didn't act fast. Someone else was called for.

Stella put a wide smile on her face and gave them a little wave. That surprised them and the displeasure turned to confusion. She wasn't supposed to be happy to see them. What did it mean?

She yawned and opened the door, extending her hand to be helped out, like the pretty, young woman she needed to be. "Thank you," she said in German with a heavy American accent. "I can't believe how long I slept."

A *Hauptmann* came forward and asked, "You are American?"

"It shows? I thought my German was getting better," she said, tilting down her chin and smiling.

"Your German is very good."

It wasn't.

"Thank you so so much. I've been trying."

"Who are you and what are you doing here in this cab?" the Hauptmann asked.

She held out her hand and nearly every Wehrmacht moved to take it, making her smile all the more. The men were young with fresh, clean-cut, and eager faces. Some younger than Stella. It'd obviously been a long time since a pretty young woman smiled and didn't hate them on sight. Despite their many hands reaching for her, the Hauptmann won out and they shook briefly.

"I'm Cathy Capshaw." Stella knew the real Cathy. The Capshaws loved alliteration and had Christophers, Carries, and Calebs. The name sounded so very American, it popped out with no thought at all and got a smile from the men. Americans had the oddest names. "I'm from Chicago. Do you know Chicago?"

They did or said they did anyway. Stella told a good tale of how she was trying to get on her ship home when *it* happened. Everything was burnt to a crisp and she had to go back to Amsterdam in the cab she hired but it had a flat tire. She didn't know how to change a tire and she was so tired, she just laid down and went to sleep.

"Why are you going to Amsterdam?" the Hauptmann asked.

"My passport's gone. Blown to smithereens. I have to go to the embassy to get a new one."

"Who told you that?"

"Zebulon Wilcox III. He's a diplomat here." She leaned forward eagerly. "Isn't it true? Can I just go home without one?"

Sadly, he told her she couldn't. That was against the rules. He proudly told her that they would be establishing order and in a remarkable time the ships would be sailing again.

"That's good to know. I was visiting friends in Berlin and my father telegrammed to have me come home in case the shipping lanes closed, but I delayed. I was having such a good time and now look. All my clothes, the gifts I bought gone and this tire." She turned to look at it in dismay. "My mother said ladies don't change tires."

Every man hopped to it. That tire was changed in record time with Stella asking their names and where they were from. Asking them questions kept them from asking her anything and they liked it. They told her about their farms and families. One missed his favorite cow. Stella didn't know farmers had favorites and the information made her happy.

They all had sisters and mothers. They wanted to know about America and Chicago. Did she know any cowboys? How about film stars? Stella found herself enjoying it. Being Cathy was easy, like putting on cozy pajamas. She could almost forget who they were, what they had done, and would do. None were professional soldiers. They were doing what the Reich said they had to. Were they doing it wholeheartedly? Some were. Some weren't. But they would do it either way and she kept that in the back of her mind, all their charm notwithstanding.

With the flat put on the back of the cab and secured, the Hauptmann opened her door and held out a hand to help her in.

"Do you know where I can get some gas?" Stella asked innocently.

It took them a second to remember what gas was, but once they did, she was rewarded with the Hauptmann sending two men off to acquire a can of it for her.

"You're so nice," she said. "I don't know what I would've done without you." It was the first true thing she'd said. She really didn't know.

"Our pleasure," he said with a big smile. "I believe our countries will stay friends for many years to come."

I seriously hope not.

"Of course, we will," she said. "Your affairs are your affairs. It's nothing to do with us. That's what my father says."

"He is a wise man."

"And the sweetest."

Two young Wehrmachts ran up and frantically asked the Hauptmann what they were doing. Command was expecting them. The Dutch were resisting in some quarters. General Student had been shot in the head. The Hauptmann told them they would be there directly and the men eyed her curiously before running back the way they came.

"What's happening?" Stella asked with wide eyes. "I couldn't understand them."

"Nothing. Nothing. The city is secure," said the Hauptman. "Not to worry."

"And the road? Will I be able to get through?"

He tapped his chin. "Yes, you are an American. You must go to the embassy."

"I hope they let me. Mr. Nagy said there might be roadblocks. What do I do at the roadblocks?"

Come on. Think about it.

The Hauptmann nodded. "There will be roadblocks. They might give you some trouble."

"Oh, no." She batted her eyes. "I just don't know what to do."

The Wehrmacht patted his chest and found a fountain pen. "I will give you a pass."

He pulled out a small notebook and wrote her a note, complete with his name and a Heil Hitler at the end.

"And I just show this at the roadblocks?" Stella asked.

"It is not official, but you are American. It should get you through."

She impulsively kissed his cheek. "Thank you."

The Hauptmann blushed with pleasure. He was a long way from his wife and daughters in Dusseldorf and missed them terribly. The man was human. Stella only hoped he would remember it when he should.

The men who'd gone off to get gas returned with two cans and filled Stella's tank, smiling at her gratitude. Stella kissed more cheeks and got in, waving as she drove off. An American losing her passport. Who knew it could make things so easy? Cathy was dead useful. Park-Welles might even be impressed, if she ever decided to tell him.

The café was still crowded on the street near the Burgerweehuis, but not loud like it had been the day before. It was hard to believe it'd only been a day. It was all so different. The streets were quiet. There were people moving about, but their heads were down and their faces pale and shocked.

Stella parked the cab in the same spot where she'd stolen it, tucking the keys and his cash in the visor. The nasty driver would find it or someone would and tell him the cab was back. She didn't really care, but it seemed the right thing to do. He probably had a family to support. She got out and listened to the quiet. Only the sound of radios came out of the windows. No voices. None at all. The people in the café silently sat around a radio, listening to news of the formal surrender being signed. The queen was safely in England where she and the ministers would lead them from afar. How that was going to work was a mystery to Stella, but she didn't spend any time pondering it. She hurried down the street until she found a deserted alley where she put on Micheline's wig and lipstick. She was filthy from Rotterdam and the soot and grit would be enough to hide her youth until she could get the makeup back on.

She didn't need to worry about it anyway. Nobody paid Micheline much attention on a normal day and it was anything but. The city was hunkered down in grief and fear with radios turned up loud. Battles were still going on. Some of the Dutch refused to stop fighting and it wasn't going well. There'd been a threat to level Utrecht and despite the surrender the radio said it might still happen. Another Rotterdam. Worse than Rotterdam.

Stella hurried through the streets, trying not to hear anything about Rotterdam. She couldn't talk about it, so she didn't want to think about it. Dam Square was deserted and the hotel lobby looked like it was, too, but Stella decided to go around back and sneak in the service entrance. To her surprise, no one was around and it was midday, too. She went up the stairs to her floor and walked down the empty hall, hearing more radios and feeling like she wasn't really there. Everything was so clean and the same when nothing was the same. She wasn't. Uncle Josiah wasn't. The Wahles gone. Hundreds upon hundreds dead and being dumped in mass graves. But there she was walking down an immaculate hall, like nothing had happened at all.

Her door was locked and her belongings untouched. Somebody had come in. Her breakfast tray was gone. Then she saw herself in the mirror. It was a wonder that she'd charmed the Wehrmacht. If she'd seen herself, she wouldn't have even attempted it. Bloody and covered in filth. What in the world were they thinking?

She tossed her wig aside and took a quick bath, washing away the blood and grime before getting dressed in fresh clothes and making a decision. Leave directly or say goodbye?

Goodbye won out. The trains weren't really running yet. She'd asked at the roadblocks. The Hauptmann's note and her American accent worked wonders. The soldiers she encountered were happy to tell her anything she wanted to know. Train service would be completely restored to areas within days. If she couldn't get out through a Dutch port, they were sure she'd be able to go to Norway for a ship or France once they surrendered, which was just a matter of time in their opinion.

She put on her makeup and found a pair of gloves to cover her battered hands. A longer skirt and hose concealed her bruised knees and shins and she took a look. Not bad. The deep purplish grooves under eyes helped her with being Micheline and there was nothing else readily visible to show something had happened. Her stomach was growling, so she had to eat, which meant not slipping out the back. After hiding her Charlotte papers back in her handbag's secret compartment, she took a deep breath and focused. She was Micheline Dubois and everything was fine. Perfectly fine.

Her hands shook when she opened her door, but that would go away as soon as she had something to eat or so she told herself. When the elevator opened, Michel gasped. "Micheline!"

"Hello, Michel." Stella got on the elevator, feeling stiff and unnatural. Maybe this was a mistake.

"Where have you been?"

He knows I've been gone. Why didn't I think of that?

"IJmuiden. I went to make sure my shipment left on time," she said.

"During all the fighting? You could've been bombed. Why would you do it?" Michel asked.

She sighed and leaned on the paneling. "I didn't want to, but my company would expect me to make sure my purchases got out in good order."

"Did they?"

"Yes, just before the surrender."

Michel put his hand on hers. "Did you hear about Rotterdam?"

Breathe. Be calm.

"Yes. I can't believe they did it," she said.

"Bastards. We were negotiating surrender. They didn't have to," said Michel.

"Add it to the list of things that didn't have to happen." She must've sounded quite bitter because he gave her a funny look. "I'm sorry. It's been a long day and I have to go see my friend. She's very ill."

He stopped the elevator and asked, "Are you well yourself?"

"As well as can be," she said. "I'm dreading what comes next."

"We all are."

Stella left the elevator and tried to get into the café without being seen, but it was hopeless. Ludwik was at her elbow before she crossed the threshold.

"Micheline, are you all right?" Ludwik asked.

"Very well thank you. I'd just like an early dinner if that can be arranged." She didn't look over at him. The sound of his voice, his concern, his fear, was almost too much.

Thankfully, he didn't question her, he accompanied her to her usual table and snapped his fingers. Ester ran up with a menu. Her eyes were large and worried.

"Micheline would like coffee immediately," he said.

Ester nodded and scampered back to the kitchen without a word and Ludwik sat down uninvited. It was so out of character that Stella could only stare.

"She knows you were gone, but she thinks the world of you and won't say anything," he said. "What did you tell Michel?"

Stella straightened her back and said, "I went to IJmuiden to check my shipments."

Relief washed over the concierge and a smile changed his whole countenance. "That's what I said."

"It's true."

Ester hurried out with the coffee and asked, "We have your favorite. Stampot. Would you like that?"

Stella couldn't have cared less what she ate, so she nodded and handed back the menu. Ester took it, uneasily shifting from foot to foot. "I'm not supposed to say anything, but I think it's just wonderful."

"I don't know what you're talking about," said Stella in all honesty.

Ester grinned and winked at her before dashing to the kitchen to yell for Stampot.

"Well, she wasn't supposed to do that," said Ludwik, "but I understand the impulse."

"What on Earth are you talking about?"

"Dr. Tulp told us."

Oh, my God.

"No, no. Don't worry. I made him, the poor man. When you disappeared from your room, I knew he had something to do with it. He was looking so odd the last time he checked on you and I had to know what was going on. You understand, don't you?"

"No," Stella whispered.

"I needed to cover for you while you were gone. A missing guest and an ill one as well. Questions would be asked, so he told me about the children. I thought you would be back from the Burgerweeshuis by five at the latest. When you didn't come back, I knew something had gone wrong. That you must've gone to IJmuiden and you did." He glanced past her to the door and then said, "Did the children get on the ship?"

Stella's mouth was so dry she couldn't speak. A tiny nod was all he got.

"You don't have to say any more. Ester and I were the only ones in your room. Everyone else thinks you were there the entire time." Ludwik stood up with tears in his eyes. "It was a very good thing what you did."

She nodded again and he headed off, saying loudly to whoever was in close proximity. "She's all better. Dr. Tulp is a genius."

Ester brought her Stampot with a broad smile and left her in peace to force the food down. It was probably delicious, but it felt like chewing yarn. The coffee did help and she drank a pot of it. Ester kept her well-supplied. Her service had certainly gotten a lot better. Other guests had come in as dusk came over the city and they got the same attentive Ester as Stella.

After she forced the food down, she paid her bill and left the hotel with quiet nods and smiles to anyone who expressed joy at her recovery. She should've slipped out the back, but she couldn't be bothered. Mussert wasn't there, but Stella probably would've let him follow her to Elizabeth's house anyway. She just didn't care anymore. She had good news to tell and hoped it would ease her friend. Some good had to come of it all. She had to remember that the children were alive and safe. It was a slender thread of joy, but she was holding onto it with both hands.

The trams were running, but almost no one was on them. The city was still quiet, blanketed in grief with only radios to interrupt the silence. Stella found Elizabeth's street the same. News of Rotterdam's destruction bounced off the buildings. Thousands dead the BBC said and Stella could well believe it. She went up Elizabeth's steps where the windows were open, but no news was drifting out to tell Stella once again what had happened. Maybe Elizabeth had had enough. Stella had. She knocked and waited. No one came. They were there. They had to be there.

Finally, after ten minutes, the knob turned and Rena opened the door, looking like she had been in Rotterdam herself. The maid's face was pale and shocked. Her full cheeks sagged and her dress seemed looser.

"Micheline," she said dully.

"Yes," said Stella. "I…are you all right?"

"I'm fine. I'm always fine. I didn't get it."

"Get what?"

A man came up behind Rena and Stella stepped back in surprise. "I should go now and leave you in peace, Rena," said Baron Van Heeckeren and then his eyes found Stella. "Micheline! I didn't expect to see you here. I thought you'd have left."

"I didn't leave," said Stella.

"I see that—oh, oh, of course," he said kindly. "You've just heard."

The baron reached past Rena, took her arm, and pulled her inside. Before Stella knew it, they were in Elizabeth's sitting room and she had a cup of tea in her hands. The baron sat in front of Stella, patting her knee and consoling her. At first, she thought he knew about the Wahles, but eventually it came to light that Elizabeth had died. She'd caught some horrible flu and her system couldn't withstand it.

Rena sat in Elizabeth's chair sobbing, beyond any consolation and Stella had none to give. It was her. She'd given it to Elizabeth. That was what Dr. Tulp had been referring to when he asked when Stella had first felt ill. Elizabeth was his very sick patient.

"I wish I could've known her better," said the baron. "After meeting Father Brandsma, I couldn't let it rest. I had to know how you'd done it, Micheline. I met Father Schoffelmeer and they told me about Elizabeth. We're going to continue her work." He touched her hand. "Your work."

Stella shot to her feet. "I have to go."

Rena looked up tearfully. "Why did you come?"

There seemed no point in concealing it from the baron or Rena. Everything was out. Nearly everything anyway. "I came to say the children got on the ship. They made it."

A smile came over Rena's face. "She would be so very happy that they're safe."

I have to leave. I have to leave.

"Excuse me. I have to go," said Stella, bolting for the door.

"I'm sorry it was such a shock," called out Rena behind her. "I thought you knew. Dr. Tulp should've told you."

Stella didn't stop. She banged out of the front door with tears stinging her eyes. It was all unraveling. The baron knew the priests and their connections with her and Elizabeth. Ester and Ludwik. Dr. Tulp. Too many people and *they* were there, coming at that very moment. If she didn't get out…

Stella didn't go for the tram. She didn't go very far at all. Footsteps pounded out behind her. She darted into an alley, running for the canal up ahead, but a hand grabbed her, yanking her back off her feet.

"I'm sorry. I'm sorry." The baron towered over her. "You've had a shock, but we must speak."

She struggled, but he wouldn't let go. "Leave me alone."

He came in close. "I know."

"What are you talking about? Let go."

"The priests. Elizabeth. The Jews. Befriending Cornelia." The baron looked in her eyes. "I see it now. You're not old and unattractive."

"I'm—"

"I want to fight for the right side and I want you to help me do it."

Stella's heart felt like it would leap out of her mouth. "I can't help. I'm just a businesswoman."

"No, you're not." He moved closer, whispering in her ear, "You're not even Belgian."

"Yes, I am."

"You quoted Oscar Wilde and it was a mistake. I saw you realize it."

"I don't know what you're talking about," Stella said with panic washing over her.

"You're a spy."

"No. No. That's crazy," she said.

"I think you're an Amer—" The Baron Van Heeckeren never finished the word. He never uttered another syllable again. A slim blade stuck out of his neck and then was retracted. His wide eyes fixed on Stella, his hands clutching on her shoulders. Blood flowed out of his mouth as he was pulled backward and lain facedown on the cobbles, his jerking body ten feet from the quiet canal.

Oliver wiped his stiletto on a handkerchief and then shoved the fabric under the baron's body. A scream burst out of Stella and he pounced on her, shoving a dirty hand over her mouth and slamming her head against the wall. "Shut up," Oliver hissed. "It's done."

She clawed at his hand until he gave way. "Are you insane? That was the baron. A good man. How could you? Are you insane?"

Oliver's brilliant blue eyes were bloodshot and his breath rank. "I had to come back," he hissed in her ear, "because of you."

"Get away from me!" Stella screamed.

He slapped her and whispered in her ear. "He knew what you are. I wouldn't risk you and the war for an unstable, useless—"

She clawed at his face and he flipped her around, pinning an arm behind her back. "You're coming with me. No more nonsense." Oliver lost his Dutch accent, his British voice coming through and traveling down the alley.

"I'm not going anywhere with you. Ever!" she yelled, and he shoved her against the wall.

"You've lost your mind!" he yelled. "He is nothing and you belong to us."

"Get off me."

"You're coming with me. We have work for you to do."

"I'm not doing it!"

"You have no choice. You have skills we need." He pushed her harder against the wall, pressing the air out of her lungs. "Nothing matters but winning this—"

There was a terrible cracking sound and Oliver jerked away from her, releasing his grip. Stella spun around and pressed her back against the wall. Oliver lay crumpled at her feet with his head cocked at an odd angle and not two feet away stood Jan Bikker, looking down at the spy's body and flexing his long fingers. "Now she belongs to us."

Nobody came. Not a single person stuck a head out a window or ran to see what happened when they heard a woman scream. It wasn't completely dark yet. Anyone could've seen two bodies splash into a canal and float away facedown, but if they did, no fuss was raised. No sirens. No police. Nothing.

Stella stood still pressed against the wall and that pleased Jan Bikker. He'd told her not to run and she hadn't. There was no point. On her little legs, she'd have gotten nowhere and then he would've killed her. She had no doubts about that.

Bikker watched the bodies for a moment, giving Stella a chance to think. She had to say the right thing, except she didn't know what he'd heard or why he was even there. He would understand strength. That's what he wanted. Tears would be the death of her, but his death would be preferable. She had her pen with the blade nestled in the bottom of her handbag. If she could get it…

Lights across the canal showed off his strong silhouette as he admired his work. Stella grasped the clasp on her handbag, sliding it slowly so as to not make a sound, but Bikker spun around to face her. "You may thank me now."

"Thank you?"

"For saving you," said Bikker with a wry smile. "I knew that fool was up to something. Always asking questions. Cozying up to the right people. I didn't realize anyone else was watching him though. I should've guessed others would notice his activities."

Stella just stared. She didn't know what to say. It was best to let him lead her down his path.

Bikker tapped his chin. "It's a shame, considering who he really was."

Stella's foot slipped in the baron's blood and a chill went up her spine. "What was he?"

"A good man. I did not think so, but I can admit my mistake."

I don't know what's happening. Who are we talking about?

"Yes, he was a good man," she said.

"When did you find out?" Bikker asked.

Stella hesitated and his eyes narrowed.

Say something. Quick.

"I don't know exactly when."

"Did he ask for the list?" he asked. "Is that how you knew?"

List?

"What list?" Stella asked.

He got in her face. "I know everything."

She clutched her handbag to her chest. If only she could open it. Distract him. "Everything about what?"

"The Jews you wrote down in *Der Totale Krieg*. Were you going to sell that list? Why did he want it?"

She shoved him back from her. "How do you know about that?"

"I have my ways." He smiled at her. He would've been so damn handsome if he wasn't completely vile on the inside.

Be who he is.

"I don't think you do, Mr. Bikker. I'm a businesswoman. I'm not going to be on the wrong side."

"And which side is that?"

Please let this be right.

"The losing side, of course. There I said it. My country and yours were always going to be part of the Reich. You people are delusional if you think it wasn't inevitable."

"Are you sure about that?" he asked. A shadow fell across his face and she couldn't gauge his expression, but it was too late anyway.

"Yes, I'm sure. You fools can't add up two and two. They walked over Poland. They were always going to walk over us."

He moved in closer. "Where did you go?"

"When?"

Jan Bikker was thinking, evaluating. "Yesterday. I had a man follow you to a Jews' house. Then he lost you. I don't think you were at your hotel last night."

"As if it's any of your business," said Stella.

He shoved her back against the wall. "Don't try to pretend there's a man. There's no man."

"There's only business and you people are ruining it," she said between bared teeth.

"Where did you go?"

"Rotterdam." It just slipped out. She hadn't planned it, but the name did back Bikker up.

"You went to Rotterdam?" he asked with wonder in his voice.

"Yes, you don't expect me to lose everything and do nothing about it, do you?"

"I…why did you go?"

"That's where my shippers are. Thanks to you people, I've lost friends, the entire warehouse is gone, the ship on fire and I spent the last six weeks working for nothing."

Bikker flexed those long fingers again. "Who are you blaming?"

"You. It's your fault. You and your stupid government. All those people dead for nothing. All my profit gone."

He cocked his head to the side and said, "Oh, really."

"Yes," she spat. "If your government had surrendered in a reasonable manner, none of it would've happened."

His shoulders dropped the slightest bit. "My government?"

"Do you deny it? You weren't going to win. It was just stupid and I'm sick of the whole thing." She went to pass him and was yanked back.

He bent over to stick his face in hers. "Why were you at that Jews' house? My man said you were there a long time."

Stella struggled and then said, "Negotiating. Thank goodness I did or I'd have nothing to show for my trouble."

"What did they have?" Bikker was full of doubt and she had to shut it down. Fear overwhelmed her, but she had to do it.

Please don't let me lose the last bit of her.

"Here." She pushed her handbag into his hands. "If you don't believe me, look for yourself."

Even in the dim light, she could see he was surprised. Women didn't generally give up their handbags, but it showed she had nothing to hide and she needed that.

Bikker opened her handbag and rooted around before he stopped and smiled, pulling out a slim black case. He opened it and the diamonds from Judith's necklace caught the light from the windows across the canal and showed their worth. "That scum had this?"

"Yes. I don't know where they got it and I don't care." Stella snatched the necklace out of his hands and snapped shut the case before grabbing her handbag and putting the case inside while surreptitiously sliding her special pen up her sleeve. "I'm going to lose my job, but at least I've got that."

She tried to walk away, but Bikker's hand shot out and grabbed her bicep. "You've got a job."

"I did. Thanks to your idiot government, I lost my company thousands of dollars." She put her hands on her hips, letting her pen slide into her hand with her finger on the button.

If this doesn't work...

"I can hear it now. You should've sent it out earlier. Rotterdam was a bad choice. Blah. Blah. Blah. You're fired."

"You could've worked for that Englishman." His voice took on a kind of wheedling tone, but she doubted that he knew it.

"I wouldn't and you know what? I *will* thank you for that. He's been bothering me for weeks. I couldn't get rid of him. So thank you for doing it for me."

"I wish I'd noticed him before it was too late. Bad luck for the baron. Tell me what the Englishman wanted." Bikker's grip on her bicep grew tighter.

"You'll probably be on his side. No, thank you."

"Tell me." A new threat came into his voice and Stella found it hard to breathe. The blade was designed to be thrust up into the base of the skull, much the way she killed Gabriele Griese with her great grandmother's hatpin. Would it be as effective through to the heart or into the throat? Was she even fast enough to attempt it?

"He wanted me to work for the English as if I would. Those idiots are next. Why on Earth would I put my hat in their ring or yours for that matter?" Stella asked.

"We don't have the same ring," said Bikker.

Stella snorted. "Oh, really?"

"That's right."

"You expect me to believe that?"

"I killed the Englishman, didn't I?"

"Only because he killed the baron. You were friends."

"We weren't, but we would've been had I known what side he was on," said Bikker.

"And what side is that?" Stella asked, sliding the pen back up her sleeve.

Bikker came in close and put a wad of Reichsmarks under her nose. "The Reich's. I like winners, too."

Stella took the money and smiled up at him. "I've misjudged you, Mr. Bikker."

CHAPTER 32

The sky was a beautiful blue over the Boulevard du Montparnasse at Le Dôme Café. It was such an ill-advised place for a meeting, but Stella didn't get a choice. She was following orders. Something she'd learned to do since Amsterdam without question or complaint. Jan Bikker liked that and so did her new contact the so-called Jean-Pierre Bernard. He wasn't really French and anyone with a decent ear would know that. His real name was Helmut Scholtz and he was from Mainz. It'd been astonishingly easy to find that out. She'd picked his pocket while they were walking down the Champs-Élysées on their second meeting and found a letter from his sad little wife, who didn't understand why he couldn't tell her where he was.

Stella swirled her glass of chilled white wine, an indeterminate vintage but still quite tasty, and tapped the book she'd brought. *Rebecca* was very diverting, but a newspaper would've hidden her and Stella needed hiding. A model sauntered past Stella's seat and posed in her couture silk dress for a photographer tracking her around the famous café, shooting her in spots where the literary avant-garde liked to meet and straddling the wicker chairs like a harlot as her mother would've said. Utterly ridiculous. Stella was going to be in multiple photos, but Helmut liked the chic spots or what he thought was chic. She thought he'd looked up famous people in Paris and ate where they ate, thinking it made him look like a native. So far, they'd met at Les Deux Magots and Café de Flore, but Micheline didn't exactly fit the clientele, being a foreigner and neither literary nor a tourist. Helmut didn't notice. He'd heard of Les Deux Magots, so they met there.

"Madam Dubois," said Helmut. "May I?"

"Certainly, Monsieur Bernard," said Stella. "I'm pleased to see you."

The Nazi sat down and peered at a menu with little interest. The waiter came and Stella ordered a second glass of wine and a Pain au Raisin in her perfect Belgian French. Then Helmut ordered a beer in whatever accent he was trying to have. A beer. Really?

"Do you have a place?"

"I do," she said.

He frowned. "Already?"

"Yes. You told me to work at the Hotel de Ville and I am now a secretary," said Stella primly.

"How did you do that so quickly?" Helmut asked.

"I had excellent recommendations."

"You did?" he asked. "Where did you get them?"

"I wrote them myself."

Helmut sat back and steepled his fingers before waving away the waiter dismissively. The man looked as though he wished he'd spit in Helmut's beer. If he ordered another, no doubt he would. Stella gave him a split-second look that said she agreed and thanked him properly for her wine and pastry. She would be getting no spit.

"You wrote them yourself?" Helmut asked.

"Naturally," said Stella. "I needed recommendations. Where else would I get them?"

"I hadn't thought about it."

Of course not.

"Well, it's a good thing I did," said Stella.

The German frowned and drank his beer with gusto that was not remotely French and attracted unwanted attention from several tables. Stella cringed inwardly, but Helmut was younger than Micheline and he was always awkward around her. He'd made it clear having a woman working for him in Paris wasn't his favorite idea, but he didn't get a choice. Stella thought she'd been given to him because he was low ranking and expendable in case she went wrong. Of course, she'd already gone wrong and enjoyed following him around to all his haunts. His little wife would not be happy about the prostitutes and his handler wouldn't be happy that she knew who he was, where he worked, and who his contact was.

A lot had happened since Jan Bikker recruited her to spy for the Reich with the promise of being on the "right" side and cash, enough for a Parisian wardrobe, a small flat, and a poodle named Bijou, who sat at her feet waiting for the piece of pastry that was definitely coming his way. The Reich was generous when it came to funds, Stella would give them that. She had so much cash she didn't know what to do with it. Money couldn't buy loyalty, but clearly the Reich disagreed on that point.

"You disapprove?" Stella asked. "I got the job."

"I didn't know you'd be so efficient," said Helmut.

"You pay me to be efficient. I'm a businesswoman after all."

"Tell me about the office."

Stella named names and gave a description of the building. It didn't matter. No one knew a thing that would help the Reich, but a foot in the door was all that Helmut was after for the moment. Later, informing on the police would become important when they had control, but right then Stella was supposed to observe and keep track of loyalties as if the French were divided on the subject of becoming German lackeys.

Helmut drained his beer and eyed her nervously. He didn't know quite what to do with an older woman who wasn't a maid, his aunt, or mother. Stella could use that. All she had to do was calmly watch the man and a bead of sweat would form on his temple. If he hadn't been a Nazi, it would've been endearing. As far as she could tell he wasn't vicious, like Jan Bikker. That man didn't bat an eye over either the baron or Oliver. She suspected Helmut would.

"I will go." His accent always got worse when she made him nervous.

Stella sipped her wine and then asked, "When do you want to meet again?"

"I will contact you."

She nodded as if she was the one in charge and he got up obediently, glancing around and then stomping off in his tight, clenched fist way. He didn't pay, naturally, and the waiter noticed with a sneer as he collected Helmut's beer.

"Please excuse him," said Stella, "even though he is inexcusable."

"May I say madam will enjoy the day better without such company," said the waiter.

"You are correct, but one must do these things."

"Must you?"

I must.

"He is the son of a friend and looking for employment," said Stella.

"Will he get it?"

"No."

The waiter gave her a rare smile and went off to serve other customers well practiced in the art of being served and it was an art in Paris. Respect being the first thing to employ. Helmut didn't understand that. He could speak French. He could wear the right clothes and be as handsome as he liked but being entitled and dismissive showed him up every time.

Helmut disappeared in the distance and Stella tore a bit of pastry off for Bijou. The poodle delicately took it from her hand and she felt a surge of affection. Someone to love when love was so hard to come by. He took a second bite from her and then gave her fingers a sweet little lick, getting him a good scratch on his topknot.

Bijou was a good distraction from the distaste that Helmut always left in her mouth, but she wasn't so distracted that she didn't notice when a certain man sat down at the table beside her. Stella concealed a smile. She could always tell without looking. He had a scent. That day he tried to cover it with a cologne that smelled of pears and bergamot, but she could still detect it.

"I hope this café wasn't your idea," said Mr. Bast.

Stella gave Bijou a two-handed scratch. "I suggested a little place near Gare d'Lyon."

"What did he say?"

"Nobody goes there."

He chuckled and when the waiter arrived he graciously ordered an espresso and took out a paper, Le Progrès, from Lyon, which, of course, matched his accent. "That gives me hope."

"Why exactly?" Stella opened her book and took a sip of wine.

"He's about as subtle as a bulldozer in a poppy field and the rest of them are no different," said Mr. Bast.

Stella's eyes skimmed the page, unable to focus on a single word. She had to go on. Being on the inside was too good a chance to miss, but there were moments when she didn't know how she could possibly stick it out another day. The losses were piling up and she probably didn't know the half of it.

"They're winning," she said.

"A bulldozer is a hell of a target and they've got a pissant private running the show."

She turned the page. "He's doing pretty good."

"So good he let 300,000 men get scooped off Dunkirk in fishing boats."

"A colossal blunder. That's true."

"And there will be more," said Bast.

"Who knows what happened there," she said.

He turned the page of his paper and thanked the waiter, who'd glided over with his espresso. When the man had cleared the area, Mr. Bast said, "I know one thing that happened."

Do I want to know?

"We survived to fight another day," said Stella, not cheered by the thought. Paris would fall within a week or two. What then? She sighed and Bijou bumped her with his little black nose. He always sensed her sadness.

"One man did, for certain," said Mr. Bast.

Stella gripped her book and the table. Was she spinning? She might've been spinning. "Yes?"

"Yes."

The words focused. Maxim de Winter saying, "We're not meant for happiness, you and I."

"Do you want to hear?" Mr. Bast asked.

I don't know.

"Tell me," said Stella.

"A certain pilot was fished out of the channel by a trawler and that lucky man is kicking up his heels at a house with an obscene amount of windows."

Bijou bumped her knee with his nose and whined nervously. Stella pulled the pup into her lap and nuzzled him. She expected tears, but they didn't come. "How do I know this is true?"

"You have friends," said Mr. Bast.

"I know. They kept me here."

"Because you are unique."

"Like everyone else."

"Not like everyone else. What do you need to hear?" Mr. Bast asked.

Stella drained her glass and said, "I don't need to hear. I need to believe he's really all right. That I haven't missed my chance to see him again."

"Then we are all in luck. The message came with something else."

She glanced over for the first time at Mr. Bast in his full French costume, dark slicked back hair, dapper suit, and a pencil-thin mustache. He was handsome and smiling, both new.

"What?"

"Another kind of message. I don't understand it, but I assume you will. It's 'The urn on the mantel next to Aggie.'"

"Abel," Stella whispered.

"What was that?"

Stella gave Bijou the rest of her pastry and then placed him gently on the ground before signaling the waiter. She paid her bill with a small but wholly appropriate tip.

"Good day, madam."

"Good day, monsieur."

The waiter left and Stella pushed back her chair. Mr. Bast hastened to retrieve her scarf that had fallen on the ground.

"I'll stay," she said, tying the scarf around her neck.

He gave her her handbag and said, "Despite what happened, I hope you know Oliver would be proud."

"I hope he's not the only one."

"Few will know of our many sacrifices," Mr. Bast said with a slight bow. "Even less will understand the pain of making them."

"As long as that pilot does and you do."

He sat back down and opened his paper. "Rest assured on that score."

Stella pushed in her chair and squeezed between his table and hers, dropping an envelope in his lap as she went through. He didn't acknowledge it and she didn't expect that he would. So much would be unacknowledged, loss, sacrifice and pain in the coming days, months, and years. She took the burden. Someone had to. Amsterdam had taught her that.

All must be given because all was required.

The End

ABOUT THE AUTHOR

USA Today bestselling author A.W. Hartoin grew up in rural Missouri, but her grandmother lived in the Central West End area of St. Louis. The CWE fascinated her with its enormous houses, every one unique. She was sure there was a story behind each ornate door. Going to Grandma's house was a treat and an adventure. As the only grandchild around for many years, A.W. spent her visits exploring the many rooms with their many secrets. That's how Mercy Watts and the fairies of Whipplethorn came to be.

As an adult, A.W. Hartoin decided she needed a whole lot more life experience if she was going to write good characters so she joined the Air Force. It was the best education she could've hoped for. She met her husband and traveled the world, living in Alaska, Italy, and Germany before settling in Colorado for nearly eleven years. Now A.W. has returned to Germany and lives in picturesque Waldenbuch with her family and two spoiled cats, who absolutely believe they should be allowed to escape and roam the village freely.

Printed in Great Britain
by Amazon